QUEST FOR ATLAN

CRADLELAND **2** CHRONICLES

DOUGLAS HIRT

QUEST FOR ATLAN

Good News in Fiction

COOK COMMUNICATIONS MINISTRIES
Colorado Springs, Colorado • Paris, Ontario
KINGSWAY COMMUNICATIONS LTD
Eastbourne, England

RiverOak® is an imprint of
Cook Communications Ministries, Colorado Springs, CO 80918
Cook Communications, Paris, Ontario
Kingsway Communications, Eastbourne, England

QUEST FOR ATLAN
© 2005 by Douglas Hirt

This story is a work of fiction. All characters and events are the product of the
author's imagination. Any resemblance to any person, living or dead, is coinci-
dental.

Cover Design: Lisa Barnes
Cover Illustration: Ron Adair
Map ©2005 Susan Kotnik

First Printing, 2005
Printed in the United States of America

Printing/Year
10 9 8 7 6 5 4 3 2 1   /   05 06 07 08 09 10

Unless otherwise noted, Scripture quotations are taken from the HOLY
BIBLE, NEW INTERNATIONAL VERSION®. Copyright © 1973, 1978,
1984 International Bible Society. Used by permission of Zondervan. All rights
reserved. Scripture quotations marked KJV are taken from the King James
Version of the Bible. Public Domain.

ISBN 1589190440

Atlan

Highwatch Tower 34

Brights Canyon Vale

Deep Vale

Mount Ke-baal

Golden Hills Passage

Execution Ridge

Rim-wall

The Atlan Ridge

DANGER!
SHALLOW WATER

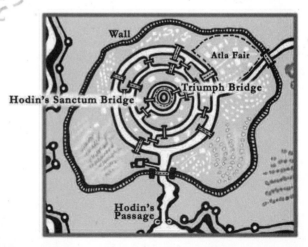

Wall

Atla Fair

Triumph Bridge

Hodin's Sanctum Bridge

Hodin's Passage

Dirgen's Navel

Redoubts

Redoubts

Eastern Passage

N

CRADLELAND

©2005 Susan Kotnik

"Be not afraid nor dismayed by reason of this great multitude; for the battle is not yours, but God's."

2 Chronicles 20:15 KJV

1

The Way

*L*amech bolted awake with a sudden gasp, his eyes searching wildly in the darkness, his face clammy with sweat, and his heart pounding. He gulped down a breath, and then another, as the nightmare slowly faded and reality flooded back. The thumping of his heart slowed. In the sliver of starlight through the narrow slit in the stone wall, the dungeon chamber came faintly into view. The shuttered moonglass mounted on the wall near the bolted door showed only dim lines of light now. *A dream.* His breathing trembled in his chest, and he let it drain away in the dark. *That's all it was.*

As the incubus of the night swiftly dissipated back into the misty netherworlds from which nightmares arise, Lamech tried to cling onto the tattered fragments before they'd completely vanished. He remembered a battle, swords ringing, proj-lances flashing their deadly missiles. Mishah had been there, fleeing for her life, with Amolikah at her side. He remembered blood, and feeling Mishah's fear. He'd seen men die ... and giant golden statues come to life.

He drew in another breath and let it hiss through his teeth, remembering how Mishah had been haunted by night visions. Was this dream like the dreams that had wrenched his wife from sleep, trembling at his side, clinging to him as if she feared being torn from his arms and plunged back into her night torments?

They're only dreams, Mishah. They can't hurt you.

The memory opened a door to the emptiness in his heart. Oh, that he could hold her now. That she could comfort him. And what of his son?

It had been so real … but it had only been a dream.

He studied the shadowy hammocks hanging about the dungeon. The other men were still asleep. At least he hadn't woken them. He settled his head back onto the rolled blanket and looked across the dark room at the slumbering bulk of one of the prisoners. Somehow, Klesc reminded him of the man in his dream. Was it because of his size? As he peered at the dark form, a glint of reflected starlight peered back at him.

Lamech looked away. So, his sudden start *had* woken one of them. Did nothing ever get past this big man?

※

The next day, at the end of their work shift, Quort Whip En'tuboc ordered the six weary men of Lamech's work quort into a row against the stone prison wall. The men dragged themselves into a ragged line. If En'tuboc had ordered them to attention, which he didn't, the results would have been only slightly improved: a straightened shoulder here perhaps, a groaning spine forcing itself from a fatigued slouch there. After fourteen hours of chopping wood for the Temple construction work fires, there was little left in a man.

Lamech stood slightly straighter than his companions, except for Klesc, whose size and muscles put him far ahead of the five other convicts of Quort Nineteen. But for Lamech, this was more than a backbreaking stint. A battle of wills had taken shape in his mind the moment they'd wrenched him from the arms of his beloved wife and had marched him down the dark stone corridor to a waiting prison wagon.

"Hear me, village grubs!" En'tuboc growled, pacing before them. He stopped and planted his fists upon his waist, his long whip held in coils in his right hand. The low sun glaring at En'tuboc's back forced Lamech's eyes down toward the crushed gravel. "You've been promoted."

His sneering tone warned Lamech this promotion might make wood gathering seem like a holiday. Lamech forced his eyes to En'tuboc's pugnacious face, framed in long reddish brown hair, a hank of it held off to one side in a blue enameled clip. He concentrated on the thick ropelike braids of En'tuboc's dark beard and endured the glare.

"Tomorrow you get to work with the animals." A contemptuous grin spread the beard.

What did that mean? Lamech owned many animals on his farm, back in the Lee-lands of Morg'Seth. But there was something else here, something En'tuboc found humorous. Since arriving at the prison, Lamech could not remember ever seeing the Quort Whip crack a smile.

Standing beside Lamech, Orm'el gave a low groan.

En'tuboc silenced him with a narrowed look. "Ah, so you understand."

❦

Later, in the dank holding cell with only a narrow slit for light and fresh air, Ker-bar and Fa-elak cornered Orm'el. "What does it mean? What's the matter with working with the animals?" Ker-bar demanded.

Lamech filled a cup from the flowing trough cut into the stone wall as Orm'el flopped on the rope hammock and stared at the moldy stones overhead. "It means we'll be shoveling behemoth girt."

"Behemoth!" Fa-elak scrunched his face into a mask of disgust and slumped to his own cot.

Mantir chuckled. "Watch your tongue, Orm'el. You might offend the preacher."

Lamech looked up from his cup of tepid water.

Orm'el, an ex-miner from the Ugmot district in the land of Havilah, only laughed.

Lamech walked to the stone slit and stared out at the darkening sky, catching a faint breeze before it had a chance to sour in the tight confine where the six men of Quort Nineteen slept. *So be it, Creator. If shoveling behemoth dung is where you want me, then that's where I'll serve. You've taken me from Mishah and put me here for a reason, though I don't see it yet.* He drew in a breath and turned back. Klesc's eyes darted away from him.

The sound of the food slot opening invigorated the men. As the tray slipped through, they dove for the bowls of gruel, the orofins and bananas, and the berries. Lamech darted in to claim his share. He had learned early on that the arrival of food turned every man for himself. If someone decided to take your share, it was up to you to wrest it from him or go hungry.

Animals. They had sunk to that level. And now on the morn they'd be tending to animals. A smile creased his face at the irony of it. He took his food back to his hammock, and after whispering a prayer of thanks, devoured it. Rule of law and civility did not apply here. Once the door was bolted and the prisoners caged together, the rule of tooth and claw took over.

Klesc sat by himself against the stones near the trough where a trickle of water flowed. He was a big man. He reminded Lamech of another big man who'd briefly stepped into and then out of his life a few weeks back ... or had it been longer?

Klesc did his work without complaining and kept to himself. He appeared simpleminded, except his eyes were forever in motion, constantly wary, never surprised. What secrets did Klesc hide?

Rumor had it he'd been arrested for killing a man over a matter of a few glecks owed to him. He'd wrecked a festival hall in the process, and it had taken more than twenty green-cloaks to bring him down. Afterward, half of the Lodath's Guards who'd been involved in the skirmish had been carted off to the local healer. Lamech gave a quiet laugh. Judging from the man's size, he could believe it.

The others were freer in their speech. Orm'el claimed to be an ex-miner, in prison for murder as well. Fa-elak and Ker-bar were thieves, arrested while leaving a precious stone merchant with pocketfuls of emeralds. And Mantir had been caught stamping counterfeit glecks out of a tin-lead alloy and, through some alchemy of his own devising, coloring them gold. The bogus money felt and looked right, but when a Web merchant accidentally set one on a stove only to return it to a silvery puddle, Mantir found himself in the clutches of King Irad's soldiers. Mantir had laughed when he'd told the story and afterward sat shaking his head mumbling how he had to get the mixture right next time.

Theirs had all been civil infractions. Lamech admitted to no crime, except that of preaching about the Creator and speaking against the Oracle in Nod City. His had been religious, and his punishment harsher than usual. Fifteen years on the Temple gang.

There must be a reason?

Night drew over the dungeon, the darkness tempered only by a rectangle of light from the moonglass set in the wall behind narrowed shutters: hardly enough to read by, had there been anything to read. Lamech peered through the stone slit to the night sky, smelling the smoke of the fires around the Temple site. He studied the stars. There, written in the heavens, was his book and the story of his hope.

He sighed and climbed into the rope hammock. Already, soft snoring filled the room. Tomorrow would be here soon enough. He closed his eyes and imagined Mishah in his arms. Had she completed her pilgrimage? Memory of the dream reared its snarling head. He forced it from his thoughts. He had to believe she was safe. To think otherwise was dangerous, yet even as he drifted off to sleep, his spirit was troubled.

❈

The sun that burned upon his naked shoulders and the acrid smoke that stung his nose were both only vague, distant annoyances....

Nothing smelled worse than the watery dung of a behemoth. The stench of it in the sweltering heat battered Lamech's nose. Its sharp odor permeated the pores of his skin and burrowed permanently into the material of his breechcloth. The Quort Whip had not permitted the men to work in their clothes, growling that he'd never hear an end to it if he allowed his charges to return to the Temple Prison reeking of behemoth dung.

"Clear the runway!" a voice from above bellowed through a funnel.

The men scurried out of the way. Lamech and Fa-elak grabbed their dump carts and moved them aside as the behemoth's knees passed by Lamech's nose, each earthshaking step covering seven spans. Lamech kept one eye on the giant beast's tail, fully as long as a cedar tree.

He parked his dung-filled dump cart and then gathered with the others under En'tuboc's watchful gaze. The behemoth lumbered down the runway, its taut harness a cable of woven spider silk, thick around as a man's arm, moving through the pulleys. High overhead, suspended by a gigantic balloon, the heavy-lifting platform dipped sharply as a block of dressed stone, harnessed in iron straps, rose off a cart and swayed a moment, three spans above the ground.

Lamech caught his breath. This was always the most dangerous part of the operation, especially in the heat of the day. The behemoth strained under the weight, while overhead the heavy-lifting platform canted more steeply to one side. Activity around the Temple site came momentarily to a halt as all watched—all but those feeding the roaring fires that drove heated air up long fabric tubes to the massive balloon.

As the block of stone rose higher, men aboard the heavy-lifting platform began signaling with flags. Here and there tether lines were adjusted, some hauled in, others let out. Lamech marveled at the precise choreography of handlers, behemoths, and signalers. Slowly the platform shifted, its massive oval shadow drifting across the construction site as the quarried block swung into place. Once the massive stone was positioned, the behemoth, following the commands of its handler, slowly backed up until the block had settled exactly in place upon the huge structure rising up out on the Plains of Irad.

The maneuver completed, En'tuboc ordered the men back to work.

Ker-bar grabbed a shovel and groused, "If they'd stop feeding them beasts, we wouldn't have to clean up after them!"

Mantir chuckled, levering a shovel over his shoulder. Orm'el followed after Ker-bar and Fa-elak. Without a word, Klesc strode to a pile and began heaving dripping shovelfuls into Lamech's handcart.

They labored far into the night; the heaviest blocks were always lifted after sundown, the cooler air giving more buoyancy to the balloon. At the third watch of the second quartering, En'tuboc marched them into the communal bath, where Lamech labored in vain to scrub the stench from his skin.

Back in their cell, the moonglass shutters stood wide open, and the soft glow of the magnetic light filled the musty room. Lamech gave a groan, put his back against the cool stone wall, and sank to the floor, lowering his head between his knees. The stagnant air smelled almost sweet compared to the stench of behemoth dung. Their food arrived and the men, driven by hunger, rallied, groping for anything within reach. The smell of cooked flesh wafting from the food tray was tempting to a famished man, but Lamech chose instead cheese, fruit, vegetables, and gruel—his usual fare.

"You'll not keep your strength, Preacher, eating like that," Fa-elak groused. "We'll all have to work the harder for it."

It hadn't been the first time Fa-elak had turned Lamech's beliefs on him like a prod. Lamech knew it wasn't his failing strength that Fa-elak was concerned about, but his refusal to compromise.

"When the Creator says I can eat the flesh of animals, then I will. Until then, the bounty of the ground will be my meat." He waited for their derision, but most were too tired to bother. Orm'el would not goad; he never did. And neither would Klesc. But the others usually scoffed at his principles.

He finished his meal and stood wearily, taking his tin cup to the trough for a drink. Klesc, sitting in his usual place against the corner, watched him, his strong jaw grinding a tough keelit husk. Lamech gave the big man a haggard smile and crossed to the slim window. A brisk breeze tonight carried the smoke from the Temple's construction fires southward over the Little Hiddekel River, and the stars showed clear.

"What is it you keep looking for, Preacher?" Orm'el tossed a bone onto the tray and grabbed the edge of his hammock, hauling himself wearily to his feet.

A question. Mishah had accused him of not knowing when to keep his mouth shut, but when one asks, how could he not answer? *Creator, watch over my tongue.* He turned from the slit as Orm'el limped over. "I look to the stars and the stories they tell," Lamech said.

"A stargazer!" Ker-bar laughed. "Always figured you was some touched in the head, Lamech."

"The preacher's got a book in the sky," Fa-elak scoffed. "Does this book have a name?"

"In fact, it does. It is called *The Way*."

"You're a dreamer." Ker-bar threw a gnawed leg bone at him. Lamech ducked, and it smacked a greasy splotch on the stone wall.

"What stories do they tell, Preacher?" Orm'el asked, ignoring Ker-bar's jab.

"From this window, I can see the story of Arieh, the Lion."

Orm'el appeared skeptical but interested.

"The Lion represents the King. And beneath the Lion's feet is the serpent, that ancient deceiver. In the midst of the sign is the cup, the divine cup of wrath being poured out on the serpent. And finally there is the sign of the raven. The raven is devouring the snake."

Orm'el looked askance. "I don't see nothing but stars, Preacher. Where'd you get all that?"

Lamech smiled. "That is all anyone sees, until they are taught. The night sky reveals twelve star pictures, but until you know the names of the stars and their meaning, you won't be able to read it."

Fa-elak laughed and tumbled back onto his hammock. "You read your star-book up or down? Or from left to right or right to left?"

"Neither. It's read according to the brightness of the stars." He looked back at Orm'el "The Creator has written his plan to redeem man in the heavens for all to see: from the Virgin to the Lion. The Creator has not left man without a witness."

Orm'el stared at him a moment, then grinned and shook his head. Ker-bar and Fa-elak guffawed.

Mantir chuckled. "In here, talk like that will get you in trouble, Preacher. You'll get a helping of En'tuboc's whip if you don't still your tongue."

Klesc just watched him with that curious expression. Lamech grimaced. Mishah would have elbowed him and whispered sternly to keep his mouth shut.

His stomach knotted with renewed concern. How was she? Was she already on her way back home to the Lee-lands of Morg'Seth?

Surely she must be. And what of their child, their son? Memory of the dream roared back, sending a bolt of fear through him. It was only a nightmare. No more than that. Still, it left him shaking, and he quickly whispered a prayer that the birth of his son would be without problem and that Mishah would be protected through it.

With a clatter of a lever from outside the cell, the moonglass shutters slammed shut, throwing the dungeon into darkness. He left the window and crawled into his hammock, listening to the others wearily climb into their own rope slings and one by one fall asleep.

2

Leenah

*E*ight behemoths worked the construction site day and night; Lamech and his fellow prisoners were never out of work. As they moved from one station to the next, there were always fresh, reeking piles of dung to be shoveled into the wooden carts. The carts absorbed the odor so completely that they smelled as bad as what they hauled.

Three days into their new routine, En'tuboc twisted the hard handle of his whip into Lamech's spine and said, "Come with me."

Under escort of two armed green-cloaks, they marched down a long stone corridor and into the correction council's chamber.

In contrast to the stark stone corridor, this room was painted a cool blue, with tapestries hung on the walls. A long table stood upon a rectangular rug woven of green and red fibers. The pattern contained the unspeakable symbols of the Oracle. It was similar to what Lamech remembered seeing on the hem of the dark blue coat the Lodath had worn at his interrogation and sentencing. A window set high in the wall let daylight into the room. Three men sat at the table. Two big-shouldered guards stood on either side of the door, naked from the waist up, arms folded across powerful chests, heads and faces shaved smooth. Lamech felt particularly vulnerable dressed as he was in only a loincloth and sandals.

En'tuboc prodded him toward the table. "This is the one you asked for."

A slight-built man at the far end studied him and then cleared his throat. "Some men never learn." His rich voice surprised Lamech. He had not been expecting such a deep timbre.

A second man, who had been reading a paper, placed it flat on the table and looked up. "You were charged with sedition and speaking against the Oracle."

He had not been seditious. He held not to rebellion, but truth. Truth would accomplish what rebellion could not: a change in hearts.

The slight-built man pressed his hands to the tabletop and leaned forward. His pale blue eyes narrowed. "And still you speak out against the Oracle."

Speak out against the Oracle? Lamech searched his memory. "I've not spoken against the Oracle." But even he could hear the uncertainty in that. Perhaps he had and just didn't recall.

The third man, watchfully silent up until then, stood. Taking a knobby walking stick in hand, he strode around the table and stopped behind Lamech. "You've been preaching this nonsense about the Creator."

So that was it. "I cannot deny I have spoken of my Creator. But to do so is not the same as speaking against the Oracle." The walking stick rammed hard into his back. Lamech groaned and lurched forward, catching himself on the edge of the table.

"You are not here to defend yourself." The man put the end of the stick to his spine and pressed. "This talk of the Creator, this nonsense of a message written in the stars. It will cease." The stick dug deeper, twisting. "Is that understood?"

Lamech bit his lip against the pain and nodded, at that moment distantly aware of footsteps in the hallway coming to a halt before the door.

"Speak it."

"Talk of the stars will cease."

"And what else?"

"I will no longer explain how the Creator has written his story of the salvation of mankind in the heavens."

"That's not what I mean." The stick drove him forward against the table.

"I'll not speak of the Constellation of Bethulah, the coming virgin who will bring forth the Redeemer."

The men seated at the table looked at each other and scowled.

"Or of the one hundred and ten stars within it that shout its glory."

The stick whacked him across the back. "Enough."

Lamech went to his knees, his back muscles screaming, his spine aching. He should shut his mouth, but something compelled him to speak. Was it sheer stubbornness? Poor Mishah would be at her wit's end if she knew. She had been too perceptive, saying he'd never leave prison, that his mouth would keep him there. He should heed her wisdom now, yet as he pulled himself straight, muscles burning, the words just came forth. "Nor will I mention again the sign of the Mozanaim, the Scales, those fifty-one stars that speak of the purchase price of the redemption."

The stick struck and broke across his back, the end sailing across the room into the wall. Lamech sprawled upon the rug. Before his blurred vision, the symbols of the Oracle swam from the weave of the rug, mocking him. Why didn't he just keep quiet?

"Get him out of here."

Guards grabbed each arm and hauled him to his feet. Scowling darkly, En'tuboc prodded him with the whip's handle. Lamech staggered toward the door, then stopped in front of an old man who had been waiting just outside. Lamech hadn't noticed him there until then.

His tangled, white beard fell nearly to the golden rope wrapped about the waist of his scarlet robe. He'd never seen anyone attired quite like this man. The green of his eyes was the same shade as Amolikah's, his wife's grandmother. They studied him with open curiosity.

The man held a long, rolled document under his left arm. Lamech's eye caught figures sketched on a part of it. A star chart. From what he could see of it, he recognized the constellation. He almost laughed at the irony in it.

The old man held him in a curious gaze, almost as if he was trying to communicate something to him by thought alone.

Lamech gave a wry grin, then glanced to the carefully penned arrangement of stars just visible upon the curve of the roll. "Tes-ark."

The green eyes widened. "This from afar." His voice was soft and thoughtful as he gave the meaning of the name exactly.

Lamech had to smile at the blank look upon En'tuboc's face. Here was a language the Quort Whip did not understand. And quite clearly, here was someone whose presence En'tuboc and the Disciplinary Council respected. Who could he be? Without understanding why—he'd certainly said enough already—Lamech said, "Eighty-one."

The man's gray eyebrows hitched up with interest. "One is of the first order." His inflection begged a reply.

"Six of the third."

"Five double."

"One quadruple." What was the game the graybeard was playing? Did he only intend to deepen Lamech's trouble?

The old man's lips worked and twitched for a moment, then shifted to the right, and he stepped aside for him to pass.

Lamech puzzled a moment over the encounter. En'tuboc nudged

Lamech down the dark corridor. If the brief exchange had indeed dug his hole deeper, it was too late now to fill it in.

Outside, sharp sunlight stung his eyes. En'tuboc started him toward his work quort. "Maybe that will teach you to hold your tongue in the presence of the council. If you've got any brains, you'll speak no more of this Creator of yours."

Someone in his quort had reported him. But who? And how could he ever keep silent? If silence was mandatory for freedom, he would surely die here as Mishah had predicted. For her sake, and the sake of his son, he would have to try.

"Who was that man?"

En'tuboc didn't reply at once as his gaze went across the bustling construction site sweltering beneath the midday sun. His glance seemed to rest a moment on the sloping sides of the Temple, already rising high above the perimeter walls. The roaring fires that kept the heavy-lifting platform sky bound added their own heat to the warmth of the sprawling place that one day would be a complex of buildings to house the Oracle.

"His name is Sor-dak. Chief Temple sky-charter and stargazer. He's a very important man. You should know when not to speak."

And how often had Mishah said that?

En'tuboc's dark look returned to him. "This was only a warning, Lamech. Take it seriously. The council doesn't tolerate trouble-makers." His eyes compressed warningly. "Accidents happen. I'll say no more."

✷

The sun crawled along the arc of heaven, burning into Lamech's welted and bleeding back. The salt of his sweat stung like nettles, but the work went on. Cart after cart of behemoth dung rolled to the stone troughs outside the walls to be flushed down to the river.

The Temple was only the first of the planned structures. It would be a hundred years or more before the full splendor of the Oracle's Temple glittered in the sunlight. Meanwhile, Lamech labored on a monument to a god he despised.

To fill the long quarterings and keep his mind off the pain and the sly glances and muffled remarks of his fellow prisoners, Lamech pondered the Creator's plan, laid out clearly in the constellations of the twelve signs that circled the heavens—a favorite pastime, and one that now seemed destined to mark his doom.

Interspersed with meditating on the Creator's comforting truths, Lamech kept his brain limber by working out the angles to each sign, calculating the degrees of separation, the years of their precession, breaking them down into days and minutes, and then turning the numbers over in his head, carefully sifting them for the pattern ... a hidden story he was certain they had to tell. He had always been good with numbers—another favorite pastime—and he believed the Creator buried deeper treasures to reward those diligent enough to search them out.

"Water?" The woman's voice pulled his thoughts back from a place of comfort to the heap of dung he, Orm'el, and Klesc were shoveling into the cart. Instantly his aching back reminded him of his morning's encounter.

She had fair hair and bright blue eyes that appeared intelligent, alert, and wary. The sun had colored her high cheeks, and it was obvious she'd arranged her golden hair to shield the scorching rays from her face as much as possible. She was very tall, slender almost to a fault, and dressed in prison gray, the shapeless dress stenciled with the symbol of the House of Cain encircled by the Oracle's pentagram above her heart.

"Thank you." He drank from the ladle and passed it to Orm'el, who drained it. She refilled the ladle and gave it to Klesc.

Lamech rolled his shoulders and groaned. Spying his wounds, the woman frowned. "I see you've met the council."

"This morning."

"Let me put some salve on it." She took a bag from the bottom of the water cart and removed a round stone box that contained a thick yellow paste. The salve stung for an instant, then the pain eased. "There, that will help you feel better."

"Are you a healer?" Mishah was a healer, but this woman in no way reminded him of his wife except for her youth, her concern, and her gentle touch in tending to his wounds.

"I was apprentice to a healer once, but ..." She gave a faint smile. "But now I'm here."

Klesc studied her as he drank.

She caught his look and smiled at him. "Thoughts of home?"

He seemed annoyed at that.

Lamech asked, "What is your name?"

"Leenah."

"Thank you for the water, Mistress Leenah, and the salve."

She looked pleased at the respectful title he'd placed before her name. How long had it been since she had been shown such respect?

Orm'el grinned and leaned on his shovel. "Come back anytime, little flower."

"I suspect I will. Your quort is part of my new assignment."

Klesc placed the ladle back in her hand. "Dirgen smile upon you."

Leenah beamed at him, "And the Creator on you." She cast Lamech a lingering glance, then left.

He felt a small smile creep to his mouth as he watched Leenah push her water cart toward where the other men in his quort were working. So, there *were* some here who believed as he did.

Klesc's eyes, dark and unreadable as usual, also followed her.

❦

His wounds burned. His sweat and the plunge in the communal

bath afterward had washed away the salve and, with it, whatever balm it had contained to numb the pain. Mishah would have known. She probably carried the same salve in her healer's bag. He tried not to think of his wife as he turned in the rope hammock, unable to find a comfortable position.

From the darkened room came the soft breathing of sleep. One of his fellow prisoners had betrayed him. Was it Orm'el? He'd been the inquisitive one. Or Fa-elak? Fa-elak had scoffed at the idea of the Creator's plan of salvation written in the stars, so why would it matter to him? Ker-bar? He seemed not to care about anything except his full share of the food and how much of it he could steal from the rest of them. And what of Mantir, the counterfeiter? He'd showed only disgust for all authority. Lamech suddenly looked to where Klesc slept. Or could it be the quiet one with the probing eyes that never seemed to miss a single detail—eyes so often directed at him? What wheels turned in Klesc's head?

Lamech flopped onto his stomach and stretched his arms, his hands hanging over the end of the hammock. Why would any of them care enough to report him? Which one of the five stood to gain the most? The questions tumbled around his brain until exhaustion stilled the commotion and a deep sleep took away the pain and worry.

One monotonous day flowed into another until Lamech stopped keeping track. Leenah, and others like her, followed their own mindless routines, hauling water to the prisoners in a never-ending circuit. Lamech was careful to whom he spoke about his faith but never refused to share it. It was what the Creator had called him to do. He was a preacher. Mantir had been the first to start calling him that, and now everyone in his work quort simply referred to him by the title.

Since their meeting outside the correction council chamber, Lamech had begun to notice whenever Sor-dak appeared on the construction site. It was impossible to miss the man in his scarlet robe and brilliant white beard. He arrived always in the company of other men, moving purposefully about, pointing here and there, peering through lenses that measured angles. Lamech longed to see what they were seeing, to gauge a slant and a distance, to calculate an elevation. His mind craved for intellectual stimulus. Cleaning up after behemoths engaged his nose only, and now even that had gone dead.

"Morning peace, Master Lamech." Leenah's smile was always as welcome a sight as the water jug she brought.

"Morning peace, and thank you." He took the ladle from her. Just then Sor-dak strode from a passageway not many paces away, accompanied by two other men. Lamech didn't recognize the second man, but the third was resplendent in a deep blue tunic and a hem embroidered with the Oracle's unspeakable symbols—the very signs he'd remembered so well as he lay upon the rug in the correction council chamber. Sol-Ra-Luce. The Lodath. The Oracle's mouthpiece.

Leenah ducked her head and shrank from sight behind Lamech.

"What is it?" Instinctively, he moved to conceal her further. He sensed she was trembling. He'd never seen her fearful like this. Leenah had always been rock solid.

"I don't want him to see me." Her whispered words held dread.

"Master Sor-dak?"

"The Lodath."

The three men continued on toward the huge monument, already standing two hundred spans tall; its four smooth stone walls tapered toward a top that one day would be capped with the purest crystal.

"They've passed. It's clear now."

She drew in a long breath and seemed to shiver as she returned to work.

"What was that about, Mistress Leenah."

"You haven't heard?"

"I've heard many things."

She dipped a ladle of water, and her voice lowered even though at the moment it was only the two of them. "The Lodath stalks the Temple grounds like a mansnatcher, and he takes whichever women he wants. Once they are removed, they are never heard from again—ever." Her eyes rounded. "Occasionally a body is discovered. Most are beyond recognition. But once in a while, a corpse is still whole enough to be identified." She trembled and burnished her arms. "It is best not to be noticed by the Lodath."

Lamech nearly trembled himself, remembering how close Mishah had come to being a prisoner here too. "I'd not heard any of this. How is such a thing permitted?"

"Who is to stop it? King Irad?" Her eyes narrowed sharply. "He's no better than the voice of the Oracle of the Crystal." She spat the words with disdain. "They're both tools in the Deceiver's hands. Between the two of them, they hold complete power."

He remembered how the dark evil had vexed his soul and filled the room as he stood before the Lodath the day of his sentencing. And he'd felt it again, a few days later, when he'd come before the Lodath to complete the interrogation. It was a struggle not of flesh, but of spirit.

Leenah gathered up the water jar, casting a worried look in the direction the Lodath had disappeared. "Someday this will all be gone." She glanced around at the Temple to the Oracle of the Crystal. "Someday soon." Her gaze came back to him, the dread replaced by the now-familiar smile. The woman seemed to possess a capacity to find peace in the midst of calamity. "I'll talk to you tomorrow, Master Lamech."

"Be careful."

"I try to be." She gathered up the heavy jar and went off to her next station.

Someday soon. Did she know of the prophecies? He glanced to the Temple encompassed about with scaffolding and ramps and overshadowed by the heavy-lifting platform, hovering day and night above it like a menacing bird. Leenah's revelation grated on the slate of his mind. How strong a hold *had* evil taken here in Nod City? It seemed it was even worse than he had suspected.

"Someday soon," he whispered.

3

Beneath Behemoth's Foot

*T*he journey south eventually took Rhone, Kenoch, Cerah, and Kleg'l past the ruins of Far Port. It was hard to believe that a handful of Earth-Borns had caused so much destruction. Yet even here among such great ruin, the indomitable spirit of men was showing itself. Already the charred structures were being cleared away, and new buildings were rising upon old foundations. Rhone pressed on past the river town, not stopping. Some of the Lodath's Guard might still remain.

He led the party down the River Road, making quick time atop the swift gerups they'd seized from some of the Lodath's troops. Rhone recalled that it was here on the River Road that the peddler, Elfin'ron, had taken Captain Jakl, Otev, and himself aboard his wagon, after the skybarge they'd been traveling aboard had been attacked by mansnatchers. Rhone wondered briefly about the two friends. Had they escaped Far Port before the giants razed the town?

He had not seen or smelled a single javian spider since leaving the Ruins of Eden weeks earlier. The spiders seemed to have all fled the encroaching evil, migrating to the Northlands. What would

Ker'ack do now without a ready supply of Web? Rhone grimaced at the pang that suddenly stabbed at him. It happened whenever he thought of the Web merchant ... and his son, Bar'ack. That one hadn't been cut out for a life of adventure and the perils of being a Webmaster. Rhone felt a frown tug at his lips. He should never have taken Bar'ack with him in the first place. What had happened to the young man, he wondered, after the Evil had entered him?

A safe distance above Nod City, they took a ferry across the Hiddekel River and made a wide detour to the west as the Wild Lands gave way to civilization. Rhone's natural wariness sharpened. Vast farms now filled the once-forested land, and small hinterland villages sprang up every few leagues: Benjinka, Oril-ee, Wada-ee. The villages grew larger and busier as Rhone, Kenoch, Cerah, and Kleg'l worked their way toward Lavin's Landing. The river-port town was a two-day march south of Nod City—far enough, Rhone hoped, to be safe from the Lodath's Guard.

※

Kleg'l strode down the plank walkway from the wharf, where four vessels were moored alongside the jetty. From the wide smile upon Kleg'l's long, thin lips, Rhone deduced the family's Good Man had managed to book passage on one of them.

"It took all of our money, Master Kenoch, but we leave at the last watch of this quartering. The captain wishes us aboard at once."

Kenoch looked at Rhone. "I regret parting, Master Rhone, but I know you have pressing business elsewhere. I only wish I could go with you." He grimaced. "I do miss Lamech. I'd give anything to hear him lecture me again on my duties to the family or my worldliness."

Cerah took Kenoch's arm. "Lamech sounds very sensible to me. I look forward to the day when we finally meet."

Sadness filled Kleg'l's long face. "I too miss Master Lamech." He shook his head. "Fifteen years."

Rhone heard the words rattle in Kleg'l's chest. "I'll tell him you miss him."

Kenoch said, "Tell Lamech we *all* miss him. And don't forget to tell him about Cerah and me." He hugged his wife's shoulder. "Tell him we'll name our first son after him. When he returns home, there'll be two Lamechs!" Kenoch forced a grin, but Rhone knew it was tears he really felt.

"I'll tell him all that has happened."

Kleg'l looked suddenly concerned. "What if they won't permit you in to see him?" His eyes narrowed worriedly. "What if you are recognized?"

"The Creator takes care of the details, Kleg'l." The confidence in Rhone's voice was only partly honest. This faith of the Lee-landers was still new to him, but he'd seen enough already to know it could be trusted. Besides, there was always Sari'el. How could he deny the Creator's protection with a companion such as the mighty Messenger?

They gathered up what few belongings were left to them, and Cerah hugged the precious book entrusted to her by Mother Eve. Cerah looked at him a long moment, then smiled and turned away with the others.

As they trudged up the plank road to the quay and the waiting boat, Cerah suddenly stopped and rushed back to him. "Thank you for helping us, Master Rhone."

"Take care of that book."

She looked at the heavy volume in her arms. "The words of our father, Adam, and of the Creator. Can anything be more precious?"

Rhone smiled and shook his head.

"The Creator be with you, Master Rhone." She looked up at him with shining eyes and hugged him, her long hair braided in a thick, fiery cord slipping over her shoulder. She stretched and kissed his cheek, then crushing the book to her chest again, returned to Kenoch's side.

A lump lodged in Rhone's throat. In such a short time these people—Lee-landers whom he had once scorned—had become closer than family. *Family?* A pit opened suddenly in his stomach as he remembered the task he had to tend to after his visit with Lamech.

Kleg'l marched across the gangplank and onto the boat. Cerah and Kenoch turned and lifted arms in the air. Rhone waved back. Then they boarded. Rhone listened to the distant idling chug of the boat's cycler; the odor of partially burned vera-logia lingering in the air from its exhaust. "Fair journey," he said softly.

They will be all right. They are watched over.

The words brushed across his brain, feather soft. He'd almost gotten used to the sensation by now. "I know."

He gathered the reins to their mounts. He considered selling the extra gerups at the livery, but since they bore the mark of the Lodath's Guard, it might raise suspicions.

Once beyond the buildings of Lavin's Landing, Rhone unsaddled the gerups and set them free. From astride his mount, he watched them gallop across a glade, flushing butterflies and birds before them. A herd of red deer moved out of their way as if annoyed to have been stirred from their lazy grazing. A pocket dragon burst from the tall grass and winged skyward.

As the gerups circled toward a distant stand of trees, Rhone longed for such freedom again. He drew in a breath and let it out. He had once run where he pleased, but that was all changed. The path before him could lead only to bondage—the sort of captivity that responsibility lays upon the shoulders of a man.

Rhone pointed his gerup north and kicked it into motion.

❦

From his hammock, if he lowered his head just so and peered up at a slight angle, Lamech could just see a rectangular patch of night sky through the stone slit in the prison wall. In spite of his perpetual exhaustion, he lay awake, watching the stars slowly wheel past his narrow view.

"Reading your book, Preacher?" Orm'el's quiet voice spoke from the next hammock over.

"Yes," he whispered; the others needed their sleep as badly as he. Unfortunately, he was cursed with a brain that sometimes refused to shut down. It had always been so. Back home he'd lie in bed bursting with ideas, while beside him Mishah would be sound asleep. Sometimes he was annoyed at her and envious that she could put her worries on a shelf and fall asleep so easily. Now he'd give everything just to hear her soft breathing at his side again.

"They must think we eat like kittens for all they feed us," Orm'el groused.

"Hungry?"

"It's the gnawing in my belly that's keeping me awake. What about you, Preacher?"

He seldom mentioned the personal side of his life, but they all knew he was married. "I'm thinking of my wife."

"I never took a wife." Orm'el gave a soft laugh. "I was always too busy taking other men's wives. That's what got me in here. Had a fling with the pretty little wife of a shift boss up in the Longrun District. She was always lamenting how her husband neglected her, so I assumed the husbandly duties, you might say. When he got wind of the liaison, he hired two strong fellows to wring my 'scrawny neck'—his words, not mine. We were mining berdeniex. Know what that is?"

"Berdeniex is a mineral in iron alloy. It's supposed to keep it from rusting." He'd already heard the story, but Orm'el seemed proud enough of his exploits to tell it over and over.

"You're smarter than you look, Preacher. The Tubal-Cain Company buys the stuff by the barge-load. I stole aboard one of them floating mountains and ended up down here in Nod City. Somehow those two head-crackers followed me, but I was ready for them. I followed them to a festival hall one night, slipped the barmaid a shaved gleck to see that their mugs stayed full of strong ale, and slit their throats at the end of a black alley when they come out. Neither one made a sound, but the alley wasn't dark enough, I reckon. Someone saw me leaving, and the next thing I know, I'm surrounded by them men in green."

Orm'el went silent a moment. "I'd do anything to get out of this hole."

Anything?

"Preacher, where did you learn all them stories about the stars and all."

The hairs at the back of Lamech's neck prickled. "Why would that interest you?" The wariness in his voice was an unfamiliar note. How quickly prison changes a man, sharpens him. A subtle shift in Klesc's steady breathing set off a warning bell. Lamech felt hidden eyes plying across him, or was it only his brain playing tricks?

"I don't know." Orm'el's voice turned thoughtful. "Just that I've been thinking maybe there's something to this Creator myth." He laughed. "Maybe I'm just too hungry and tired to think straight."

Was Orm'el's interest genuine? Or was he setting him up? It was dangerous to preach here, yet not to do so would be as hard as ceasing to breathe.

Lamech inhaled quietly and told Orm'el of his grandfather Enoch, of the Creator, and of the prophecies.

※

Ker-bar slopped a dripping shovelful of behemoth dung into the cart, his nose wrinkled like a dried grape. "I thought I'd gotten used to it."

Lamech's defense was to hold his breath. Over the weeks he'd developed mighty lungs. "Try to think of something else."

"Nothing else works, Preacher. I'm so hungry all I can think of is food, but with this smell in my nose, I always imagine it tasting like behemoth girt!" Ker-bar leaned on his shovel and seemed to shudder all over.

Fa-elak heaved a shovelful into the cart. "Look busy, men; here comes somebody."

Lamech and Ker-bar glanced at the white-bearded man accompanied by two muscular workers, each carrying tripods and heavy bronze lenses. It was Sor-dak. Seeing Lamech there, he altered his steps. He wore a faded robe today, its once bright scarlet hue muted to a dull umber. His swarthy face had seen many years and too much sun; deep lines crisscrossed his cheeks, and furrows radiated away from his green eyes.

"Ah, the young man with a curious grasp of star mechanics."

Lamech lowered his shovel. "I'm honored you remember me, Master Sor-dak. Our meeting was brief and not under the best of circumstances."

"So, you know who I am."

"Your reputation as a master builder and learned stargazer is well known."

Sor-dak's mouth crinkled at the corners, his green eyes catching a glint of sunlight. "And you are called by what?"

"Lamech."

"Oh, yes. Lamech. The Sethite." His smile widened a little, and a long finger shook before Lamech's nose. "You too have a reputation."

"Unfortunately."

Sor-dak laughed without making a sound, then pointed to the Temple. "What do you think of it?"

Be wise as a serpent. Now seemed a good time to take Amolikah's advice. "It's an engineering marvel. When completed, its height alone will surpass any other structure built."

Sor-dak nodded. "Yes, over six hundred spans."

"Six hundred and sixty-six," Lamech said.

The engineer's eyes widened. "Precisely. How do you know this?"

He hadn't really thought about how he knew. He just did. Probably from one of the many mathematical games he'd played to keep his brain engaged and distracted from the labor of the prison. He shrugged. "The base is already in place, and the angle of the walls are set at forty-one units. The calculation is a simple one."

En'tuboc showed up just then. "What's going on here?"

Sor-dak held Lamech a moment in a bemused gaze, then looked at En'tuboc. "I apologize for keeping your men from their task, Quort Whip. We were simply admiring the Oracle's Temple." He waved a hand in the direction of the rising edifice, then smiled and strolled off with his instrument-bearers in tow.

En'tuboc scowled and unfurled his long whip. "To work!"

Lamech turned back to the mound of dung, and as his shovel stirred up a swarm of flies, Fa-elak mumbled, "Your stargazing is going to get us all in trouble, Preacher."

❈

It had become the high point of Lamech's day. He could count on at least some reprieve from the drudgery toward the middle of the fourth quartering when Leenah would come by with her heavy crock of cold water. At first she seemed nothing at all like Mishah, but as he got to know her, he began seeing similarities. Leenah was a woman of strong faith, yet, like Mishah, cautious when speaking of it. She was caring and, like Mishah, very pretty. His mouth bent in a wry smile. Such comparisons brought on the fierce ache of separation.

Alone, they'd speak of the Creator and how he was working in both their lives. If others were nearby, she'd just share the gossip circulating about the prison camp. News traveled quickly. In practice, each work quort was kept isolated from the others. But in reality, nothing could happen to even a single member of one quort without the whole camp knowing about it within a few hours.

Today, Leenah was later than usual. When she did finally arrive, he noted the strain in her face and the worry in her eyes. Instead of the friendly conversation he had grown fond of, she spoke little as she ladled out water for each of them, then giving him a guarded look, hurried on to her next station.

Lamech tried to ignore his disappointment, but worry subtly worked its way into him. He sensed she had wanted to tell him something and wished they'd been alone so he could have spoken freely with her. Had it been the presence of Ker-bar and Fa-elak that had stayed her tongue? Or something else?

Night brought a cool breeze that afforded the men the chance to work upwind of the dung. It helped.

"Clear the runway!" came the now-familiar call from the heavy-lifting platform above.

Lamech shoveled up one last load and grabbed the heavy cart. Already the great footfalls of the approaching behemoth rumbled through the ground. As he started away, Fa-elak turned and pointed. "Preacher! You left a shovel on the runway!"

Lamech halted and wheeled back. There it was. How did it happen? Had he been so wrapped in his thoughts, so worried about Leenah? If En'tuboc saw his carelessness, it would be double work duty and the biting end of his whip to be sure. He dashed back to snatch the shovel out of harm's way and caught a glimpse of movement to his right. Something slammed into him, catapulting him out onto the gravel. The ground seemed to be rumbling all around him, and voices shouted. As he rolled over and looked up through blurred eyes, a shadow suddenly blocked the light of the fires. A circle of blackness hovered over him. The behemoth's immense foot descended. He flung an arm over his head. Someone grabbed him by the shoulders and heaved him to one side. Something hard punched his shoulder, and the ground shook.

"Fool!"

Lamech's head cleared to a vision of swinging ropes of braided hair and scowling dark eyes.

"Fool! If you get yourself killed, it's me who'll have to stand before the Lodath and explain why his Temple Crew is short a man!" En'tuboc's fiery glare narrowed at him, the reek of his breath a hot wind in his face. "What was the cause of this?"

Lamech discovered Klesc holding him steady on his feet. It was he who had snatched him from beneath the behemoth's feet.

"I'm not sure." Lamech looked around. Fa-elak was helping Ker-bar to his feet.

"It was my fault," Ker-bar said, standing a little unsteady. "I saw the shovel in the runway and went for it. I guess I wasn't paying attention. Me and the Preacher, we ran into each other."

En'tuboc snarled his disgust, barely restraining anger. "I'll teach you to keep your eyes open. You'll work all night!" His hot anger flared across the six men. "All of you!" He pointed the furled whip at Lamech and Ker-bar. "Next time something like this happens, I'll flay your backs."

4

A Break for Freedom

With the dawn still only a gray hope in the eastern sky, Lamech leaned against the cool stone wall near the corner of a building and closed his eyes. Every muscle in his body burned. If he stood like this for very long, he'd certainly fall asleep on his feet. What would En'tuboc have to say about that? A grim smile cut his face.

Out on the runway a behemoth trudged in its slow, powerful way, lifting another great stone toward the platform floating high above the Temple scaffolding. The night seemed endless. Was En'tuboc going to permit them any rest, or did he intend to work them clear through their next shift? And where had the Quort Whip gone, anyway? Likely off someplace napping. Lamech hadn't seen him for most of the last quartering.

Lamech and Ker-bar had endured the angry stares from their fellow workers all night. He couldn't blame them. It hadn't been their fault. He opened his eyes. Fa-elak, Mantir, Klesc, Orm'el, and Ker-bar each looked as worn out as he, slumped against walls, heads hanging. He sunk to the ground and drooped his head to wait out the passage of the behemoth.

"Psst."

He opened his eyes and cocked an ear.

"Master Lamech." Leenah's whisper came from around the corner.

He glanced over as she peeked out at him, then drew back. "What are you doing here?"

Her finger appeared and crooked. He stood, cast cautiously about, and slid surreptitiously around the corner.

"I heard what happened last night." She spoke softly, her eyes constantly on the lookout.

He grinned in spite of his weariness. "News travels fast." He saw her heavy water vessel sitting beside the wall. "Why are you here, Mistress Leenah?"

"My shift is about to start. I managed to get away from the others earlier than usual in the hope I might speak with you. You're in danger."

His mouth tightened. "Danger? From whom?"

"I don't know. All I know is the correction council has heard you've been speaking of the Creator again. They wish to deal with it permanently, but because of some oversight council above them, their hands are tied. They let it be known that if an accident were to happen, the one who caused it would receive favorable treatment. That's why I couldn't speak yesterday." Her quick eyes darted left and right. "This has happened before, Master Lamech. And each time, the *accident* was caused by a member of the victim's own quort."

Lamech's neck bristled as he sidled up to the corner and peeked around at the five haggard men. One of them wanted to kill him. "You shouldn't be seen with me. You can be in danger too."

She nodded. "But you had to know."

"Thanks."

She touched his arm. "Be vigilant. If I hear of anything, I'll tell you." She took up her water jar, bent beneath the weight, and moved off to her first station.

He glanced to the behemoth, nearly finished with its task, then at Ker-bar and Fa-elak with their backs against the wall, talking. Mantir sat alone. Orm'el and Klesc both leaned against another wall, half dozing, half watching the behemoth trudge back to its shaded pen, where a work quort fed it and sprayed it down with cool water.

It could be any one of them.

The Quort Whip came from one of the buildings, yawning and stretching; his tangled, braided beard a swaying mop at his chin. With a crack of his whip, En'tuboc ordered them back to work.

❧

Rhone stood over the small fire, his cloak drawn tight about him, beaded with the morning mist while a gray sky to the east welcomed a new day. These early hours at the end of the second quartering always filled him with a sense of well-being. He bent to fill his cup from the pot on the fire. Hot, strong carrog and the first rays of daylight! He drew in a deep breath and let it out, sipping the carrog that steamed against his face. All around him were the sounds of the deep forest waking to a new day. His gerup rustled about in its hobbles some distance away, grazing the branches of omis and keelit trees.

"We should make Nod City by this evening." He still felt foolish speaking to an entity who, most of the time, he could not see. Sometimes he'd get an answer and sometimes not. Sari'el was full of surprises. Rhone never knew if he was around or off on some errand of the Creator.

We must not delay in Nod City. I will be up against much resistance there.

So he *was* around. Rhone hadn't exactly heard the Messenger's voice. When Sari'el spoke, it was like a gentle stirring against his brain. Yet his words were so clear that they might have been whispered directly into his ear. And then again, if he were not paying close attention, the Messenger's words could easily have been passed off as a distant thought of his own.

"Do you want some carrog?" He didn't know what Messengers ate or drank, or even if they needed to. Only that, if they wished to, they were quite capable of mimicking anything human ... *anything*. Rhone grimaced, recalling the giants. Sari'el had explained what they really were—the children of human women and fallen Messengers—and how through them a vile pollution was entering the world. It had sent a cold shiver through him—a thing almost too incredible to believe. But believe it he must, for he had met the frightening results: met, fought, and killed them.

A shimmer in the midst of the darkness drew his eye as a rift opened and golden brilliance spilled out, momentarily illuminating the dark tree with its yellow glow. The touching of two worlds. Another marvel he had not quite gotten used to. From the golden light stepped the Messenger of the Creator. The rift folded in on itself, and the dawn's gray darkness once again closed in.

Sari'el wore a dark jerkin over a blue shirt. His trousers and boots were black. The Messenger was nearly as tall as Rhone, though not as large across the shoulders. But among these beings, size did not equate to strength. They were vastly more powerful than any human, than any army of humans, but their ability to exercise such power was limited by their obedience to the Creator. They did nothing outside the Creator's will.

Rhone filled a second cup for him. Sari'el sipped it with no outward show of pleasure or displeasure.

"I would like to visit my old friend Ker'ack. He should know about his son." Ker'ack's son, Bar'ack, had accompanied Rhone on what had begun as a routine trip into the Wild Lands to gather Web. The trip turned out to be anything but routine. Among the casualties—himself included—had been Bar'ack. Although the young man still breathed, his body had become inhabited by the vile spirits of the dead giants. Where Bar'ack was now, Rhone didn't know. That Bar'ack had left the Cradleland with the Lodath's Guards—who had unsuccessfully stormed its gates—was all he knew for sure.

Sari'el nodded. "Visit your friend if you must, Master Rhone, but I will not be able to accompany you."

"Oh?" Sari'el's jarring habit of dropping in and out of his life was becoming almost predictable.

"I have urgent business elsewhere. When this task is over, I will have to leave you."

"I understand." Rhone regretted the loss of his mostly unseen companion. Over the weeks since he'd first met the being from the Creator's realm, Rhone had grown close to him. It seemed a lifetime ago that he was happily engaged in the simple pursuit of gathering Web. That life of a Webmaster now seemed remote indeed. "And once this new task of yours is finished?"

"I am needed on many fronts, Master Rhone. If Elohim wills it, I will return to you. Yet take comfort in knowing he is with you always."

"This is still too new for me to understand."

"You have learned much already. Growth always takes time."

Rhone huddled the warm cup in both his hands as the first rays of morning sunlight streaked the sky in rose. "I worry only that I will not be able to do the Creator's will." He preferred the name the Lee-landers used, even though Sari'el always referred to the Creator as Elohim. His understanding was still shallow, yet he knew it made little difference to the Creator which name was used. The Creator first appeared to him as a simple gardener, but he was so much more than that. No simple gardener could have healed Kenoch's wounds or have instantly re-formed little Noah's lungs as he struggled for breath in those first few moments of life. *No simple gardener could have raised him from the dead.* For a while at least, he'd left his body and stood with Sari'el in that realm of golden light, but the details of that memory had been taken from him.

"You will do his will to the best of your ability, Master Rhone. The Creator expects no more than that."

And what was his ability? Up until a few weeks ago, he had been a Webmaster. Before that, a Makir Warrior and an exiled heir to a chiefdom and his father's high seat on the Council of Ten. "What the Creator asks of me is difficult, Sari'el."

"He would not ask it if it was not necessary." The Messenger sipped his carrog, at the moment appearing every bit as human as Rhone. "You worry how the task will be accomplished."

These beings from the realm of the Creator were perceptive. "By now Zorin would've consolidated his hold on Atlan. With his right to rule firmly entrenched and protected by Atlan's army, how will I overthrow him?"

"You are an exceptional man, Master Rhone. You will find a way."

"The skills I once had languish from years of neglect."

"Yet you can easily hold your own against any ten green-cloaks."

Rhone gave a short laugh. "Yes, but against even a single Makir Warrior in the prime of his training, I'd fare poorly."

"You misjudge in thinking you will be alone, Master Rhone."

"I know the Creator is with me always, and you," he made a wry face, "at least sometimes. Am I to assume you will be fighting at my side?"

Sari'el's very human smile was almost enough to make Rhone

forget whom he was speaking to, but then he'd be wrenched from his comfortable misconceptions remembering that it was Sari'el who had lassoed Leviathan with a golden chain and bound him in the depths of the sea.

"There will come, many years hence, another man who will lament that he is the only one left to do Elohim's will, when in truth, the Mighty Elohim will have more than seven thousand waiting in readiness."

Rhone raised a quizzical eyebrow. "Many years hence? You see the future, Sari'el?"

"Eternity—the past, the present, and the future as you comprehend them—is difficult to appreciate, Master Rhone. There is no concept in your world that encompasses it. You had a glimpse of eternity in Elohim's Garden, but because you were destined to return, your vision was clouded. The best way to describe it is to say eternity is not time unending. It is the cessation of time."

"I guess I will just have to wait to understand it, Sari'el."

"Every human does, eventually." Sari'el glanced at his cup, then handed it back to Rhone. "Thank you for the carrog. The dawn is upon us, and we must be on our way." Abruptly, the air behind him began to shimmer and split with a golden light. Sari'el stepped into the brilliance and was gone, leaving the lingering scent of lilac.

His comings and goings were dramatic, to say the least. Rhone doused his fire, packed his gear, and readied his mount for the final leg of his journey to Nod City.

❦

The morning quartering dragged on interminably. Lamech's weariness moved beyond exhaustion to a mental stupor that clouded his vision. Each of them, except Klesc, felt it. Klesc's great size and seemingly indomitable strength carried him on after other men failed. But a numbing weariness had begun to cause them all to make blunders, and more and more their naked, sweating backs felt the impatient sting of En'tuboc's whip.

Distantly, a commotion of some sort impinged upon Lamech's deadened brain. Fa-elak and Klesc, working at his side, heard it too. Lamech looked up. A woman, struggling in the arms of two prison guards, was being wrestled across the Temple compound. He blinked sweat from his eyes, and his vision sharpened. "That's Leenah!"

Fa-elak put down his shovel and leaned onto the handle as if it were the only thing keeping his weary body upright. "The water girl?" He slung sweat from his forehead. "What trouble has she got herself into?"

Strength surged anew within Lamech. He'd come to care for the young woman, in some ways seeing his own beloved Mishah in Leenah. As the guards hauled the struggling woman toward a low portal in the stone wall, their path brought them close to Lamech. Her face flushed with desperation, and her eyes held the same fear he'd noted days earlier when she'd hid from the Lodath. Had her natural beauty, her inborn innocence, her iron will finally caught the Lodath's eye?

Then a chilling thought crashed in on him. Had circumstances been but slightly altered, this could be Mishah instead of Leenah!

Klesc grabbed his arm. "Where are you going?"

He hadn't realized that he'd begun moving toward the struggling woman. "Someone's got to help her."

"You can do nothing, and you know it. Not here." That was the most that Klesc had spoken all day. The concern in his eyes was real.

Fa-elak backed away. "I want no part in this. You stick your nose in this, Preacher, and it's"—he dragged a finger across his throat in a meaningful way—"for certain."

Lamech wrenched free of Klesc's fingers. "I can't just let them take her." His thoughts were muddled, but his feet carried him forward even as he struggled to devise a plan. Mishah always accused him of thinking with his heart rather than with his head. Was he about to prove her right … again? *Creator, I'm at a loss as to what to do next. Be at my side.*

"Preacher, don't." The concern in Klesc's voice was so painfully real that Lamech wondered for an instant why the big man would care if he went and got his head broken.

Before a plan could take shape, he was in front of the guards, barring their way. They drew up and glared at him, obviously seeing his intent.

"Back to your quort. This doesn't concern you."

"Lamech." She looked at him with frightened eyes. "The Lodath has sent for me."

One of the guards unfurled a whip. Out the corner of his eye, Lamech saw En'tuboc rushing to intercept him. *Lamech, you've dug your grave this time!* The thought flitted through his mind like a wisp of smoke. Mishah's warning reverberated in his head. *You'll never come home. You'll clash with everyone you meet; you'll talk yourself into a new sentence, then an extension of that one. Sentence upon sentence will pile up because you'll not keep your mouth shut.* How well she knew him. He would never come home. Life without Mishah was not worth living. But what difference did it make now what he did here?

Lamech grabbed Leenah and yanked her to his side. Instantly a rush of guards closed about them. A whip cracked across his shoulder. He wheeled and raised his shovel. Leather whirled around the handle. Lamech tugged sharply and pulled the whip from the man's hand. He fended off another whip with the shovel. Stinging leather coiled about his neck, cutting off his breath. He cracked the iron blade of his shovel against a guard's skull, then grappled at the strangling coils of leather as hands clambered to grab hold of him.

Someone wrenched the shovel from his hand as he went down beneath their weight. Suddenly the press of men lifted. Leenah's hand was still in his grasp, and now someone was hauling him up by the arm while all around him something hummed like a swarm of hornets.

Klesc's shovel whirled like the blade of a harvester cutting swaths of vera-logia. Out of this cyclone of destruction, Klesc glared at him. "Preacher, youuuu—" the anger in his voice strangled his words as he shoved him toward the nearest portal.

Lamech pulled Leenah along, glancing over his shoulder. At least ten guards sprawled in the dirt, and more were rushing in from every direction. Klesc wheeled and parried and thrust with his shovel. Lamech had never seen such movements, except once, in the marketplace in Nod City…. But he didn't have time to ponder that now. He and Leenah dashed under the portal into the deep shadows of a tunnel. They pounded down a long, empty hallway with Klesc closing in behind them.

Two guards, apparently unaware of what had just happened, rounded a corner. Lamech slammed a shoulder into one of them, startled at his sudden aggression. He'd never lifted his hand against another man in all his life. As the man fell, Leenah drove an elbow into the throat of the other, then bent and retrieved their swords. Thrusting one into Lamech's hand, she turned and tossed the other to Klesc. The big man expertly snatched it out of the air by the hilt, and a large smile grew across his face.

"The proper weapon for a Makir!" Leenah shouted as they fled down the dark tunnel, the sound of pursuit echoing in the hall behind them.

Lamech heard the pride in her voice. *A Makir?* In his confused brain, he struggled to recall where he'd heard that before. The tunnel made a turn up ahead where daylight brightened the arched walls. Klesc put on a burst of speed and shot past them. As Lamech rounded the corner, his heart sank. An iron grate stood between them and freedom.

Klesc grabbed hold of the bars and strained against them, his huge muscles standing out like mighty straps of steal. Lamech set the sword aside and lent his own strength. Leenah took up the weapon and turned to face their pursuers. By the sound of their pounding footsteps, the Temple guards were not far behind.

The grate groaned and then lifted a span. "Under!" Klesc ordered.

Leenah tossed the sword through the bars and tumbled under the grate, rolling to freedom. She grabbed the grate from the outside and lifted with them.

"Now, Lamech!"

He crawled beneath the bars to freedom and stood with Leenah, holding the ironwork in place as Klesc scrambled under it. They let go, and with a crash, it slammed back in place. A double fist of guards burst into view and piled up against the bars.

The three of them took off across the open, dusty ground where beast and men and carts wound their way along a well-worn construction road toward towering gates that stood open. A warning horn blared from the wall, and from different quarters shouts rang out as guards filed from open doorways.

His heart pounding, Lamech fought to keep up with Klesc and Leenah, striving to put as much distance between himself and the Temple Prison as his legs would allow. Klesc was making for the distant buildings of Nod City, casting back over his shoulder to be certain he and Leenah were still there.

Suddenly Klesc veered and stopped. From the city, a troop of green-cloaks rushed toward them. Klesc dodged to the right. Soldiers had suddenly appeared from everywhere. Leenah's wild eyes flashed between Lamech and the big man in the lead. Lamech snatched her hand and hauled her after him.

"The river," she puffed. "He's heading for the river."

"Klesc seems to know what he's doing," Lamech managed, his lungs burning. But how could he? Klesc was running blind, seeking any avenue of escape. But all avenues were methodically being shut off. The big man drew to a stop again, and Lamech and Leenah caught up to him.

"It's no good." Klesc cast about, his breathing still regular and controlled, unlike Lamech's and Leenah's. "We'd need wings to escape this noose!"

A contingent of green-cloaks appeared among a traffic jam of stone-laden carts and three-points. Klesc gestured and dove beneath the belly of a three-point, rolling to his feet on the other side. Leaping to their feet, they wove their way among the snorting animals. Klesc glanced up to the tiled roof of a nearby building, overhanging the road where a row of carts and three-points and spike-tails waited in a queue.

Without warning, he scooped Leenah up, put her in the back of a cart hitched to a spike-tail, and leaped up after her. Surprised by this sudden move, Lamech scrambled up into the cart at their heels. The big man climbed over a hewed block of white stone and, to the startled surprised of the driver, leaped to the seat. He hauled Leenah to his side.

The driver threw his hands into the air. "Heya, whatsya doing here?! Getsya offa my cart!"

Klesc sprang from the driver's seat to the spike-tail's spine, landing between its double row of bony plates. The startled beast snapped around and nipped at Klesc. Klesc kicked the head aside and turned, urging Leenah to follow. She leaped. Klesc caught her in his big hands and, continuing the fluid motion, tossed her to a nearby roof. Leenah appeared shocked at her sudden relocation, but she recovered instantly and scrambled up toward the ridge line. Klesc planted a foot upon the spike-tail's small head. It lifted, and he bounded to the roof behind her, turned, and thrust out an arm to Lamech.

With green-cloaks closing in from every side, Lamech was too frightened to think about what he was doing. He grabbed Klesc's wrist and sailed upward. The next instant, the three of them were racing along the tiles.

The whole compound was in an uproar, green-cloaks streaming in from all directions. Some carried ladders and tilted them against the building.

Their headlong flight took them to the edge. They skidded to a stop. On one side, Lamech could see a hundred or more guards rushing across the grounds. On the other side, the land lay flat and relatively empty of people, clear down to the Little Hiddekel River where a copse of trees hugged the water near the Temple docks. If they could reach those trees and slip unseen into the river, they might hide until dark under the Temple wharves and slip aboard a barge heading back upriver. For the first time, the chance of escape seemed real to him. It was right there, almost in reach. Klesc must have realized it too, by the cunning look that had come into his eyes.

There was no way down from this roof, but the next building over had a convenient staircase running down from a rooftop patio. Even as Lamech took in this detail, Klesc was putting a foot to the edge of the roof and drawing back like a spring going under tension.

Lamech grabbed Klesc's arm. "You're not going to jump?"

"It's our only chance, Preacher. From that building we have an open road to freedom."

Breathless at his side, Leenah said, "We can make it. The distance is not that far."

But the fall, should one's foot miss, *was* that far!

Klesc levered back and sprang out into open space. There was a sharp crack as a tile broke under the pressure of his foot and crashed distantly on the ground below. The big man easily cleared the span, landing safely on the other side.

"Jump!" Klesc urged.

Lamech grimaced. If Klesc could make it, he could too! "You go next, Mistress Leenah. I'll be right behind you." He glanced over his shoulder. The roof was still clear, but any moment it would be swarming with green-cloaks.

Leenah positioned herself on the edge and leaned far back. As she did so, a tile weakened by Klesc's leap gave way beneath her foot. Flailing her arms wildly, she plunged over the edge.

5

A Sentence Worse Than Death

With his tattered cloak bunched around him, shoulders stooped, and face averted, Rhone strode along the crowded streets of Nod City. Even hunched over as he was, his height and size were apparent. He regretted leaving his gerup, but the Lodath's mark would have been sure to raise suspicion.

Sari'el kept pace at his side, a gnarled, wooden walking stick in place of his usual gold and ivory staff rapping the pavement with each step. No one looked twice at the Messenger. A woman bearing a bundle on her head nearly walked into Sari'el but sidestepped at the last moment and cast an apologetic smile at him. He nodded to her and then his eyes returned to probing the buildings, the parks, and the passing carts piled high with merchandise bound for the marketplace along the river. Sari'el clearly saw things Rhone could not.

"The Deceiver has Nod City firmly in his grasp."

"His Watchers?"

"They are all around us."

"Won't they reveal our presence?"

Sari'el shook his head. "They don't notice us. They are occupied."

Occupied? What exactly did that mean?

"When I take human form, I become less apparent to the other side. They have business of their own to concern them."

Rhone was amazed by the way Sari'el sometimes seemed to know exactly what he was thinking. The Messenger of the Creator claimed he could not actually enter into a human's mind, but that humans were so guileless that their inflections and their expression easily gave away their thoughts. There was much about the Messengers Rhone did not understand, just as there was much about this hidden war—this struggle between the Deceiver and the Creator—that he did not yet grasp. Only recently had he even become aware of this combat taking place in the other realm.

Lamech had often remarked that there were no accidents in the Creator's providence. It wasn't, however, until later that he recalled this proverb. At that instant, he'd been standing quite near to Leenah, glancing worriedly over his shoulder.

At a moment when his head was turned away, Leenah gave a startled "whoop!" Out the corner of his eye, her arms windmilled frantically and then disappeared. Instinctively, Lamech lunged, catching hold of an arm, feeling it slip through his grasp. Only at the last instant did he manage to grab her wrist, and then Leenah's other hand latched onto his. Locked together like that, her plunging weight slammed him down upon the edge of the roof.

His shoulders wrenched at her sudden stop, but his grip held strong. The jolt sent fire up his arms and across his back as she dangled there swaying above nothingness. He groaned and tried to haul her up, but in his wearied state, her weight made him helpless to accomplish any more than to hold.

"Preacher! Don't let go of her!" Klesc backed up and took a run for the edge of the adjoining roof.

"No! Save yourself, Klesc!"

But the big man was already airborne and crashing into the tiles by Lamech's side. He tossed aside his sword, took hold, and drew Leenah up and set her on her feet. A hoard of green-cloaks swarmed up from the eaves just then and charged. Klesc snatched up his sword and met the attack, cutting the soldiers down left and right, his sword seeming to know exactly where to strike next. Stunned by such a fierce attack, the soldiers retreated behind a second wave of men who formed a line across the roof and snapped weapons to their shoulders.

Klesc halted, glaring at this new threat. His lips curled in disgust. "Proj-lances! Weapons of cowards!" He raised his voice in a challenge to the lancers. "Fight me hand to hand like real men!"

Lamech rose shakily to his feet and placed himself in front of Leenah, but she stepped around him and stood at his side.

A young lieutenant forced his way to the front of the line of lancers and stared at the bodies of his men strewn across the roof, then at Klesc. His face hardened.

"I'll show you the price for bringing a weapon against the Lodath's Guard." Drawing his sword, he raised it to give the signal to his lancers.

Lamech's chest tightened. Leenah drew herself up to her full height, squared her shoulders, and thrust out a proud chin. Her bravery sent a surge of admiration through him and bolstered his resolve to meet his own death with defiant dignity.

The lieutenant's sword hovered a moment, then a hand shot out and grabbed his wrist. The troops parted, and an officer Lamech instantly recognized stepped to the fore. Captain Da-gore! It had been Da-gore who had taken him and his family captive all those months ago. It had been he who had stood them before the Lodath.

The lieutenant glanced at him. "First Shield Da-gore!"

First Shield?

Da-gore's dark eyes found Lamech's face and remained there a moment, locked in an unreadable gaze. "There will be no executions here, Lieutenant Buz-ot." His view shifted to Klesc. "Drop the sword."

Klesc flung the bloody blade to the tiles, where it skittered toward the edge of the roof, then disappeared. From below, a three-point bellowed and a startled cart master's voice yelled, "Hey, watch it up there!"

"Shackle them."

Iron cuffs and heavy chains bound their wrists, and they followed without resistance, climbing clumsily down a ladder. They followed Da-gore out across the compound, where now a hundred or more guards marched alongside and behind them.

"You've sealed your fate this time, Lamech," Da-gore said as they angled toward the tall gates into the construction site.

"My wife predicted this would happen." Now that the rush was ebbing from his blood, he trembled at the thought of what lay ahead. From what he had heard, capital punishment was not a thing to face lightly here in Nod City.

Da-gore gave him a curious look, then shook his head. "I would have liked to interrogate you."

"Me?" What did Da-gore expect to learn from him? As far as he knew, he had no knowledge the Captain—the First Shield—would want. "The last time we met, you were Captain of the Guard. What happened?"

Da-gore's eyebrows pinched and a sudden frown bent his lips, but he remained silent.

※

They were buried so deep in the bowels of the prison that Lamech wondered if he would ever see daylight again. Down here, the air weighed heavy and damp, foul to breathe, and laden with the biting odor of rat urine. There was a single aperture high up near the ceiling, which presumably vented to the outside. Maybe it had become clogged? Maybe the rats lived there? The room, six spans square, would have been dark as a grave if not for a single shard of moonglass mounted in a recess of one of the stone blocks.

Lamech sat upon a cool stone ledge, his back against the clammy wall. Leenah slouched near his side. Klesc sat across the cell. All three wore iron wristbands fastened to the stone wall with lengths of heavy, rusted chain.

None of them spoke. Lamech listened to the guards' muffled voices beyond the door, then their receding steps, and finally a silence so profound that even the steady plop ... plop ... plop of some far-off drip was a pounding drum in his ear. He shifted on the hard stone. "You shouldn't be in here, Klesc. Why did you do it?"

The big man's head rose slowly and looked at him. Leenah gave her chain a sudden, sharp tug, but it was a fruitless gesture. Klesc had already tried that, and the chains had held.

"Neither one of you should be in here!" she said.

"I couldn't leave you to them." Lamech paused. "To *him*." He turned back to Klesc. "But you, my friend. You could have stayed out of it. You know there can be only one end for what we did today."

Klesc still didn't speak.

Lamech grimaced and glanced back at Leenah. Her high cheeks and strong jaw caught the faint light. Her mouth took a determined set, and she jerked the chain again and again. "It's no use."

"Where could we go even if we could break these chains?"

She looked to the door. "I heard the guards leave."

That was a hopeless notion. On their way down they had passed through no less than seven doors, every one of them probably bolted and guarded.

The silence stretched out. Klesc said suddenly, "You ever hear voices, Preacher?"

The question caught him by surprise. "Voices?"

Klesc's staring eyes reflected the pale light of the moonglass. "Not exactly like speaking … not like you and me talking right now. But voices … like whispers."

Lamech almost laughed. How many times had Mishah chided him on the voices he heard? As real as they seemed to him, she was never quite convinced. And her doubts had caused him to suspect. "I've been known to hear voices from time to time."

"What do they say to you?"

"Go here, go there. Do this, do that. Speak to this man or that. He needs to hear the truth." He made a wry face. "Encourage your wife to make the pilgrimage to the Mother. The child she bears will be a son."

"Whose voice do you hear?"

Lamech shrugged. "The Creator's. At least it is to him that I attribute the voices."

In the darkness, Klesc looked puzzled. He frowned suddenly. "I don't believe in your creator. It can't be that."

"Can't be what?"

"The voice. Ever since I first saw you, it's been telling me to do things."

Lamech's attention riveted in a way it hadn't for a long time. "What things?"

"The voice says to watch Lamech. To protect Lamech. Crazy things." His arm shot forward, snapping the chain taut. "Things that get me bound in shackles." The chain strained a moment, then the big man relaxed and slumped back against the damp wall. "I heard it again, when the guards all piled onto you, Preacher." His lips knotted. "Should have ignored it."

Lamech's neck prickled. "Perhaps you should have."

Klesc shifted his view to Leenah. "How did you know about me?"

Her chains rattled as she straightened on the stone ledge beside him. "My mother was a granddaughter of Hodin. She has two brothers, both Makir."

Lamech detected a quality in her voice that, if the room had been brighter, he was certain would have revealed itself as a smile upon her face.

"I know what to look for, Master Klesc. I knew the first day your quort walked out onto the Temple grounds."

Klesc nodded. "Of course. Hodin's blood flows in your veins. One can see it in your eyes, in your bearing."

Leenah nodded "My father was a Sethite. We left Atlan after the rebellion, when I was but a baby. My Uncle Debne came with us; my other uncle, Sirt, remained to serve the new High Councilor, but Uncle Sirt has little respect for him. After the rebellion, when their Pyir disappeared, the Makir fled Atlan. Those who didn't are now unbound. They long for the days of honor, when the old High Councilor ruled Atlan."

Klesc made a low rumble deep in his throat. "I will never serve Zorin."

Lamech tried to piece together what little he knew of distant lands and cultures. "I've heard the Makir are renowned warriors."

Klesc nodded.

"And you are one of them?"

"I am no longer bound."

"Bound?"

Klesc dropped his head and looked away.

Leenah said, "It means he is not attached to a kal-ee-hon—a company of Makir Warriors. He is unbound. They are all unbound. There must be a Pyir."

"A Pyir? What's that."

"A powerful warrior to lead them," she said.

He did not fully understand the deeper meaning he sensed in that. "Can't you name a new Pyir?"

Klesc shook his head. "A Pyir must be chosen by the Council of Ten. But Zorin sits at the head of the council, and no ..." Pounding footsteps stopped outside the door, cutting his words short.

The heavy cross bolt clanked and the door groaned open. First Shield Da-gore at the head of a fist of armed guards waited as a man with a chisel and hammer split the rivet on the iron wall ring. At Da-gore's order, they followed the guards out of the dank dungeon and along the dark corridor.

❧

The cool blue walls, the bright tapestries, and the rectangular rug of red and green all stood in stark contrast to the three dark, unsmiling faces. Ranged about the room were six frowning green-cloaks. Quort Whip En'tuboc and First Shield Da-gore stood on either side of the prisoners.

Neither Lamech, Leenah, nor Klesc had been permitted to speak. The slight-built council member Lamech had encountered before took the floor.

"Each of you is in this place because you've violated the dictates of either Irad, Chief of Nod City, or Sol-Ra-Luce, the representative of the Oracle of the Crystal." His sonorous voice seemed to resonate off the stone walls. "Any rights you may have had before arriving here have been stripped from you. As wards of the prison, your fate is absolutely within the hands of the Disciplinary Council."

Lamech slid a glance toward Klesc. The big man's face gave no indication of what he was thinking or feeling. Leenah's face showed a fear held in rein by a resolute spirit. He took encouragement from both of them and prepared himself for what he knew was coming.

"This morning you interfered in the affairs of the Prison Guard, under order of the Lodath." The little man's view rested momentarily upon Leenah before moving to Lamech and then Klesc. "In doing so, you killed a guard, fled the Temple grounds, and during your failed attempt at escape, killed six more of the Lodath's Guard." He glanced at his two companions at the table, somber faced, listening to the facts. "We have deliberated on the proper punishment. The attempted escape alone would have cost you your lives."

Lamech struggled to control a twitch that had begun to prod at his cheek. Klesc was a rock. Leenah stood tall, her strong, indomitable chin thrust out.

"But your actions today went far beyond mere escape. Discipline must be maintained, or other weak-minded prisoners such as you three may attempt this foolishness again. Therefore, punishment will be swift and dramatic. Prisoners Lamech and Klesc, tomorrow morning at the second hour of the third quartering, you will be bound between behemoths and drawn and quartered."

Leenah gave a sharp gasp.

Lamech's brain momentarily reeled. He drew in a breath and steadied himself. *So be it.* As his brain cleared, Lamech thought not of the sentence, or of dying in that manner, but of his dear Mishah and the son he had never seen.

"And what of me?" Leenah demanded.

Yes, what of Leenah? Lamech realized she hadn't been named in the punishment.

"You?" The man sitting to the left of the speaker leaned forward. "You are to be spared. The Lodath has requested you, and so it will be."

"No! I'd rather die! Set my place with Masters Lamech and Klesc. I am as guilty as they. It is only fair."

The man at the far end—the one who had beaten Lamech with the rod on his first visit—spoke. "Guilt? Fairness?" A thin smile moved across his swarthy face. "You forget where you are, woman. Ward Officer Dar-sett has already reminded you that any rights you may have had were taken the moment you entered the Temple Prison."

Dar-sett nodded. "Our decisions are not based on fairness. We do what is best for the construction of the Temple. We bow to no authority except King Irad, the Lodath, and the Temple Overseer." He smiled. "And of the three, only the Lodath has spoken on behalf of one of you."

"I will not go to him!" She rushed a guard, grabbing his proj-lance. Before she could wrest it away from him, three guards seized her.

Dar-sett laughed. "That was a futile display. Take her away."

Da-gore motioned and the guards seized her. Leenah tried to wrench free. En'tuboc gave her a sharp rap at the back of the neck with the hilt of his whip, and she went limp in their arms.

Lamech moved to her aid as a swarm of guards fell upon him and beat him to the floor. Again, Lamech's cheek lay upon the carpet emblazoned with the Unspeakable Mystery Symbols, those angles and spirals that spoke of the Oracle's dark and hidden secrets. He tried to rise; the weight of the men held him down, crushing the breath from his lungs.

Once Leenah had been taken from the room, the guards

released him. En'tuboc jerked him to his feet and struck him across his cheek with the back of his whip. Blood flowed warm down his chin and dripped to his naked chest.

He pressed a hand to the wound. Klesc scowled at him as if to say, *When will you ever learn, Lamech?* He grimaced. Guards encircled them. The man at the table said to Da-gore, "Return them to the pit. Make ready for the execution in the morning." Then to a prison officer, he said, "See that every prisoner is present, Warder Bote. This will be an example to the inmates. I do not want a repeat of what happened this morning."

"As you order, Ward Officer Turlun. Shall I also post word in Nod City?"

"Yes. The more the better." Turlun dismissed them with an impatient flick of his hand.

Surrounded by guards, Lamech and Klesc were ushered out of the presence of the Disciplinary Council. Lamech's thoughts for his own safety seemed less pressing than his concern for Leenah. It wrenched his heart to think what she might be facing, yet what could he do to help now? Prayer was the only weapon he had left to him, and in earnest he flung his petition at the Creator's feet.

The corridor descended and twisted like a burrowing worm, and somewhere deep within the prison's bowels, the guards unceremoniously shoved them into the darkness of their cell. The big-shouldered man with his heavy hammer reattached their chains to iron rings, finalizing the task with a sharp tug to test the rivets.

When all was in order, Da-gore turned to leave, then hesitated, and held Lamech for a long moment in a slowly narrowing gaze. It seemed he wanted to say something, but at the last moment decided against it. With a look akin to regret, he removed his men from the small holding cell. The door groaned shut, and the clank of the locking bolt rang with finality, driving home the hopelessness of his situation as the sound of footsteps receded down the long tunnel.

In the faint glow of the single moonglass, Lamech saw Klesc staring at him. "I'm sorry my rashness will cost you your life, Klesc."

The big man jerked his chain, as if just making sure the rivet was secure, then settled back in silence.

Lamech put a hand back to his cheek. The stinging wound had stopped bleeding.

6

Children of the Gods?

*E*ven though Leenah came to almost at once, she was too groggy to resist her captors. Her brain buzzed, and for a while the roaring in her ears drowned out every sound. She was being hauled down a wide hallway, but it seemed a hazy reality; the ache in her neck from En'tuboc's whip was a much clearer one. Slowly her focus sharpened, and the muffled sounds floating all around formed as words:

"... she's that, all right. A fighter."

"Our *beloved* Lodath will have his hands full with this one."

"Be careful what you say, Oris. Sol-Ra-Luce deals harshly with those who cross him."

"Who, me?" He laughed. "I meant every word."

The other guards chuckled. She discerned four, maybe five voices.

Through slit eyes she saw that this part of the prison complex was a section she'd never been permitted to enter. The walls stood wider apart, and stark stone had given way to an intricate paneling of finished wooden strips, arranged in angular patterns that rose and fell along the length of the hall. The light was bright here and came from overhead as if from skylights. She resisted lifting her head to see. If they thought her still unaware, she might yet find a way to escape.

Where the tunnel ended, sunlight spilled through iron bars. With a clatter, the bars rose into the ceiling. Beyond waited a prison wagon and more guards. They were removing her from the prison? Her destination must be the Lodath's palace. She knew that once she was in the wagon, all would be lost. She sorted through her options. Not many presented themselves, but one thing was clear. If the Lodath wanted her, these guards would not dare harm her. *Victory lay in bold decisions*, her uncles would often tell her, *but defeat resided in a quavering heart.*

She dug in her heels and wrenched swiftly to her left. Her right arm came free. Turning left, she raked the man holding her on that side with her nails. He gave a cry and flung his hands to his bleeding face. She was free!

She tried to speed away, but she had not yet fully recovered her balance from the blow to her neck. Someone tackled her from behind, and the next moment a crushing weight fell upon her. Arms wrapped about her waist, lifted her off the ground, and flung her into the prison wagon. The door slammed shut.

The guards lurched back as she sprang for the bars. If she had Klesc's strength, she'd have ripped them from their moorings, but the ironwood held fast. The growl from her throat surprised even her. Could a beast of the forests have sounded any more ferocious ... or untamed?

No, she'd not show herself a wild, untamed woman. Releasing the bars, she crossed her arms and stared back at them.

"She's a fighter, all right." The one with the gouged face stared at the blood on his hand.

Another bent for his helmet and fixed it upon his head. "The Lodath will have to chain that one to his bed."

"He'd better watch himself," the man with the bloodied face said.

The wagon gave a lurch. Leenah grabbed a bar to steady herself and turned her eyes toward Nod City, the walls surrounding Government House just visible in the distance. Was that her destination? She glanced south to where Irad's palace lifted high, pink stone towers above the city, but the wagon continued toward Government House. Then it made a sudden turn to the river, and the gleaming spires and parapets of the Lodath's palace swung into view.

The mettle that boiled her blood earlier now suddenly chilled to ice. She remembered the whispered rumors about those doomed young women snatched from prison cells. Then her breath congealed inside her lungs as another memory came to her. It was of her mother fleeing the flames of their burning house. She heard the voices again of the soldiers ... the lusty laughs ... the obscene remarks....

No! She would not permit the past to overpower her. Not now, not here when she needed her wits about her!

The prison wagon turned down a tree-lined lane and rattled toward the lush bottomland along the Little Hiddekel River. Four mounted men, their green cloaks fluttering behind them, galloped into view. The upper echelon of the Lodath's elite guard. Her mouth soured. The riders fell in alongside and escorted the wagon under a portal of brilliant ebony onyx. The gateway's artistry momentarily captivated her, but the leering eyes of the outriders, brazenly appraising her through the ironwood bars, instantly doused any fleeting wonderment.

The Temple construction site receded in the distance, while Nod City seemed to stretch on forever to her left. The placid waters of the Little Hiddekel, mostly hidden now by the palace complex, flowed to the west, partly obscured by a row of smaller buildings. The Lodath's administrative offices? Ahead, the palace spires grasped at the blue sky like grotesque fingers trying to claw their way into the heavens. She had heard that the Lodath had an entire floor of Government House at his disposal, but those rooms were for administration and the daily functions of the Temple. Here, at his private residence, it was reputed that the Oracle of the Crystal himself actually took on human form and met with Sol-Ra-Luce face-to-face.

This palace, however, was where Sol-Ra-Luce escaped the public's eye. Stories of what went on behind its white walls ran throughout the lands around Nod City, always related in hushed words—stories that frightened children and made even brave men quiver.

The wagon rocked to a halt. Leenah drew in a breath and thought of her uncles and their indomitable spirits. She would try to be like them now, although she had never had Makir training— or ever learned the Katrahs and Kimahs. Instead, from her father, she had learned of the Creator of all the world, and it was to him now that she prayed. Whatever this man might do to her body, he could never harm her soul. It wasn't much, but it was all she had to cling to.

And what of Lamech and Klesc? Their fate was every bit as repulsive as hers. Even so, she was sure they were facing it with dignity. And she would too.

The driver came around back carrying a big black key and unlocked the door. Heavily armed guards moved in close. Two men dragged her out and escorted her along a shaded walkway between fountains and rolling landscaping filled with colorful flowers. Butterflies—kaleidoscopes of color beneath the dappled light—fluttered about the flowers, cooling them with the breeze from their large wings as they feasted on the abundant nectar. Birds added their own colors and filled the warm air with music, while the sweet scent of the river, pleasant and untainted by the stench of human sweat and animal dung, wafted up on an amiable breeze. It twisted a knot in her gut to see the beauty of the Creator's handiwork surrounding the black heart of the Lodath of the Oracle.

The guards led her around to the side of the palace and through a door. An attendant quickly closed and locked it, then turned and scrutinized her with a critical eye. "This is the one?"

"She is."

His thin mouth took a disappointed plunge. "She stinks."

The guard gave a short laugh. "We weren't ordered to bathe her, just bring her."

The attendant glowered. "This way. Come quickly." He scurried on ahead, a mouse about the rat's business.

A guard slammed her shoulder with the palm of his hand. She glared at him, then tossed her head around, her long hair undone and tangled, and followed the attendant.

Their footsteps echoed in the long, vaulted corridor, then rang with each step as they ascended a marble staircase. Stone gave way to warm wood paneling and thick tapestries. They stopped at a towering door and the attendant knocked, then glanced back at them, his dark, tiny eyes nervously appraising her again, and apparently finding her still wanting. Did he expect the smell of hard work to have dissipated by virtue of her being within these pristine walls? Her anger flashed and burned hotter. The door opened, and two guards from within stepped aside to permit them to pass.

Almost at once, a heavy weight seemed to suffocate her spirit. Before her, Sol-Ra-Luce lounged upon an immense wood and gold chair, a hundred times more garish than the honor seat she'd seen in some homes. Leenah scrunched her lips. His reclining form was half buried in thick pillows of purple silk, while three women, scantily clad, attended to him. One was carefully filing the nails of his right hand into long, tapering points, while a second applied a dark blue polish to the nails of his left hand. The third, standing behind the garish honor seat, massaged his shoulders and neck. Amid all this attention, the Lodath's eyes were closed, and a contented smile puckered his face.

A personal bodyguard stood nearby, his right hand resting upon the hilt of his sword, unmoving as a statue. He watched her with a strange coldness, as if death itself dwelled within him.

Leenah shivered, directing her view back at the man being lavished over.

"You have brought her, Captain El-ik?" Sol-Ra-Luce spoke without opening his eyes.

"Yes, Your Eminence."

The Lodath's nose twitched and wrinkled. His eyes opened and peered along the offended protuberance, looking her up and down, openly evaluating her assets. "She should clean up nicely."

Clean up nicely? Her jaw quivered.

Sol-Ra-Luce rose from the deep cushions and stepped down off the dais. The bodyguard standing nearby him remained as if stone.

She met his arrogant gaze head-on, holding it in her own unwavering glare. *Clean up nicely ... indeed!*

A thin smile moved across his face. "You're different from the others."

A burning contempt came rushing to the surface, and she wondered what had caused such a violent reaction. She remained silent, the fury of her breath hot upon her upper lip. Whatever evil there might be in the world, here it seemed concentrated and focused upon her—upon her spirit.

Sol-Ra-Luce took a handful of her long, golden hair, frowned, then wiped his fingers upon a light blue towel one of his attendants rushed to put into his outstretched hand. "You don't like me."

She glared. Words spoken now could only blunt the depth of her feelings.

He shrugged. "No matter. If you perform well, your stay here will ..." his smile stretched, "be more pleasant." The Lodath strode back to the gaudy honor seat and peered down at her. "You understand, I don't do this for my own pleasure?"

She worked her jaw, marshaling her emotions. "You take whom you wish and discard her when you are finished."

He shook his head. "Your understanding is so shallow. Appearances and rumors, this is what you judge me by?"

How else might she judge him? But she remained silent.

"Do not so easily accept as fact the rumors whispered in private." He pursed his lips. "What charges put you in the Temple Prison?"

He didn't know? He hadn't even investigated her that far? He'd selected her on appearance only. A small part of her was flattered, but caution kept a tight rein on her emotions. "My mother refused to pay the New Day Temple Tithe."

"And for *that* you were sentenced?"

Memories crept unbidden into her brain. She forced them back; her jaw tightened again. "I struck one of King Irad's officers while protecting my mother."

Sol-Ra-Luce lifted an eyebrow and his mouth cocked into an amused smile. "You struck a guard?" He laughed. "It seems a minor offense for so severe a punishment."

"I struck him with a harvesting blade."

"Oh." The smile wavered and he cleared his throat. "I see." He studied her. "You have Hodinite blood?"

"My mother."

"Ah. That explains it. No doubt, your mother struck a guard or two herself that day."

Leenah's arms tightened about her waist. She struggled to restrain the memories, her clenched teeth aching, the muscle across her temple burning. "What is to become of me?"

He lowered himself back onto the chair. The guard at his side still hadn't moved. "Your tone is offensive." He raised a fist. "I hold life and death in my hand. Remember that, daughter of Hodin, and you may even enjoy your future ... brief as it might turn out to be." He settled into the silk pillows. "Soon the Oracle's Temple will be completed. When it is, the Oracle will move his abode from the stars to it, and a glorious new day for every man and woman will dawn. Knowledge will increase throughout the world. Already, through the help of his emissaries, our technology is advancing. And someday, when the gods and man finally mingle, their children, and their children's children, will become gods themselves. We will leap a million years of plodding development in but a few generations."

Did she care about millions of years? *What was to become of her now?* He was taking the long way around to answering her question.

"When the Oracle resides with man, the highest calling will be to serve him and to serve his priests. You, daughter of Hodin, could very well be one of those blessed women who will dedicate her life, and her body, to the service of the priests."

What was he talking about? Had she misunderstood?

His lips thinned. "But first I must judge you worthy for such a calling." He leaned forward. "They like long hair."

"They?"

"The emissaries, of course."

She didn't understand. Distractedly, she grabbed a handful of greasy hair and fingered the tangled knot. She'd have a hard time pulling a comb through it. *Emissaries like long hair?* If she understood him, he was to test her, to see if she was worthy of being a—

a Temple prostitute! What did the emissaries have to do with any of this? They were beings from the stars. They weren't even human.... Her blood turned to ice. Could it be ...? No! The thought was too horrible to entertain.

Sol-Ra-Luce must have read her thoughts. "It will be but one of the many functions of the Temple. The transformation will start slowly at first. Already it has begun in the Mountains of the Singing Sky. In the generations to come, we will be as they are. The Oracle has declared it true. If you please me, daughter of Hodin, you might very well be one of the first to bring forth the next race of mankind."

She felt suddenly ill.

Sol-Ra-Luce waved a hand. Two guards who had escorted her there were instantly at her side. "Take her to the bath."

She jerked her arms from their grasp. All this time she'd been concerned for herself. "What of the two men who were with me?"

"They are of no concern."

"But say the word, Your Eminence, and their lives will be spared." The title gagged in her throat, but she got the words out. She'd kowtow if she must, if it would save Lamech's and Klesc's lives. "As you rightly put it, you hold life and death in your hands."

"They murdered Temple guards. Death is what they have earned."

She loathed what she knew she must say. "For me—for my compliance—would you not do this?"

Anger stormed into his dark eyes. "Your compliance is already assured." He looked around. "Captain El-ik."

"Your Eminence."

"See that the executions come off as decreed."

"Yes, Your Eminence."

Sol-Ra-Luce leaned back into his pillows and fixed his gaze on El-ik. "Your predecessor failed me. Now he strides the prison corridors and lives in a stone barracks, instead of in the fine quarters you now occupy." His eyes flashed, his tone turning threatening. A long finger stretched out, the sharpened nail a polished blue claw. "No one is indispensable in the Oracle's service."

Captain El-ik's expression remained flat. Was everyone near the Lodath made of ice? Did feeling not exist in this place? Was that the weight that had burdened her soul the moment she'd entered his presence?

"The executions will be carried out as ordered by the Disciplinary Council, Your Eminence."

The Lodath's anger passed as swiftly as it arose. "Take her away."

Leenah struggled in their grasp and glared over her shoulder at him as the guards forced her toward a door to the side of the meeting room. The bodyguard turned toward her. So, he hadn't been made of stone after all, yet his eyes remained vacant and cold, and somehow, horrible.

The Lodath laughed. "You'll not find any harvesting blades here."

She was too transparent. She'd have to do better.

❧

First Shield Da-gore finished making his rounds. Finding the prison secured and quiet after this morning's attempted escape, he turned over charge of it for the night to a junior lieutenant. The near success of the breakout had emboldened some of the prisoners, but once the swiftness with which the council had moved to set an example of Lamech and Klesc had been made known, any beacon of hope promptly burned itself out.

With the light fading from the sky, the ex-Captain of the Lodath's Guard strode down the long, stark corridor of the barracks to his bleak quarters on the second floor.

He shut the door behind him, tossed off his green cloak, and stood staring at himself in a mirror, frowning at the gaunt visage staring back at him. He ought to eat more and drink less. He drew himself up and momentarily squared his shoulders, then sighed and turned away. What was the use?

His view traveled around the little room: a bed, a desk, the private room, a cupboard, and a small hearth where he could heat a kettle of water or cook a meager meal. He frowned. His own cooking had never appealed to him. As Captain of the Guard, that chore had been seen to by a collection of servants. Now ... his frown lengthened ... he either fixed his own or rubbed shoulders in the barracks dining hall. He didn't mind the bland cooking. What he did mind was the circumspect looks, the sudden pall of silence whenever he came into earshot. *There goes the great Captain Da-gore, run afoul of the Lodath and demoted. Now he does the grunt work with the rest of us.*

He exhaled and stared out the window. The rumors of how he'd tumbled from power would eventually go the way of such things. It was still too new for the guards he'd once commanded—and ... for him.

The sky was a deep evening orange. Black shapes winged in the distance. A long, undulating pocket dragon landed upon a wall and tucked its wings. Buildings blocked his view of the construction site from here, except for the top of the rising edifice encased in its cage of scaffolding and, of course, the heavy-lifting platform high in the sky, which was visible for leagues around Nod City.

He had been shocked to come face-to-face with Lamech this morning. The sight of the Lee-lander had opened wounds that had only begun to heal. It brought those nagging questions back to the front of his brain.

There was nothing more to do about it now. Tomorrow, once he escorted the prisoners up from their holding cells, the duty of overseeing the executions would fall to the new Captain of the Guard.

Captain El-ik was cold as a dead fish and unemotional as a machine. Da-gore huffed. Maybe that's what Sol-Ra-Luce needed. Would El-ik have fared any better than he? El-ik hadn't been sent to overtake the fugitives. Da-gore remembered how he had pursued the Lee-landers clear to the Ruins of Eden. He had done all he could. How does one fight beings from another realm when they choose to inject themselves into the affairs of men? Even the giants were helpless against the cherubim.

Sol-Ra-Luce's anger hadn't been rational, but come to think of it, little in the orders that the Lodath and the Oracle had given to him seemed rational. *Kill the woman and her companions?* And why had they been aided from the other side? If the Oracle was truly the power of this world, why hadn't he been able to stop the Tyrant's warriors?

He snatched a bottle of garlberry wine from the cupboard and filled a mug. What was really going on? Why had the Oracle insisted on the woman's death? How was *she* a threat to *him*? He'd not received any explanation, only a sharp reprimand for his failure and a demotion. And the only other man alive who might answer his questions was scheduled to be ripped apart by a pair of behemoths in the morning.

He gave a sardonic laugh as he toasted himself in the mirror. "To the morning!" He tossed back a mouthful of wine. "Why do I stay in this business? A man with my experience could find other work. What do I owe the Lodath?" The mirror remained mute. He could transfer back to King Irad's lancers and work his way up the ladder again. It might take another sixty or eighty years, but he was still a young man.

He drained the mug without really tasting the wine and refilled it, anxious for the effects to take hold. His world had been rocked by all he had seen in the last few months, and he had yet to come to terms with it. That he was being lied to was certain, but if the Lodath's truth was in fact error, what *was* the truth? He took another gulp. And what did it matter anyway? He'd numb his brain with wine tonight and dutifully go about his assigned tasks in the morning.

Such was the slow, downward spiral his life had fallen into.

7

Beyond the Realm of Man

Ker'ack's *Cabling and Tackle* carved into a wooden sign announced that they had arrived. Rhone paused at the iron gate to the big warehouse-like building and briefly entertained thoughts of leaving. He grimaced and shook the notion from his head. Ker'ack deserved to be told, and it was his duty to do the telling. Dusk was almost upon them, and Ker'ack's door was open to vent the lingering heat of the day. Rhone had counted on his old friend's habit of working late. He preferred meeting Ker'ack here, alone, rather than at his home where he'd have to face Sarsee as well.

Inside, the smell of javian cables and the oily tang of wooden block brought back memories. Ropes of immensely strong spider silk hung like vines along the walls and from the ceiling. The usual clatter and slap of weaving machines was silent. The workers had gone home already. Good. The things he needed to tell Ker'ack were best spoken in private.

They entered and passed the big weaving machines where Ker'ack's son, Bar'ack, had once spent his days weaving the javian spider silk collected by Rhone and other Webmasters like him in the Wild Lands. Javian rope was big business now that the Temple construction was in full swing.

Rhone missed his life as a Webmaster, but those days were gone. The Creator had shown him a corner of the tapestry he was weaving—a vast and wonderful design of which Rhone was a thread.

Rhone found Ker'ack in his counting room. The single window was dark with the coming evening. A fist of candles in a stand at the corner of his desk cast a wavering light upon the big book over which he was bent, carefully entering figures.

Rhone knocked on the doorjamb. Ker'ack jerked about, his eyes went large, and the pen fell from his fingers. "Rhone?"

"Have you forgotten me so soon?"

Ker'ack's lips quivered. "You … you're dead. They said you were dead. But you're not dead … *you're not dead!*" Ker'ack shot to his feet, his chair crashing to the floor as he enfolded Rhone in a bear hug. He stepped back to look at him, eyes glistening. "The reports were wrong! Praise be to the Creator, they were wrong!"

Rhone's mouth tightened into a grim smile. How did one explain? It was easier not to try. "I was injured, but there was a healer."

"She must have been skillful, judging from the reports that came back." In his excitement, Ker'ack had ignored Sari'el. Now he composed himself and bowed slightly toward the stranger.

"This is my traveling companion, Sari'el." Like his own death and subsequent return to life at the hand of the Creator, explaining Sari'el's true nature would have been complicated, and Rhone did not have time enough to explain.

"Evening peace, Master Sari'el."

Sari'el returned the bow. "May your servant find favor in your eyes."

Ker'ack turned back to Rhone. "Where have you been all these months?"

Another question he could not answer. "It's been a slow journey from the Wild Lands."

"Ah, your wounds. I understand. You look remarkably well for a man back from the dead!"

Rhone grimaced. Ker'ack had spoken truer than he realized.

Ker'ack laughed. "I am so pleased the reports were in error! Sarsee will have a thousand questions for her favorite dinner guest."

"I will not have time to honor your home, Ker'ack."

Ker'ack's eyes shifted warily. "I don't understand. The Lodath thinks you're dead. Surely you can spend a few days at least. I must know how you managed to get yourself embroiled in such trouble. Nod City was filled with talk and rumors for weeks. Then when the green-cloaks returned with that giant creature, announcing that you had been killed ..."

"I cannot stay, Ker'ack."

"But you're back."

A lump hardened in Rhone's chest. "I came back to tell you about Bar'ack."

"Oh." He staggered slightly, righted his chair, and sat in it. "He's back, too."

"He is?" The last Rhone had seen of Bar'ack, who had gone with him to learn the art of collecting Web, the young man had been fighting on the side of the giants, empowered by some force Rhone did not, at the time, comprehend. It was only later that the Creator had explained to him what had happened.

"Bar'ack returned with the green-cloaks, but he had changed. He is not the same boy who left here with a head full of dreams, Rhone. I don't know what happened, only that he now lives in the Lodath's palace and refuses to speak to his mother or me. He doesn't even seem to recognize us. We've tried to see him. At first we were permitted entrance. Now the guards turn us away at the gate." Ker'ack drew in a long, rattling breath, tears spilling silently down his cheeks. "We're heartbroken, but there is nothing we can do."

Rhone grieved too, almost as if the boy had been his own. "Bar'ack is not himself. Don't take his refusal to speak with you as a sign that he no longer loves you. His spirit has been taken captive."

"Spirit? Captive?" He dragged a shirtsleeve beneath his eyes.

Rhone glanced at Sari'el but saw no help in the Messenger's eyes. "I don't understand it myself. There are deep mysteries at work here, Ker'ack. The giant you saw is called an Earth-Born. There are more—how many, I don't know. What I do know is that their numbers are increasing.

"Four have died—one by my hand. The fifth was wounded in Chevel-ee and returned to his home, somewhere on Mount Ermon, in the Mountains of the Singing Sky."

"Chevel-ee?" Ker'ack's mouth fell open.

Rhone grimaced. "Much has happened since we left here. Someday I will tell you. For now, you must know about Bar'ack. The spirits of three of those Earth-Borns now dwell within your son."

"How can that be? I've never heard of such a thing."

"It has never happened before."

Ker'ack sat shaking his head. "Why Bar'ack?"

"He was susceptible. He took the Lodath's pledge pendant. He listened to the Lodath's words."

"How can any boy raised in Nod City help but hear them? They are preached from the streets, taught upon the steps of the knowledge halls, pronounced from the stage, and exalted in song!"

Sari'el nodded. "The lies that lead unto death are a powerful message in Nod City."

"Lies that lead unto death?" Ker'ack's voice cracked, and he dabbed his cheeks with a sleeve again. "What are these lies?"

"That man can become God. That life arose of its own volition. That all things continue as they have from the beginning. Denying that, by the word of Elohim, the heavens were stretched out and the earth was formed from the water. These are the lies that lead unto death."

"Elohim? Who is Elohim?"

Rhone said, "The one we call the Creator."

Ker'ack stared at Sari'el, his eyes narrowing suspiciously. "You're a stranger to this land."

Sari'el nodded.

"I thought so." He looked at Rhone. "What can be done for Bar'ack? Is there no hope for my son? Would the Oracle not intervene on his behalf?"

Rhone glanced at Sari'el, and again, saw no help from the Messenger. "Bar'ack is a tool in the Oracle's hand. I don't know what can be done, Ker'ack, but if there is any way I can help him, I will. This I promise you."

❧

Rhone despised the smothering helplessness that pressed down upon him. He had left Ker'ack confused by what had happened to his son, and he had been powerless to ease his friend's mind. The only solace he could give Ker'ack was a promise—one he had no idea how he could fulfill.

"You must know something of this matter, Sari'el." They were walking back into the heart of Nod City, the night streets bustling and bright with the glow of a hundred moonglasses embellishing the walls of the buildings.

Sari'el remained thoughtfully silent for the moment. "I have knowledge of what has happened, Master Rhone. But I am forbidden to interfere in matters such as this."

"Then I will interfere. Tell me what to do."

Sari'el paused and leaned on the gnarled-wood staff with both hands. "There are powers here greater than you can imagine."

That wasn't anything new to Rhone. "Greater than even your powers?"

"You misjudge power. What I am able to do in your realm flies far beyond what humans are capable of, but in my realm, the balances even out. Some Maliks are lesser, and some much greater. The ruler of this world, the Deceiver, is far more powerful. His power is surpassed only by Elohim. If I were to drive the spirits from your friend, the Deceiver would crush me as you might a worm."

Such strength was incomprehensible. "But you *could*, if you wanted to."

Sari'el nodded. "The commingling of humans and Maliks produces a brittle spirit. Like the mixing of miry clay and iron. We have named these spirits. We call them demons."

Demons? These were a new class of beings he'd not heard of. A *Malik*, Rhone knew, was what Sari'el called beings such as himself. Even the Deceiver's emissaries, the Unshackled Ones as they called themselves, were Maliks.

"The spirits of the Earth-Born are incomplete and without power, except when possessing a body," Sari'el continued. "The deaths of the Earth-Born have unleashed a new evil in the world, Master Rhone. From now on, demons will stalk the earth seeking susceptible humans to occupy."

"Is there no way I might drive these demons from a human once he is possessed?"

Sari'el pursed his lips. "Man, in himself, is powerless against the Deceiver's forces. But man is not without a source of power to draw upon."

"What is this source of power?" Hope sparked anew in Rhone.

If he could but touch the power Sari'el hinted at, perhaps he might help Bar'ack.

"There is power in the name of Elohim. But only those who are worthy can call upon it, Master Rhone. You must strive for righteousness. This is not a light matter. The spirits of the Earth-Born, when they inhabit a tent such as Master Bar'ack's, are tenacious creatures."

The Creator had told Rhone about the vile creatures formed by commingling the seed of man with that of the fallen Maliks. The offspring, the giants called Earth-Borns, were neither human nor Malik, but an unholy aberration to the blueprint of life that the Creator had crafted.

Rhone did not understand how such a thing was possible, but it had happened. This pollution of the human bloodline was so foul that the Creator had declared that the Earth-Born would never be raised from the dead. Demons, as Sari'el called them, are cursed to wander in search of a body to possess until the end of the ages, when everything is to be broken down and consumed in Holy Fire. Then all evil will be purged, and a new earth will be created. It will be a glorious time, but one still so far in the future as to be completely hidden by the misty veil of time.

Rhone and Sari'el left the rows of busy festival halls and crossed the darkened Meeting Floor outside Government House, then passed through shadowed courtyards. Their footsteps rang upon the paving stones, making a lonely sound. As they moved between the buildings, Rhone probed the dark corners and shadowed places. His habits and training endured, though in the company of Sari'el, nothing would overtake them by stealth.

As they left Nod City, the great wall of the Temple construction site loomed ahead. The Temple Prison's long, low row of stone buildings lay to Rhone's left. The area was well lit by the huge fires and mirror arrays; overhead, the huge balloon of the heavy-lifting platform glowed orange from roaring fires below.

They directed their steps toward the prison. There was still enough activity in the area that they, so far, went unnoticed. Rhone wondered how Sari'el would get them inside.

Sari'el stopped suddenly and leaned again on his staff, looking around. To Rhone's right, a line of carts bearing quarried stones wound its endless way through the towering gates into the construction site. He glimpsed the scaffolding's wooden timbers showing brightly in the glaring light of the many bonfires that pumped heated air up a silk umbilical cord to the heavy-lifting platform.

"Why are we stopping?"

Sari'el moved to a nearby wall and stood in its shadow. "We must wait."

Rhone was anxious to speak with the man whom he'd briefly met on the Meeting Floor all those months ago. That first encounter with the *zealot,* Lamech, had left a bitter taste in his mouth. Now that he had come to know and understand Lamech through his wife, Mishah, Rhone was anxious to form a new opinion. "Wait for what?"

Sari'el gave a small, enigmatic smile. "Preparations are being made."

❦

The guards put Leenah in the charge of two women who escorted her down a long hallway. There appeared to be no place to run, and no way out of the Lodath's palace. The Lodath was always surrounded by guards. Leenah couldn't erase the memory of the face of that strange bodyguard standing near the honor seat; his vacant eyes had been like spears of ice piercing through her soul. Would he be invited to watch while the Lodath "tested her worthiness"? She hugged herself to quell the sudden tremor.

"Follow us," said a tall woman with a nose like a mansnatcher's beak and small rattish eyes. She wore her shiny brown hair in a swirl piled high atop her head, held in place with gold and silver combs. Leenah's view darted nervously along the bright hallway— its smooth, stone walls, adorned with carved flourishes of leaves, vines, and animals of every kind. The textures appeared so real one might mistake a leaf, or a gerup, for being alive.

A silver chair rail ran the entire length of the hallway, while overhead a ceiling of pure crystal reflected the light of moonglass paneling.

The second woman walked at her side, her hand firmly upon her elbow.

"Where are you taking me?"

"To the bath." Her escort's voice held no trace of threat, but her grip remained firm.

Leenah's eye was drawn to the way the light glinted off the taller woman's shimmering dress and the golden combs ornamenting her hair.

They turned into a room with tall windows overlooking the wide, peaceful Little Hiddekel River. Servants undressed her and carried away the grimy prison garb in their fingertips.

They took her to a tub lined with the swirling colors of mother-of-pearl and rimmed in gold. She stepped into the warm water, which flowed steadily along a trough made to look like a stream in a stunning landscape relief. Attendants scented the water with vials of oil, then began scrubbing her with a coarse sponge. She fought them at first. She was perfectly capable of washing herself! But their attention to her was unwavering, and after a little while, she succumbed to the lavish attention.

The warm water browned with the residue of the prison, and soapy scum spilled out over a channel in the rim of the tub. Fresh, clean water rinsed away the filth until all was but a distant, vaguely troublesome memory. The aches in her neck, spine, and shoulders seemed to seep into the water, drawn out by the aromatic oils that softened her rough skin. At first she resisted an attendant's attempt to untangle her hair, but relented beneath the bath's comforting embrace. The spiraling aroma of oils engulfed her, and a thick drowsiness muddled her head. Why did she fight it so? Her eyelids fluttered, suddenly heavy with sleep.

Leenah noted, in some remote part of her brain that still managed to remain on guard, that the two women who had led her here remained apart from the servants bathing her. And she noted too, in a dreamy haze, the peculiar rotation of the staff. One would begin to comb her hair, then leave after a few minutes, and another would take her place. The same with the women who'd scrubbed the dirt from under her ragged nails. Curious, but unimportant. Sleep. Deep, warm sleep drove away her worries and care.

Some time later, she found herself reclined upon a couch, dressed in a sheer silk chemise with a plunging neckline and a wispy skirt that revealed the pale hue of her thigh and hip. Her hair had been tended to, and now hung in a golden waterfall about her shoulders, thick and sprightly. She looked down, startled at the revealing cut of the chemise, and how her shape seemed more pronounced through the light folds of material that ceded little to modesty. "Oh my. How ... daring." She should have been shocked, but her thoughts flitted along, her brain content to drift, buoyed by remnants of the soothing perfume from the bath.

Across the room, the large, gold-rimmed tub gave off wisps of steam as warm water continued to flow through it. The room was momentarily deserted. Tall poles supporting broad circles of bronze each held a steady blue flame. But the flames gave off little light compared to the ceiling of crystal and moonglass.

She stood and the room shifted. "Oh!" She grabbed for the edge of the couch. Her head cleared after a moment, and she became aware of a weight upon her chest. It was a necklace of several large teardrop crystals. She lifted one of the heavy crystal dangles and watched it sparkle as if radiating light of its own: shifting patterns of reds and greens and gold, swirling like the Dancing Lights in the night sky, as if a living force. Magnetics, she decided. A kind of moonglass, no doubt.

Nearby was a table laid out with files and nail polish. A dusky light through the windows told her it was almost dark. Where had the day gone? She shook her head to clear it, was unsuccessful, and staggered for the first few steps until she regained control of her legs. Beyond the windows stretched a broad porch. The tall double doors were unlatched. Hope momentarily swelled within her breast as she pushed one open and quietly slipped outside. The hope died. Beyond the porch lay a broad sweeping curve in the Little Hiddekel River, and beyond that the patchwork of distant farms. But from the porch to the ground was a sheer drop of forty spans or more, with no stairs or ladder, or even a convenient vine to shinny down. She craned her neck the other way. There was no convenient passage to the roof, which rose a good twenty spans in the opposite direction.

"No wonder the doors weren't locked." She frowned and scooped her hair from her face, arranging it behind her shoulders. The air held a fragrance of orange blossoms. She paced the porch then leaned over the balustrade. Gardens ran to the river's edge, and here and there, winding paths followed an easy switchback down to a heavy stone pier where a moored barge was bedecked in the Lodath's colors and standards of the Lodath and King Irad.

A servant girl spied Leenah. "Oh. There you are." There was a clear note of relief in her voice. "I need to finish your nails."

Leenah swayed slightly. The girl was at her side, an arm wrapped about her waist, guiding her gently back through the doors into the bath and back onto the couch.

Leenah shook her head, trying to clear the wool from her brain.

With numbed fingers, she lifted the warm stones around her neck. The heat spread into her hand as the crystals swirled through a spectrum of ever-changing color.

"You leave that alone." The servant unfolded her fingers from the necklace and began working on them with a long nail file.

"What's wrong with me?"

"Nothing is wrong. Hold still and let me do your nails."

Leenah's vision drifted in and out of focus. The sensation made her vaguely ill. A nagging voice at the back of her brain was struggling to tell her something. She tried to listen, but her concentration drifted.

Desperate to settle her stomach, her view latched onto the nail file, sliding back and forth … back and forth … back and forth …

8

Lamech's Curious Visitors

*D*a-gore wheeled impatiently at the knock upon his door. Who would be coming to his quarters now? He shot a glance out the window. Nearly dark. The lieutenant in charge? Some new trouble? He stood sluggishly and glared at the empty mug on the table. How many times had he filled it? Three? No, four. He paused as a momentary dizziness passed. Straightening himself, he crossed to the door and pulled it open.

"Captain El-ik?" Finding the new Captain of the Guard at his door instantly sobered him. "Come in." He stepped aside as his superior entered. "What is it?" He and El-ik had never been friends, exactly, but they had never gotten crosswise either. A visit from the Lodath's right-hand man this late could not bode any good.

"First Shield Da-gore ..."

Formality and a curt tone. This was business. Well, he hadn't thought it would be a social call.

"... I've just come from his Eminence."

"Yes?" How many times had he begun an interview in just such a manner, to impress and intimidate. He had to believe

Captain El-ik intended that now.

El-ik's glance went to the bottle on the table, then came back to him. "The Lodath has expressed some concerns that tomorrow's execution will *not* proceed as planned."

Da-gore's lips tightened. He'd nearly managed to drown Lamech from his thoughts. Now he was back, and so were all the questions. Questions whose answers would die on the next morn.

"Has Sol-Ra-Luce any reason to believe there might be a delay?" Da-gore understood the tactics of the Captain of the Guard and refused to be cowed by them. El-ik held the position that rightfully belonged to him! Resentment burned, fueled by the wine, no doubt. *Watch yourself.*

A thin smile moved across El-ik's face. "You have to ask? You of all people, *First Shield*, should know the curious streak of good fortune that seems to favor these Lee-landers."

"Good fortune?" He exhaled sharply. "You understate the matter."

El-ik's right eyebrow hitched up, questioningly.

"You must have heard my report, Captain El-ik. You know of the emissaries who watch over them?"

"The Lodath told me all that happened. How you failed to run down seven fugitives—women and farmers—and how you lost them in the wilderness beyond the Ruins of Eden."

"Women and farmers? You forget that one of those fugitives was a Makir Warrior."

"And *you* had the Earth-Born."

Da-gore's jaw tightened. "At every turn they found allies to protect them."

"As I said, fortune favors these Lee-landers."

Da-gore knew it was hopeless to try to explain all that he had seen and encountered: the delays, the Lee-landers' miraculous escape from Chevel-ee, the freak storm at sea that sank one boat and prevented their army from reaching Eve's Weep before the fugitives could flee into the Ruins of Eden ... the golden guardians at the portal to the Cradleland.

"The executions will come off as ordered."

El-ik pointed a finger at him. "I like my new command, First Shield Da-gore. I would very much hate to have it taken from me. Do you understand?" El-ik glanced back at the bottle. "Try not to drink yourself into a stupor tonight, Da-gore. I'll want you sharp in the morning." The Captain of the Guard left.

Da-gore shut the door and leaned against it. Why shouldn't he drink himself insensible? He went to the table and snatched up the bottle, then stopped and stared at it. It hit him again: The answers he needed were going to die in the morning!

What did he care ...?

No, that wasn't it. *Why* did he care? He didn't understand this compulsion to know, but if he was ever going to have the puzzle solved, it would have to be done tonight.

He put the bottle back in the cupboard.

❧

Rhone fidgeted as he slid a wary glance along the busy thoroughfare that led past the Temple Prison. His hand remained under his cloak, clutching the hilt of his sword, squeezing it out of a need to release energy. His muscles tingled; his nerves were on edge. The sounds of the never-resting construction site filled his ears, and at any moment he expected guards would spy them.

Incredibly, Sari'el hadn't moved in almost a quarter of an hour. Perhaps he wasn't even there? Just the body he donned when he presented himself in the world of men. Rhone stifled the urge to poke him to see if he'd respond. Instead, he said, "How much longer?"

"Soon."

So, Sari'el was there after all. Rhone suspected that if the Messenger had desired to, he could have remained motionless for a year. Such patience. Such control. *Control.* Rhone had long since ceased practicing what the Katrahs and Kimahs had once taught him. Self-control like Sari'el's had once been his as well— before his exile.

He paced a few spans, turned, and stared across the busy grounds at the arched gateway into the Temple Prison where four guards stood before an iron gate. Somehow, he and Sari'el would have to make their way past those guards, the gates, and through a series of barred and guarded doors. He had tried to work out a plan, but not knowing the prison layout, his musings were simply a way to burn off pent-up energy.

Suddenly, Sari'el stirred from his self-imposed paralysis. "It is time."

Finally! "How do we get inside?"

Sari'el lifted his gnarled staff and pointed at the gate. And as they began to walk, a faint blue light slowly grew around them, and the fragrance like sweet lilac filled the air. Sari'el's cloak faded away, replaced by a dark jerkin over a robin's egg blue shirt. His britches and boots were black and shiny. The gnarled walking stick metamorphosed into the gold and ivory staff Rhone was used to seeing the Messenger carrying.

Other curious changes met his eye. Now, alongside the guards, other Messenger-warriors stood about as if they too were guarding the way to the gate. The warriors looked disheveled, their clothes giving off faint wisps of sulfurous smoke. At first Rhone made no sense of what he was seeing, but as they drew nearer to the gate, he discovered the Creator's Messengers holding other Messengers hostage, and all at once he understood the reason for the delay.

The men at the gate paid them no attention as the iron door

shimmered into nothingness before Rhone's eyes.

"This is too easy."

"It was not easy." Sari'el's voice was stern.

What had happened while he and Sari'el had waited? Rhone saw more hostages—some pinned beneath nets of fine, golden chains—all cowering before the ivory staffs of Messengers much like Sari'el, watching him with glaring eyes and snarling lips as he and Sari'el passed by.

Rhone chilled at the sight of these fallen Messengers. He and Sari'el descended passageways, passing guards unaware, passing more scenes of a recent battle.

"If we hadn't secured the Deceiver's Maliks, they would have reported to their master what we do now." Sari'el turned a sober eye on him. "They are forbidden to harm you in your own realm, Master Rhone, but here, in our realm—" He paused a moment, then gave a small smile. "You're fair game."

That revelation held little comfort.

He and Sari'el burrowed deeper, descending the maze of dark tunnels. They passed through one final timbered gate, then stood before a locked door. But as Rhone had learned, locked doors were as ephemeral as the blue mist that engulfed them.

"We have arrived." Sari'el waved a hand at the door.

Beyond the door was Lamech, Mishah's husband. It pained Rhone now that he had once had designs on this man's wife. Thankfully, nothing had come of that. He put the memories out of his head. He had pressing business here. This was his whole reason for coming, the whole reason the Creator had sent Sari'el to deliver him safely deep inside the bowels of the Temple Prison.

Sari'el nodded toward the door and stepped through it. Rhone followed.

In the dimly lit room, two men sat chained to the wall.

Lamech to Rhone's left, another to his right, his face hidden in shadows. Two of the Creator's Messengers were there with them. "Welcome, Sari'el," one said.

"We have been waiting for you," the other added.

Sari'el nodded. "Meren'el. Laes'el. Did you have difficulty?"

"No more than expected. The devils want Lamech badly. They taunt him mercilessly," said Laes'el, who was Lamech's Guardian.

Sari'el considered Lamech. "You are to stay near to him."

Laes'el gave a broad smile and took a pugnacious stance with his golden staff. "I'll keep the Fallen Ones from tormenting Lamech."

Sari'el rapped the end of the ivory staff upon the stone floor. The haze slowly dissipated, and with it the shapes of the two Messengers, until finally it was just he and Sari'el and the two men in the cell.

❦

His failure as a husband, and the heartache he'd caused Mishah, hurt Lamech more than the thought of his impending death. The family would watch over Mishah, and someday another man would fill the empty place left in her heart by his rashness. Another man would raise his son.... He made a fist and strained at the chain, then dropped his arm in defeat.

Klesc hadn't moved in over an hour. *Is quiet resignation how a Makir Warrior faced death?* Lamech gave a weak smile. No, it was just Klesc's way. "Have you any family, Klesc?"

The big man stirred, the soft clink of his wrist chains coming from the shadows. Then the silence resumed.

Lamech grimaced. When would he ever stop sticking his nose where it didn't belong? He closed his eyes and leaned his head against the gritty stone. The stale air in the cell took on a subtle change. He sniffed, imagining flowers in a green field. A flash of pale light played across his closed eyelids.

"What in Dirgen's name!" Klesc boomed.

Lamech's eyes sprang open to a wavering sheet of light brightening before him. A golden flash tore a ragged gash in the darkness, then faded. As the rift closed, two men stood there. He gasped and shrank from them.

"Peace, Master Lamech."

The pounding of Lamech's heart drove the breath from his lungs.

"I am Sari'el, a Messenger of the Creator."

"Great Dirgen! A spirit of the dead! Begone from us!"

Sari'el glanced at Klesc. "I am neither dead, nor a spirit, Master Klesc."

Startled as he was, Lamech noted how the second visitor's head came sharply around at the mention of Klesc's name. This man was larger than Sari'el, and there was something vaguely familiar about him.

"You have come to free us—!" Lamech's words fumbled. What was the proper way to address a Messenger? Surely such formalities didn't matter to a representative of the Creator of all. A deep awe suddenly overtook him, realizing that the Creator had sent a Messenger to *him*!

Sari'el shook his head. "No. I have brought you a visitor."

"Visitor?" Lamech stared at the second man, fighting to bring some order to his jumbled thoughts. "A visitor! Klesc and I are to be executed in the morning!" His voice rose in a way he could not control.

"The Creator knows your needs, Master Lamech. Take peace in that, and hear the news Master Rhone brings."

Lamech forced himself to draw in a calming breath. Where was his faith? A wry smile tugged at his mouth. It was quivering at the prospect of being ripped asunder by a pair of behemoths. He swallowed and his view shifted. "You are Master Rhone?"

"I am."

There was a sudden rattle of chains as Klesc shifted positions. Lamech glanced at him. The big man's gaze seemed riveted. Lamech looked back at Rhone. "Have we met?"

"Many months ago upon the Meeting Floor, here in Nod City."

Klesc leaned forward with sudden interest.

Lamech searched his memory, his eyes widening. "You're the one who stood up for us when the crowd turned against us." He stopped and stared, trying to remember. There was more. Where else had he seen Rhone? "The dream. I dreamt of Mishah and Amolikah and ... and you. You were there with them!"

Rhone nodded.

"What happened? What went wrong? Mishah was only making the traditional first-child pilgrimage to Chevel-ee, to present herself to the Mother."

Rhone's lips thinned in a way that sent a shiver down Lamech's spine. "The Mother is dead."

"Eve ... dead?" His breath momentarily froze in his lungs. "It's true then? The giants. Mishah fleeing for her life. The Cradleland, where man has been forbidden for ages. It wasn't a dream, was it?"

"It was no dream. The Creator obviously permitted you a glimpse of what had happened."

"Mishah!"

"She is well and safe."

A shudder of relief shook him. "I awoke before it ended, and it has disturbed me ever since, but I consoled myself in that it was only a dream." As he spoke, the memory of it again filled his head. "Mishah and Amolikah were fleeing toward a gate ... no, a portal. The giants were almost upon her, but Kenoch ... and you, you two stood ground before the giants." Lamech closed his eyes and saw the gleaming portal, flanked by two immense golden statues. He remembered something else, too. "You were wounded. No," his eyes sprang open, "in my dream you had died!" Lamech exhaled a trembling breath. "But that apparently didn't happen."

Rhone's face bore the sober look of a man who had seen the incomprehensible. "It did happen, Master Lamech."

Lamech stared. "What manifestation of the Creator's power is this? Am I speaking to a spirit?"

"No."

"Then, the Creator must have—"

"Raised me."

The plop ... plop ... plop of that distant drip filled the sudden silence. "Incredible."

"Our Creator has sent me to you."

Lamech's brain was still stuck on Rhone's revelation. He was speaking with a dead man made alive. He pulled his thoughts off that notion. "Sent you to me? Why?"

"Because he loves you, Lamech. You, like your grandfather before you, and like your son, have been called to his purpose."

"My son!" In the shock of this visitation he had momentarily forgotten. "He is born. He is well?"

Rhone's tight expression eased some. "Both Noah and Mistress Mishah are well."

Noah! He'd dreamt he had walked with Mishah and told her what to name their son. So, that had been real as well. What a faithful Creator he served! "Where are they?"

"They are in the Creator's Garden where they will be safe."

"Safe? They're in danger?"

"The Deceiver knows Noah is a chosen one, although he yet

does not know what Noah must eventually do."

"What he must do? What are you talking about?"

"The Deceiver is bent on destroying Noah and all who are near to him."

Lamech felt the despair returning. "Beginning with me. Tomorrow."

Sari'el said, "You will not die tomorrow, Master Lamech."

"Then you will take me out of here?" He looked hopefully between Sari'el and Rhone.

Rhone shook his head. "You will remain here. You are in the very heart of where the Creator wants you to be."

"Come tomorrow I will be in a grave."

Sari'el said sternly, "I very much doubt that."

"Will you overturn the council's orders?" Even as he spoke, he knew his words were foolish—the words of a doubter. Before him stood a man raised from the dead! Could a Creator who had performed such a marvelous miracle not accomplish a simple task such as repealing a death sentence? "I'm sorry. My human-ness oftentimes tries my faith."

"Such is the testing of all humans, Master Lamech." Sari'el glanced suddenly at Rhone. "We must hurry. He's to have another visitor shortly."

Rhone said, "The Creator intends for Mishah, Amolikah, and Noah to remain in his Garden until your task is finished here."

"Is ... is it as wonderful as legend says?"

"More so. It's a haven where the Creator and Messengers like Sari'el will protect your family. It is where the Creator will walk with Noah, and instruct him as he once did with your grandfather, Enoch."

Lamech winced at the pang in his heart at not being able to instruct Noah himself. But his heart was immensely relieved that they were safe.

Sari'el said, "When you have finished with the task Elohim has set before you, I will come for you, and you will be reunited with your family."

"When?"

"I don't know. He tells me only what I need to know. But rest assured, His timing will be perfect."

"What am I supposed to do here?"

Rhone shook his head. "I don't know that either."

Lamech looked to Sari'el. The Messenger had been staring at the closed door, yet somehow he felt Lamech's stare and looked back. "Your task is to do what you do best."

"What do I do best?"

"Preach." Rhone reached under his cloak. "One other thing." He removed a small pouch, extracted something from it, and placed in his hand a finely braided hank of hair the length of his finger. "Mishah asked me to give this to you."

"What is it?"

"A bit of Noah's hair, and Mishah's, woven into a strand as one. It was all she had to send. And she instructed me to be sure I told you how much she loves and misses you, and dreams of the day when you will be reunited."

Lamech's eyes stung as he stared at the memento. He clutched it in his fist. "Will you see her again?"

"Yes. Soon."

"Tell her I miss her and love her." His voice cracked. "Tell her not a day passes that she doesn't fill my thoughts."

"I will. And there is one more thing—"

"Master Rhone." Sar'iel's voice held an edge of urgency.

"I'll be quick." He looked back at Lamech. "Kenoch and his wife send their regards."

"Wife? Kenoch has taken a wife?" This was certainly unexpected.

"They were married in the Garden."

"Master Rhone." Sar'iel's face was stern, matching his voice's impatience.

Rhone nodded. "We can leave now."

"No, there is still one more thing to do," Sar'iel insisted.

Rhone glanced at the Messenger. "I've accomplished all the Creator asked of me."

Sari'el inclined his head toward Klesc. Lamech watched Rhone stiffen. Sari'el said, "The pattern is vast and wonderful, the threads many."

Rhone drew in a breath and looked at the big man. "Klesc. It has been many years."

"Pyir Rhone," the man's deep voice replied from the shadows. "For a moment, I thought my ears and eyes were deceiving me."

"You know each other?" Lamech shifted on the stone slab upon which he sat.

"From long ago." Rhone's voice had taken on a hard note.

Sari'el said, "Elohim arranged this."

"He didn't tell me."

"It was not for you to know until now, Master Rhone."

Rhone worked his jaw.

Sari'el touched Klesc's shackles, and the heavy iron crumbled away in a fine dust. The big man stood, freed from his bonds. "I have been instructed to watch over Lamech."

"You have completed your responsibility, Master Klesc. Now you will come with us."

Rhone frowned. "Why?"

Sari'el turned to him. "The task that lies before you is a difficult one, Master Rhone. Did I not say you misjudged in thinking you would be alone in it?"

Rhone shot a glance at Klesc.

Sari'el said, "Now, we must go."

"Wait!" Lamech leaped to his feet, his chains snapping taut.

"Leenah. Someone must help Leenah!"

"Leenah?" Rhone's eyes narrowed, his view shifting to Sari'el. "Who's Leenah?"

Lamech said, "A friend. A follower of the Creator. I don't know what the Creator's plans are for me, but I know Leenah is part of this somehow. She was taken by the Lodath. She'd have died, rather than to be used by the Son of the Deceiver!"

Klesc said, "I will do what I can."

Sari'el's face pinched at this new complication.

Was this something the Creator had kept from the Messenger? It seemed that Rhone was not the only one. "Promise me, Klesc. Promise you will help her."

"I promise."

"You can't make such a promise," Rhone said. "We must be away from Nod City."

Klesc shot Rhone a stare. "I've given my word … as a Makir."

A scowl darkened Rhone's face. "Now is a fine time to be remembering your oaths."

Klesc looked stunned.

Sari'el said to Lamech, "You will have a visitor soon. He needs to hear what you have to tell him."

"Visitor? Who is it? What does he need to hear?"

But there was no time for an answer. The air shimmered in a wavering blue light turning suddenly to gold. The darkness behind the three men split wide, and the brilliance that filled the dungeon stung Lamech's eyes. When he opened them, he was alone, except for the sweet, lingering scent of lilac.

They had to help her. Klesc promised. He lifted his eyes to the ceiling. "Please watch over Leenah and all of them." He opened his fist and looked at the braid. "And thank you for this."

Footsteps sounded outside the door, then the clatter of the heavy bolt being thrown. Lamech pulled his thoughts together and shoved the braid into a pocket of the gray prison clothes. He sat back down, took a calming breath, and whispered a plead for guidance.

The squeal of hinges announced the arrival of the visitor.

9

A Two-Makir Job

*T*he dark maze of passages bored deep beneath the prison had grown more chilled as Da-gore descended. The way took him through four doors and past two barred gates. At each, a pair of guards gave him entrance to the next lower level. After the last door swung wide for him, he paused and peered down the gloomy tunnel. Bolted doors led off to each side.

"Shall I accompany you, sir?" one of the guards asked.

Da-gore knew the answers he sought might best be listened to in private. "The prisoners are shackled, aren't they?"

"I checked their chains myself."

"I will speak with them alone, Warder." He hitched his cloak tighter against the damp chill and strode briskly into the murky passageway. At the cell door he paused as the guards up the tunnel watched from their posts. Should he encounter any problems, they'd be but a call away. He threw the bolt and pushed it open.

The prisoner leaned against the wall, arms folded across his chest ... *alone!*

Da-gore's gaze darted to the right. Klesc was gone. He spun, expecting the big man to attack from behind the door, but no one was there.

"Greetings, First Shield Da-gore."

"Where is he?"

"Klesc has left."

"Left?" He turned to summon the guards.

"If you call for help, your questions will never be answered."

A chilling dread unlike anything he had ever known sent cold fingers probing his chest. *Lamech knew.* Somehow, he *knew*! Da-gore called upon his years of training to overpower the shock of finding things topsy-turvy from what he had expected. He turned back and carefully surveyed the cell, lifting what remained of the iron chains still attached to the wall.

"Tell me how this can be."

"I'll answer all your questions." Lamech glanced toward the open door. "Perhaps you should close that lest we be interrupted."

Da-gore reached back and shoved the door, too bewildered to care that he was taking orders from a prisoner.

※

They strode through the tunnels, Sari'el at the lead. In the haze of the Messenger's blue light, Rhone glanced at Klesc. He knew of few men larger than himself. Klesc was one. Klesc had once been as solid as the Pillars of the Sun, but now, like himself, he had grown soft. Although still a powerful man, and no doubt a skilled warrior, Klesc needed the rigors of the Katrahs and Kimahs to hone the edge. The mock battles in the marketplace had been all show. How long had it been since Klesc had faced a real enemy?

The same might be said for himself. Rhone grimaced. Until a few months ago, he too had neglected the disciplines of the Katrahs and Kimahs. A Webmaster had no need of such skills.

Klesc's eyes opened wide in amazement. The scene of the recent battle was all around him. The Messenger-warriors with their captives caught beneath staffs, or held within a net of golden chain, seemed to intrigue him.

"What is all this?" Klesc asked softly.

Rhone gave a silent laugh. Klesc couldn't know that he was hardly the one qualified to answer that; this was all new to him, too. "There is a war being waged that until now has been kept hidden from the eyes of man." That was almost all he knew of this eternal battle between good and evil.

Klesc looked ahead with interest.

It was now dark outside the prison, and the big moon wore an eerie bluish cast. As they left the city, heading toward the river, the blue haze dissipated, and the beings of Sari'el's world faded from sight. Near the dark water's edge, Sari'el stopped and turned toward them. He retained the gold and ivory staff. Rhone understood that meant his job here in the realm of man was over.

"I am needed elsewhere."

Rhone nodded. "On the Creator's business?"

"Always, Master Rhone. As you need to be."

"You leave us?" Klesc was a conspicuous sight in his gray prison garb. The first thing Rhone needed to do was find him different clothing.

"I must, for now."

"But what of Leenah?" he demanded

"I am called elsewhere, Master Klesc." Sari'el pointed to the palace by the river's edge, gleaming like a jewel of light against the black water. "You will find her there." Sari'el turned to Rhone. "Be wary of the Deceiver's temptations. He knows who you are and what you must do."

"I understand."

"Fair journey. Elohim be with you both."

"Fair journey, Sari'el."

Sari'el walked down the river embankment toward a sheet of shimmering light, then winked out of sight.

Klesc shook his head. "Great Dirgen! Does he always come and go like that?"

"It takes some getting used to." And he hadn't quite gotten there himself.

"I'm going after Leenah."

"Not dressed like that, you aren't." Rhone swept off his cloak and handed it to him. "This will have to do until we can find you other attire."

"We?" Klesc took the cloak and gave him a suspicious look. "You don't want me with you. I see it in your face. I hear it in your voice."

"I try not to question Sari'el's wisdom."

"What manner of being is he? And why did he remove me from prison and not Lamech?"

"He is a Malik, a Messenger of the Creator."

Klesc fastened the cloak over his shoulders and gathered it close in front of him. "Then the legends and myths are true?"

"Yes. And the truth is stranger than the myths."

"Sari'el must be very powerful."

"Sari'el is a created being, like we are, Klesc, and his power is unimaginable, yet he is limited by the will of the Creator. He freed you because *I* need you. He did not free Lamech because the Creator needs him there. Don't ask why. I don't know."

"You need me?" He snorted. "I am unbound. You resent me for that, Pyir Rhone?"

He shot Klesc a sharp look. "All the Makir are unbound. And I am no longer their Pyir."

Klesc's face softened. "For years many of us thought you dead."

"I might as well have been." They started toward the Lodath's palace. Rhone had hoped to put Nod City far behind them before Klesc had been discovered, but Klesc was determined to free this woman, Leenah. Although Sari'el had refused to be a part of any rescue, he had told them where to find her. There was more here than met the eye, and Rhone had come to learn that the Creator moved people in mysterious ways.

"Then what have you against me?" Klesc asked.

"You've broken the oath."

Klesc looked stunned. "How?"

"The games in the marketplace."

His lips tightened. "You saw that?"

"The Usito forbids such."

Klesc gave a low growl. "After all these years, am I still bound by the Usito?" His eyes flashed with anger. "If I have broken the Makir Oath, how much more so have our brothers who remained to serve Zorin? I was cut adrift from my kal-ee-hon. I could not return home. How was I to live, save by marketing the only skills I possessed?"

"The oath constrains you until you draw your last breath—bound or unbound." Rhone remembered reciting the words himself as a young Makir. His father, High Councilor Khore, had presided over the ceremony first instituted by Hodin, which was later refined and written into verse by the first Makir leader, Pyir Torc.

Klesc strode beside him in a brooding silence. "You don't have to do this. I can find Leenah myself."

Rhone winced at the hurt he heard in Klesc's voice. Was the offense as dire as he was making it out to be? Could a man who takes an oath then breaks it be trusted? Rhone weighed this in a moment of thought. But if the Creator deemed it so ... "There must be more than a hundred green-cloaks and servants in that place. No, this is a two-Makir job."

"A two-Makir job?" Klesc slid a glance, gave a tentative smile, and then a low, belly-rumbling laugh.

Streaming bands of reds, golds, and greens swirled across the northern heavens as Rhone and Klesc scaled the stone wall surrounding the palace grounds. Some called the Dancing Lights a gift from the Creator. Others simply noted it was a wonder of the magnetic veil. Up until a few months ago, Rhone hadn't given the debate much thought one way or the other. But right at this moment, he wished the lights would simply go out.

Dropping lightly into the shadows on the other side of the wall, he went to his haunches, listening. Klesc, taut as a bowstring, sniffed the air for the spoor of danger. So, the old training *was* still alive within him.

"How will we locate her?" Klesc peered at the great building with light spilling from every window. A pair of guards strolled along a path, chatting idly as if their job was merely the necessary trappings of official grounds. To the left of the palace sat a row of dark, official-looking buildings. To the right, a copse of dark trees. Klesc sniffed. "Barns in that direction." He glanced toward the trees.

"The stables and barracks for the court green-cloaks." Rhone waited as the two guards disappeared around a shadowy corner. "Someone there will know where she is being kept."

They moved toward the black copse, keeping to the shadows. The grove was alive with flashing starlight flies and lantern beetles, and the softly glowing greenish tendrils of the low-growing lambent creepers that trailed across the ground and into the trees. A fire flickered beyond the thicket. Silently, they crept toward it. The Lodath's stables came into view, flanked by a low stone building.

Between the stables and the barracks, flames licked skyward from a large iron basin. No one was in sight, but shadows within the stone building cautioned Rhone that the Lodath's green-cloaks were not far off. They sprinted to the back corner of the stables, reaching it moments before a guard emerged from the barracks and made for the barn. He disappeared inside the barn, and a moment later Rhone heard the sound of something heavy being dragged across the floor. He slipped through a window into an empty stall. Klesc silently joined him, pressing his bulk against the dividing wall. A gerup in the next stall chortled, a horse down the row gave a soft whinny.

Rhone crept toward a stone arc that opened onto the next room. He peeked around it. The guard, dragging a crate, paused at his labor, drew in a deep breath, then bent over again, and went back to work. A piece of moonglass gave off a weak glow.

Rhone motioned to Klesc, and they crept toward opposite walls. Just then voices reached him from outside. Rhone pressed against the wall as two more men appeared.

"Wol-vic said you'd have trouble."

The struggling guard growled, "Wol-vic can come fetch his own Kingle Stone."

"Ha. When you get to be Warden, you can give the orders. In the meantime, we grunts just follow 'em."

He straightened up and sat upon the crate. "What put it in his head to play this game anyway?"

The second newcomer gave a short laugh, set his weapon aside, and bent to lend a hand. "Some men take their Kingle seriously. I've seen Warden Wol-vic leave the Stone after a night's gaming with a thousand glecks in his purse."

Rhone gave a nod. Klesc crept quietly to a place of advantage, just out of sight of the three guards who were busily wrestling a broad, flat stone out of the box. In the poor light, Rhone couldn't make out the lines inscribed on the stone, but he knew what the designs were and what they meant. He'd played Kingle himself. It was a favorite pastime for fighting men the world over.

They moved in unison, and in spite of not having practiced the Katrahs and Kimahs for so long, Rhone could still feel their minds momentarily linking—the binding was not completely severed. He sprang left while Klesc darted right, and between them, they braced the three men so swiftly that not one of them realized what had happened until it was over.

Rhone's sword flashed in the pale light and touched one of the guards above his heart, backing him up against a wall. The man gasped and stared at the blade. Klesc caught the other two in each arm, his mighty biceps bulging around their necks, giving just enough pressure to make breathing possible—and to assure them how easy it would be for him to shut off the air.

Rhone narrowed his gaze at the guard beneath the point of his sword. "A woman was brought here from the prison. Where is she being kept?"

"Many women come to the Lodath."

"Not good enough." Rhone pressed harder, and a bead of bright red blood formed at the point of his sword. "Speak now or your two friends die. And then you."

Klesc tightened his hold, and the men began to sputter.

"I think I heard of one brought in today," he croaked.

Klesc let up a fraction, but Rhone kept up the pressure as a trickle of crimson streaked the tip of his sword. "Where is she now?"

"I have no way of knowing." His wide eyes had riveted on the steel above his heart. "Bu—bu—but I would expect her to be in his private quarters. On the third floor, overlooking the river."

With a sudden jerk, the hilt of Rhone's sword shot out and cracked the man alongside his skull. The guard slumped. Rhone caught him before he hit the ground.

Klesc merely tightened his hold until struggling ceased. He dropped the unconscious men and checked to see if they were still breathing. "I timed that about right."

"You haven't lost your touch."

Klesc glanced up. "Nor you."

Rhone smiled at him. "I'm as rusty as those old chains you left hanging in your cell. These were practice fodder. Wait until we meet up with my brother's soldiers."

"Zorin?" Klesc's eyes compressed. "When do you intend to face your evil twin?"

"When we return to Atlan."

Klesc was momentarily lost for words. "Return to Atlan? Why?"

"Because the Creator has told me to."

They dragged the men into a stall and bound them with the leather straps of a bridle.

Rhone fixed a gag about each man's mouth. "They will be missed shortly. We must hurry."

Klesc went to the door, peeked out. Then he lifted the Kingle Stone and angled it against the door. "That will slow them down a little."

Rhone found a coil of rope. He tossed Klesc the guard's proj-lance.

Klesc scowled. "A coward's weapon!" He flung it aside and relieved one of the guards of his sword. "This is the weapon of a warrior!"

Rhone smiled as they slipped out the back of the stables and made for the Lodath's palace. How well he understood that.

10

A Stab of Desperation

*E*le-se!"

The servant girl filing Leenah's nails looked around with a start at the sound of her name. Leenah stopped fiddling with the crystals about her neck and peered toward the door.

"Ele-se, where are you?" a woman's voice inquired sharply from the hallway.

"I'm in here." She set the nail file down and stood.

In the doorway appeared one of the women—the shorter of the two—who'd escorted Leenah here. "Oh, there you are. Mistress Mag-eli is looking for you."

"I'm just finishing the woman's nails, as Mistress Mag-eli commanded."

Through a dreamy haze, Leenah noted sudden concern flash across Ele-se's face.

"That should have been finished already. Mistress Mag-eli wants you now."

"But her nails?"

"I can do my own nails, thank you." Leenah was vaguely annoyed at the disturbance that, for a brief instant, had drawn her from her blissful lassitude. But now that she had sobered a little, a sudden sense of dread, like a sea wave drawn far back and then released, came crashing back.

Ele-se hesitated. "Very well." She glanced down at Leenah. "I'll be back as soon as I can."

"Don't hurry back." She grinned. "I've filed my own nails before." The euphoria was swimming back, and Leenah fought against it, willing the intoxication from her head. The crystal necklace seemed to burn hotter against her skin the more she resisted. As soon as Ele-se had gone, Leenah lifted the stones from her chest. At once the fire faded, and her thoughts became slightly clearer. Under Ele-se's watchful eye, she had not been permitted to do more than examine the necklace with her fingers. Though her euphoria had slightly lessened, the light-headedness continued. She took a cloth from the manicurist's tray and held the necklace in it.

Almost at once her head began to clear and her wits sharpened. Whatever power the crystals possessed to numb the brain, they apparently needed to be in contact with skin to transfer it. She quickly unfastened the crystals and set them on the tray. She had to devise a plan quickly. Ele-se would never permit her to go without wearing the necklace. She fumbled through the jars of lotions and nail paint on the tray. Then she scanned the room with a growing fear that Ele-se or another servant might return at any moment. Her mind, still groggy, was coming around too slowly.

She shut her eyes. *Think, Leenah. How do you protect yourself against the necklace?* Her hands balled into fists, and the newly manicured nails dug into her palms, smooth and without the familiar raggedness she had grown used to feeling. Ele-se had nearly finished with them and had but only to apply the paint when she'd been called away. Leenah could hardly remember the last time she'd seen her nails cared for and pretty. She opened her eyes and looked at them. But that was a waste of precious time. She cast about the room again.

Still nothing helpful that she could use…. A thought suddenly brought her gaze back to her nails with a lurch.

Swiftly, she uncapped jars of paint until she found what she'd hoped she would. Grabbing a brush and the jar of clear glazing, she turned the necklace over and got to work. With an eye on the door and her heart racing, she quickly covered each stone with a thick coat of clear paint, careful to coat only the flat undersides where they touched the skin. Would the paint dry in time, and would the crystal's swirling colors mask the ploy?

She finished even as footsteps sounded in the hallway outside. She grabbed the necklace by the clasp and hid it under the couch.

Ele-se came in, her face scrunched, her attitude changed. Without a word, she sat in the chair and grabbed Leenah's hand. "I thought you said you could do this yourself?"

"Hum? Oh. Oh, I'm just so sleepy." She giggled.

Ele-se's grip tightened belligerently. What had happened? A reprimand by her overseer for some mistake? Leenah turned from the servant girl so the missing necklace might go unnoticed.

Ele-se finished with the nails, a rushed job at best, and as she blew across the paint to speed its drying, Leenah's two escorts came through the doorway, impatience plain in their carriage. "The Lodath is ready for her," the taller one said.

"Yes, Mistress Mag-eli. I'm just finished."

"Is she … prepared?"

Something in Mistress Mag-eli's inflection sent a shiver through Leenah, but she didn't let it show.

"Yes, Mistress."

"Good." The two women each took an arm and lifted her from the couch. "Stand straight now. You must make a good appearance for the Lodath."

Somehow, Mag-eli's concern sounded self-serving and made Leenah wonder what would happen if the Lodath was not pleased with his servant's efforts to "clean her up." Her temper climbed with the thought, and she redoubled her self-control.

Mistress Mag-eli gave her a final inspection: her hair, her eyes, her fingers. A whiff of her breath and some minor adjustments to the plunging neckline of the sheer chemise. All at once the fussing stopped. "Where is the necklace?"

Leenah smiled innocently and shrugged, swaying slightly on her feet.

Mistress Mag-eli glared at the servants. "The necklace is gone. Find it."

The servants bustled around, looking under cushions, scanning the floor.

"Here it is." One of the women stood, holding the necklace with the tips of her fingers. "It must have come loose."

Mistress Mag-eli scowled impatiently.

Leenah smiled inwardly at the servant's caution. How many other women had been unfortunate enough to wear it, to be captured by its beauty and weakened by its power? As the servant refastened it about her neck, Leenah's breath caught, waiting for the warmth to spread, but the crystals remained cool. With her heart pounding her ribs, maintaining the charade was becoming a challenge. Fear and desperation pressed in and taunted her.

As of yet, all she had to defend herself with was her wits. What she needed was a weapon.

"Come with us. The Lodath does not like to be kept waiting."

Fear clawed at her throat. It must show. She was supposed to be in a walking stupor, numbed to fear. She tried to hide it with a giddy smile. A carefully calculated misplaced step sent her reeling, and she caught herself on the edge of the manicurist table at the last moment.

"Don't be a clumsy gorion!" Mistress Mag-eli's scowl darkened.

"Sorry." She smiled innocently, but her anger helped defuse

some of the fear. *Gorion, indeed! We'll see whose snout shovels the earth for grubs.*

The two women helped her up. Mistress Mag-eli's face, pinched in an impatient frown, looked at that moment more gorion-like than she'd likely care to know.

"Wait, I'm all crooked now." Leenah fussed with the waist of her chemise, straightening it round. When she got it to lay just right, she giggled. "I'm ready."

They led her from the bath and into the hallway.

She fingered the nail file secreted within the flimsy folds of the chemise, and prayed that it would not show.

✿

Rhone and Klesc advanced on the palace, moving silently through the premises where an occasional guard walked his lonely rounds. Any moment the missing men in the stables would be discovered and an alarm raised, but Rhone refused to let that pressure him into rashness.

He and Klesc halted in the shrubbery above the dark slow waters of the Little Hiddekel and peered up at the imposing sprawl of the Lodath's palace. The entire third floor was lined with balconies. Any one of them might be the Lodath's quarters, and there would be little time to try each.

Klesc whispered, "We need to hurry."

Rhone heard the impetuousness in Klesc's voice. "We can't barge in without knowing where we're going."

Klesc glanced around. "We'll not find her by hiding in these bushes."

Maybe impetuousness was all they had left. Rhone sprinted across the dark grounds and flattened against the palace walls. The joint lines between the hewed stones offered finger- and toeholds and they climbed to the first balcony, then ascended to the second floor where light spilled from windows. Keeping to the shadows, they clawed and toed up to the third floor and scrambled over a balustrade onto a bright balcony. The curtains were drawn. Rhone peered through a slit where the curtains joined imperfectly. Across the room, a tub rimmed in gold wafted steamy vapors toward a crystalline ceiling. A couch, some chairs, and plain bronze torchères holding steady blue flames were the only furniture. Servants scurried about collecting towels and arranging soaps and oils.

No sign of the Lodath or a woman. Rhone peered down the length of the palace. At least ten more balconies hugged the side of it. The Lodath's quarters could be off any one of them. His view lifted to the dark roofline one more story overhead, and he frowned.

Klesc peeked through the gap, and then suddenly his head snapped around and cocked to one side.

"What is it?" Rhone cast about for trouble.

"I heard a voice." He stared at Rhone. "You didn't hear it?"

Rhone had been listening for an alarm to rise from the stables. "No. We'll make better time on the roof." Rhone shifted the weight of the coils of rope and started his final ascent.

"Wait." Klesc gave a shake of his head as if to clear it of some annoyance. "Not the roof."

"What is it, Klesc?"

Klesc looked worried. "A voice. The same that told me to protect Lamech."

Rhone had learned not to ignore the softly whispered voices that came to men. Was a Messenger speaking to Klesc? "What is it telling you to do?"

He frowned, then peered down the row of balconies, some aglow from windows and moonglass, some laying in gloomy darkness. "That way."

A servant led the way, while Leenah's two escorts stuck near her side. A fourth woman followed ten paces behind. She was trapped, though the trap's jaws gave the pretense of being fur lined. The nail file hidden in the folds of material at her waist was a feeble weapon at best. She needed more.

Her face flashed past in a wall mirror, and as she glanced at herself, a plan came to her. She stopped and stared at herself, touching her long golden hair into place. Her entourage came to an impatient halt.

Mistress Mag-eli's reflection scowled over her shoulder. "No more delays."

Leenah lifted her hair in both hands, let it fall, then shook her head. "This will never do."

Mag-eli tugged at her arm.

"I want to make a good impression." She narrowed her eyes at the overseer. "You *do* want me to make a good impression, don't you?" Maybe she'd read more into the woman's inflection earlier, but right now she was out of options.

Mag-eli hesitated, her scowl widening.

So, she'd read her correctly. These servants were rewarded or punished by the results of their grooming the Lodath's next victim.

"Your hair is perfect." Mag-eli quickly fussed with the long truss and arranged it over her shoulders.

"It needs something else." Leenah kept her voice dreamy and whimsical. She was, after all, under whatever strange intoxicant the crystal necklace emitted. "It needs something …"—she paused and turned her head to one side to see the back—"… to hold it away from my face." She flashed a girlish smile.

"I said it's perfect." Impatience stormed back into Mag-eli's eyes. But the other women looked concerned and glanced worriedly toward a door down the long hallway. "Oh, very well! Here, let me pin it back." Mag-eli snatched a silver comb from her own hair, turned Leenah's trusses into a long, looping coil, and stabbed it in place. "There. That keeps it out of your face. Better?"

"Now it is perfect." Leenah beamed and cast a carefree face at the tall overseer.

They escorted her down the hall, through the doorway, and marched her inside a large antechamber. "He will be here shortly." Mag-eli and her entourage left her, and the door shut firmly behind her.

She stood there alone in the sudden hush of the room; the sound of her breathing, harsh and determined, filled her ears. Beneath her slippered feet was an orange and black tiger rug. A pale light filtered down from the ceiling. It didn't quite penetrate the shadowed corners. The walls dripped silk in pale waterfalls of blues and whites, and huge tapestries draped about, depicting images she did not recognize: great ruby red and emerald green bridges arching over rivers of pearlescent water; distant cities of towering, spired buildings stabbing toward the heavens. The fanciful world of someone's imagination. As far as she knew, no place like that existed on earth.

To her left stood a pair of tall black doors, presently closed. What lay behind them? Her imagination could conjure up only the worst images. She backed a step toward the red lacquered door she'd entered by. At least she knew what it opened onto. To her right, huge, arching sheets of glass overlooked a balcony and beyond to twinkling, distant lights of vessels upon the Little Hiddekel River, ablaze with the reflected greens, golds, and reds of the swirling Dancing Lights.

"I've been waiting for you."

His words startled the breath from her. Her heart crashed into her ribs and rebounded into her throat as she lurched around. The Lodath stood beneath a low arch in the far wall. A silken veil floated back across the opening. Through its sheerness was the muted outline of a bed. It stood between two bronze torchères shaped like men's arms with upturned hands, each palm holding a blue flame.

A thin smile slanted up one side of the Lodath's face. "You're frightened."

She wrapped her arms about her waist, feeling the hard file hidden there. It gave her no confidence now as he approached. The pale peach robe that he wore swirled about him with each step, every bit as sheer as the flimsy chemise his servants had dressed her in. She concentrated on her breathing and tried not to think what the garment she wore was revealing to him.

"I'm in awe in your presence, Your Eminence." She fought down the disgust that rose in her throat. She had to cling to her wits in order to play this game.

"Let's forsake with decorum. For tonight, I am simply Sol-Ra-Luce."

Her fingers clawed her waist as he stopped in front of her. "As it pleases you."

The hard line of his lips crept higher, and his eyes greedily devoured her.

She crossed her arms over her chest.

He laughed. "You don't mean that."

Her heart raced. He'd detect a lie the moment it left her lips. His fingers rose to her neck. Her throat constricted at his touch. She flinched as his fingers encircled her, then fell to the heavy necklace, and lifted the crystals. His eyes narrowed briefly, and he set the stones gently back upon her heaving chest.

"So, you discovered their secret. Intelligence as well as beauty."

Her chest constricted, her brain reeling slightly as blood pounded in her ears.

Sol-Ra-Luce laughed and went to a nearby table that had escaped her notice until then. "Never mind. We won't need their ... how should I say ... influence tonight, will we?" An opened bottle stood beside two goblets. He took the goblets from the table and handed one to her.

"What is it?"

"The Oracle's Whimsy. It's quite delicious."

Another potion to muddle her brain again? "I ... I'd rather not."

The smile vanished, and the cords of his neck thickened. "But I insist."

She peered down into the goblet, then at his. With a playful smile that did not spring easily to her face, she took his and gave him hers. "After you, Sol-Ra-Luce."

He hitched up one eyebrow, then laughed again, and took a long draught of the wine. "Harmless, but delicious."

She took a small sip, hardly tasting it.

"That's better." He fondled her hair, curling it about his fingers. "Lovely, indeed. The emissaries will be pleased."

Leenah shivered as visions of being taken by those inhuman creatures filled her brain.

"Chilled?" He took her arm and started her for the room beyond the veiled arch. "We'll see to that in a few moments." His dark eyes narrowed as his lips thinned and drew another hard line across his face.

Her eyes riveted upon the bed as fear gripped her. She shook free of its hold and shot a glance toward the windows overlooking the balcony. No escape that way except a swift plunge and certain death. Would that be any worse than what she faced here? Any more horrible than being a mistress to those ... those creatures?

He parted the veil and pulled her inside the bedroom.

With her heart testing the resilience of her ribs, Leenah folded her left hand around her waist and grasped the nail file hidden within the thin layers of material.

At the bed, she saw the terror in her eyes reflected in a long mirror. Sol-Ra-Luce's sharp blue nail ran along her collar bone. "One final item to see to." With a sudden jerk, he wrenched her hand from her waist, and the nail file dropped silently to the thick fur hide that carpeted the floor.

She gave a gasp. He flung her to the bed. "Did you think I would not know? Foolish woman. Nothing happens in my palace without my knowing it." He stooped, retrieved the file, and sneered at it in the light of the blue flames. "Not quite a harvesting blade, is it? What did you expect to accomplish? Are you so simpleminded as to think you could defend yourself against me with such a puny weapon? Or do you believe you've inherited Hodin's valor? Do even his granddaughters fancy themselves Makir Warriors?"

"I'd use my teeth if that's all I had!"

A dark cast suddenly overshadowed his face. "Is that so? Your own words have spoken your punishment. After tonight, you will have no teeth." He laughed.

Leenah saw his fingers bunch into a fist, and when they shot up suddenly, she was prepared. She rolled with the punch, and it glanced off her chin, momentarily stunning her and toppling her onto the bed. In an instant Sol-Ra-Luce's weight was upon her, his hands clawing at the flimsy material of the chemise.

Leenah strained to roll him off, but Sol-Ra-Luce had greater strength than she. He grasped her arms and wrenched them up behind her head. She drove a knee into his side. He snarled at the feeble attack, releasing her long enough to backhand her across the face. The stinging slap jerked her head to one side, but she didn't feel the pain. A surge of vitality filled her blood. Her fingers grabbed for the silver comb Mag-eli had fixed into her hair. The comb's blunted metal teeth were long and heavy. In a maneuver he hadn't expected, she swung out with all her strength—strength toughened by her time hauling water to the Temple prisoners, strength that the ancestry of Hodin had bequeathed to her muscles.

The finger-length silver teeth found the Lodath's neck. Leenah felt resistance. She drove the blunt silver spikes in as deep as she could. There was a gush of blood. Sol-Ra-Luce's eyes went wide as blood gurgled and bubbled from his throat, and a look of shock sprang to his face. His hands released her and clutched for the comb. She rolled out from under him.

The Lodath staggered, one arm clawing the air. Then she saw what it was he was desperately seeking. She leaped to stop him, but it was too late. His fist grasped a thick maroon cord hanging from the ceiling, and as he collapsed, he tugged down hard on it and an alarm rang out.

She had but moments. Casting a final glance to the man gagging on the floor, oddly suffering no remorse at the sight, she plunged through the veil of silk into the antechamber. Her view swung from the red door to the black one. She already knew where the red one led to, and that left only ...

The black door slammed open, and guards burst in on her. She dodged for the red door. It, too, exploded with a barrage of guards. Caught in their pincers, she grabbed the flagon of wine off the table, smashed it, and waited for them with the jagged piece of crockery in one hand and the little table in the other.

Creator, forgive me for killing that man, and grant me a swift, painless passage to Adam's Bosom.

11

Escape

hey had conquered two balconies, and upon neither had they discovered the Lodath's quarters. Klesc was determined to press on, while Rhone could almost feel the bound guards in the stables being discovered. He could hear an alarm ring inside his head, even though, up until now, the grounds remained silent. He'd hoped to be away from Nod City by now. Rhone cast about across the dark grounds below for roving bands of guards. This woman was nothing to him. His instructions from the Creator had nothing to do with saving a girl from the romantic overtures of the Lodath of the Oracle.

These thoughts raced through Rhone's head as he clung to a wall, fifty spans above the ground, creeping along a rough seam in the huge stone blocks. If there was only a faster way! But the arrangements of the balconies along the river-facing side of the palace precluded any swift way of checking them except by tackling one after the other.

He had clawed his way nearly to the next balcony when, from within the palace, he heard a clanging of bells. At first he thought it was the stable guards, but that quarter remained dark and quiet.

Something else was happening.

Rhone slipped silently over the railing. This balcony was larger than the others and brightly lit from panels of moonglass and light from an adjacent room. The curtains were partway drawn. He reached out to Klesc. Just then a young, scantily clad woman burst into view slightly beyond the curtains. She had a pretty face framed in long, scattered yellow hair. The panic in her eyes was clear as she hesitated in the middle of a huge orange and black tiger rug. Panic showed in her eyes as she cast about.

Suddenly guards stormed through the doors.

At that instant, the panic hardened into lines of grim determination as she grabbed up a bottle and table as weapons and turned to meet her fate.

❧

"… so, you see, the war is between the Creator and the Deceiver, and you and I, First Shield Da-gore, have chosen sides in that war, whether we know it or not."

Da-gore tried to digest it all, but his mind rebelled at the notion of being a dupe in this spiritual war. *It couldn't be true,* he told himself, yet his heart was whispering something else entirely. The bits and pieces he'd been gathering for months began to make sense in light of what Lamech had told him so far about this struggle—this eternal battle he'd just described. And according to the Lee-lander, the consequences, if true, would not bode well for those who followed the Oracle. But who could he believe?

"There can be no doubt of the outcome." Lamech peered earnestly into his eyes. "This world is to be destroyed, but it is not too late to turn from the evil."

"Destroyed?" He'd heard that before, and he refused to acquiesce without a fight. "From man's earliest memories, all things have continued as from the beginning."

"It is not for slackness on the Creator's part. He delays judgment only so that man might repent and turn back to him. He does not wish to destroy, yet destruction is near. A greater evil than this world has ever known is even now being unleashed." Lamech's face held a sudden, deep sadness. "You've seen the budding of it already in the Earth-Born." He paused as if to let that sink in. "The Creator promised my grandfather, Enoch, that when his son, my father, dies, that very year the judgment will come."

Da-gore frowned. "Then I wish your father long life." He glanced around the dark cell. "At least I still have time to decide on this matter, but there is nothing I can do to help you. If all you tell me is true, tomorrow morning, you will stand before your Creator."

"I will not die tomorrow."

"You think not? Your Creator can save you from the Lodath's hand?"

Lamech nodded.

"You have much confidence in this unseen god of yours."

"And you have so little."

Da-gore remembered what it was about Lee-landers he disliked. Their annoying confidence bordered on arrogance. He almost laughed, except he remembered those Lee-landers he had pursued across the Wild Lands, across the Border Sea, and clear up into the Ruins of Eden to the very entrance to the Cradleland. They had been protected by beings so powerful that even the Oracle's emissaries could not fight them. He grimaced. That did not prove the good or the bad of this eternal struggle, but it did hint at who held the true power … and the Oracle fared poorly. Lamech may be smug in his self-righteousness, but he had the evidence of his Creator's might to back it up.

"Tomorrow you *will* die."

"And if I do not?"

Yes, that was the question. Da-gore drew in a breath and glanced at the chains hanging cuffless against the wall where Klesc had been bound. If Lamech did escape this, then what?

Lamech said, "If I miss my appointment with the executioner tomorrow, take it as a sign, and remember what I have told you tonight."

At the door, Da-gore turned back. He had felt a slight stirring when Lamech had explained the message. Lamech claimed his Creator had written across the sky, yet Da-gore could no more explain this feeling than he could the mysterious absence of the second prisoner. Da-gore clenched his jaw and felt his fingers balling into a fist at his side. "I'll consider all that you've said."

Lamech nodded.

"I'll be back in the morning."

"I'll be here."

Da-gore glanced one last time at the dangling, cuffless chains, then left, bolting the door behind him. *As if a bolted door would make a difference.* He halted at the guard station. "One of your prisoners has escaped."

The two men on duty stared at each other. "That's impossible!" one said.

"Nonetheless, it is so."

The other guard rushed down the tunnel, flung open Lamech's cell door and stared inside. "It's true."

"Sound the alarm and scour the city." Da-gore strode away. He wasn't looking forward to reporting this to Captain El-ik. Climbing out of the tunnels, he stood alone outside the prison in the warm night breeze and stared up at the stars. *Do you really have a message up there for me?*

He frowned and started for Captain El-ik's quarters. All at once the distant clanging of alarm bells rang from the Lodath's palace. *What now?* Altering his steps, he hurried for the palace.

❦

The Lodath's guards piled into the room and paused for a heart-beat. They seemed to grin at her weapons. One of the men stepped to the fore; the same man who earlier had stood near the Lodath. His eyes were no longer empty; they now blazed as they held her for a long, agonizing moment. Leenah could still hear the gagging and gurgling from the bedroom, as if to shout out her crime to them.

The man pointed, and three guards peeled off to investigate the sounds. "Drop the weapon." His voice rumbled as if issuing from the throat of a much larger man.

Leenah retreated toward the balcony door, her muscles quivering as she stared at their swords.

"Bladesmen!"

Swords hissed from scabbards. Her prayer was about to be answered. Her end would indeed be very swift.

Then glass shattered all around her, and a chair from outside landed in the room, carrying with it glass, curtains, and window framing. She wheeled to face this new danger. Instead of a company of the Lodath's green-cloaks, a single man dove through on the heels of the chair with a sword in his hand. Whoever he was, she knew instantly he was not one of *them*.

The next instant a second man appeared at this stranger's side, and his face was one she did recognize.

"Klesc!"

Klesc grabbed her arm and whirled her behind them.

"Take them!" an officer shouted.

Klesc and the stranger put their backs together, their swords striking, parrying, slashing with a dazzling precision, as if a single mind controlled both their swords. Almost as if ... and then suddenly she knew. The stranger was a Makir!

The battle reminded her of the Katrahs and Kimahs her uncles had shown her when she was but a child. But back then it had only been practice. This was real!

Klesc shot her a glance. "Out the window!"

She discovered she was still holding the jagged bottle and table. She flung them at the advancing forces, grabbed up a fallen sword from a dead soldier, and plunged it through the heart of a guard who had moved to stop her.

Outside on the balcony, Leenah nearly tripped over the coil of rope. Setting the sword aside, she quickly fastened an end around a fat marble baluster and tossed the rope coil far out, watching it unravel as it plummeted to the ground.

❧

Vigor flowed through Rhone's veins. He sensed a renewed bonding with a way of life he'd thought he had left forever behind as he and Klesc struck and parried and held the guards at sword's length. As they backed toward the broken window frame, their only way of escape, Rhone regretted not having prepared the rope beforehand. But at the time, from his perspective upon the balcony looking in, there appeared not to be a moment to waste.

Over the din of ringing steel and the grunts of men, a voice growled Rhone's name … a voice that sent a startled chill coursing through him.

"He's mine!" the voice ordered. Immediately a space expanded around Rhone as the guards gave way for this new threat.

"Bar'ack!" The Web merchant's son! Only, this wasn't Bar'ack. It was merely his body. The life forces that now dwelled in that body, Rhone knew, were the spirits of the Earth-Borns—demons, Sari'el had called them. And he'd fought them before.

Rhone's concentration focused on this single adversary. The last time they had met, the strength of the spirits dwelling inside Bar'ack had easily overpowered him. Rhone remembered how desperately Bar'ack had wanted to escape his tedious life as a Web weaver, forsaking it for adventure in the Wild Lands as a Webmaster. A frown shaped Rhone's lips. Well, Bar'ack had found adventure—more than he'd counted on....

The demon-possessed man lunged. Rhone threw his sword up to deflect Bar'ack's blade. Steel clanged, and Rhone staggered a step from the blow. Bar'ack reversed his swing and drove forward, slicing the material of Rhone's shirt. Bar'ack had grown in skill since their last fight! Even so, Rhone's trained reflexes and superior mastery of the blade leveled the scales. Although he towered over Bar'ack a good head, no mere mortal could stand on strength alone against a man possessed by a trio of demons.

They fought back and forth, each countering the other's strikes, Bar'ack pressing the advantage of strength, Rhone relying on skill. In a glance, Rhone saw that Klesc had nearly emptied the room of standing swordsmen. As the last of the house guards fell, Rhone shouted for Klesc to escape with the girl.

"I'll not leave you, Pyir Rhone!"

Focusing his concentration on the battle, Rhone sensed more than saw the big warrior at his side. "The girl! Quickly, before they summon more guards! I'll catch up!"

Klesc hesitated. "I'll be back!" He plunged past the splintered woodwork.

Perhaps thinking he could catch Rhone off guard, Bar'ack feigned a lunge. Rhone saw through the ploy and caught the demoniac's wrist in his left hand, but he might as well have grabbed hold of a wild gerup! Bar'ack rammed him up against a wall, and the breath exploded from Rhone's lungs. Bar'ack's blade climbed. Rhone held it off with his own. The sharp steel hovered near Rhone's throat as the two men pitted muscle against muscle, a game Rhone could not hope to win against these creatures. His arms burned, quivering, weakening under the strain. Two handbreadths from his face, Bar'ack gave a snarl of victory, his eyes fierce and wild—terrifying eyes, partly human, partly something else.

Rhone quavered beneath the inhuman strength, Bar'ack's breath hot upon his face. Trapped with his back against a wall and his shoulders afire, his vast strength failing under Bar'ack's demon-possessed muscles, he had but moments left.

How could he fight creatures from Sari'el's world? Sari'el had said something about that. His brain blurred as his strength failed. What had Sari'el told him? Then he remembered! There is only one way to defend against these demons, one name that can defeat them … the name Sari'el knew the Creator by.

Through gritted teeth and Bar'ack's blade touching the skin of his neck, Rhone hissed, "*Elohim.*"

A wail of terror and pain exploded from the demoniac's throat, and in that moment Bar'ack's strength returned to that of a human. Rhone flung him back. Bar'ack tripped over the body of a fallen guard and hit the floor hard. Rhone leaped and pressed his blade to the man's chest—but stopped. In spite of the vile creatures now in possession of Bar'ack's body, somewhere submerged beneath their influences was his friend's son. Though he might have ended this threat here and now, he couldn't do it.

Wielding his sword to keep the remaining guards at bay, he turned and dove out the window, onto the balcony.

Klesc took him by the shoulders and looked him over in a glance. "I was about to return for you."

"The girl?"

"Making for ground now."

"After her!" The pounding of feet out in the hallway announced the arrival of a fresh contingent of guards. "Quickly!"

Klesc grabbed the rope and leaped over the edge. Rhone leaped to the balustrade, grabbed the rope in both hands. He paused only long enough to see the guards burst into the room and draw to a halt, momentarily stunned by the sight that met their eyes. Another alarm began to wail, this time from the direction of the Temple site. A call for more guards? As if in response to this new summons, a third alarm began clanging to his left. The stable guards had been discovered, and just then, so had he! One of the green-cloaks pointed, and they all charged toward the broken window.

Rhone dropped swiftly to the dark ground.

Klesc drew off his cloak and draped it about the woman's naked shoulders. They moved off along the palace walls, keeping the balconies between themselves and the guards with their proj-lances. Once beyond the range of the weapons, the three fugitives raced for the river. The sounds of men beating the bushes for them became louder. They drew up in the deep shadows of the garden shrubbery.

A canic howled nearby. Rhone glanced to Klesc. "They'll have our trail in a moment."

Klesc drew his sword. "I'll see to it."

"We'll meet you down there." Rhone nodded toward the river. He took Leenah's arm and started off, keeping to the shadows, out of the moonlight and the glow of the fiery bands of Dancing Lights in the sky. Below them a stone quay stretched along the river's edge, pale gray in the moonlight, like the bleached spine of a behemoth. The canic's baying grew louder. They had almost reached the quay when the canic gave a yelp and then went silent. Leenah's head came around, a frown impressed upon her pretty, moon-drenched features.

"It couldn't be helped."

She looked at him. "I know. Who are you?"

"Rhone."

"You and Klesc know each other?"

"We ... were friends once."

"*Were* friends?"

"I haven't seen Klesc in almost one hundred years. Not until tonight."

"How did he escape? You?"

"A long story that will have to wait."

"And Lamech?"

"He'll be looked after."

She scowled. "What does that mean?"

He took her arm and hurried her along. "It means the Creator has plans for him that don't include you, me, or Klesc."

She stopped and held him in a long, wondering stare. "Are you a believer?"

"I am." He got her moving again.

"I must hear of this."

"Later."

Klesc came trotting silently up beside them. "There will be others."

"We need to hurry."

They stopped just before reaching the quay. Guards had already begun prowling it. Rhone led them to a place where trees overhung the river. They slipped quietly into the warm water and struck out into the current.

12

The Unexpected Ally

*L*amech shifted nervously upon the stone slab. It was impossible to sleep. How much longer before the dawn? Buried in this deep dungeon, it was impossible to know. The Creator's Messenger had assured him he wouldn't die, yet fear crept back into his soul, stealing his peace. It seemed an eternity as time drifted slowly toward dawn. And the worst of all was not knowing when the sounds of footsteps outside his prison door would signal his forthcoming execution.

Maybe there would be a simple reprieve? Maybe the security council would change its mind? Lamech gave a sardonic laugh. No chance. So, how was he to be spared execution? His faith wavered.

I will not harbor unbelief!

Had not a Messenger of the Creator visited him? It hadn't been a dream! He shot a glance across the room, fearing he'd see Klesc still bound to the wall. His heart leaped as a wave of relief filled him. Klesc was indeed gone.

He tried to fill the time with prayer, but worry kept rattling the door of his heart. Only when he thought of Mishah and imagined holding his baby son in his arms did anything resembling peace take hold.

He claimed to have faith and to trust fully in the Creator. Yet he trembled before the coming dawn. Faith, indeed. He was like any other man facing execution. How often had he been vain in his own faith? How often had he judged others for lack of it? He regretted all the angry things he had said to Kenoch. At least his brother-in-law had been honest enough to openly question his faith. Lamech lifted his face to the dark ceiling. "Forgive me, Creator, for my judgments. Here I sit a hypocrite, no different from any other man."

His head snapped around at a distant sound. His pulse was racing, his breathing suddenly shallow and quick. Footsteps! They grew louder, taking on the cadence of a drumbeat. Then the bolt slammed aside, and the door opened.

Two guards began unfastening the iron cuffs. Two more waited just outside the door. First Shield Da-gore stepped inside and studied him with a stern face. Dark shadows rimmed his eyes.

Lamech willed his breathing to settle. "I take it neither one of us slept."

"It's been a busy night. Your friend, Klesc, and another, attacked the Lodath."

"Leenah?"

"She is gone. We will find her."

Relief flooded over him. Even if he didn't make it out of here alive, at least Leenah and Klesc were free. "And what of the Lodath?"

Da-gore's mouth shifted to one side in a grim half-smile. "He was well enough when I left him to order the woman's immediate execution upon her capture—and the other two men who helped her escape."

The guards pulled him to his feet. "Have you considered what we spoke about?"

Da-gore hesitated. "I have."

"And?" They moved him toward the door.

"The execution will proceed as ordered. I haven't yet seen the intervening hand of your god."

"And when you do, what then, First Shield?" They started up the tunnel.

Da-gore didn't answer him. He appeared to be a man burdened with a decision. Lamech left it at that, trusting the Creator to do the rest. Sari'el had said someone needed to hear what he had to tell him, and last night, Lamech laid before Da-gore all he needed to know to cross from darkness to light. It was out of his hands now. He had his own worries. Although he struggled to put forth confidence, the fear of his impending execution still showed him how tenuous his own faith could be.

The bright morning sky stung his eyes as he emerged from the dark tunnels. Through his tears, Lamech could see crowds of onlookers lining the road leading into the Temple site, flinging jeers and taunting remarks at him. Within the circle of guards, he was at least safe from the stones and rotten fruit with which some condemned men were tormented.

The half-built Temple, encased in scaffolding, dripped onlookers dressed in prison gray off almost every beam. Ranks of townsfolk filled the construction site and packed along the top of the walls surrounding the project. The heavy-lifting platform had been drawn down by its cables to accommodate a bird's-eye view; its railings were crammed with faces. Before him two behemoths stood in harness. To his left, a hastily erected booth of bright fabric with rising rows of benches had been constructed. Lamech recognized some of the occupants of this stall; they were the officials of both the prison and the construction site, including the three-man council that had sentenced him. Among the dignitaries, one was conspicuously absent. The Lodath never missed an execution. Perhaps his injuries were worse than Da-gore had let on.

Guards escorted him to the execution platform between the two behemoths. Lamech solemnly climbed three steps and stood there as his wrists and ankles were fastened to chains. Da-gore and Captain El-ik examined the chains.

"Nothing had better go wrong," the captain said quietly to Da-gore.

Da-gore said solemnly, "The chains are secure and the beasts are already in harness. What can go wrong?"

But Lamech heard the wariness in Da-gore's voice. The First Shield would be on the lookout for any attempt to free him. He closed his eyes and tried to shut out the noise of the crowd. *Faith. I must have faith.*

"Is all in readiness, Captain El-ik?" the court executioner asked.

"The execution may proceed." Under his breath, he added, "And let's get it over with quickly, before something else goes wrong."

Lamech opened his eyes and scanned the masses of faces crowding the construction site and its walls. It seemed as if all of Nod City had turned out. The two officers stepped down from the platform and positioned themselves on either side. Overhead, several scarlet dragons cast their shadows across the ground as if they, too, were curious to see this human ripped apart by the giant work beasts.

It brought to mind an old field hand's adage: *Mansnatchers forlorn, red dragons at morn.* Lamech shivered ... and waited.

※

"Mansnatchers forlorn, red dragons at morn." Leenah's gaze followed the flop of scarlet dragons across the hazy blue sky. Her words had been whispered, as a thought that sometimes sneaks out. "This will be a good day."

Rhone glanced at her, his eye held momentarily by the graceful line of her cheek and the curve of her lips. The old saying had been whispered from them unconsciously. What was she remembering? Another place? Other dragons? The dragons, a big drake with six hens and four yearlings, winged over them and then out toward the Little Hiddekel River.

"Sometimes I feel as if I understand what they think," she said softly.

Rhone was huddled in his cloak and Klesc in his. Leenah stood between them, her long yellow hair bound up beneath a hat, her form hidden beneath over-large clothes bunched up in the sleeves and cuffs. They blended in perfectly with the crowd … so long as neither Rhone nor Klesc stood at his full height. Nevertheless, Rhone kept a lookout for danger from the occasional green-cloak prowling along the top of the Temple site walls. But the crowd was thick, and the chance of discovery remote.

"Perhaps you can." Rhone returned his gaze to the drama being played out below. He had to be here this morning, even though it placed them in danger. They could have easily stolen away during the night, but he could not return to Mishah without seeing for himself how her husband cheated the executioner's chains, to give her the assurance of having seen it with his own eyes.

Leenah pulled her view off the dragons. Her hands clutched tight as her fingers wormed within each other.

Rhone took her arm and leaned close. "He will be all right." His grasp lingered longer than absolutely necessary.

She leaned close and her blue eyes held him a moment. "I wish I shared your confidence. It will take a miracle."

Her pretty face seized his breath. "Miracles are simple matters for the One who speaks worlds into existence."

❦

Da-gore's shoulders tensed as if suddenly wrapped in bands of iron. His neck muscles burned. He could almost feel his heart banging its way through his chest. Why should he feel as though it was he upon the execution stand? His eyes shifted warily and momentarily followed a flop of dragons, their shadows skimming the crowd. If an escape was attempted, it would be from that quarter.

The court executioner moved from the dignitary booth and stood before the behemoths. "Beast handlers, make ready!"

Da-gore knew what his problem was. Somehow, Lamech's words had reached down inside him and touched him. Strangely enough, he believed the preacher. *He actually believed him!* This unseen war made sense to a man with a military mind and an eye to see the evidence. Hadn't this Lee-lander's Creator shown his hand in protecting Lamech's wife and family? Hadn't he snatched Klesc from beneath the noses of the prison guards? Da-gore had no doubt he could do so now. Only, how …?

The executioner raised a purple flag at the end of a long pole. "Beast handlers …" His words suddenly halted.

A murmur arose from the dignitaries' booth as a red-garbed man emerged from a doorway and strolled between the executioner and the prisoner. Master Sor-dak came unhurriedly, as if unaware of the magnitude of the proceedings he was interrupting. Under the arm of his faded red robe, he carried several rolls of papers. He strode toward Da-gore and El-ik, combing his long white beard with his fingers.

El-ik intercepted him. "Master Sor-dak. Why are you here?" He spoke with impatience barely held in restraint. Master Sor-dak, chief stargazer and overseer of the project, was the third most powerful man on the Temple construction site, just below the Lodath and King Irad.

"Why, I must speak with Master Lamech."

"We are in the middle of an execution."

Sor-dak's eyes widened. "No, no, no." He waved a hand. "My business can't wait. I must speak with him." He brushed past Captain El-ik and climbed the platform.

A murmur of wonderment rippled through the crowd.

El-ik's mouth worked itself into a knot, and folds of skin deepened around his eyes.

In spite of the magnitude of Sor-dak's intrusion, Da-gore had to restrain a grin. At the dignitaries' booth, four men arose and made their way to the outside.

"Master Lamech, I've looked all over for you. A guard down in the cell block told me I'd find you here." Sor-dak looked around as if seeing the circumstances for the first time and gave a brief scowl.

"Why do you seek me, Master Sor-dak?"

"I just can't get a grasp on it!" The long beard wagged back and forth. "I've been up all night."

So, that made three of them.

He dropped three rolls of charts to the platform and quickly unfurled them in front of Lamech.

Da-gore kept one eye on the Disciplinary Council marching toward them, and the other on Lamech and Sor-dak.

"The figures just don't work out. See, the alignment is correct for the next 4,266 years; then we completely lose the ecliptic!"

"Why come to me?"

Sor-dak's green eyes expanded in a bewildered look. "I'm not certain. I was struggling with this problem when the thought occurred to me to go speak to Lamech." He blinked. "I tried to ignore it, but this issue so confounded me that I had to act on the notion. Curious, this is somewhat unlike me." He looked at the crowds, the behemoths, the scowling Captain El-ik, and finally the council members who had just arrived.

"Master Sor-dak, we are in the middle of an execution!" the

short man with the booming voice said.

Sor-dak's eyes peered up from beneath snowy brows at Lamech, but now Da-gore saw a cunning in them he hadn't noticed before.

"Master Sor-dak." The big voice grew impatient.

Still Sor-dak ignored the man. "Can you help me, Master Lamech?"

Lamech peered at the chart Sor-dak held in front of his face.

"Did you bring your calculations?"

"I did." Sor-dak rummaged through the pile on the platform and unfurled another sheet.

Da-gore glanced at El-ik. The captain's face glowed scarlet, and his eyes had narrowed to two angry slits. The crowd filling the Temple site was growing impatient. Any lesser a personage would have been tossed out at once, but Sor-dak was not any other man. Da-gore was aware of a growing excitement and a quickening of his breathing. An interruption like this was unheard of, yet it was happening! Lamech's words rang in his brain. *I will not die tomorrow.*

"I think I see your problem, Master Sor-dak." Lamech's chains rattled as he put a finger to the paper with—to Da-gore's eye at least—its indecipherable scribblings.

"You've not accounted for the back-creep of the equinoctial points along the ecliptic."

Sor-dak looked to the low morning sun, then back to his scribblings. "Precessional back-creep! Of course! So simple, yet so foolish of me to overlook it!" The stargazer gathered up his papers. "Wonderful! Ah, but you have an eye for the stars and a brain for numbers, Master Lamech!" He crammed the charts under his arm and grabbed Lamech's elbow, pulling him toward the platform steps. "I must have you with me!" They both jolted to a halt at the end of Lamech's chains. Sor-dak stared at the chains as if he had only just now noticed them. "Release this man!"

The council members looked at each other. "He has been condemned to death."

"I have need of him." Sor-dak glared at the spokesman. "The *Temple* has need of him!"

"The Lodath has approved of the execution," the spokesman stammered.

Da-gore almost laughed. It was a hopeless cause, with the kind of help Lamech was getting. What Lamech had told him was true after all! Da-gore saw Lamech's small smile, the glow of sudden peace that seemed to radiate from his eyes. *To have that assurance in life.*

"The Lodath?" Sor-dak glanced to the booth. "I don't see his Eminence here to refuse my request. Where is Sol-Ra-Luce? Tell me so that I might speak with him."

Captain El-ik cleared his throat. "The Lodath is in his palace. He is ... not well today."

"Oh? Then King Irad. Where is the King that I might petition him?"

The council spokesman glanced to his companions. No help there; no one was prepared to speak against Master Sor-dak. "Er, King Irad is off on a hunting trip."

"Hum. Then it seems there's no one here to contravene my order to free this man." Sor-dak seemed to struggle to contain a smile; then his face hardened, and his voice took on a rare tone of authority that Da-gore seldom heard from this mild, self-absorbed man. "Release him into my service. I have need of a man with Master Lamech's abilities."

But Da-gore had caught that fleeting glint of mischief in Sor-dak's eyes. The *absentminded* stargazer wasn't so naive after all. He knew exactly what he was doing.

❧

Atop the broad wall encircling the Temple project, Rhone, Klesc, and Leenah made their way with the crowds to the packed staircases.

"Where to now?" Klesc asked.

Rhone, holding Leenah by the arm so they'd not get separated in the press of people, said quietly, "Now we make for the Cradleland."

"The Cradleland?" Klesc stared at him a moment. "It's only legend."

"It's a real place. I've been there." Rhone felt Leenah's muscled arm tighten beneath his grip.

"But even if it is real, its location is supposed to be lost."

Rhone glanced at him. "It has never been lost, only forgotten."

"I'm going with you," Leenah said.

They looked at her. Rhone said, "Why? Once away from Nod City, you're free to return to your home."

"I have no home. My mother and father are dead, my Uncle Debne is somewhere on the coast of the Border Sea, and Uncle Sirt is still on Atlan." She looked into his eyes, and Rhone was again struck with her beauty. "And besides," she looked down at the baggy clothes Rhone had found for her in the cottage he rented from Master Mav-duruc, "I can go around dressed like this."

"She's right, Pyir Rhone."

Rhone cast Klesc a scowl. "Don't call me that."

Leenah's momentary smile faded. "The Creator is obviously using you, Master Rhone, and I feel he will use me, too."

"Feelings are a poor ruler to gauge your actions by, Mistress Leenah."

"In that case, Master Rhone, I will have made a mistake." She smiled again. "But it's worth it for a chance to see the Cradleland."

Sol-Ra-Luce's ashen face was drawn in a mask of pain and anger. He glared at them from his bed, his throat wrapped in bandages and two healers in attendance at his side. Da-gore had heard that the vicious attack had ripped the large vessel that carried blood to his brain. The wound had nearly drained him, and only the swift arrival of the guards and the skill of the healers had saved his life.

"The woman?" The Lodath's voice rasped from the brutally punctured larynx like gravel grinding underfoot.

"My men are searching the city at this moment." Captain El-ik's stiff spine and sweaty chin told Da-gore he greatly feared for his newly won position. "Every home will be searched if need be, Your Eminence."

Da-gore stifled a smile. *Sweat a little more, Captain.* A grilling from the Lodath of the Oracle was a sure remedy for pride. He knew firsthand.

"She will be found!" El-ik's brow glistened in the morning sunlight that streamed through the window.

A promise you cannot keep. Da-gore stood at rigid attention himself. The woman had been helped by the escapee Klesc and another—one whose description sounded suspiciously familiar—but that was impossible. He'd seen Rhone cut down before the entrance to the Cradleland; his injuries so catastrophic that no man could have survived them. And even if he had, he'd be a cripple the rest of his life. The one described to him had been vigorous and powerful, a Makir Warrior, judging by the reports. A friend of Klesc, no doubt. Da-gore frowned. He was under the impression that the old order was no more, although it was widely known that a few Makir remained, scattered far and wide.

Da-gore felt certain the woman would not be found ... not if the same pattern played out. The Lee-lander's Creator had taken a hand in this matter. *Had somehow managed to save Lamech from a certain death.* At that thought a cold finger teased his spine. The Tyrant of Old had awakened from his long silence, and now there was a new wind blowing across the land. Da-gore feared being in its path. He'd once attempted to shake a fist at this sleeping God and was crushed along with the Oracle's giants.

"Da-gore." The Lodath winced, snarling back the pain. One of the healers put her hand to his shoulder as he feebly attempted to rise. His finger stabbed out, the long blue nail broken, the paint chipped. "You failed me—again," the tortured throat grated.

El-ik appeared relieved that the object of the Lodath's scorn had changed. Oddly enough, Da-gore didn't care.

"I have no explanation for what happened last night, Your Eminence. What we are dealing with is beyond man's understanding. We are in the realm of the Oracle, I fear."

"Excuses! The prisoner was yours to hold. Find him! I will have an execution that will not be interrupted—that will not fail this time!" Sol-Ra-Luce's lips curled back, and he trembled with the pain, on the verge of exhaustion. "Be it the prisoner's, or—" the finger thrust out again, "—or a substitute's." His dark glare narrowed threateningly.

"What of Lamech?" Da-gore asked.

"I will see to Sor-dak's meddling later. Now be gone! Both of you!" He fell back exhausted, each breath a torment that contorted his face.

※

Back in his quarters, Da-gore packed the few mementos of a life spent in the service of his King and the Lodath. *Be it his or a substitute's. Indeed! I'll be no one's scapegoat.* Nor would he any longer be a dupe of the Lodath.

He set the small rucksack and an extra cloak on the bed with his sword and a proj-lance. He made his rounds through the Temple

Prison, listened to the reports on the search in progress, issued orders to his lieutenants, and then returned to his quarters.

The fires on the construction site spread their perpetual glow across the darkening skies as he watched the sun play out its nightly death scene beyond the distant rooftops.

A knock on his door pulled his eyes from the daily drama.

Four guards stood outside his quarters. "First Shield Da-gore." The one who spoke saluted.

"What have you found?"

The guard put a flimsy bit of material into his hand. "It was in the cottage on Master Mav-duruc's grounds, exactly where you told us to look. Mav-duruc said the cottage is rented to a man named Rhone, a Webmaster, but the man hasn't been seen or heard from for months."

"Rhone? Hum." Da-gore let the material unfurl. A woman's shift, barely anything at all. Just as the Lodath liked it. "Did you find anything else?"

"No, sir. Most of the clothes were missing and no weapons. Like Mav-duruc said, the cottage appeared to have been empty for a long time. But we did find fresh smudges in the dust. Someone was in there within the last few quarterings."

Da-gore peered at the bit of clothing, then handed it back to the guard. "See that Captain El-ik gets this, and tell him what you just told me."

When the guards left, Da-gore looked back out the window. Night had once again defeated the sun, and darkness had settled over the city. At least some things never change. "You three are long gone from Nod City, aren't you? Long gone." He grinned. "But I know where you'll be going—Leenah, Klesc ... and Rhone." He frowned at this new and intriguing puzzle piece.

In the dark hours of the second quartering, Da-gore removed the crystal pendant from around his neck and peered at its softly shifting colors in the darkness. It was a struggle to set it aside, but as soon as he did, he felt a sudden release such as he'd not known for years.

Shouldering his pack and taking up the proj-lance, he slipped away from his apartment and quietly out of Nod City.

13

The Garden

Somehow, the trees sensed Mishah's melancholy mood and shifted their songs to one that helped with the loneliness. In their own way, the animals too tried to comfort her. She'd been overwhelmed with marvelous and new sensations, and now she understood how a man like Rhone could communicate with the spiders. Every now and again a Messenger of the Creator—or two or three together—would appear, as if on a mission, clothed in light more beautiful than the finest silks and the most skillful tailoring. She recalled the tattered garments of animal skins Mother Eve had kept in her home, and the lament in the ancient woman's voice when she had compared them to the first clothing the Creator had provided.

In most respects, Mishah was happy—how could she not be in the presence of the Creator, with her baby to her breast, and her grandmother at her side almost constantly—yet her loneliness pressed heavily upon her today. She ached for Lamech: to walk in the cool of the evening with her husband; to hold his hand; to feel his touch, his kiss.

Mishah sighed. Lamech was in the center of the Creator's will, exactly where he had always wanted to be, where she wanted him to be. Nonetheless, the separation was bitter.

"Take heart, Mishah, for this trial is only of the moment, and it will pass."

She looked at the Gardener, strolling beside her. His understanding smile helped melt some of the burdens of her heart. Although he always appeared to her as a caretaker of the Garden of the Creator, she knew he was so much more—yet what exactly, she still didn't fully understand.

Noah wiggled in her arms. The Gardener took him, held him to his chest, calming him. "He will need to know many things before he is ready."

Mishah recalled the frightening dreams that had once haunted her. Since coming to the Sanctuary … the Cradleland … the Garden of the Creator, the dreams had ceased to trouble her. "The Deceiver will try to hurt my child? In my dreams, he was a black dragon, filled with hate."

"The Fallen One will do what he must to prevent the coming Redeemer of man."

She took Noah's small arm into her hand and held it a moment. Her son … destined to carry the seed of mankind beyond the coming judgment. She trembled at the gravity of the responsibility, released the tiny arm, and looked around the Garden. So much beauty headed for such utter destruction. This coming destruction was not a new thing to her. Enoch, Lamech's grandfather, had walked with the Creator years earlier and had come back with word of the pending judgment. But few had heeded his words; few had believed.

She looked up and discovered that she and the Gardener had wandered into an area of the Garden that she had never been to before. It had been five months since her brother, Kenoch; her new sister-in-law, Cerah; their Good Man, Kleg'l; and Rhone had departed from the Garden. In that time, she had walked daily with the Gardener, but this was the first time he'd led her into this section of the Garden. Her senses sharpened, and she cocked her head toward the distant roar of a rushing waterfall.

They walked upon a path of verbiscus: tiny yellow and blue flowers with petals so fine that, at a glance, their appearance was that of a finely woven carpet. They smelled a little like crushed vanilla beans. The trees around her stood straight and tall, stretching leafy umbrellas to the clear sky, spreading their shadows upon lawns of silvery-green grass. Sunlight streaming through the leaves cast a soft, emerald light upon Mishah's hands and her white, silken dress—only it wasn't silk, but some material she had never seen before. She took a fold of it between her fingers and thumb, likening it more to a silky skin cream rather than to fabric. It even gave off the faint aroma of winset and roses as she moved. The material didn't soil, it didn't rip, and it draped her so lightly that she might not have been wearing anything at all, yet it completely and discretely covered her. Both she and Amolikah had been given complete wardrobes and a cottage to live in. The Garden provided every fruit and vegetable and root and seed they could ever hope for. All her needs except one had been met. She tried not to let her loneliness intrude on the beauty of the day.

"Where are we going?"

"To the Father."

She inhaled sharply, and a sudden panic gripped her. "But no human can look upon the Father and live."

The Gardener smiled. "You will see him in a manner fit for your eyes, Mishah."

What did one say to the Father? The very thought of him conjured up images of awesome strength and a fierce countenance—like the fearsome King Irad of Nod City.

The path made a bend and entered a tunnel of colored light. Mishah had seen such tunnels before during her stay in the Garden.

They seemed to appear randomly and flow around her like the Dancing Lights in the night sky, only more intense, more real, and ever changing according to her mood. The colors appeared brighter when her mind was free of worry, darker when Lamech's absence weighed heavy on her spirit. But in the Gardener's presence, they radiated a golden hue that even her longing for Lamech couldn't dim. She stretched out a hand into the shimmering wall, and the colors rippled along her skin; she felt the warmth of the reds, the chill of the blues. Golden hues sent a tingle of well-being through her, while the greens in deep leafy hues and brighter emerald bands somehow always settled a troubled spirit.

"This light is very much like the glory that once clothed the son and daughter of God," he said.

"And the Messengers?"

The Gardener nodded as Noah chattered contentedly in his arms.

Mother Eve had spoken of the brightness that once clothed both her and the Father. "When they fell, the light left them?"

"Yes. After the Fall, the glory left them, and they saw their nakedness." The golden hues dimmed a bit, and she sensed sadness in his voice. The tunnel opened out to a wide green glade stretching toward a high overlook. The overlook was paved in a sheet of pure green marble, with no seam or joint anywhere. At the edge of the overlook, a railing of the blackest stone shone in the sunlight. It seemed to float at waist height. When Mishah leaned upon it, the railing was as solid as a mountain. The view stole her breath.

The roaring of water muted the sounds of birds and trees. Below them flowed a wide river where water tumbled over ledges of rock and billowed in a fine mist high into the air. The Gardener stretched out an arm. "The Great River that divides into four and waters the whole earth."

Arching above the cataract, a bow of colored light stood bank to distant bank: brilliant red blending to pure yellow to vivid blue and to deep, royal violet.

"Beautiful." She couldn't take her eyes off the bow of light.

"One day I will make a covenant with the sons of men. When I do, I will place this bow in the heavens for all to see and remember. For now it must remain in my Garden."

They continued down the path meandering between trees bearing fruits of every kind. The roar of water was muted as they left the terrace and walked amid the trees. Ahead, the path widened, and a paving of translucent amber stones replaced the blue and yellow flowers. They proceeded down a long gallery lined with trees, each bearing a different fruit. Ahead, a pure blue flame of fire arrested her eyes. It stood before a spreading tree of silver leaves, heavy with a pale yellow fruit.

Mesmerized by the single tongue of fire, twice as tall as she, she felt curiously drawn to it—as a moth to candlelight. It burned brightly upon a circle of grass in the midst of the amber pavement. Amazingly, the grass did not burn.

A booming voice spoke from the flame. "Remove the sandals from your feet, my daughter, for you stand upon holy ground."

She gave a start, and an overpowering presence drove her to her knees, and she trembled as her strength was suddenly sucked from her being.

"Stand, my child, and come forward." The voice from the flame seemed to reverberate all around her.

Gently, the Gardener reached down and helped her up. She stared at him. He smiled and nodded.

Trembling, even though she knew she shouldn't be fearful, she slipped off her sandals. The Gardener placed little Noah back into her arms. As she approached nearer, she realized the flame gave off no heat.

"I am the God of your father Adam, the God of Enoch, the God of Lamech. Tremble not, my daughter. Let me behold the son of Lamech." As he spoke, a dove fluttered to the Gardener's shoulder and roosted there. Together, the dove and Gardener stepped into the flame. It burned brighter, parting into three tongues. Two of them reached out. Mishah felt the gentle touch of the fire as it lifted Noah from her arms and drew him into itself. Noah's eyes shown wide with wonderment in the midst of the flame. Mishah felt a pang of concern, but almost at once it dissolved in a strong aura of unexplainable peace.

"The child will grow strong and wise even as his world fills with evil and the filthy abomination." The voice was a mighty wind blowing through the trees, yet the air was perfectly calm. "And in that day when the cup of corruption overflows and consumes the whole earth, as maggots devour the carcass of the dead, I will be stirred to fury and will cast Rahab upon the wicked. And in that day of my wrath, the earth will be broken asunder, yet Noah will be found perfect among his generation, and by him will the seed of man be preserved through the season of my judgment."

The roar of his voice swelled louder with each proclamation, and the flame went from blue to orange to white. Then suddenly the voice became as soft as the flutter of butterfly wings. "But for now, my daughter, dwell here in peace a little while longer, until the days of Lamech are fulfilled." The flame returned Noah to her arms.

She was quaking again. And suddenly the Gardener was at her side; His peaceful face helped to still her shaking knees. The dove that had rested upon his shoulder winged into the sky and was lost to sight in the bright disk of the sun.

The flame had returned to a steady blue tongue of light, the voice from it like a gentle breeze against her cheek. "Go now, my daughter, for visitors have arrived."

Visitors? Master Rhone? "Thank you." She bowed low to the

flame, then backed up and slipped her sandals onto her feet. The experience left her numbed, yet an odd peace such as she had never felt before filled her. She, Noah, and the Gardener were back in the tunnel of light when she finally found words to say, "It must be Master Rhone. Who else could it be?"

"He and two more."

Two more? For an instant the hope that one of them might be Lamech seized her heart; then reasoning returned. No, the Creator had a job for Lamech to do, and that required him to remain in Nod City. Rhone had left the Cradleland with her brother, Cerah, and Kleg'l. They were to return home to Morg'Seth. So, who might these visitors be?

Amolikah met them on the path. Her pale green eyes shone with excitement as she took Mishah's arm and pointed toward the portal. "Master Rhone returns, and he brings others with him."

They hurried to the portal where the two golden cherubim kept guard. Beyond them stood the ranks of tents of the Lodath's Guards and King Irad's soldiers—permanently bivouacked there after the great battle with the giants. In the midst of the encampment, shrouded in a faint blue haze and in the company of a Messenger, strode Master Rhone, another man—a large man strikingly similar to Rhone—and a woman. They came through the encampment unseen, yet Mishah saw them quite clearly. She had discovered shortly upon entering the Cradleland that her senses had been expanded far beyond anything she knew outside the towering walls of the Garden of the Creator.

❧

Stepping into the Garden was like having every one of his senses stirred from sleep. Where before Rhone was able to understand only the quiet, probing voices of spiders and had made his living gathering their Web, now every animal had a voice. And not only the animals, but the trees and the flowers and even the grass whispered a music designed by the Creator to please man. Here Rhone felt more alive than ever before.

Leenah seemed spellbound by the sudden awakening of so many sensations. Her face glowed, and her eyes and mouth took the shape of big ovals as she turned a full circle. Tall, in a plain green traveling dress and sturdy shoes, with a short sten-gordon-claw handle dagger at her side, Leenah, in Rhone's way of thinking, was a perfect complement to this place of rest and beauty. He caught himself staring, as he had many times since their escape from Nod City weeks earlier.

Mishah and Amolikah hugged him.

He took Noah into his big arms and held the infant close. Somehow, it felt good, felt right to him. He'd never considered having children of his own, until that moment. Then he remembered he hadn't introduced Leenah or Klesc.

"Welcome!" Mishah grasped Klesc's big hands, then Leenah's. She seemed excited to see a new face; she must long for outside contact.

"Did you see Lamech?" Mishah asked immediately, her eyes widening hopefully. "Did you give him my gift? You must tell me everything!"

Rhone did. She marveled and thanked the Creator for his escape from execution, then worried for his well-being, then reaffirmed her faith that he was indeed where the Creator wanted him to be and it was up to the Creator to protect him. "After all, the Gardener says we will be together again one day."

It occurred to Rhone that he hadn't seen the Gardener. "Where is he?"

She looked around. "He was here a moment ago."

Amolikah said, "Come to the cottage. You must be weary after your long journey. We have food and drink."

Rhone took Leenah gently by the arm and urged her along. Would she have stood there all day, reveling in all that her eyes and ears and nose could perceive? Even the air had a different feel here in the Garden of the Creator—the first home of man.

Rhone was still not completely used to the new vistas opened to his eyes. Here the Messengers of the Creator were not hidden from view but strolled freely beneath the arching treetops, along groomed pathways. Even their appearance was different in this place. Instead of the apparel of war that he was used to seeing on Sari'el and the one who had guided them safely through the encampment, these beings were clothed in a light so bright and pure that it was difficult to look upon them.

A ribbon of candy-colored light caught his eye as it drifted past, split into two parts, and wove through a cluster of blue crystalline rods, vibrating like distant bells, the music changing as the ribbon passed through.

※

In the cool of the evening, Rhone stood alone outside the cottage, which, in contrast to the singularity of this place, appeared quite conventional: It was made of stone and had a thatch roof. As the sun lowered in the sky, a flock of iridescent birds winged overhead, their wings glowing in the evening light.

The Gardener strolled up the path. "Walk with me, Rhone."

The One who had raised him from the dead was inviting him to walk! He got his feet moving.

"You marvel at this beauty?"

"Your Garden is more wonderful than any other place on earth."

"It is a faded beauty, Rhone. A shadow of what I had first prepared for man." The wistful quality in the Gardener's voice struck at his heart.

"Can it not be restored?"

"It can, and it will, but that road is long and hard, and the cost will be great."

Rhone didn't understand how cost could make a difference to the One who had created everything from nothing. He wasn't comfortable pursuing that thought. He sensed the Creator had another purpose for this meeting.

"Are you prepared for what you must do next?"

"I am not sure how to prepare for such a task. But I will go forth anyway."

"You will not be alone."

"You have given me Klesc. And Leenah wishes to accompany us. Three against my brother and the Kingdom of Atlan is like flinging a handful of sand to turn a raging sten-gordon."

"There will be others, Rhone."

"Your Messengers?"

"They will be there too." The Gardener smiled. "You will find you are not alone in this quest. Many desire to see the end to Zorin's reign."

He suspected as much, but since his exile over a hundred years earlier, he'd had no contact with the land of his birth. "Why is this important?"

"Rhone, you have been given but a glimpse of what is to be. You know judgment is to come."

"I understand that Mishah's son is to be part of it." He really knew little more than that.

"The Father of Lies will use every means to stop Noah. Here, in my Garden, he is safe. My cherubim stand at the gate to keep the Deceiver from this place, to protect the Tree of Life, which he desires to destroy. But the tree will be preserved until the consummation of the ages, when man once again will have access to it."

"And what is my role in this?"

"One day, after Noah leaves this place, he will need a protector."

Rhone swallowed hard at the implication of the Gardener's words. "Am I to be his protector?"

"He will dwell in Atlan until the time of judgment comes and the bowl of my wrath is poured out on this world."

Ⅸ

When Rhone returned to the others, he kept his meeting to himself. Klesc and Leenah, with the help of Mishah and Amolikah, had already packed provisions for their long journey.

Early the next morning, Rhone, Klesc, and Leenah left the Cradleland under the protection of a Messenger and passed unseen through the encampment of the Lodath and King Irad's soldiers.

On the forest road, safely beyond the enemy's lines, the Messenger said, "This is as far as I go, Master Rhone. Fair journey."

"Fair journey."

The Messenger disappeared in a ripple of golden light.

Klesc still stared in amazement every time that happened.

Rhone looked back at the towering walls of the Cradleland, now but a distant line of white stone shimmering in the sunlight; the soldiers were mere specks on the plain before it. Then he turned his eyes eastward. The Ruins of Eden lay off in that direction, and several weeks' journey beyond it was the great Border Sea.

He briefly considered the task before him. It daunted his imagination. How would he ever accomplish such a thing? He halted that line of thinking and glanced heavenward. "Not by my power but by yours."

They set off on the road to the Ruins of Eden.

14

The Stalker

*L*amech awoke thinking of Mishah, missing her, and of his new son, whom he had yet to see and hold. They were never very far from his thoughts. He had dreamed of Mishah, a dream so real he could remember her touch, her scent, as if she had been in this very room.

He went to the window and stared out at the silken undersides of the heavy-lifting platform, glowing orange from the reflected rays of the morning sun still out of sight just below the rooftops of Nod City. Then with a sudden blaze of light, it rose into view.

It still amazed him how swiftly his fortunes had turned. Granted, he was still a prisoner, but the prison had taken on a softer hue. Guards still stood at each of the eight exterior doors, but here at least, in Sor-dak's official residence, he was free to roam from the deep basement where the vats of chemicals bubbled, producing the life force that filled the copper wires, all the way to the open rooftop where the stargazer's huge crystal lenses pointed heavenward. And in between lay the design rooms, the models of the Oracle's Temple spread out in gigantic scale, the long tables of scribes and mathematicians poring all day over numbers and drawings, and Sor-dak's personal research area, filled with instruments of finely crafted gears, levers, dials, mirrors, moonglass, and sparks that flew between balls of copper.

Lamech's room faced the Temple site. In an adjoining chamber he spent much of his day checking the numbers and the angles on star charts Sor-dak had painstakingly constructed. But he sensed Sor-dak had another reason for rescuing him, though the crafty old stargazer had yet to divulge it.

In the cycle of one full year, there were two critical days when measurements had to be taken, each one hundred eighty days apart—and today the earth would enter one of those critical measuring points when it was farthest from the sun in its yearly circuit.

Lamech stretched, watching the partially built abomination in the distance catch the first rays of the sun and flare in its fire. Even encased in its scaffolding, it shown like an unfinished jewel, a foreshadowing of its future beauty. No expense had been spared in its construction. Someday, when finally encased in its brilliant sheath of white stone, it would shine like the sun itself on these early mornings, as if it were the source of that light. He frowned. That was the whole idea. He had gleaned a smidgen of what was going on here, and in those minute particles of knowledge, he had learned there was a critical alignment the Temple had to achieve, and that alignment, oddly enough, had much to do with the gathering of Oarion and the sunrise on this very day.

In the story given to his grandfather, Enoch, Oarion meant light. It represented the Glorious One, the Prince, the Redeemer of man, who would someday come forth as light. Could this building, and the brightness of it when it was completed, be a counterfeit attempt by the Oracle to convince man that *he* was the coming light of the world, the redeemer of mankind?

Lamech chilled. He was determined to learn all he could of this travesty. At least here, in his new status as a bondsman to the Chief

Builder, he was in a position to learn … to influence … if only a little. He smiled suddenly. How easily had the Creator arranged all this. "Thank you."

A flash of red caught the low sunlight. A flop of dragons lifted above the morning mist still clinging to the far line of forest and winged lazily over the Little Hiddekel River, then swooped low toward the farmland to the west. The grains were coming into season, and the tillers and harvesters would be busy chasing opportunistic dragons off their fields.

Lamech turned from the window at the sound of a knock on his door and slipped on a robe. "Come in."

Sor-dak, wearing the faded red robe and holding a slender, polished gopherwood staff, entered. Instead of the usual bundle of scrolls and charts under his arm, Sor-dak held a single slip of heavy reed paper.

Lamech bowed to his benefactor and nodded at the paper. "The final calculations?"

Sor-dak looked him up and down, his eyes narrowing some behind bushy white brows. The long white beard was tangled and needed a comb run through it. Perhaps he'd never retired from his labors at all. The man seemed to need little sleep.

"You're not dressed yet?"

Lamech looked down at the robe he wore. "But it's just now dawn."

"Dawn?" His sea-green eyes darted toward the window and widened in surprise. He felt among his deep pockets and dragged out a heavy bronze suntracer, peered at it a moment—then frowned, shaking it near his ear. "Confounded machine!"

Lamech suppressed a grin. The old mathematician had forgotten to tension the spring again. "Is that the star chart I'm to examine?"

"Hum?" Sor-dak shoved the useless suntracer back into his pocket and handed Lamech the paper.

"I've spent all night checking my figures, but you must check them again for me." His lips thinned behind the white tangles, then spread into a humble smile, his eyes crinkling. "You know how I sometimes get, Master Lamech." In spite of his lofty position, his immense intelligence, Chief Stargazer Sor-dak was not in the least a vain man. And the more they had worked together, the more open Sor-dak had become, even willing to discuss philosophy. Lamech had held his tongue on many occasions. Sor-dak was a man who, if Lamech could earn his trust, would be a powerful ally.

"I'll see to them immediately."

"Good. We have only today to complete our preparations. The lenses have to be properly adjusted before nightfall if we are to take exact measurements."

When Sor-dak left, Lamech hurried down to the kitchen for breakfast and carried a flagon of coffa back up to his room where he set about methodically going over the stargazer's calculations.

That afternoon, he, Sor-dak, and three other stargazers carefully adjusted the long tubes atop Sor-dak's observatory, carefully cleaned the pure crystal lenses, then minutely nudged bronze dials one last time so that finely scribed lines joined and the symbols upon the huge bronze disk of the constellations stood in exact positions.

Tonight, one of only two nights out of the year, the blazing bonfires in the Temple complex did not burn. The heavy-lifting platform had earlier been deflated and now rested on the ground in the construction site. Fires were outlawed in all of Nod City, and any window showing a flame would be visited by green-cloaks.

The moon was one thing they had no control over. All week Lamech had watched it wane, and this evening at least, its razor-thin edge would present no problems to the stargazers. Only the Dancing Lights would have stood in their way, had the measurements Sor-dak required been in the northern sky. But tonight the lenses were angled to the west where they had almost a full quartering to make their measurements before what little light the waning moon gave off would intrude upon the precious black sky.

Long after nightfall had closed around them, with the stars bright before their instruments, Sor-dak pressed a lever that put in motion a set of precision suntracers, and the measurements began. Lamech was relegated to the sidelines as the stargazers worked. Sor-dak climbed onto the saddle and peered into the lens, while assistants carefully adjusted the tracking wheels, and scribes studiously recorded their measurements.

Lamech studied the stars in his own way, reveling in the story they told him. It was the plan of redemption, a testimony to the Creator's promise to return one day and set man free from the curse under which the whole world groaned. The Creator had written that promise in the heavens for all who had an eye to see.

Indeed, the curse had affected not just the world but even the far-flung stars. The ripples of Mother Eve and Father Adam's Fall had spread out to every corner of the creation. It had caused much change, even in Lamech's short lifetime of 182 years. Animals were turning, the magnetic veil was failing, and the Dancing Lights were not as vibrant and alive as he remembered them from childhood. He suspected the curse had even affected moonglass. It was why people got sick, grew old, and died—or worse, murdered each other. The curse enabled the Oracle to gain a foothold. Lamech frowned. The world was slowly decaying around him.

He thought of Mishah again. The curse was why he was here in prison and so far from his beloved wife. A tear stung his eye, and he put those thoughts from his head.

❦

They'd been on the road a few days when the hairs at the back of Rhone's neck rose in warning. At the same moment, Klesc's hand drifted near the sword in his belt.

Rhone narrowed his view up the slender path they were following, then glanced at Klesc. "You sense it too?"

"Someone watches from the shadows," Klesc whispered.

Rhone dropped back a step and put a hand to Leenah's shoulder. "Keep a lookout behind us."

She came instantly alert and nodded, grasping the gold-braided handle of the long dagger they had appropriated from a careless guard during their escape from Nod City.

Rhone and Klesc advanced cautiously, eyes probing the deeper shadows, the dense brambles, the high, overarching branches that turned the path into a dim tunnel. Suddenly Klesc stiffened, then dashed into the forest. When Rhone caught up, Klesc was scowling, turning a slow circle.

"I saw someone move, Pyir Rhone."

Rhone spied a snapped twig and crushed moss behind a thicket. "You did." A single pair of footprints left a clear trace to follow. "Looks like only one." He gazed off in the direction the man had fled.

"Let's follow him." Klesc started on the trail.

"No."

The impetuous warrior wheeled back.

"It might be nothing. An inquisitive wanderer. A lost seeker." They couldn't pursue every curious soul ... although something about the footprint had left Rhone unsettled. More important, he didn't want to leave Leenah on the road alone. "Let it go for now. We will be more watchful."

Reluctantly, Klesc sheathed his sword.

※

That night they made camp among a pile of moldering stones in the Ruins of Eden, in what once had been a village and fertile fields, now reclaimed by the jungle. Rhone built a fire, while Leenah cleared a place against an ancient stone wall for their sleeping blankets and drycloths. Klesc went off to gather fruits, roots, and berries for dinner.

As Rhone fed twigs and small branches to the feeble flames, his eyes were upon Leenah, watching the way she carefully cleared the ground of sticks, stones, and the decaying nuts of last year's season of falling. Tall and lithe, pretty and efficient, she was both pleasant to the eyes and a valuable traveling companion. He remembered her unflinching bearing back on the road when he'd told her there might be trouble and how she had faced the Lodath's Guards single-handedly, prepared to fight and die. He also recalled her wince of pain and the sadness in her voice when Klesc had been forced to kill the canic on their trail as they fled the Lodath's palace.

A smile came unexpectedly to his face as she drew her dagger and began working it around a stubborn boulder planted in the middle of their sleeping ground.

Klesc returned and deposited an armful of food by the fire. "Let me help you with that, Mistress Leenah!" He drew his sword and levered the boulder free, then wrenched it from the ground and heaved it to one side.

"Thank you, Master Klesc." Her smile shone warm, her eyes wide and pert in the late first-quartering light.

Later, when Rhone and Klesc divided up the watches, Leenah insisted on having her turn. "I won't sleep through the night anyway so I might as well bear my share of the load. And if we should encounter trouble along our journey, it would be better met by Makir Warriors who are well rested."

"Her logic is sound," Klesc said.

Rhone agreed, so they split their watch into threes, and Klesc drew the first stint.

Upon his blanket, under his drycloth covering, Rhone found

that sleep evaded him. He was too aware of the woman's soft breathing beside him. In the end, sleep won out, and the next moment Klesc was quietly nudging him awake.

He threw off the drycloth, already beading with moisture, and stretched as he stood. "All quiet?"

Klesc inclined his head, and they stepped apart from the sleeping woman. "When the breeze is just right, it carries the odor of smoke." He glanced at the great, wide sliver of the lesser light, low in the sky. "It comes out of the west."

"Our follower is a determined man."

"I could track him down."

Rhone shook his head. "We know he's out there."

"There might be more than one, Pyir Rhone."

Rhone winced at the title. The big warrior seemed determined not to let him forget that part of his past. "I saw only one set of tracks. There might be others, but I don't think so, Klesc."

He nodded. "As you wish."

"Get some sleep."

Klesc turned back to his waiting blankets. "One more thing. Mansnatchers hunt tonight. Three drifted over not an hour ago, and I heard the hunting calls of others."

"I'll watch for them."

Klesc frowned. "Unusual—so many here." His eyes narrowed suspiciously. "Come to think of it, I haven't seen any scarlet dragons about lately." He shook his head and went to his blankets, arranged his sword near at hand, and crawled under his drycloth.

Thinking it over, Rhone hadn't seen any scarlet dragons recently either. But dragons weren't a problem that greatly troubled him. Their unseen stalker was more vexing. Rhone buckled his sword around his waist and cast a quick glance to the projlances leaning against the tree, ready at hand should he need them. He sniffed the air, but the breeze was now out of the east.

In the distance a mansnatcher screeched, too far away to be of concern. From time to time, beasts of the forest made their presence known as they lumbered through the darkness, going about their nightly scavenging.

Turnlings—those creatures that had grown aggressive toward man and each other—were Rhone's chief concern. He peered into the forest's darkness, dotted here and there with the shimmering flicker of luminescent insects, broken only by the soft greenish coils of lambent creepers looping from the tree branches. The mansnatchers were the most notorious, but others had turned too. The sten-gordon; the hook-tooth; certain canics, the low, shuffling black and yellow hefler that burrowed underground at day and stalked at night; and the scale-back river snapper with its long snout, fierce teeth, and powerful tail. There were many others as well. The Wild Lands were becoming a dangerous place.

Even the beautiful scarlet dragons had turned—but fortunately their favored prey was mansnatchers, not humans. Where red dragons lived in abundance, man was relatively safe from being carried away by a mansnatcher.

Rhone sat against a tree, watching the quarter moon creep toward dawn, its smooth, silvery surface a comforting companion for a night watcher. The waning light touched the cheek, closed eyes, and tousled hair of the sleeping woman.

Leenah stirred and sat up, rubbing the sleep from her eyes. Rhone quickly glanced away and peered at the stars. She had somehow known it was the time of the third watch. She looked around, then stood and came over. "You weren't going to wake me?"

"I would have. It is only now mid-second quartering."

She combed the hair from her face, quickly binding it in a thick braid. "Anything?"

"Klesc smelled smoke, but I have not detected it. Mansnatchers in the area. Keep an eye out for them."

"Smoke?"

"Likely the follower we ran across earlier."

She cut the thick, fleshy stem of an alecup fern and squeezed the sweet water into her mouth. "Who could be following us? The giants that you told me about? The Lodath's Guard?"

"The footprint was that of a man, not a giant. And if it's the Lodath's Guard, they would have made a move by now."

She frowned. "So we wait?"

"We wait."

She startled at the nearby screech of a hunting mansnatcher and scanned the night sky past the overarching tree limbs. "I hear their talons hold a poison."

"It's true. It won't kill you, but it will make you go mad—at least for a while." He smiled. "People scratched by a mansnatcher have been known to do crazy things."

"Like what?"

"Like stop strangers, claiming to be their long-lost child; or leap into rivers, suddenly thinking they are fish; or become thieves and steal food and hoard it under their beds. Sometimes it takes weeks before they are right in the head again."

Leenah frowned. "I'll keep the proj-lance nearby."

Rhone smiled. "They don't like tight places. They need room to stretch their wings. We're safe so long as we remain under these trees."

"Just the same, I'll keep it at arm's reach. You ought to get some sleep, Master Rhone."

"I'm not tired yet. I'll sit with you awhile."

Leenah began to protest, but stopped. The idea of company must have appealed to her. She took up a proj-lance and sat against the tree next to him with the weapon across her lap. Then she cocked her head to one side, listening. "What bird is that?"

"It's not a bird. A golden eye monkey."

"I never would have guessed."

"They play all night and sleep during the day."

A pretty smile came to her face. "The Wild Lands are not strange to you, are they, Master Rhone?"

He smiled back, as if he could have helped himself. "I've spent the last hundred years collecting Web in the Wild Lands."

"You have the gift?"

He nodded.

She stared at the crescent moon. "I think everyone still has the gift, Master Rhone. It's just harder for some of us to touch it. While in the Cradleland, my senses sprang to life. I could hear the animals talking. Some more clearly than others. But once outside its walls, everything went dull." She looked at him. "How can I hold on to it?"

"I don't have the answer, Mistress Leenah. I suspect the farther we get from the beginning time, the duller our ears and eyes grow."

"Do you think a time will come when no one will remember how it was?"

"That time has already come for many. Generations from now, what you and I know to be true will be called myths and legends."

"That's sad ... sad to think of all that we've lost because of what happened."

Rhone remembered the Mother's despondency when he and Bar'ack had been ushered into her presence. If Leenah felt the loss now, how much more had the Mother felt it? Eve had walked with the Creator and his Messengers. She had spoken freely with all of creation. But once she and the Father disobeyed, the shining glory the Creator had clothed them in had been stripped from them. Standing naked in their transgression, they were cast out of the Garden—and death leaped triumphant into the world. Then, as if to emphasize the tragedy of it all, the Creator Himself killed the first animals and prepared their skins for the first covering of man.

Leenah drew in a breath. "But someday it will be restored, all of it, just as the Creator intended it to be."

"Who told you that?"

"I heard it from my father. He was a Sethite too. A distant cousin of Laeoch, a cousin of Enoch. It was Enoch who was given an account of the restoration to come at the end of time."

"And your mother was from Atlan, you said?"

"Of the House of Ergne." Her sudden smile stole his breath away. "My father gave me a Sethite name, but Atlan flowed in my mother's blood ... and it flows in mine." Her voice took on strength when she spoke of her mother's homeland. But then a sudden sadness seemed to sweep away the vigor. Rhone suspected Leenah was remembering how her mother had died. She said softly, "Her brothers, my uncles Sirt and Debne, were Makir, as yourself."

Rhone searched his memory, but the names were unfamiliar. "I've met with the leaders of the House of Ergne, but I do not recall your uncles."

"They were not leaders."

He nodded, spying the dark silhouette of a distant mansnatcher passing before the smooth surface of the moon, a limp shape in its talons. Perhaps Leenah's uncles were not leaders, but she clearly possessed leadership qualities. She could even be a queen.

The thought startled him. How had it leaped so easily to his brain? He shook the notion from his head and stood. Being near to this woman was oddly unsettling. "I'll try to get some sleep before the dawn. If trouble comes near, wake us."

"I will." Her mood seemed to have darkened. Had he caused it by inquiring of her mother? "Evening peace, Master Rhone."

"Evening peace." He went to his blanket and drycloth, trying to think of some way to bring back the cheer and the captivating smile to her face. But as he lay staring at the stars and the tattered ends of the Dancing Lights filling the northern sky with color, his thoughts moved to his own mother. Was she still alive? Still a virtual prisoner in her own house? And what of Zorin? Born only moments apart, Rhone wondered how two brothers could be so different.

How strong was Zorin's hold over the land? By what method could Rhone hope to wrench the Kingdom of Atlan from Zorin's grasp and take his rightful place as head of the Council of Ten?

15

Marin-ee

For six weeks they marched eastward, through the Ruins of Eden, through the lands of Yerran, Kaz-ak, and into the land of Havilah. Here the mountains grew tall, pitted with mines and garnished with small villages. From these mountains, all roads seemed to eventually converge and point southeast, toward the shipping port of Marin-ee.

The mountain folk were friendly and not overly suspicious of travelers. Lodging was easy to find and cheap. The mines produced gold, onyx, and berdeniex—a mineral used to harden iron. The Tubal-Cain Company bought the stuff by the bargeful.

On the northern slopes grew scrubby qwall trees, widely spaced and planted in long rows. Their fruit was delicious, but it wasn't the harvesting of qwalls that kept the people employed. Upon the tree's squat, thick trunks hung copper pots beneath reed spouts that dripped a thick white sap. It was from this fluid that bdell-m was extracted and sold in spice markets around the world.

At a crossroads, Rhone stopped and looked over his shoulder.

Leenah followed his glance. "He is persistent." Her golden

hair was twisted into two thick chords that looped over her head and knotted together at the back. Her dress was worn from travel, though carefully patched. Her shoulders square and strong, her arms, darkened by the sun and roughened by wilderness travel, showed the long, powerful muscles of her Hodinite heritage. Rhone found it hard to take his eyes from her.

"I still say, let me grab him," Klesc growled lowly. "How long are we to permit it?"

For over a month, their elusive shadow hadn't gotten close enough for them to catch a glimpse. And though either he or Klesc could have easily circled back and seized the follower, somehow Rhone felt the time wasn't right. One of the hardest things he struggled with in his new life as a believer in the Creator was to let things unfold according to the Creator's timetable, not his own. "He's ours to have whenever we want him, Klesc. We can afford to be patient."

Klesc's expression showed he disagreed. "You've changed, Pyir Rhone. You would have never permitted this when you ruled the Makir."

"Those days are over."

"Yet you return to reclaim your rightful seat at the head of the Council of Ten. How will you rule if not with a strong hand? Do you think Atlan will be simple to hold on to once Zorin is gone?" Klesc scoffed. "Not if his followers have anything to say about it."

"We will deal with Zorin's followers when the time comes."

"Like you are dealing with this follower?"

Leenah stepped between them. "This bickering will only drive us apart. We all want to see Atlan liberated. And that can only happen if we cease this rivalry."

"Maybe I should be Pyir here?" Klesc grumbled.

Leenah's blue eyes flashed. "Talk like that is exactly what I mean." She put a hand gently to his big arm. "Klesc, division among us is not good. We will need each other's strength to accomplish the task set before us."

He backed off. Leenah had that power over both of them. Neither could refuse her when she looked at him with those determined eyes. Rhone knew, for his part, it wasn't a matter of *could not*, but of not wanting to deny anything Leenah asked. Yet she asked so little.

Klesc hesitated, then drew his sword. Taking it by the blade, he turned to Rhone. Rhone drew his own, and the two men rapped their hilts together and held them crossed a moment.

"Peace 'n passing," Klesc mumbled.

"Peace 'n passing." Rhone sheathed his sword, and the three of them resumed their journey, though under a cloud of discontent.

❧

The small village of Aron-ee was nestled in a valley amid huge groves of qwall trees. A wooden stockade surrounded the twenty or thirty colored roofs, and an aged gate warden sat in the shade of the wall to collect an entry tax from strangers. A dyte per person came to less than a quarter shaved gleck for the three of them, and Rhone paid it from his purse. It had been days since they'd set foot in a village, and Rhone intended to do some business here. Over the past few weeks he had returned to Web collecting. With two spools of the valuable silken fiber in his pack, he sought a place to sell it.

Leenah sniffed the air as they strolled into the village. "Bdell-m." She shut her eyes, and a wide smile filled her face. "Mmmm."

"I'll buy you some," Klesc offered.

Her face beamed. "But it is so expensive, Klesc." She drew in another breath.

"Not in this place. That's all they make here."

She looked delighted, and Rhone wished he had made the offer first.

Klesc maneuvered her toward a bdell-m distiller. "Rhone?" She looked over her shoulder at him.

"I'll catch up." It gnawed at him to see her with Klesc. He tried to shrug off the pair as he set out in another direction. He inquired and eventually found a merchant who was interested in the Web. After the usual haggling—which he never had to do when selling Web to Ker'ack—they settled on a price, and Rhone pocketed the coins. He found Klesc and Leenah under a big canopy where three kettles of a bdell-m distiller bubbled away. Rows of the solidified spice, formed into the shapes of animals or simple geometric designs, lined shelves.

Leenah was holding a thick cylinder, the length of her hand and wrapped in fine rice paper, to her nose. Klesc handed over a coin as he walked up.

She thrust the bdell-m under his nose.

"Very nice." Bdell-m had many uses, not the least its pleasant aroma. In food, it added a candied tang. Shaved into a fire, it gave off a wonderful smell and kept insects at bay. Eaten straight, it sweetened a sour stomach. Boiled in tea, it made one drowsy. But mostly people just liked smelling the stuff. Women kept it with their clothes to freshen them. Thinking of clothes, Rhone looked around at the rude shops and tiny houses.

"It was really inexpensive, like Klesc said." Then she stopped and asked suddenly, "Did you sell the Web?"

"I did. I have enough money to see us through to the coast and then some." He looked at her shabby, patched clothes. "There is enough to get you something more sturdy for the remainder of the trip."

Leenah looked down at herself and plucked at a patch that had begun to tear away. "Are you sure?"

He took her hand and led her away. "The trouble is, where in this place would one find a proper traveling dress. If this were Far

Port ..." he broke off. Far Port was no more. It had been razed by the giants.

Klesc caught up. "You won't find that kind of thing here. Best to wait until we make the coast and Marin-ee."

A sudden clamor arose from outside the village walls. There were shouts of, "Dragon in the field!" Men dropped their tools and grabbed up proj-lances. Rhone, Leenah, and Klesc joined in the rush of people out the gate.

In the middle of a grove of qwall trees, a scarlet dragon was ravaging the copper buckets with their precious white sap.

With a shout, the villagers charged through the fields, waving swords and proj-lances. The dragon remained as long as it dared, spilling buckets of sap in its attempt to get at the very last drops, then with a sudden flap of its immense wings, it leaped to the sky. "She's beautiful," Leenah said. The hen's heavy ruby body caught the sunlight as her huge wings lifted her skyward.

Men shouldered their weapons, and in an instant a volley of projs hissed skyward.

"They're trying to kill her!" Leenah cried.

The first two missed. A third smacked the tip of her wing and exploded, sending the dragon into a spiral toward the ground.

Leenah flinched as if feeling the blow in her own body.

The dragon managed to right herself, angling toward the dense forest beyond the qwall fields. Another barrage of projs streaked skyward on long plumes of smoke. One hit her in the thigh.

Leenah staggered and went to one knee. He helped her up. "You all right?"

The dragon tumbled in the air. A second caught her low in the big belly, and her wings folded. Leenah grabbed at her stomach, and her face went stark white. The trees groaned and cracked as the great dragon crashed to the ground.

A blaze of anger flared in Leenah's eyes, and she took off in a run after the hunters moving toward the place the dragon had fallen.

Rhone glanced at Klesc, whose lips were bent into a hard scowl. "There was no need to kill her," he said.

"No." Rhone looked back at Leenah, now far ahead of them. "Come on." They moved with the crowd toward the forest where people had gathered around the carcass. Some made drumming victory hoots, others just looked on with sober faces. Leenah went to her knees beside the great, fallen head and touched it gently. Rhone pushed his way through the crowd.

"She's dead," Leenah sobbed. But just then the dragon's eye blinked open. Leenah went suddenly stiff. The two stared at each other a moment; then with a flutter, the great golden eye dulled, and life went out of it. But in that moment, Leenah's eyes had leaped wide. Instinctively, Rhone understood the surprise that registered in her face.

She sprang to her feet, looking around.

He was fascinated and certain now of what he had seen.

"What happened to her?" Klesc asked.

"She's a sensitive."

Klesc stared at him. "You mean, she's like you?"

He nodded. "Only with dragons. And she's only now discovered it."

Leenah rushed off a little way into the trees, looked across the ground, and then began tracing back and forth as if searching for something.

A voice cried out from another direction. "I found her nest!"

The crowd moved.

"No!" Leenah raced toward the place. Rhone leaped to her heels with Klesc right behind him. But when they arrived, it was too late. Two men were already smashing the eggs with clubs.

Leenah dove into one man and tackled him onto the ground. In an instant she was on her feet. The other man retreated, raising the club to fend her off. She yanked the claw-handled dagger from her belt. The crowd surged forward. Leenah wheeled to face them. Rhone burst through the onlookers and stood before her. Klesc rounded to his left. The bdell-m harvesters halted.

"This is none of your business," one spoke up.

"You've done enough damage here," Rhone said.

"Not near enough. Not until every one of them thieving creatures is gone."

A grumble of agreement rose. A man leveled his proj-lance. Rhone's sword leaped from its scabbard and struck the weapon from the man's startled hands. It was only then that the crowd settled down long enough to look at Rhone and Klesc—to look really hard.

A hush settled over them. Someone whispered, "Makir," and they backed away. A few stood still, staring. This little village was close enough to the coast to have heard the stories and likely to have met firsthand some Makir of old. The island nation of his homeland lay but a day's journey by boat beyond the Border Sea and the Pillars of the Sun.

Leenah fell to her knees, eyes glistening as she stared at the eggs. "They were about to hatch." There were tears in her voice and her eyes. The tiny bodies lay strewn and bleeding. "She told me ... she pleaded with me ... but I was too late."

Among the litter of the broken nest came a soft cracking sound, and then something moved. She brushed away the heavy branches. Somehow, the branches had caught the blow of the club, sending it glancing off a hard shell, cracking it. Leenah took up the heavy egg in both hands, and as she held it, the crack widened and ran around the cap of the egg. A long neck with a tiny head covered in gray scales pushed it off, and with a squawk, the hatchling took its first breath.

"Kill it," someone shouted.

Leenah clutched the egg to her heart.

"It will grow to be a ravager of our crops."

Rhone stepped forward, his long sword still in his hand. "Back to your village. You are finished here."

There was a tense moment of uncertainty, and then they backed away, reluctantly heeding his words and his sword. When they had gone, Leenah sat back and picked away the rest of the clinging shell and wiped the little creature dry with her dress. The tiny dragon mewed.

"She was just trying to collect enough to feed her hatchlings. She knew they would be emerging soon." Leenah wiped a tear but seemed to find solace in the little dragon curled up in her hands.

"What are you going to do with it?" Klesc asked.

"Keep it." She sounded surprised he would even ask.

Rhone peered at her for a long moment, remembering when he first discovered he had the gift. "She spoke to you?"

Leenah's eyes rounded. "It was the most amazing feeling. I've never known anything like it before. Not at all like it was in the Garden."

"How?" Klesc asked.

Rhone knew she could not answer. Leenah stared at him, then shook her head.

He looked toward the village where men were gathering. "We'd best be away from here." He helped her to her feet.

"We'll need to find it food."

"Later."

They hadn't gone but a hundred spans when he came to a sudden halt at the head of a shallow ravine, stopped by a foul stench. Leenah gave a soft groan and looked away.

Klesc made a low growl and stared at the pile of bleached bones and the rotting, fetid flesh. A cloud of flies hovered over the mass grave. "They kill off the dragons to protect their precious bdell-m sap, and mansnatchers multiply and take their children." He shook his head.

Rhone looked skyward again. "No wonder there are so many mansnatchers about."

Leenah sucked in a ragged breath and whispered. "Red dragons in sight, mansnatchers take flight." Tears filled her eyes as she held the tiny new life to her breast.

He took Leenah's arm and turned her away from the place.

※

Marin-ee had become an important city since Rhone last saw the place. As the major shipping port in this region of the Border Sea, it was prospering. Buildings gleamed in the sunlight, their flat roofs of green and dusky burnt orange tiles spreading out below them as he squinted down at the vast wharves and piers stretching out into the blue water.

As they entered the city, Leenah's eyes drank in the sight. She bent for a shard of pink seashell from the wide avenue and held it to the hot midday sun, watching the colors shift.

Rhone recalled the history of Marin-ee, told to him after they had left Mother Eve. He had already known some of it, but Cerah had filled in the missing details.

Long ago, when the world was still new, his grandfather, the mighty Hodin, had fled the Plains of Eden to Marin-ee with his new wife, Atla. Trying to avoid war with a close cousin, he lodged in Marin-ee, which at that time was a tiny seavine-gathering village, nothing like the prosperous town bursting before him now. Here Hodin lived three years in peace with his brother, Marin ... until Gabli, a grandson of Cain who had wanted Atla for his own wife, found him.

He glanced at Leenah, and his heart filled with a strange

delight at the wonder he saw in her face at something so simple as an iridescent seashell. Only since traveling with her could he begin to understand the power of such passion—a passion that caused Gabli's death. Gabli's brother, Imo, together with the sons of Cain, raised an army to have their revenge.

With twenty-four fighting men from Marin-ee at his side, Hodin fled with his wife and their young son. They landed on an uninhabited island not far beyond the Pillars of the Sun that could be defended against Gabli's kin.

Rhone envisioned defensible cliffs—the Rim-wall—from which Hodin, renowned for his size and might, and supported by his small band of warriors, routed the attackers. Imo and his brothers retreated to the coast above Marin-ee and built the fortress Imo-suk. Although now abandoned, Imo-suk's ancient wall and parapets and bastions still stand on a naked rocky cliff overlooking the Great Sea.

Imo raised an army of several thousand men. But the first-borns—Marin, Chevel, and Gark—joined forces with their brother Hodin. The war lasted eighteen years, and when it was over, the family was forever split.

Once secure in a land of his own, Hodin stayed on the island to which the other warriors brought their families and pledged themselves to him. They first built the Rim-wall highwatches, the high lookout towers to watch the sea lanes, and then a vast, beautiful city that Hodin named after his wife. And finally they constructed Hodin's Passage—a wide canyon through the Rim-wall cliffs into the island. Over the years, Hodin expanded the harbor to three concentric canals that connected to the Golden Hills Passage and distant points in the island.

Leenah's gaze traveled the wide streets of Marin-ee like a quick, inquisitive tree banti, examining the shops of every description, missing nothing. "It's not as big as Nod City, but there is so much here." Along with her pack, a wicker basket hung by a strap over her shoulder rested on her hip. Rhone had been unable to separate her from the baby dragon inside it. But he understood the deep connection she felt to the creature, this being her first experience as a sensitive.

Rhone nodded. "Marin-ee sells goods from around the world." They halted where a bend in the road offered a wider view of the harbor below and the Border Sea, bending to the far horizon. The deep-blue water caught the sunlight.

Leenah drew in a long breath, her face filled with wonderment. "It's beautiful."

"The sea stirs men's blood. I grew up surrounded by it. I learned to pilot a boat when I was only waist high to my father." He had put that life behind him, but now suddenly his hands ached for the solid feel of a pair of stout oars. He remembered the rhythmic clanking of the oarlocks and how his legs shoved against the toe board with each powerful stroke. Like Leenah, he inhaled the sea air. It brought a smile to his face. Seabirds squawked overhead: white gulls, gray kormens, the yellow and green divers.

He looked at her. "The sea is beautiful, but dangerous. It hasn't always been so." He watched a kormen dive into the water and return with a large fish dangling from its massive beak. Turnlings weren't restricted only to the land. "Leviathan haunts those depths."

She peered at him with wide eyes. "The creature that attacked you on your last crossing?"

He nodded.

Klesc stared toward the far breakers that arched out into the water. Where they touched the horizon, a rocky spit of land shot skyward. The Pillars of the Sun—two spires of rock soaring a thousand spans into the clear sky, separated by two thousand spans of deep, open channel. This narrow gap at the mouth of the Border

Sea had built Marin-ee into what it was today. It was the only passage out onto the great waters that lay beyond. Rhone frowned. The last time he'd passed through that channel, he'd been leaving Atlan.

"What's our next move?" Klesc surveyed the street, warily examining each building, every face.

Rhone felt Klesc's alertness in a way that was impossible to describe to anyone not of Hodin's blood and not schooled in the ways of the Katrahs and Kimahs. He'd tried to explain it to Leenah, but she only understood it in her head, not her heart.

Marin-ee could be as dangerous as the Wild Lands. With multitudes of people from all over, the Lodath's spies might lurk anywhere.

Leenah said quietly, "Perhaps there are Atlanders here who would join with us?"

"No doubt there are those who'd wish to see Zorin gone. But finding anyone to admit it might be hard." Rhone glanced at the busy street behind them. A man ducked his head and stepped into a convenient doorway.

Atlan was well represented in Marin-ee—her tall men and women a common sight on these busy streets. Not surprising since the island lay but a long day's journey by boat to the east. Because of this, Rhone had let his beard grow. If anyone knew Zorin's face, he didn't want to raise eyebrows upon them seeing his.

Just the same, he and Klesc kept their faces averted and their cloaks drawn over their swords so as not to attract attention to themselves. Their proj-lances would raise fewer eyebrows than their swords. To most folk, they were simply impressive people, likely just returned from the Wild Lands, but to an Atlander, the bearing of a Makir Warrior was hard to hide. Rhone recalled Klesc telling how in prison Leenah had spotted him for a Hodinite and a Makir immediately. If she, half Atlander and raised in a far country, could spot the signs, how much more easily could a full-blooded native Atlander see them?

"I can begin to make," Klesc lowered his voice, "inquiries."

Rhone turned his gaze ahead, feeling a tingling grow at the back of his neck. "That's a start."

The road dipped toward the harbor where boats, barges, and skimmers of every description hugged the wharves.

"Are we to stay here?" Leenah studied him with large eyes.

Rhone nodded. "We must have news of Atlan before we decide our next move, and what better place to find it than Marin-ee?" Around another bend lay an open-air market. "Ah, look what we've stumbled on." He appraised Leenah, tall and lovely in spite of the tattered dress. "No doubt we will find you suitable clothing here."

She patted the wicker basket. "And something for little Gur to eat or his squalling will draw attention to us. I've run out of the keelit fruit we gathered on the road."

"Gur?" Rhone raised a questioning eyebrow.

She grinned. "Someday he will strike fear in his enemies. Anyway, I can't keep calling him 'Little One.' That name would only be appropriate for just so long."

"As if 'Gur' will ever be appropriate!" Klesc gave a deep, rumbling laugh. "A scarlet dragon striking fear?" His laughter rumbled on.

She scowled. "Who knows?"

Rhone glanced at the basket. "You intend to keep him?"

"I do."

"But no one keeps scarlet dragons," Klesc said, the rumbling winding down. "Monkeys and cats and canics, yes, and even little pocket dragons. But a scarlet dragon? Where will it live once it's full grown?"

"I'll shuttle that thread when the pattern calls for it."

"We'll find you a dress and Gur something to eat." Rhone leaned near to Klesc. "We're recently arrived from the Wild Lands, if anyone asks. Been away from Atlan a long time. See what you can learn."

Klesc nodded and drifted off to mingle.

Taking Leenah's arm, Rhone led her in among the crowded, gaudy booths and noisy vendors. Crushed seashells crunched beneath their feet, and the aroma of baking biscuits and fried keelit rinds teased his empty stomach.

Rhone glanced over his shoulder. The crowd was thick around them. It would be easy to blend in and get lost among so many people from so many lands. Still, he kept one eye on the lookout as they searched for a booth selling traveling clothes ... and baby-dragon food.

16

The Temple Secrets

A calm sea lapped the rocky shoreline near the path they followed down to the gleaming water. The bustle of Marin-ee was behind them. The road they followed was narrow and led out onto the rocky breakwater that separated the Border Sea from the Great Sea beyond. In the misty distance rose the Pillars of the Sun, their tops hidden in the hazy light of the late fourth quartering. To the east, Rhone could just make out the flat gray waters of the Great Sea. To the west, the jewel-like azure blue of the Border Sea lay at their feet.

He looked at Leenah. She cut a handsome figure in her new shiverthorn dress. Though there was nothing stylish about the sturdy traveling outfit, there *was* something about Leenah. Anything she wore seemed just perfect on her.

"There." She pointed at a grove of teris palms overarching a pink sand beach. Here and there a few people gathered as the sun set in the west. Four children splashed in the warm water, and a family or two had spread reed mats near the firm sand where gentle waves whispered to within a few spans of their bare feet. Rhone noticed a man and woman strolling hand in hand.

Lovers, no doubt. Why hadn't he noticed lovers before?

Klesc had been filling him in on what little he'd learned back in the marketplace. "They're a tight-lipped bunch when it comes to Zorin and the Council of Ten," he'd said just before they negotiated the rocks down to the beach and dropped their bags in the shade of the palms. That temporarily ended the conversation.

Leenah dug out the bundles of roasted orofin and mushroom-stuffed peppers, wrapped in radish leaves, still warm from the food merchant's booth.

Rhone chewed a warm black roll with a crisp, buttery crust, as Klesc continued with what he'd learned from mingling among the crowd. "Zorin still rules Atlan, but that's old news. His heavy hand is a burden to the people. I had to piece that together. No one will admit to wanting to see Zorin's rule overthrown."

"Cautious, they are."

"He's put a mighty fear into their hearts, Pyir Rhone. There are whispered words about something called the Bloody Pikes." Klesc's eyebrows dipped together. "Apparently it's how Zorin deals with his enemies—and he has many enemies."

Rhone scowled. "Atlanders are warriors at heart; they are a people who speak their minds without fear of their leaders taking vengeance on them. If the High Councilor led well, the people spoke well of him. If he led poorly, he did not punish the people for that, but mended his ways. At least, that was how it once had been. What of the Council of Ten?"

"One man I spoke to said that the Council of Ten is made up of Zorin's men. He was surprised I didn't know that. I have the feeling this has been going on for a long time, Pyir Rhone."

"What of the Makir?"

Klesc shook his head. "The old order long ago disbanded. Being unbound, what could they do?"

Rhone winced. The unbinding had been his fault. Was it too

late to change that?

Klesc continued, "If there were any Makir left on the council, Zorin must have arranged for them to relinquish their oaths."

"Then they are no longer Makir!"

Klesc looked away. "Sometimes men do what they have to. They may have families to protect."

Rhone regretted having said it that way. Had his own choices been any more honorable?

Leenah opened the wicker basket's lid in the shade of the palm tree, and the small dragon stood up on its hind legs, miniature clawed forelegs grasping the lip. Its tiny head swung back and forth on its long neck, snatching bits of keelit from Leenah's fingers. Its small, undeveloped wings still lay flat along its back. In the few days since rescuing the little creature, its scales had brightened to the distinctive reddish color of its species. It suddenly threw back its head and gave a high-pitched squawk.

"All right, all right, I hear you. Patience, my little ..." Leenah caught herself and grinned. "Patience, Gur." She scraped at the soft green pulp.

Rhone scanned the shoreline where children played, and he listened to the sounds of people up on the road above, but down here he couldn't see them. For the moment, they were alone. Anyone wanting to follow them out this far would have to reveal himself, but no one was watching them here—no one of any concern. The scampering children had caught sight of Leenah feeding her pet and came rushing over. She invited them closer, laughing with them and sharing the keelit so that each might have a chance to feed little Gur.

Rhone realized he was staring at her again. He averted his eyes, relieved that she hadn't noticed. He unlatched his boots, stood, looked at Klesc, and hitched his head down the beach where they could speak in private. The warm sand working between his toes reminded him of home and youth, when life was easy and every problem intercepted by a proud father and loving mother. "Any word of my mother?"

Klesc shook his head. "I tried to turn my conversations to her, but I didn't think it wise to carelessly bring up the subject."

"You were right not to probe too openly."

Klesc picked up a stone and skipped it across the water. "We don't want to arouse anyone's interest in us."

"We already have."

Klesc frowned. "You certain?"

"I glimpsed a man following us. He ducked into a building when he knew he'd been seen. It might be nothing at all, but I don't think so."

"Our follower?"

"That would be my guess."

Klesc bent for another stone. "In spite of your feelings on this matter, Pyir Rhone, I think it's time we speak with our elusive friend."

He nodded. "Tonight."

Klesc spread a smile. "Good," he said, and skipped the stone far out across the blue water.

Lamech had been shocked that he'd received the invitation. He didn't want to go. He didn't want to mingle any more than necessary with officials of the Temple project. But Sor-dak wanted him there.

On the morning of the gathering, a servant in Sor-dak's household arrived at his door with a new robe—one similar to what the stargazers of the Temple project wore. Lamech would have refused it had it come from anyone else. He loathed being associated with the project.

That evening, the guards permitted him to pass unharassed to the gathering room. Not that harassment of any serious nature was a problem anymore. That had all but ceased once he had been taken under Sor-dak's wing, but tonight it was evident that the order had gone out to treat him as everyone else.

The room on the second floor was the largest in the building. This evening it was filled with dignitaries, officials of the Lodath and the Temple Guard, and the planners and stargazers. In his new bright green robe with its immense sleeves and sable collar and hem, he blended right in with the other stargazers. Would Mishah be disappointed in him if she knew? He frowned. Maybe dressed like this no one would recognize him.

He knew a few of the men there. The three members of the Disciplinary Council were in attendance. The prison commandant. The Captain of the Lodath's Guard ... Lamech particularly wanted to avoid Captain El-ik. He'd been warned by Sor-dak that El-ik had been smarting since the aborted execution—too much explaining to the Lodath and to the hundreds of spectators who had come expecting blood and torture and had left grumbling their disappointment.

Perhaps he should have tried to beg Sor-dak's release of the obligation on the pretense of finishing his review of their mathematical calculations from the measurements they had taken a few nights before.

A table along one wall held flagons of ale and wine, cheeses, fruits, vegetables of every kind, and for many, the seared flesh of animals. The Creator had provided every green plant and herb for food, yet men had turned to flesh to satiate their wanton, never-ending desire for that which the Creator had never permitted.

His view was drawn to a table in the center of the room where an object was covered by a sprawling, emerald green sheet. He knew from the vague outline that poked the cloth here and there that beneath it was a large model of the future Temple. He'd watched artisans constructing it over the last few weeks.

Across the room, Sor-dak was in earnest conversation with two Temple officials. Lamech strolled to a window and looked out at the heavy-lifting platform that hovered above the half-built Temple, glowing a dull orange from the fires below, obscuring most of the night sky. How many more years must past before that device was dismantled? Of course, then the Temple would be functioning. He glanced at the covered table and sighed. Given a choice of the two, he'd take the heavy-lifting platform.

"Master Lamech."

He turned at Sor-dak's summons.

The stargazer waved him over. "I want you to meet Masters Sevins and Tor-een." Sor-dak had the courtesy not to mention that he was a prisoner.

Lamech bowed stiffly to them, and both bowed to him as courtesy dictated.

Sor-dak said, "I've been telling them how we've completed our measurements."

"With these final calculations, you will be able to track the star from now until ...?" Tor-een left it open for Lamech to finish.

Lamech spread his hands. "Provided the earth remains unchanging in its course, forever."

Both officials smiled and nodded at what Lamech was certain Sor-dak had already told them. Sor-dak, for his part, seemed not the least put out that Tor-een had seen the need to check out his opinion.

The measurements they had taken were the final ones in a long series of sets. By noting the minute differences over the years, it was possible to extrapolate exactly where the constellation of Oarion was five hundred years ago or where it would be five hundred years hence. But why such precise knowledge was needed was still a mystery.

A server came around carrying a tray and handed each man a flagon of wine. Sevins seemed about to ask another question when the door opened and a line of guards filed in and stomped briskly to a halt, forming a corridor through the crowd. King Irad marched into the room, a scowl on his lips, a pinch at the bridge of his nose. The place went silent, every eye following the magnificently bedecked man to a pair of honor seats. Though short, Irad's stout form commanded attention. A moment later the Lodath entered, his brooding view casting about like a serpent looking for something to strike at. He strode to the second of two chairs set apart on an elevated platform, his blue cloak streaming behind him, hemmed in a golden band of the Oracle's Unspeakable Symbols.

Sor-dak cleared his throat and said softly, "The show's about to begin."

Lamech nodded. "I'll just melt in to the background." Cleaned up and outfitted like the other stargazers, would anyone even recognize him? It was a risk he didn't want to take. More than ever, he wished he could have declined the invitation.

A grim smile tightened Sor-dak's mouth. "Disappear." He flicked a hand as if conjuring the deed himself. "Poof. Go away."

Lamech slipped through a side door packed with interested faces into an adjoining chamber that had taken the overflow of people. He found a place past someone's shoulder where he could observe the event in the next room.

"I've heard it said he doesn't talk anymore," someone in the crowded doorway whispered.

"Heard he can't," another replied.

"Why didn't the Oracle heal him?" a third wondered.

A murmur of conjectures followed.

Sevins took the floor and called for silence. With a bow toward the honor seats, he acknowledged the distinguished guests, then went into his announcement. Most of what he had to say was nothing new. But when he flung back the green cloth, the crowd gasped. The finished Temple as it would appear one day, a miniature of that jewel rising on the vast track of ground beyond these walls, gleamed before them. Crowning the Temple was a four-sided crystal, tapering to a point that, when fashioned for the real Temple, would be immense! It pulsed with its own light, a flowing spectrum of living colors, not something imbued to it by the overhead panels of moonglass.

"And now I am excited to tell you that there is more here than meets the eye. For years we thought the Temple was to be a magnificent monument to the Great Oracle, a dwelling place fit for the Master of the Heavens. But the Oracle has revealed to his Lodath," Sevins turned to Sol-Ra-Luce and bowed slightly, sweeping an arm his way, "the deeper mysteries of the Temple." He paused for effect as his view traveled around the crowded room. "It is to be much more than merely a god's earthly home."

Not a sound rippled the silence except Lamech's own breathing, the thumping of his heart, and the muted thud of blood in his ears.

"When it is completed, it will become the place where the Oracle's emissaries will join with us who live here upon his world. The Temple will be the incubator of a new order of life, one that will lift us in only a few generations from mere animals to godhood!"

The room caught its breath, then as if finally understanding what had been spoken, it gave forth a shout of praise for the Oracle. Lamech's stunned mind suddenly went blank. He tried to remember the prophesies his grandfather, Enoch, had told him about this.

Not everyone in the room was applauding. An inscrutable look clouded Sor-dak's green eyes. But the most notable was the scowl that darkened King Irad's face. Did Irad understand something the others didn't? Would a future generation of god-men permit him, a mere mortal, to hold onto his kingdom? Lamech managed a thin smile. Here was a new wrinkle.

Sevins lifted his hands and quieted the cheers.

Lamech shouldered through the crowded doorway into the main room. This was too important to miss.

"There is more. You've all heard of the silly sacrifices some people offer up to an impotent god." He barked a sarcastic laugh. "The blood of lambs and goats covers nothing but crude rock altars and does no one any good! An empty tradition left over from primeval days when men feared a being who couldn't walk among them ... or who would not! Except for some foolish men who spin tales of walking with this so-called Creator, we've not seen him or any display of his power!"

A slow rumble of agreement moved through the crowd. Lamech's cheeks warmed, his lips compressing as he fought against his own nature to speak out. *Your mouth has gotten you in trouble all your life. Keep it shut now.*

"Who here has ever been visited by this so-called Creator?" He paused for a show of hands and when none appeared, he continued, bolstered. "I thought not. But I have seen the Oracle. I've spoken with him. I've touched him! As have many of you. And his emissaries are among us. Some have even taken wives of our women. Who can deny the Oracle's presence to any of us who wear his pledge?" Sevins drew out the crystal pendant that hung around his neck. It swirled with the same living light that the Temple crystal held.

Lamech's slowly boiling anger suddenly turned to fascination.

In a moment men and women around were holding high their

own crystals. His chest constricted and his head prickled with sweat. His spirit suddenly seemed on fire.

"Even our great King Irad has seen the Oracle. But he has not seen this fable, the Creator!" Sevins grinned at the faces riveted upon him. "So I ask you again: What good is it for these deceived individuals to sacrifice the blood of animals to a myth? But you are not deceived. You live in the Oracle's light, and when you begin your sacrifices to him, they will not fall upon deaf ears. Your petitions will be heard, indeed."

"Sacrifices? What sacrifices?" someone asked.

"Sacrifices that will show your love and devotion to the Oracle. And he will respond to them as surely as the sun lights the morning sky!" Sevins went to the model of the Temple, lifted the crystal capstone, and held it high. "This is the difference between the faith of fools and the science of the wise. As I speak to you tonight, the Temple's crystal is being forged in the ancient furnaces of Rahab! Beneath this crystal he will dwell among mankind, and every morning, with the coming of a new sun, Holy Fire will shine forth from it and consume your sacrifices! There will be no spilt blood! The shed blood of innocent beasts accounts for nothing! The Oracle will consume your offerings, and through his power and by the mysteries of his Temple, the offerings will be sent across the vast expanse of the heavens to the stars!"

The crystal seemed to warm in Sevins's hand, its colors growing vibrant and swirling, and as if in tune with each other, every crystal pendant in the room took on the same fire. The crowd became chaotic. Some people groaned with delight; some fell writhing to the floor, while others threw up their hands, jabbering nonsensical sounds.

Lamech had difficulty breathing. He staggered and fought off a wave of smothering heaviness from some unseen force.

Sevins let the people have their way, then placed the crystal capstone back atop the Temple model. Its fire dimmed and slowly the frenzy died, and people emerged from their ecstatic wrenching and jabbering. Lamech took a breath, his lungs suddenly able to fill fully. The heaviness lifted.

"Now as to how it is to be done." Sevins leaned over the model, and one of the four sloping walls swung open at his touch. Inside was a circular platform. If the scale was accurate, Lamech judged the platform to be over four hundred spans wide. "This is the altar. It's here you will place your offerings each morning before sunrise."

An altar the size of a meeting floor? Lamech frowned.

"With the coming of the sun, the Oracle's Holy Fire will blaze upon the altar, and in a moment, he will consume them and send all the offerings through this passage in the wall that will forever be pointed at the constellation of Oarion."

This intrigued Lamech on several levels. How was the Oracle planning to track the stars of Oarion? It would require a vast network of gears and wheels and some immense power source. Literally, the whole Temple would have to shift positions daily! Now he understood the necessity of their measurements a few nights before and Sevins's keen interest in them. But he had a deeper concern. What exactly did the Oracle expect his people to offer as sacrifices? Sheep and cattle? If so, they might run whole flocks and herds onto an altar that huge.

When the announcement ended, Sevins left the room, refusing to answer the scores of questions cast at him. "Later," was all he said as the guards formed up around him, keeping everyone else at bay. In frustration, the questions turned to Sol-Ra-Luce, who also refused to answer or was unable to.

King Irad stood suddenly and stomped out of the room, twisted ropes of hair flying, face dark, eyes narrowed, his mouth screwed tight in the tangled nest of his dark beard.

Lamech caught the brief smile of victory that touched the Lodath's face.

Someone grabbed Lamech's arm and swung him around. Captain El-ik's glare slowly appraised the new garment, noting its occupant's groomed hair and beard. His glance stopped at the flagon of wine in Lamech's hand. "You're looking fit ... for a prisoner." El-ik's eyes held both a challenge and a threat.

A lump lodged in Lamech's throat. He swallowed it down. "Master Sor-dak treats me well."

"Perhaps Sor-dak needs to be reminded of your status. Not long ago you were shoveling girt. One careless move on your part could put you back there. You escaped execution by the thinnest of threads, and I bore the brunt of the Lodath's anger." His face darkened and his breath smelled sour. "You will be here a very long time, prisoner, and so will I. Your luck won't hold out forever." With a shove, El-ik released his arm and spun away.

Lamech's heart was pounding as he started for the exit. He should have stayed hidden in the adjoining chamber. He shouldn't have accepted Sor-dak's invitation! Hindsight. Carelessness. When he reached the doorway, he glanced over his shoulder. El-ik had snared the Lodath's ear, and the two of them were staring at him.

He pushed past the crowd into the adjoining chamber and out another door. He was still clutching the flagon when he reached his room. He set it upon a table, and in the darkness went to the window, breathing in the cool night air. He stared at the monstrous orange heavy-lifting platform hovering above the unfinished Temple. What had Sevins said? *Even now the true crystal was being forged. On Rahab?*

Lamech peered heavenward. In the glow of the heavy-lifting platform, the stars and the stones of fire were mostly obscured.

Oric was just visible in the night sky, its reddish orange light distinctive. And somewhere beyond Oric's path lay Rahab....

Rahab? Mishah had dreamt about Rahab—he was certain of it. But the exact details eluded him as he hurried into the next room where he kept the star charts.

17

Da-gore

*T*wo and a shaved," the innkeeper said flatly, not budging on his price.

Rhone knew rooms would be expensive here in Marin-ee. His purse would not sustain many days at such rates. "Two."

The innkeeper, an old seafaring man with a leather-hard face and a permanent squint to his eyes, gave a shake of his head and turned away, starting for his welcoming room.

"How many beds?" Leenah asked.

The innkeeper halted and rolled his shoulders around, squinting at her. "One bed a room. That's what I let here in the *Busted Bow*. A bed, a table, a chair. Take it or leave it. I'm full up every night."

"We'll take it," she said looking at Rhone. "I'm tired."

It was already dark, and Rhone doubted the deal would be any sweeter at the next inn down the street. They'd already tried three others. Maybe tomorrow he could find more suitable accommodations. "All right. Two and a shaved. But I want a room on the top floor."

Leenah cocked her head and gave him a look as he counted out the money.

The innkeeper scooped the coins into his hand. "Green door. Top of the stairs."

Rhone hefted his pack, and they climbed the creaking staircase to a tiny landing facing three doors. The color had faded long ago, but green, yellow, and white were still identifiable.

The room was as cramped as the landing. It smelled of moldering seavines and old boots, and reminded him vaguely of the holding cell in the seaside tower in Derbin-ee.

Leenah sat on the edge of the bed and bounced once. "Must be a mattress under here somewhere."

Klesc's view circled the walls and ceiling. "The *Busted Bow* raises spiders."

Rhone opened the shutters and leaned out upon the rough sill. They faced the sea, and the freshening breeze helped clear the stuffiness from the room. Below, boats large and small lay alongside rocky quays, the lights from their moonglasses and torches stretching across the still, smooth water. From time to time, a distant bell clanged softly. A canic barked somewhere off in the night.

"Friends of yours?" Klesc batted at a spiderweb, then dragged his fingers across his vest.

Rhone glanced at him. "Not mine."

Klesc gave a single low laugh.

Leenah set her basket on the bed and pealed back the dark covers. "So, there is a mattress hidden here." She looked up at Rhone. "How are we three going to manage this?"

"You take the bed. Klesc and I will spend the night in the welcoming room."

"You won't get much sleep down there."

"We'll be fine." Klesc was still trying to wipe the sticky web from his hand.

Leenah opened her pack, removed a moonglass, and opened the covers. The room brightened, though still far from cheery. She set it on the single table and placed the basket beside it, carefully peeking inside. "Gur's asleep."

Rhone fell into the creaky chair. "It's only for tonight."

"Why did you insist on the top floor?" She quietly closed the lid.

"If we have visitors, I'll hear them go upstairs."

Her eyebrows arched. "You're expecting visitors?"

He shrugged, keeping his suspicions to himself. "Places like Marin-ee are full of thieves."

She seemed to accept that. "When will we go to Atlan?" Her hands went to her head, skillfully undoing her braided hair.

"I need to learn more before I set foot there."

Klesc paced to the window and leaned out. "About your mother?"

Rhone winced at the prick in his heart. "That and other things." Was she still a prisoner in her own home, or had she regained her freedom? And why hadn't he heard from her? He frowned. Why should he have? He had been, after all, a wanderer.

Later, he and Klesc went down to the *Busted Bow's* welcoming room, but there was no private place to discuss their next move, so they took themselves outside.

"Our Watcher will be nearby." Rhone looked toward the dark jetty where wide-spaced torches cast a weak light. A few shadowy people moved down there, none whom he could identify.

"He needs sleep too. Might he have taken a room?"

"Maybe." Rhone turned his view up the street where at least five inns were located. "Let's have a peek into some welcoming rooms."

They visited every festival hall and every public room on that street and the next one over. Rhone did not spot anyone who looked like the man he'd gotten a glimpse of earlier. Circling the square of buildings, they searched for anyone who might be taking an interest in them, but no one took his bait.

They went down to the jetty, but by now the night was getting late, and the torches flickered low, their wicks needing to be trimmed and smelling of vera-logia—'gia that was perhaps grown on Lamech and Mishah's farm in the Lee-lands of Morg'Seth.

The stone walkways along the jetty were deserted. Rhone drew in a breath and blew it out. "Perhaps tomorrow."

"Our Watcher hides well, Pyir Rhone"

In the Wild Lands he would have been simple to find, but here, in a city with a thousand places to disappear, the task was nearly impossible. "We'll keep our eyes wide tomorrow. Let's get some sleep."

Back in the *Busted Bow*'s welcoming room, Klesc settled onto a hard-back bench. Rhone went up to the room to fetch a couple of blankets. At the top of the stairs, a line of light beneath Leenah's door told him she was still awake. He mounted the landing and raised his knuckles to the door when a man's voice from the other side arrested his fist.

In an instant he realized what had happened. Grabbing his sword, he burst through the door.

Leenah jumped in surprise. The man looked up casually from the chair and smiled. "Master Rhone. We've been wondering if you'd show up tonight."

Rhone stared, and it took a moment to recognize the man. The green cloak was gone, and with it, all the symbols of authority. And like Rhone himself, a full beard now filled his face—but the eyes were unmistakable.

"Da-gore."

"I thought now would be a good time to drop in. Here, in this inn, you are less likely to spill blood … at least until you've given me a chance to explain myself." He was holding the baby dragon on his lap, running a finger down his long neck. Gur's eyes were closed, and he purred with contentment.

Da-gore's proj-lance leaned against the wall nearby. Rhone tossed it on the bed. "Where are your men? Why the disguise? Answer quickly." His sword hovered above Da-gore's heart.

"Kill me now, and I may never know if what Master Lamech told me is truth or fable."

"Lamech? What did Lamech tell you?"

"Everything. That very night you and the Messenger came for Klesc."

His sword wavered then lowered. "So, it was you Sari'el spoke of." He remembered passing Da-gore in the prison tunnels. Being enveloped in Sari'el's blue haze and not really in the world of flesh and blood, the three of them had strode past him without the officer realizing they were there.

Da-gore shrugged. "I know nothing of this Sari'el of whom you speak."

There was a sudden pounding on the stair outside the door, and the next instant Klesc burst in, his sword drawn, his eyes darting, searching for danger. He took in the situation in a glance, drew in a breath, and lowered the sword. "I heard."

"Your ears are keen, Master Klesc."

Klesc scowled at Da-gore a moment then crossed to the window and peered out. "Is he alone?"

Rhone nodded and glanced at Leenah. "Why did you let him in?"

"He knocked on the door and said he carried a note from you."

"And you believed him?" Klesc rumbled.

"I didn't think anyone intending me harm would simply knock. And besides, I was ready." From the folds of her dress, she extracted the long dagger.

Da-gore's eyebrows lifted, and a small smile came to his face.

Rhone's skin prickled at the calmness of his foe sitting before him. Any moment he expected to hear the pounding feet of a hundred of the Lodath's Guard rushing up the stairs. "What are you up to, Captain Da-gore? You've been following us for weeks."

"You knew? Ah, but of course. You're Makir."

Klesc shut the door and leaned his bulk against it. "We could have slit your throat a dozen times."

"Why didn't you?"

Rhone slid his sword back into its scabbard, his ears tuned to the noise outside the window. So far nothing out of place. "Curiosity? Patience? I knew you'd reveal yourself in due time."

"Did you?" He stopped stroking the dragon, which appeared content to doze on his lap. "I'm up to no intrigue. And I'm no longer a captain."

Klesc crossed his arms. "That's true. He was demoted to First Shield."

"Not even that, Master Klesc. I walked away from all that the day Lamech was spared."

Rhone grabbed Da-gore's shirtfront and ripped it open. "The pledge pendant. Where is it?" He remembered the sway that faceted piece of crystal held over men and how difficult it had been to relinquish his.

"I left it behind as well."

"Why?"

"Many reasons. The giants were powerless to stop you even though they were the children of gods. It seems the Oracle's power is limited after all, in spite of all that we've been told." He considered Rhone a long moment. "I saw you killed, Master Rhone. Yet here you stand before me."

"I *was* killed." A chill filled him every time he thought of it, even after all these months.

"Yet the one called the Creator had the power to raise you?"

"In his Garden."

Da-gore's expression turned solemn. "Lamech explained his power to me, and perhaps that is the greatest reason why I left. I want to know more about your God, the One you call the Creator. The One whom the Oracle seems bent on destroying."

"The Oracle can never destroy the Creator."

"I've almost come to believe that. There is a battle being waged that is hidden from our eyes, and I want to be on the winning side."

Leenah sat up a little straighter. "Your reasons for wanting to believe are flimsy."

"Perhaps. But for now it's all I have to offer. Would you rather I be a seeking ally or a pursuing enemy?"

Klesc pushed away from the door and stalked back to the window, peering askance along the wooden frame to the harbor below. "We don't need allies. And by Dirgen's beard, our enemies are easily enough dealt with."

Leenah said, "That's not exactly true. We are in the market for allies."

"For Hodinites," Klesc growled. "Not the likes of him."

Rhone stood in front of Da-gore. "What could you offer us?"

Klesc swung around and stared. "You don't seriously believe him?"

Da-gore looked at the sleeping dragon in his lap, and his finger traveled along its neck. "When they are hatched, their necks are extraordinarily long, but soon the head grows to fit it. Isn't that the way of new beliefs? They grow to fit the one who is seeking?"

"Or the seeker abandons the beliefs before they have time to take root," Leenah noted.

"And only *time* will tell, Mistress Leenah."

Klesc's face hardened. "In the mean*time*, what do we do with him?"

The situation intrigued Rhone. The Creator was moving here in a way he was yet unable to discern. "We keep an eye on him."

Klesc's gaze burned. "This isn't about religion, Pyir Rhone. It's about our homeland."

It was bigger than that, but Rhone couldn't explain it with Da-gore sitting there. "We'll talk later."

❧

The men slept in the welcoming room. Rhone dozed shallowly, certain he would wake if Da-gore tried anything, but when the gray windows blushed with the first rosy light of dawn, the ex-captain was still curled in his cloak, asleep, his head upon his traveling pack. Klesc slept on a bench near the door and would have been a formidable barrier to pass by if Da-gore had turned to treachery.

Had what Da-gore told them the night before been true? Had Lamech's words touched even his hardened heart? Rhone still didn't understand the Creator's methods—he doubted he ever would. Mishah once told him that what mattered to the Creator was not so much what a man understood, but what he believed. Faith is what the Creator valued.

They ate at the inn with the proprietor glaring contemptuously at the extra mouth to feed. Rhone pressed half a shaved gleck into his sweaty palm to appease him when they were finished.

Out on the streets again, Da-gore said, "May I accompany you?"

"A spy, that's what he is!" Klesc said.

"He's been following us for over a month now, Klesc. Is it not better to have him where we can keep an eye on him?" They were a long way from Nod City—beyond the Lodath's influence—who would he tell? "What do you expect from us, Da-gore?"

"I want to learn of your Creator."

"Great Dirgen!" Klesc threw up his hands.

Leenah scowled. "I wish you'd stop invoking that name."

He glared at her. "Sorry. Old habits die hard."

Rhone said, "For you to accompany us requires a certain amount of trust, which you have not yet earned."

Da-gore glanced at the three of them. "I would be suspicious too. But what I told you is the truth. I have quit the Lodath, and I have no plans for the future except to ferret out the truth in this matter of the Creator. I have many questions." His view settled on Leenah. "I know you to be a believer. In prison you were cautious with your tongue. Have you nothing to say now?"

She opened her mouth, then closed it and shook her head.

Da-gore gave a thin smile and nodded. "You are not cut from the same pattern as Master Lamech."

She averted her eyes, adjusted the basket at her side, and then suddenly looked up at him. "Ask your questions."

As Leenah and Da-gore spoke, Rhone quietly drew Klesc aside. "We need to find homelanders willing to talk."

"Their tongues are difficult to loosen. I learned that yesterday."

"Perhaps the bartering grounds and market squares aren't the places to be trying."

Klesc slid him a suspicious look. "You have somewhere else in mind?"

"A place where tongues are easily loosened." They were passing a festival hall, and a whiff of stout conger ale reached Rhone's nose. He nodded toward the open door. "Tonight."

That evening they took their dinner in the welcoming room of the *Lone Traveler Inn*, some distance away from the harbor. It was cheaper and cleaner than the *Busted Bow*. The innkeeper was an amicable, black-faced woman named Mini-ai. Her hair was the color of corn silk and her manner friendly and talkative. Three little girls clung close to her skirts. Her husband worked an ore barge and was even now making the dangerous crossing to Wen's Slip on the southern shore of the Border Sea. Rhone sensed her concern for his safety. Leviathan stalked the waters of the Border Sea.

After dark, he and Klesc left Da-gore and Leenah chatting in Mistress Mini-ai's welcoming room. They walked to the nearest festival hall where business was booming and hardly a vacant chair was left.

Rhone spied two chairs at the back of the hall and wove through the crowd, past dripstone tables that seemed to grow up from the floor like squat, milky gray mushrooms. Around each table hung six chairs on chains anchored to stone girders overhead. Polished shards of seashell paved the floor, and scattered panels of moonglass bathed the hall in a muted light. Rhone carefully scanned the room. Among the patrons, six men and three women were plainly of Atlanian descent. Size alone would have given them away, but there were the subtle traits, usually hidden to the eye of off-landers. At least one of the men had the clear manners of Makir training. Rhone dug through old memories, but did not recognize him.

If he could spot one of his own kind so easily, surely they had already taken note of Klesc and him. That might work in their favor.

They sat on either side of a slab of stone that stuck out from a wall. The proprietor brought over a bowl of crisp keelit rinds and pickled tormatins.

"What's your drink?"

"Conger ale," Rhone said.

The innkeeper grinned. "Thought so."

Klesc's eyes shifted warily around the crowded hall. "Sure you want to advertise that we're Atlanders?"

"I hear advertisement is good for business. Besides, they already know we're Atlanders."

The proprietor returned a little while later with two brimming mugs. Klesc took a sip of Atlan's highly prized export. Rhone brought the flagon to his lips and stared over its rim at two big men who sat around a gaming table, tossing colored stones onto the lines etched into the tabletop. It appeared to be a private game, but there were two vacant seats.

"How about a game of Kingle?"

Klesc looked at him. "Here?"

He jutted his chin toward the gamers. "There."

Klesc lowered his voice. "I've been watching them. The one with the long hair has been stealing glances at us since we walked in. He heard you order the ale."

"Then perhaps we should introduce ourselves."

"All right."

They carried their drinks across the floor. The men's conversation broke off when he and Klesc stepped up. The man with dark brown hair bound in a leather thong and hanging down his back looked up.

Rhone set his flagon on the table. "Kingle's a whelp's game with only two stones." He was careful of how he stood and the way he exchanged looks with this man. Little hints gave away much to someone with an eye and the knowledge to read them. "It's rightly a four-stone game."

"This is private." The man's eyes hardened like brittle emeralds and shifted between Rhone and Klesc.

"It's said that a man who wins a four-stone game is a man and a half." Rhone concealed a smile at the surge of vigor that seared his blood. Here was one of his own kind. "I can see the bottoms of your flagons. Let me take care of that." He plopped his pouch onto the table next to his own cup. "We're just looking for a friendly game and some news of home. We've been off Atlan a long time. I hear Zorin the Minck still sits at the head of the Council of Ten."

The man glanced to his partner, a flushed-faced fellow with a red beard, high forehead, and thinning hair more gray than red. His small eyes shone like tiny black beads. They captured Rhone's eyes and held them, unblinking. Two bush buffalos vying for dominance.

Rhone broke off the contest first, signaling a submissiveness he hoped would hide his Makir training. He reached for the pouch.

The first man's hand came down and stopped him. "Sit. We'll talk."

They took the two hanging seats on opposite sides of the Kingle board. "I'm Ehron and this is Storc."

Storc's tiny eyes still hadn't blinked.

"Rhone and my friend, Klesc."

Storc said, "My brother is named Rhone."

"It's a common enough name for an Atlander." He signaled the proprietor over and ordered conger ale for the two men and asked for a second pair of stones.

The proprietor delivered both, and once he left, Ehron gathered up a blue pair, rattled them in his fist, and tossed them out. "Why inquire about Zorin?" The stones tumbled to a stop just shy of the foer'd line.

"He still rules Atlan, doesn't he?" Rhone took his turn. The two red stones tumbled past the goer'd circle and into the foul corner.

Ehron's eyes narrowed as Rhone advanced his peg one hole. "Zorin still sits at the head of the council. You must have been away a long time not to know that."

He heard cautious suspicion in Ehron's voice. He nodded. "We've been gathering Web for the Temple project in Nod City. There's a big market for Web these days."

Storc finally blinked. "You've come all the way from Nod City?" He scooped up the blue stones and made his cast. One stone stopped in the goer'd circle and the other on the twer'd line. Storc grinned and advanced his peg four holes.

"I've started missing Atlan's rocky coast, the smell of lemon and rinerun groves, and the taste of home-brewed conger ale." Rhone raised his flagon and took a small sip. He would make it last all evening. It was *their* heads he wanted foggy.

Ehron's frown spoke volumes. Clearly he missed all that too. Another displaced Atlander like himself. Marin-ee held many such men. Still, Ehron would have news of Atlan, living so near to its shores. The night lengthened, but neither Ehron nor Storc drank much ale, and neither readily gave up any information. Instead, Ehron seemed to grow more interested in them. Somehow the tables had been turned.

The game went round, each player making his cast and each advancing or retreating his counting peg. Klesc became intent on scoring points. Rhone refrained from playing his best. A game sloppily played might put Ehron and Storc more at ease. He sensed there was much these two were keeping to themselves. Whenever the conversation came around to the ruling power in Atlan, both men went silent and looked worried.

This was going nowhere, so Rhone tried a more direct approach. "What of the old Councilor's wife?"

"She's well, from what I hear," Storc said offhandedly and pretended to concentrate on the red stones Klesc had just tossed out. But his brow had suddenly furrowed, and his teeth ground against his lower lip.

"You've seen her?" Rhone tried not to sound overly interested. He desperately wanted word on his mother.

"No one's seen the Lady Darha." Ehron grabbed up the stones, shook them, and threw them carelessly across the lines. "Zorin keeps her in the old palace. Maybe she's dead, after all. All we hear is what Zorin and his partisans want us to hear. Some say she died years ago. Others claim so long as she lives, Zorin has no need to fear the return of his brother." He narrowed his eyes. "What is it you want, anyway? Whatever it is, you won't get it from me or from Storc." He stood. "We've business elsewhere."

The two men left. Klesc leaned back in the swinging chair and drained his flagon of ale. "That was fruitless."

18

Return of the Pyir

O ther than Leenah and Da-gore, the welcoming room at the *Lone Traveler* was deserted. Mini-ai and her daughters had already retired to their sleeping quarters, and the lamps had been extinguished. A sleepy, soft glow came from moonglasses in wooden frames scattered about. The sounds from outside had diminished to a few late-night revelers. For the most part, the *Lone Traveler Inn* was located in a quiet part of Marin-ee.

Leenah watched them enter and come over. "Well, do we sail for Atlan?" Her eyebrows lifted with a hint of impatience.

Rhone dropped into a chair and looked from her to Da-gore who sat stone faced, staring. "What's wrong with you?"

Da-gore pursed his lips and shook his head.

Leenah said, "For some, the decision comes hard."

He recalled his own rocky path to belief. It had taken the Creator's mighty hand intervening in his life more than once and finally reaching down, snatching him and Mishah from the jaws of Leviathan before he broke. And like Rhone, Klesc had seen enough to convince most men, but Rhone still didn't know where his friend stood.

"Well?" Leenah asked.

Rhone looked back at her. "Atlan is still in the future."

She frowned.

Klesc dropped heavily in one of the chairs. "No one wants to talk."

"Even with their tongues loosened?" Da-gore gave a wry smile as he had temporarily put aside the thoughts that held him.

"They are careful," Klesc said. "Too careful."

Rhone nodded. "What do they fear? What do they hide?"

"Zorin, I dare say." Leenah yawned again and stood. "I'll worry about this in the morning. I need to check in on little Gur. Evening peace."

"Evening peace," they mumbled as she padded quietly through a door that led to the rooms at the rear of the inn. Tonight they could afford two rooms, and each of the travelers had a bed. Da-gore had helped with the fee, paying his and Leenah's portion from a heavy purse he wore under his cloak. When he'd left Nod City, Rhone mused, he'd apparently done so well prepared.

Da-gore asked, "Is there some way I can help?"

Klesc's dark look held a challenge. "Why would you want to?"

He smiled. "I'm an opportunist."

Rhone leaned forward. "The opportunities we offer can get you killed."

He shrugged. "I'm a soldier. I've been behind the lines too long." He leaned forward, putting his face half a span from Rhone's. "Chasing you and those Lee-landers halfway across the continent reminded me why I became a soldier in the first place." His view shifted to Klesc. "You two haven't said much about what you're doing here in Marin-ee, but I'm not blind. You're both Makir, and I know you have your eyes set on Atlan. I have no idea what your purpose is, but this I do know: If the Creator smiles upon this quest, as he smiled upon your leading those people to the Cradleland, you will be successful."

Klesc snarled. "He's a spy."

"Maybe," Rhone said, remembering that the Messenger, Sari'el, promised he'd not be alone in this quest. First Klesc, then Leenah ... and now Da-gore? "We'll continue this conversation in the morning."

The inn's four rooms stood two abreast off a narrow, stone-floor hallway. The dark, cool walls were plastered in lime, and as they passed Leenah's room, Rhone listened, but there came no sound from behind the door. He stopped and stared at it.

Klesc gave him a questioning look.

"Didn't Leenah say she was going to look in on Gur?"

"She did," Da-gore said.

"She's not in there."

Da-gore looked skeptical. "How can you know that?"

"She chatters like a bird to that animal."

"And it to her," Klesc added.

Rhone's skin had begun to tingle. "Something's wrong."

Klesc silently drew his sword. "I feel it too." He cast about.

"Feel? Is this a Makir thing?" Da-gore frowned.

Rhone's sword hissed from its scabbard. He felt the energy radiating from all around them as he rapped upon the door. Leenah didn't answer. The hairs on his neck bristled. He quietly lifted the latch and pushed it open. The dark room set every nerve on fire.

A long-forgotten memory awakened. The Katrahs and Kimahs, those exercises that honed a child into a man and a man into a Makir, had become rusty with disuse, but skills once imparted still resided in his brain. Like a moonglass suddenly exposed, he knew what it was that had touched his subconscious....

The dark walls had begun to move all around him. In a blur of motion, the shapes of men separated from the blackness, and a double fist of swords suddenly caught the dim light from the hallway.

Rhone put the tip of his sword to the floor and crossed his arms over the hilt.

Soundlessly, it was taken from him. From the hallway came more men clad head to toe in black sutas—the battle garb of Makir Warriors. They shoved Da-gore and Klesc into the room, confiscated their weapons, took the Webbing knife Rhone carried in his boot top, and then forced them out the open window into a black courtyard behind the inn where Leenah stood between two more black-garbed men. They spoke to each other in signs that Rhone clearly understood.

The statre of the kal-ee-hon motioned three Makir to gather their belongings. Making no more noise than a shadow, the men were gone. Others bound their wrists.

Leenah glared at one of the men. "Only cowards and thieves hide behind masks."

"Hold your tongue woman, or I'll cut it off," the statre said softly.

"He means it," Rhone warned quietly.

Klesc gave a solemn nod.

A moment later the men returned, bearing all their gear. In the morning, Mistress Mini-ai would discover their rooms empty and their beds not slept in. She'd probably shake her head at the mystery and think no more of it. Rhone grimaced. To be in the hands of a kal-ee-hon of Makir Warriors was a dreadful thing to someone who didn't know their ways. Even Da-gore understood the futility of resistance.

Their heads were covered in black sacks and fastened tight about their throats. Then they were led away. They walked for most of an hour. The sound of the sea grew louder, and the ground beneath their feet became uneven and dipped sharply in places. To his right came the sound of breaking waves. An occasional sea spray drifted across on the light breeze. The party turned sharply to the left, and the sea sounds lessened. Now their footsteps gave a hollow echo as if in a cave or grotto. The ground began to climb, and here and there, the way became so narrow that they had to walk in single file. More than once a hand moved his head aside from some unseen object.

The air turned musty, tinged with the growing odor of smoke. Eventually a wavering light filtered past the weave of Rhone's head covering. The scraping of many feet sounded all around them as if men were gathering in a small room. They stopped; the knot was untied, and his hood was removed.

The glare of the fire momentarily blinded him as slowly his vision sharpened. Leenah, Klesc, and Da-gore were still hooded. The cave was inky beyond the cast of the firelight. The smoke of the fire spiraled straight up into the blackness. There had to be a breech to the outside somewhere up there. All around him stood men in black hoods—many more than had captured them.

They were all large men, and Rhone noted the bearing and confidence of Makir Warriors. A kal-ee-hon of Makir here in Marin-ee?

"Who sent you here?" one of the masked men asked.

He shifted his view, but the source of the voice was not apparent. "Who asks?"

A man stepped into the light. He held a long sword with the writhing serpent of the House of Ergne etched along the blade. "I speak."

"Are you Pyir?"

The man stiffened. "There is no Pyir. How did you find us out? Speak quickly and truly, and death will come easy."

"Death?" He fixed a wry smile to his face. "You said yourself there is no Pyir. Who lends his approval to executions?"

Another man said, "He understands our ways."

"An agent of Zorin would. A Makir with no honor, perhaps?"

"We don't honor Zorin," Klesc growled from under his sack.

The leader turned. "Uncover this one and let me look upon him."

Klesc's mask was yanked off, and he shook out his head and beard as a canic might shed the water from its fur. "Zorin the Usurper is as much our enemy as yours."

Another man spoke up. "I would expect spies for the High Councilor to say no less."

Rhone recognized the voice. "Ehron. I might have guessed it was you."

From among the triple fist of garbed men, Ehron stepped forward. "And because you know my face, you will have to die." His glance shifted toward Klesc. "And you."

Rhone strained at the ropes binding his wrists. "What makes you think we are allies of Zorin?"

Ehron advanced, placing himself within arm's reach. "You slipped when you called Zorin the Minck. Only people like you who support his villainous reign address him so."

"Truly? Much has changed since I left the land of my youth. A hundred years ago, the Minck was the accepted title for the villain who holds the high seat on the Council of Ten. Has a split grown so wide? Zorin can no longer hold Atlan by force alone? The time seems ripe for rebellion in the land of Hodin."

The first man said, "Which is why Zorin sends out his spies to search for the kal-ee-hons. And when they find us, we cut their throats and cast their bones into the sea."

"And what of the old Councilor's wife, Lady Darha?"

A murmuring uneasiness moved through the ranks of men.

"Again you ask!" Ehron growled. "Our love for Lady Darha is all that stands between Zorin and our blades. If not for her, we'd have seized a council seat years ago! But you already know this. It is you who must answer the questions. How did you discover us? Who is the traitor who told you?" Ehron's sword caught the yellow tongues of firelight as its cold steel rested lightly in the hollow of Rhone's throat.

Another voice spoke. "Such accusations are not called for, Ehron."

Leenah stiffened, her hooded head swinging toward the source of the voice.

"All they do is eat away at the kal-ee-hon. We cannot afford division within our ranks." His reasonableness seemed to calm the growing restlessness in the cave.

"It must be true, De—" he almost blurted out the name, then caught himself. "How else would he have singled me out, and why pry for information on Atlan and lie about being away? Even now, a boat of Zorin's warriors might well be skulking along the coastline, searching for this place. If he had accomplices and they followed us here, we may already have sealed our doom."

Ehron turned back and ripped the hood off his own head, his eyes narrowing dangerously. "My wife and my daughter were murdered when Zorin scoured Atlan, grinding out the seeds of rebellion. I swore then that I would kill him and everyone who stands with him."

The voice of reason spoke again. "We are Makir. We must deal with this in a proper manner, as we always have."

Ehron pressed the sword harder to Rhone's throat, his hand trembling, his Makir training suddenly submersed by the ardor of his loss.

Leenah took a sudden step forward. "Uncle Debne! Uncle Debne, I know that's your voice!"

The man who had tried to calm them stared, then stepped into the firelight, and pulled off her mask. "Leenah!"

"You know this woman?" demanded the statre in charge.

"She's my niece. She cannot be involved with Zorin. Her parents fled Atlan years ago!" He looked at her, then engulfed her in a huge hug. "I heard what happened to your mother ... my sister."

A murmur of confusion rippled through the men standing there.

Leenah looked at them. "I can explain everything. Oh, Uncle Debne." She threw her arms about him and buried her face in his wide shoulder.

Rhone saw the first hint of doubt come to Ehron's eyes.

The statre said, "Lower your sword, Ehron. We will hear the woman's words. Let us not be so quick to draw blood. It would be bad business to be known as rogues."

The Makir reluctantly put the tip of his weapon to the stony floor in a watch position. Someone removed Da-gore's hood and released him into the circle of men holding their weapons at watch.

"This one is not Hodinite."

The statre's eyes narrowed as he considered Rhone, then Klesc, and finally Leenah. "Tell your story."

Leenah glanced at Rhone. He nodded. She looked back at the statre. "We are here because Zorin has stolen the high seat of the Council of Ten. The very reason, I judge, that you've banded together, even though all of you are unbound and in exile."

The men stirred uncomfortably. The statre said, "You need not remind us of our shame."

Debne said, "We may have lost the true binding of the Katrahs and Kimahs, but we have retained our honor."

Rhone slumped a bit at that, but hadn't they all lost honor? And whose fault was that? His. Instead of here, leading his warriors, he'd tried to flee who he was, chasing spider silk and money. Had Klesc done any worse in the gaming rings putting on exhibitions for those curious enough to pay to see the legendary warriors from a distant land? And what of these men? They tried to retain honor by banding together here in Marin-ee. But without a Pyir to lead them, they were just so many children playing a game.

"And how did the four of you expect to liberate Atlan?" the statre pressed.

"We were hoping to find allies." She glanced at Rhone. "That is why Master Rhone asked the questions he did."

Ehron said, "Then why did he call Zorin 'the Minck'?"

"I told you. I've been away a very long time … too long. Customs change. I did not know."

A thickish man separated from the men and stood before the fire, staring through the holes in his mask.

The statre said, "Your interest in the Lady Darha convinced us you were working for Zorin. We thought you were testing us, to learn how much we knew of her. That is something Zorin would want to know in order to assess how secure he was."

Leenah said, "Master Rhone desires news of Lady Darha because she is his mother."

The cave went silent.

"That cannot be!" Ehron declared.

The thickish man took Rhone's chin in hand and turned it to the firelight. The firm grip began to tremble, and suddenly the man released him and drew the mask from his head. His was an old visage, one that stirred long-forgotten memories. It took Rhone a moment; then the name from his boyhood came to him.

"Larik!"

Larik's stern gray eyes stared at him, filling. "You've grown into your father's face, Pyir Rhone."

Every sword clattered to the floor. Ehron's eyes lowered, and he fell to his knees. Larik slashed the ropes that bound Rhone's wrists, then threw his arms about Rhone, and crushed the breath from him. He turned to the men there. "Pyir Rhone has returned. We are no longer unbound! Atlan will be ours again!"

"Larik, I'd heard you'd been hunted down and killed." Larik had been his father's—High Councilor Khore's—First Statre before Zorin's treachery and Khore's murder.

The old face beamed, the battle scars deepening with the huge smile. He dragged a thumb along one of the scars. "I got this killing the rogues who stood by Zorin! They tried to stop us, but I held them off and killed every one of them while our brothers loaded our wounded, our women, and our children onto a waiting boat." He grabbed Rhone by the shoulders and stared at him as if not believing his eyes. "I heard how you defeated the executioners in the Pit of Ramor."

"Zorin had been forced to follow the custom back then. He'd yet to consolidate his hold on the land."

"Yes, yes. He released you into exile and made Lady Darha prisoner, claiming he was protecting her from you. But we Makir knew that Zorin was only using her as a shield against you."

"What is the word on my mother, Larik?"

The old warrior's delight faded. "She lives yet, but as a prisoner, and well guarded. Zorin understands that the day Dirgen cuts her off from the living, Atlan will suddenly become too hot to hold. We love Lady Darha. Every man here would die for her. Yet we are helpless to free her. At the first signs of insurrection, Zorin will have her killed."

Rhone drew in a breath. "I must know everything that has happened. First, I will free my mother, then Atlan."

As if with a single voice, the men erupted in a roar of approval that shook the stone walls around him. The exiled Makir in Marin-ee had a Pyir, and Rhone had the beginnings of an army.

You will not be alone.

The Creator had given him a start, and with his help, he intended to make a finish!

19

Mysterious Rahab

*L*amech immersed himself in his research the next few days, poring over every chart in Sor-dak's library. Up until then, Rahab had merely been the fifth stone of fire locked in its heavenly circuit around the sun. He knew something of these heavenly stones, but not as much as he knew about the stars. The Creator's message to man had been laid out in the stars—the brightest star in any one gathering being the name star, the dimmer ones each adding their part to the story. But the stones of fire were different. Two circled the sun inside Earth's circuit. After Earth was Oric, the red stone, and then Rahab, the pale, milky stone. Beyond Rahab raced the gas giants, and beyond them were the lumps of frozen rock circling at the very limit of the stargazer's best starglasses.

For the last four days, however, it had been Rahab that held Lamech's attention. He tried to remember Mishah's dreams, but the details were sketchy. In her dreams she'd seen Rahab shattered, yet the pieces drawn back and held together in the Creator's hand. And Sevins had said that the Oracle's emissaries—those powerful beings from another world—were even now forging a crystal on Rahab. What sort of furnace could create such a thing? Could it be that the

fire in the heart of Rahab was the furnace Sevins meant? He scowled.
A shattered stone held together by the Creator's hand. He remembered this much from his wife's dreams. What sort of heat could be
generated if somehow the very elements of creation were being
used? The same fire that lights the sun, perhaps?

He turned back to his notes. One thing he'd discovered was that
Rahab's path was unstable. He'd plotted it over the course of seven
hundred years. The passage had grown wider with each passing year,
while at the same time the period of its circuit had grown shorter.
Rahab was speeding up. And although the observations of its poles
were not as well documented, Lamech had detected a gradual shifting in them as well.

Rahab was a doomed world, destined to rip itself apart!

The knock at his door jolted him from his thoughts. "Yes?"

Sor-dak entered. He didn't smile, and a worried scowl clouded
his usually bright green eyes. He peered down at the charts and
papers scattered about the floor and atop the wooden desk, and
behind the wild beard his lips rolled together, then puckered. His
bushy, gray eyebrows hitched together. "So, this is what's been keeping you holed up here like a squimit."

"Let me show you something, Master Sor-dak."

The old stargazer held his beard to his chest as he bent over and
studied the notes where Lamech's finger touched them. "Hum.
Interesting, but I don't see how this is any part of our work."

"Look at this." He showed him another sheet, with the orbit of
Rahab hastily sketched in the upper left-hand corner. "I've calculated
its velocity increase over the last seven hundred years. Projecting forward, at some point, gravity will rip Rahab apart." He didn't mention
Mishah's dream. If indeed the Creator was holding Rahab together,
then no amount of increase would be of any import. But if he wasn't
... or if he released it ...

Sor-dak seemed distracted. "It's all very interesting."

"I'd like permission to use your starglass tonight."

He absently tugged his fingers through the beard as he considered him. "Master Lamech, we have more urgent matters to discuss."

"Oh." He was suddenly aware that Sor-dak's distraction ran deeper than usual today. He unloaded a chair and pulled it around for the old man, taking one for himself. "What is it?"

"I've just gotten a resounding reprimand from the Lodath. It seems he and Captain El-ik decided that you are not being treated *prisonerly* enough here." Sor-dak made no attempt to hide his scorn. His beard ruffled with a frown, as he withdrew a paper from an oversized red pocket and handed it to Lamech.

Lamech read that he was to be kept confined to his room and the door guarded. That he no longer had free roam of the building, and that when his services were required, he was to be accompanied by Sor-dak himself. He looked up from the orders. "I'm still better off here than down in the Temple Prison or in En'tuboc's work quort."

Sor-dak's eyes widened with curiosity. "I thought you'd be upset. I was."

"I wish only to do the Creator's will, and if his will is to keep me under closer scrutiny by the Lodath's Guards, then so be it."

Sor-dak shook his head. "I admire your simple faith ... as misplaced as it is. I once had such faith." He sighed.

"What happened to it?" Lamech had never heard Sor-dak speak of anything but work.

"I took my training at the knees of a great stargazer. He was wise in the movement of the stars and the stones. I was innocent and naive. I'd accepted the words of my forebears who said they knew the firstborn; some even claimed to have known the Mother and Father." He gave a short laugh. "But of course all that is a clever fiction. It can't possibly be true."

"Why? What did your master tell you that crushed your faith?"

Sor-dak gave him a patronizing look. "You're an intelligent man,

Master Lamech. All you have to do is look to the stars for the answer."

He glanced at the ceiling, following the jerk of Sor-dak's hand. "I have, and they have strengthened my faith."

Sor-dak rolled his eyes. "Tell me how the Creator made this whole world a little over a thousand years ago. We've measured the distance to some of those stars, and we've measured how swiftly light flies. Surely this world of ours has been here tens of thousands of years. It must have been for the light from even some of the nearer stars to reach us."

Lamech felt the smile come to his face. "Oh, is that all?"

"You can explain it?"

"Not exactly. But if my Creator can speak a world into existence, then surely he can see to that challenge."

"That's a lame answer; one that doesn't satisfy a curious mind."

He thought a moment, then reached for a moonglass in a wooden case and opened the shutters. In the bright light of day, it appeared to be only a smooth, pale-green stone. "Have you not noticed how the light from a moonglass seems just a little dimmer than when you were a child?"

Sor-dak's face took a suspicious cast. "No. Well, now that you mention it ..."

Lamech drew the shutters and draped a blanket over the window. In the deep shadows, the moonglass gave off a soft glow, bathing the room in a greenish tint.

"Your point, Master Lamech?"

"Watch." He took a lump of magnetized rock from a shelf. "I really only noticed this when Mishah and I first arrived here in Nod City. We were on the balcony of an inn, watching the Dancing Lights, noticing that they seemed to have faded."

Sor-dak screwed up his lips. "I thought it was just the dimming of an old man's memories."

"I did too, at first. But then I began to think through the problem. What causes the Dancing Lights?"

"The mystical elements of the sun impelled into the magnetic veil."

"Exactly. And what makes the moonglass glow?"

He huffed. "Every child knows that. The magnetic veil energizing the life force within the stone."

Lamech smiled, surprised how easily he had led Sor-dak down the path he wanted him to go. "And what do the two have in common?"

"The magnetic veil, of course," he snapped, growing irritated.

As Lamech brought the rock near to the moonglass, it brightened. "Is this how you remember it from your childhood?"

Sor-dak stared.

Lamech said, "It's how I remember it. Master Sor-dak, I believe the magnetic veil is failing. Now I ask you, if the magnetic veil is failing, could not the speed of light be failing also? Maybe in the beginning it traveled in a day what it now takes a year to travel."

Sor-dak's eyes flashed from the moonglass. "No. Impossible. It goes against all our understanding."

Lamech set the glass aside and removed the covering from the window. "How long have we been able to measure the speed of light?"

"Three hundred years, give or take a few. Since the first reliable suntracers were constructed."

"So there must be records available to us?"

Sor-dak's beard slid up and down his chest with the nod.

"I wonder what one would discover if he were to study those measurements?"

Sor-dak stood with a jolt. "I'll hear no more of this." He strode toward the door and wheeled back. "What you suggest is scientific heresy!"

"Perhaps, but isn't science about finding truth? Or is it in fact only a thin disguise for just another philosophy—the Oracle's philosophy?"

Sor-dak's face hardened, and he reached for the door.

"What about the starglasses, Master Sor-dak?"

He expelled a sharp breath. "I'll come by tonight for you." He glanced at the paper still in his hand, shoved it into his pocket, and left.

❧

Although the heavy-lifting platform cast a bright orangish light across the night sky, the area Lamech was interested in was out of the direct glare.

"Ready," Sor-dak said.

Lamech climbed onto the smooth saddle slung beneath the big instrument. "You may begin."

With a small grunt, Sor-dak shoved a tall lever and set the whirring gears of the suntracer in motion. The glass swung to its position, halted, and would remain pointed in the same direction so long as the suntracer was running. Lamech put his eye to the bronze lens and Rahab, a bright, milky point of light beyond the path of the red orb of Oric, came into clear focus.

As he gazed upon the stone, glowing in the light of its distant star, the sounds of the nearby construction and the smell of behemoths all slipped from his consciousness as the vast distance between him and Rahab diminished to nothingness. Within the unsearchable workings of his brain, Lamech was transported to that far world.

Slowly, a curious feature emerged from the pale glow. "The Vale of Merinse." He'd hoped he would be able to see it tonight in a sky less than perfect for viewing.

"Good. It is often hard to see." Sor-dak's words intruded upon his fancy and reminded him where he really was.

He willed himself back to Rahab. A normally cloudy planet, tonight its skies were clear. He nudged the focusing wheel, and the Vale crisped up. He reviewed the theories. Some thought the Vale was a great canyon that encircled the stone. Others declared that it must be a river, wider than the Hiddekel, Euphrates, Pison, and Ghion combined. He tried to imagine how those four rivers must appear in the Cradleland....

Immediately the planet dimmed as his wife's image filled his thoughts. Unexpected tears swelled his eyes. He blinked them away and coaxed Mishah back into a special nook of his brain where he kept her safe.

Some thought the Vale was a ridge of volcanoes, and it was from these that Rahab's clouds were formed. There was some credence to that theory. But now, as he considered the great, snaking feature, a new possibility blossomed—one that Mishah's dreams had given him. Could the Vale of Merinse be the place where Rahab had been shattered? Could it be the scar of that violent upheaval, split clear through, held together now only by the Creator's will? The notion was too incredible, and he laughed inwardly. Who would believe such a tale? He could already hear Sor-dak's learned objections—and they'd be correct! It was only if you were willing to allow the Creator's hand in the matter, his ability to twist the rules of his own creation to do his bidding, that such a theory made any sense.

Lamech gave the saddle over to Sor-dak who was anxious for a clear view of the Vale. "Don't often have the opportunity to see it so sharply," the old stargazer mumbled excitedly, adjusting the focus to his eyes.

After they had finished for the night, Sor-dak erected the sturdy, shiverthorn tent over the machinery to protect it. Lamech put his back to the glow of the heavy-lifting platform. The stars appeared hazy. He'd have to be far away from Nod City for a really clear view. In spite of that, the comforting gathering of stars was there—the Creator's message for man, His promise of a coming Redeemer who will crush the serpent's head and buy back mankind for himself.

Sor-dak stepped quietly to his side and waved an arm toward the night sky. "I hear you have tales about all this beyond your curious theories on the speed of light?" he chuckled. "Some say you see patterns in the stars that tell a story."

He'd said it casually, but Lamech detected something deeper. Was Sor-dak setting him up? That made no sense.

"Patterns in stars?" He allowed a small smile and tried to sound equally casual. "Do you gaze up there and see nothing, Master Sor-dak?"

Sor-dak gave an amused snort. "If I let my imagination run, I can perhaps claim those stars look like a river across the sky. Or that band—a fish, or those three—a warrior's belt. I see no more than that."

"Yet you see Oarion."

"I see only what the Oracle expects me to see, and I see nothing at all. They are stars, and if four or five or twenty of them form some slight resemblance to a fish, so be it."

"And you are exactly right, Master Sor-dak."

The stargazer narrowed his view suspiciously. "I know you well enough to suspect a trap, Master Lamech."

Sor-dak wouldn't be tricked as easily this time. "No trap."

"Then you don't see pictures in the stars?"

"I see them because, like you and the Oracle telling you what to see, I've been told. You're right; there are no pictures in the stars." He smiled. "In the usual sense of the word."

"Aha! I knew you'd spring that on me."

"Hear me out. The stars all have names; the Creator has personally named each one."

"Impossible. Too many!"

"Nonetheless, it's true. And the names have meanings. The Creator has simply grouped stars together to tell his story. Take Oarion for instance. The name the Creator has given those stars is Ha-ga-t. It means 'This is he who triumphs.' The brightest star is in his right shoulder. The Creator named it Bet-el-euz, and it means 'The coming of the branch.' The next in brightness is in the foot of our imaginary image. Its name is—"

"Ri-go," Sor-dak huffed. "I know the names of the stars!"

"But do you know the meanings of the names?"

His bushy eyebrows crawled together. "I suppose you do?"

"Ri-go—the foot that crushes. See how appropriate the meaning is to its location? That's the hook that helps us remember the story."

Sor-dak flung his hands in resignation. "I can see you're warming to this and nothing will stop you now."

In spite of Sor-dak's casual attitude, Lamech detected a hunger within him for what he had to say. "The next brightest star is in the left shoulder. Bel-at-ix means 'Quickly coming.'"

"Names. Words. What does it all mean?"

"You read the story according to the brightness of each star. Take for instance the gathering of Oarion. When you know the meaning of the names, it says, 'The Creator is coming again ... he will come swiftly ... and when he does, he will crush his enemy underfoot.' The enemy is the lying serpent who's plagued man from the beginning. It's confirmation of the first prophecy spoken to our Mother and Father in the Cradleland. In the day that this all unfolds, the serpent will bruise the Creator's heel, but the Creator will crush the serpent's head." Lamech paused at Sor-dak's blank look. "Don't you see?"

He didn't speak right away. "The meaning of the names is really the story. The stars ... they're only place markers to help you put the meanings together?"

"Exactly. It's the way the Creator communicates with his people today. It is the witness of his future promises. In days to come, he may choose other ways to speak to his people. I have no special knowledge of that. But I do know that he has promised not to leave us without a witness."

Sor-dak's thick eyebrows formed a thoughtful, bushy "V."

Had his words touched Sor-dak? Or was everyone in Nod City immune to the truth?

Sor-dak huffed. "We'll talk on this matter later."

20

Sor-dak's Request

*L*amech's footsteps snapped hollowly upon the polished stone floor as he hurried down the hallway. At a door, he adjusted the bundle of scrolls under his left arm, then knocked.

"Come in."

At the far end of a huge room crammed with tables, shelves, and books was Sor-dak, dressed in his faded scarlet robe. He stood at a large table, hunched over something, surrounded with scrolls and books rising in teetering piles shoved out to the corners of the table to make room. A small bronze machine, half buried beneath a sheath of papers, clicked quietly. At his left elbow, a flame sputtered from a sooty copper brazier. Above the table hung a slab of moonglass.

As Lamech crossed to the white-haired man, he noted that it was a scroll upon which Sor-dak was marking, spread out and weighted at the corners with a book, a rock, a wedge of faceted crystal, and a bunch of carrots.

Without looking up, Sor-dak said, "Sit, Master Lamech."

He glanced around at six chairs, each one occupied with papers, boxes, and glittering brass devices for measuring angles and decided to remain standing. "You sent for me, Master Sor-dak?"

"I did. Thank you for coming so promptly." He still hadn't looked up. Aligning a straightedge of black ironwood, he scribed a thin green line, returned the pen to the green ink bottle without taking his eyes off his work, and plucked up a blue one. He shook it twice, then drew a curved line that intersected points on the chart and bisected the green line. "I've been giving what you said careful thought."

Lamech searched his memory but couldn't recall what Sor-dak was referring to. "You have?"

"Yes, yes." He straightened up and spied the scrolls under Lamech's arm. A question came to his face.

"I brought them for you to approve."

"My approval?"

"The Temple alignment uncertainties. I thought you'd called me here to check on the progress." He had been two weeks wading through Sor-dak's calculations for his latest geometric construct.

Sor-dak sighed and looked at him. "My dear Lamech, I very much fear I'm underutilizing your talents, having you checking columns of numbers like a counting clerk."

"It is why you rescued me from the executioner's stand."

A small smile lifted Sor-dak's mouth. "Is it? Look at this, Master Lamech."

He cast about for a place to deposit his scrolls and finally set them on the floor.

Sor-dak put a finger on the paper and traced the green line. "I searched back three hundred years for every measurement made of the speed of light. You were correct! It is decreasing!"

Lamech studied the figures. "Can it really be? What about errors in the measurements?"

"There is always a margin of error. I've accounted for it. The decline is real!"

Lamech marshaled his thoughts. It had only been a guess on his part, but Sor-dak had dug out the numbers and verified it. "What does it mean?"

"It means our whole understanding of the world has been in error." The chief stargazer stared at him. "It means you and I need to talk." He reached up and touched the moonglass suspended over the table. Lamech hadn't noticed until then, but the light that shone from it seemed brighter than the last time he'd stood here. "See, I've encircled it with a magnet."

Sor-dak had put to practical use the demonstration Lamech showed him that day in his quarters. A rim of iron, wound tightly with thin strands of copper, had been fashioned around the edge of the moonglass. From the iron, copper strands stretched overhead to glass beads on the wall, then ran down the wall, and disappeared through a hole in the stone floor. Lamech had seen the huge clay jars of chemicals in the foundation room far beneath Sor-dak's building. Within those jars, Sor-dak brewed a force both wonderful and dangerous. Lamech understood only that it was somehow akin to the magnetic veil surrounding the entire earth, which gave moonglasses their glow and energized the Dancing Lights.

Sor-dak took him by the arm and led him to a window overlooking the Temple construction. From here the vastness of the complex was evident. Beyond the walls, the distant forest was being swept aside by dozens of work quorts to make room for the final footprint of the Temple complex. The Temple itself was only one small part of a vast network that, in another hundred years from now, would sprawl across the land in the shape of an immense pentagram. Lamech felt a scowl develop. He had cleared some of that forest himself when he'd first entered the prison, and since then the forest had retreated considerably.

"Don't think I snatched you from the executioner's clutches because I thought you clever with numbers."

"I don't," Lamech replied with a bit of smugness that he always had a hard time suppressing whenever he thought of how the Creator worked in his life.

Sor-dak's gray eyebrows hitched up wonderingly. "You don't?"

"I was saved by my Creator." He tried not to sound ungrateful. "You were the method my Creator chose to use, and for that I am pleased."

"I'm used by him?"

"He uses whom he wills."

Sor-dak pulled at his tangled beard and gave a series of quick puffs.

"If not my usefulness with numbers and my understanding of the heavens, what did you perceive my usefulness would be, Master Sor-dak?"

"Hum?"

He had caught the stargazer out of some thought.

Sor-dak drew his lips into a tight "O" and peered back out the window. "I want to learn more about this ... this story in the stars." He looked back at him with earnest eyes. "The *Way* that you speak of."

For the briefest of moments Lamech was at a loss for words. "Why?"

Sor-dak gave him a sudden, impatient scowl. "I don't know why." He drew in a sharp breath. "No, that's not entirely true." He paused, organizing his thoughts. "I've heard of it before ... many years ago. I've always thought it superstitious nonsense, but the thing stayed with me. I'd almost forgotten it since coming here to work on that thing." His eyes cocked toward the Temple. "And then I began hearing it again, in whispers that hushed whenever I came near. I questioned one of the prisoners. He named you. When I heard that you'd been taken to stand before the Disciplinary Council—" Sor-dak's eyes shot back to him "—I made a point of being in the hall. Remember?"

"You carried a star chart and tested me with questions."

Sor-dak nodded. "Something about you piqued my curiosity, and I was determined to learn more." He smiled. "Why else would I have made a fool of myself in front of all those people at your execution?" His face crinkled with a boyish mischievousness. "I purposefully incorporated a glaring precessional error in my figures. I have watched you all these months—I had to be certain."

"Certain?" His heart quickened. Was this yet another door opening?

"That your faith and your knowledge were genuine."

"And your conclusion, Master Sor-dak?"

"I am certain you are both honorable and brilliant. I want to learn about this thing you claim your Creator has written across the night sky. I want to hear all of it."

His head momentarily swam, feeling the Creator orchestrating events in a way he never would have guessed. "And so you shall, Master Sor-dak." He took a breath to clear his brain, then settled a solemn look upon his face. "But I must warn you, holding such knowledge here, in this place, can be dangerous. It might very well be the undoing of a man even as powerful as yourself."

"You speak of Sol-Ra-Luce?" Sor-dak gave a short, mirthless laugh. "I do not fear the great Lodath of the Oracle."

"It is not the Lodath I speak of. Sol-Ra-Luce is only a puppet. The real threat comes from the Dark Deceiver himself, the one who pulls the puppet's strings."

21

Noah and the Gardener

*S*even years later ...

"Mother, why are you smiling?" Noah's small strong fingers tightened within Mishah's hand, and his brown eyes widened beneath the shock of black hair that tumbled across his forehead. He definitely had Lamech's nose.

"I dreamt of your father again last night." They were following a path to the lake. Suddenly a tunnel of light developed before them. These marvels of the Garden seemed to appear at random, and as she and Noah stepped into it, its colors brightened. She called them mood tunnels, a sort of visual gauge of how you truly felt. She was sure the Creator had constructed them for just that purpose.

His face suddenly brightened. "Is he coming soon?"

Mishah smiled. Here was a child who thought it not the least amazing that his mother's dreams were more than visions within her brain, but real events. "I don't know. Your father has a few things he must finish."

Noah's glow dimmed, and his disappointment tugged at her

heart. They emerged from the tunnel of light and stood upon the long, sandy beach of a small, sparkling lake. He cast off his robe and scampered down the golden beach, flinging himself into the clear water. He disappeared for a moment, then surfaced, clutching a shell that glinted like opals in the sunlight. "Come in, Mother. The water's warm."

How her little man was growing up. She marveled that already seven years had passed since she'd come to the Garden. "Not now, dear. You have fun. I'll wait in the shade."

He laughed and threw his arms about two shiny blue fish that had came beside him. With a whoop of delight, he skimmed through the water, holding tight to his two new friends.

She let a contented smile touch her lips as she sat upon a pink marble bench beneath spreading branches bursting with pink and purple blossoms. *If only Lamech could see you now.* A pang squeezed at her heart, and her smile faltered a bit, but she kept the brave face, watching her son frolic with the fish.

"They love him," the Gardener said, sitting beside her.

She gave a small gasp of surprise. Would she ever get used to his sudden appearances?

"It's his birthday today," the Gardener said.

She smiled. "He's grown so tall in seven years."

"I've brought him a present."

She hadn't noticed until just that moment the long boat that the Gardener held upon his lap.

"Come." He took her hand, and they walked down to the beach.

Upon seeing them there, Noah spoke to his friends, and they swam him back toward shore.

"I love swimming." He stood waist deep, the blue fish beside him, their heads lifted from the water.

"I made the lake to be enjoyed." The Gardener smiled. "I made it just for you."

"For me?"

The Gardener nodded. "And I've made something else for you."

"What is it?" Noah's eyes widened with expectation.

The Gardener held out the boat. "You can play with it while you swim." He gave Mishah a smile, and her heart filled with warmth, her cares evaporating like the morning mist that watered the Creator's Garden.

Still holding her hand, the Gardener started toward Noah. The water parted before them, and the sandy bottom was powdery dry beneath Mishah's toes. The expanding pathway raced ahead, split into two, arched out, and encircled Noah, leaving the laughing child standing waste deep in a sparkling pool, now completely isolated from the rest of the lake. Mishah could clearly see the blue fish swimming round and round and darting between Noah's legs.

Noah reached out. The Gardener stretched across the pool and put the long boat into his hands. "Happy birthday, Noah."

Noah examined it with a careful eye, which was his nature. More and more, Mishah was seeing Lamech in him. He turned it over and looked questioningly. "There's a hole in the bottom."

"Indeed, there is."

"Won't it sink?"

"Put it in the water and see."

Noah set it upon the shimmering surface. "It doesn't sink."

"Splash and try to overturn it."

Noah lunged up and down, and the long boat rode the waves with ease. He smiled up at the Gardener. "Why doesn't it turn over?"

"Because its length and width are just right. And it doesn't matter if you build a boat one span long or one hundred spans long. As long as the length and width are correct, it won't overturn."

The Gardener never missed an opportunity to teach a lesson, but she wondered about this one.

Noah pressed down on the boat until the water nearly spilled over the roof, which had a long raised window section along the center of it. He let go and the boat popped up. He laughed again. "But what about the hole in the bottom?"

The Gardener only smiled. "That is a puzzle I want you to figure out. When your father returns, he can help you."

The longing squeezed its way back into Mishah's chest, but the gentle pressure of the Gardener's hand upon her arm eased the pain.

"Is my father coming back soon?"

"Soon," he said, smiling at Mishah.

She hoped that would indeed be true, but over the years she'd come to learn that the Gardener seemed to reckon time differently than she.

✿

The ruins of Imo-suk crouched over the Great Sea on a rocky perch. The once mighty fortress had been built in the days of Imo, when he and the Sons of Cain had tried to wrest Hodin from Atlan. Upon its ancient walls, Leenah stood by Rhone's side, smelling the tangy sea breeze, feeling its warm fingers stroke her cheek and fondle her hair as a new day emerged from the gray waters to the east. On Rhone's left stood First Statre Larik. Together, they oversaw the exercises below.

"Today is my birthday," Rhone said quietly, looking out over the courtyard where a hundred Makir Warriors moved through their routines. The Katrahs and Kimahs had once again become a daily part of their lives.

"Yes." She pulled her eyes off the expanse of water where, just beyond the horizon—just out of her reach—lay Atlan. Seven years ago today, Rhone had been touched by the Gardener, and new life had filled his dead corpse. He spoke of it even when he didn't realize it—little remarks that to a stranger's ear would pass by unnoticed.

Seven years. How much longer would he wait? It had been almost five years since coming to Marin-ee. He'd raised his army and acquired a fleet of ships that he'd hidden up and down the coast. He'd sent spies into the land. Their cause had been blessed by the Creator. Many exiled Atlanders had built successful businesses in Marin-ee, and they were willing to give it all for a chance to take back their homeland. From the start, money never seemed to be an issue.

Rhone drew in a sudden breath as if taking in the sea breeze, but it wasn't the sea breeze he was sensing. "Can you feel it? Feel the energy flowing among them?" His eyes remained riveted upon the Makir below, a small smile stretching his lips.

She watched how he studied them as they moved through their daily rituals, how he seemed to move with them. "No, I don't feel it, Rhone."

She wished she could sense what he sensed. He'd often told her how, when the Makir went into battle, they drew energy from each other in some mysterious way. *The binding.* She watched the men going about their exercises, moving together as if under the control of a single mind. Why couldn't she feel it? His warriors seemed able to. She scowled. This had become his life, and where did she fit into it? A corner of her mouth twitched. There were yet secrets hidden inside Rhone. How she wished she could find the key to open him up.

She willed her impatience back to its dark corner. True, there were secrets even she didn't know, but that was for the best. What she didn't know, she couldn't accidentally reveal. He had a plan, and he was steadily working toward accomplishing it. His spies had entrenched themselves in Zorin's army, even in his personal guards, and in spite of her impatience, she understood his need for carefulness. Her Uncle Debne was abroad, searching out and regathering the displaced Makir, while her Uncle Sirt, who had never left Atlan, was quietly moving key people into place.

"Where's Gur?" Rhone scanned the sky.

"I don't know." She'd seen him earlier roosting upon the garrison's crumbling watchtower.

"He's with his flop," Larik said, pointing to seven scarlet dragons soaring against the faintly pinkish sky.

Even at this distance, she sensed the dragon's contentedness. He'd grown strong and powerful, as comfortable among his own kind as he was at her or Rhone's side. She'd raised him well.

Her thoughts went back to the Garden, the Cradleland of mankind. That wondrous place that had momentarily expanded her senses and had first made her aware of the voices of animals and plants. Watching the distant dragons loom larger, she was still amazed that a creature like a scarlet dragon was able to understand her at all. She could touch his thoughts but still didn't know how much of her thoughts he was aware of. Being a sensitive was confusing at times. The more she honed her abilities, the more she realized how different the workings of a dragon's brain were from hers.

Rhone's head came up and cocked to one side, and he turned and peered down a deserted passage between two crumbling stone walls. She wondered what had caught his attention, then distantly came the sound of hurried footsteps. In a few moments, Ka-Larik, Larik's son, came sprinting into view, leaping the steps three at a time.

"Pyir Rhone." He gasped, drawing himself straighter. "The boathouse has been penetrated."

Rhone's dark eyebrows dipped above his suddenly concerned eyes, and he shot a glance at Larik. The old warrior's battle-scarred face took on a sudden, worried look.

Ka-Larik said, "Klesc is questioning him now."

"Stay here with the men, Larik."

Rhone, Leenah, and Ka-Larik jogged down the stone steps and hurried to the huge stone building that sat near the water's edge, a quarter league north of Imo-suk. A canal ran from the building to the shores of the Great Sea, and as they drew nearer, Leenah could see a contingent of Makir guards standing outside the boathouse, some peering into the long, narrow waterway to the sea.

They halted before a door ten spans by five, and a hopeful spark lit inside her.

"Wait here."

So, she wasn't going to get a glimpse of the secret inside of the boathouse after all. She'd heard Rhone speak of the gormerin, but had never seen the secret project he'd been working on for years.

He read the disappointment in her face. "It's better if you return to the compound."

Imo-suk, six leagues from Marin-ee and perched on a rocky cliff overlooking the Great Sea, had become home to her and over two hundred Makir Warriors. Some had wives, some even had families. It wasn't as if she was alone … except that she *was* alone.

Rhone could keep his secrets secure in Imo-suk. Once in a while a boat from somewhere would moor offshore, and the occasional glint of a spyglass from its deck would reveal its true nature. But few strangers ever came near the old garrison. There were too many Makir who blended in too perfectly with the rocky landscape. That was one of the things they did best … blending in … like the night of her and Rhone's capture.

She frowned. The real concern wasn't the infrequent boats, but the skybarges that drifted westward over the sea from Atlan. Rhone worried that Zorin's curiosity had been aroused. Rhone made certain the Katrahs and Kimahs were not observed, and for all Zorin knew, they were merely a cult of disgruntled expatriates, struggling to keep the last flickering flame of an old way of life from being snuffed out.

Until now. *A spy?* A double fist of questions flashed through Leenah's brain, but she'd have to wait for the answers.

She glanced at the door, then to Rhone, and nodded. There was no point in arguing. When the time was right, she'd know this secret, just as she was determined to know the deeper secrets of his heart.

Rhone ordered one of the warriors to escort her to the compound.

"I know my way back."

22

The Spy

She strode away, tall and strong, her shoulders thrown back and her head held high, her golden hair bound up in leather lacing that hung down her back. Leenah had a warrior's heart, and he was treating her like an outsider. *Why?* Rhone wondered. He almost called her back but stopped himself. What lay inside was too important to risk news of it leaking out.

His face hardened. News must have already leaked. At least they had captured the spy. Had there been others? How much did Zorin know? Concern forced thoughts of Leenah into the background as he hauled open the heavy door and stepped into a tall, wide hallway.

Their footsteps rang upon the stone pavers and echoed against the stark walls, and then suddenly a huge room opened before them, its roof soaring upward. In the center of the room, wooden scaffolds arched up over an iron boat in dry-dock. He called it a *gormerin.* Perhaps he should have named it something fiercer than the huge carrier fish that had snatched him and Mishah from the deadly jaws of Leviathan and then transported them in safety to the shores of Eve's Weep. He refused to call it Leviathan. Memories of that encounter were too terrifying. No, gormerin was a good name. It fit. The idea of building a gormerin—a boat that could travel underwater—had been forming in Rhone's brain ever since that day.

The rumble of turning wheels and the muffled thumping of a cycler competed with the clanging of the riveters' hammers. In the corner, sparks flew from the forges as a small army of skilled smiths battered unwilling sheets of white-hot iron into useful shapes. Overhead, the open roof, masked with teris palm leaves, filled the room with a diffused light.

"This way, Pyir Rhone." Ka-Larik marched them toward a door that opened into the room where, three years earlier, Rhone and a bevy of builders had pored over drawings and plans.

"Was he alone?" Rhone asked.

"It appears so, Pyir Rhone," Ka-Larik said.

For a moment the culprit's face was hidden by three of Rhone's warriors. Klesc was among them, holding the man upright by a fistful of strange straps buckled over his shoulders and around his waist. Rhone inclined his head toward the door. "Close it."

He was a very young man, maybe forty years old, and in some ways reminded him of another young man. Bar'ack's once naive and curious face swam before his mind's eye, only to be replaced by the snarling beast he had become—his body now home to the spirits of the three dead giants.

Why did Zorin send children? The boyish face looked full at him. One eye had already swollen shut. His split lip wore a fragile brown crust of dried blood. He was barechested except for the odd harness made of heavy shiverthorn fabric. A red welt graced his shoulder and another his ribs, vaguely the shape of a knuckled fist. The bruises would be bright purple come morning. The young man held a rag to his tongue and looked like a practice dummy for the Katrahs and Kimahs. His pitiful visage and youthful face couldn't hide the anger and fear in his gray eyes.

When he spied Rhone, his expression went wide. Rhone could guess why; the resemblance between himself and Zorin was often startling. "What's your name?"

The youth glared at him.

"Your name!"

"Ooarun," he mumbled past the cloth in his mouth.

"Lorun?"

He nodded.

Rhone glanced at Klesc. "Where did you find him?"

"Inside the gormerin."

"Inside?" He looked back at the youth. Anyone who could sneak past his Makir had to be very good … or very desperate. Somehow, he guessed it might be the latter.

"How did you get past my men?"

"Wam."

Rhone tossed a questioning glance to Klesc.

"Apparently from the sea. Underwater. The net under the sea doors was cut. We found this resting on the bottom near the dry-dock's water doors." Klesc picked up a sealed iron tube with a pair of cork floats on either side. A long hose ending in a ring of cork came off one end, and a lever and second, shorter, flared piece of rubber tubing off the other end.

"What is this device?" He worked the lever, listening to the hiss of air being sucked into one end and out the other. "Clever. Your design?"

Lorun remained silent, his eyes following him as he crossed the room to a narrow stone slit in the wall. Rhone stopped and peered out at the iron boat. "What were you looking for?" He really didn't expect an answer and wasn't disappointed. "Who sent you?"

More silence.

"He was carrying these." Klesc held a waxed shiverthorn pouch with a watertight, rolled seal.

Rhone opened the pouch and extracted five sheets of heavy paper, each with a sketch and notes: the air-intake mechanism; the cycler that propelled the tail fin; the air bladders that would be deflated to allow seawater into the iron fish and sink it beneath the sea, and then reinflated to force out the water and bring the iron gormerin back to the surface. A scowl crossed Rhone's face as he studied the final sheet and the detailed sketch of the gormerin's saw-tooth blade running from its long, pointed snout, up across its back, and rearward over the tail.

"With those drawings, Zorin might construct a fleet of his own gormerins," Klesc said.

"With these, he'd know how to build boats to withstand an attack." Rhone drew in a breath and looked back at Lorun. He didn't enjoy using hard methods, but he needed answers! Too much was at stake here not to use every means to get the information out of the young man.

"Once more. Who sent you?"

Lorun had been staring at Ka-Larik. His answer to Rhone was a glare of defiance.

"Klesc."

The big man swung a fist. Lorun buckled, breath exploding from his chest, his tongue gushing blood again. Klesc yanked him erect.

Rhone leaned near the battered face. "Have you ever watched men die at the hands of Makir executioners?"

Lorun's lungs heaved, drawing in a painful breath. His rounding eyes told Rhone he had at least heard the stories of such things.

Once, long ago, violence had been a way of life to him—to every Makir. It still was to men like Klesc and the other warriors who did not know the Creator. But for him, the old ways, although still useful, had become more and more difficult to use. Had this new faith made him weak? What sort of ruler could he be if seeing his enemies suffer brought on an ache in the very heart of his being? "Will you talk?"

The young man put the cloth back to his tongue. "Ah caunt auk."

"Can't or won't?"

His eyes had lost their defiance as a flush of helplessness filled his face. There was something more here staying Lorun's words than a gashed tongue and a loyalty to Zorin.

"I'll make him talk." A dagger flashed in Klesc's hand. "When I'm done with him, he'll plead for death."

Rhone caught Klesc's wink. "Don't kill him right away."

"I'll leave enough of him to get what we want. I'll start by whittling away at his ears."

"No. Ah … ah … caunt. 'Ell kol em if ah auk."

Rhone stopped Klesc's hand. "Kill who?"

"My 'ife, my 'oy."

"Your wife and son?"

He nodded quickly.

"And if you don't talk," Klesc rumbled, "you'll end up a pile of bloody parts on the floor."

Lorun shrank from him. A Makir caught him by the shoulders and shoved him back.

Rhone held the papers under his nose. "Who sent you to make these? Zorin? It has to be. I saw it in your face when you first laid eyes on me. For a moment you weren't sure I wasn't my brother, were you?"

Lorun nodded.

"How much does Zorin know about this?" He swept the handful of papers toward the wall where beyond sat the gormerin in its dry-dock.

"All I know es, 'e knows son'thing goin' on 'ere."

Klesc put the knife to Lorun's chin. "Who's the spy who told him?"

Lorun shook his head.

"He doesn't know," Ka-Larik said. "Zorin wouldn't send someone who had that knowledge. He knows any man can be made to talk."

"No Makir could be forced to talk," Klesc said.

Rhone nodded. "But this one is no Makir."

"Why didn't Zorin send one?" Klesc cast a demanding look at Lorun, who shrank back again.

"Thew aw few left who aw loyal to Zowin," he said thickly.

Rhone dragged the toe of his boot through the pool of blood on the paving stones. "Then how does he hold onto the land?"

"By taw-wa."

Terror was always Zorin's way. Even as a child, Rhone had seen the seeds of it in his twin brother. "How large is his army?" Rhone already had a good idea from his own spies.

Lorun shook his head.

"How many Makir?"

He shook his head again. "No Makir."

Rhone signaled the two warriors guarding the door.

"Take him out of here. When he's better able to talk, we'll get more out of him." But would they? Or had Zorin indeed sent someone who knew no more than he needed to?

After they had gone, Rhone, Klesc, and the two remaining warriors went to the sea channel inside the building. The closed sea doors came down to the water's surface, and the morning sunlight slanting through the water beneath them showed the thick rope net that hung to the bottom of the canal. The hole Lorun had cut in it was obvious.

Rhone looked across the boathouse to where the top of the gormerin rose above a heavy, watertight door. "He was clever to have gotten this far."

Mortok, a red-haired Makir with a flushed, battle-scarred face, peered at the water as a slender, iridescent fish slithered through the netting into the shadows. "Who could have guessed he'd come from the sea, underwater, using that breathing device?"

How much information did Zorin already possess? "He must have entered under the cover of night and have been inside a long time to make such detailed sketches."

Ka-Larik said, "If Zorin knows what we are up to, our very existence is threatened."

Klesc frowned. "I'll double the guards. Now that his suspicions are aroused, he's sure to send more spies."

Ka-Larik's eyebrows came together in a scowl. "We may have a traitor among us, Pyir Rhone."

"Who?"

Ka-Larik shrugged. "Someone with something to gain?"

Rhone frowned. "If you have any suspicions, speak them now, Ka-Larik."

"No Makir would trade secrets with Zorin, no matter what the gain," Klesc growled.

"There are none among us but loyal Hodinites, the Makir, and their wives and children." Rhone considered that a moment. Could one of the non-Hodinite women be a traitor?

"That's not exactly true," Klesc said, a rumbling reluctance in his voice.

Rhone stared at him. Klesc was right. There was another. A knot twisted in his gut. There was one they'd taken in after years of reluctance who was not Makir or Hodinite. The knot bound up tighter. But he'd been so careful, so sure of the man! Could he have been so mistaken? "What would Da-gore have to gain?"

"What he lost," Klesc said solemnly. "An army of his own to command. Zorin will give him that, if only until his usefulness is past."

Had it been an act all along? Even his abandonment of the Oracle and his professed belief in the Creator? Rhone shook his head. No, he couldn't believe they'd been so cleverly fooled!

"What makes you think this, Klesc?"

The big man hesitated. "Something someone said."

"Who?"

Klesc briefly glanced at Ka-Larik, then back. "First Statre Larik."

23

The Cloth Merchant

Working in unison, the sixteen oarsmen pulled swiftly toward the rugged jut of land rising from the sea. With each rotation, the bow beneath Da-gore's boots lifted then fell back with a slap of the waves breaking across it.

He gripped a taut rope strung to the tall mast and glanced up at the basket perched near the top of it that held three half-naked lookouts with proj-lances. So far the crossing had been uneventful. The humid air hung heavy and still; the boat's sails had remained furled the whole trip. Turning back, Da-gore studied the sheer rocky cliffs growing larger and looming higher with each forward lurch of the boat.

The clear water showed the shallowness of the crossing. Schools of silvery fish skimmed the white, gravely bottom, which looked near enough to reach down and touch. Pyir Rhone called these shoals the Atlan Ridge, and only shallow draft vessels could pass over them.

Captain Akin, a thick man with a florid face, scattered, white hair, and a long, slender beak of a nose, stopped by Da-gore's side and squinted at the mass of land ahead. "We will be putting into

Atlan in less than a quartering."

Da-gore nodded.

Akin's eyes crinkled, and his ruddy face smiled as he peered at the rocky shore. "Don't let that coastline fool you, Master Jael-ik. She's got a fine harbor—the best I've ever dropped anchor in."

Da-gore had used the name Jael-ik for over a year now, yet it still rang strange to his ears.

"First time to Atlan?"

"No."

"Ah, a regular visitor?"

"Business brings me from time to time." He'd paid for transportation, not company.

"Well, then you know all about the harbor."

Da-gore looked back at the island.

Akin lingered a moment, grew uncomfortable in his silence, and wandered off. There were few men Da-gore could trust these days. He watched the captain out the corner of his eye sidestepping mounds of cargo as he made his way to the stern of the boat and leaned on the rudder. The boat veered northward and the water grew shallower, from time to time grinding the keel.

He watched the cliffs—Atlan's Rim-wall—grow closer. It wasn't yet visible from here, but there was a passage through those frowning cliffs—a long, hand-dug channel two hundred spans wide, sixty spans deep, and almost two leagues in length. The passage, know as Hodin's Gallery, opened out into the first of three concentric harbors. In past trips he had estimated the first harbor—Merchant's Harbor—at twelve hundred spans, perhaps more. The second and third harbors, separated from each other by a ring of land, were considerably smaller. From a skybarge it looked like a gigantic bull's-eye laid out on the fertile Atlan plains, and in the very center of it all, on the man-made island called Hodin's Sanctum, rose the Government Houses and Zorin's stronghold.

Da-gore brought his thoughts back to business. Would Batok be waiting for him? There was no way to know if he'd gotten his message. Birds could be—and often were—intercepted, but the code was clever. He doubted anyone could break it. If Batok wasn't waiting, he knew where to find him. He drew the heavy sea air into his lungs and shaded his eyes toward the jut of land coming into view.

Now he could make out the Rim-wall towers strung along the cliffs like a strand of pearls encircling Atlan's neck. They were ancient structures from the days when Hodin was securing this island for his own land. Now the old Highwatch Towers stood mostly abandoned, but there was a new feature up there. The Pikes—sometimes called the "Bloody Pikes." The place was known as Execution Ridge, and if he squinted, he could just make out the bodies of traitors and rebels impaled upon the Pikes—Zorin's warning to all who entered Atlan.

His view shifted toward the jut of land, and anticipation stirred in his chest. He was not a man who particularly relished works of art, but every time he rounded this point and the passage came into view, the majestic statues took his breath away.

As he waited, the rhythm of the oarlocks played a taunting melody. *One more stroke ... just one more stroke.* He craned his neck. The point drew nearer, teasing him in its reluctance to give up the sight behind it.

Then suddenly they came into view. One moment nothing, the next two immense figures stepped out from behind the island, gleaming in the sunlight like gods.

"Hodin's Gallery ahead!" a lookout called.

Da-gore marveled at the images of Hodin and his beloved wife, Atla, carved from the living stone of Atlan, towering four hundred spans above the sea, facing each other on either side of the passage. The great warrior stood with his sword thrust into rock at the water's edge in the traditional Makir watch position, signifying the end of war. Hodin seemed to radiate strength and protection, while, on the opposite side of the passage, Atla beckoned to the incoming boats with grace and beauty. The two figures towered over the passage with arms stretched out and fingers entwined, forever immortalized in stone, a welcoming sight to all who arrived here. Da-gore inhaled sharply to cleanse the stale breath in his lungs. The work had taken a thousand artisans twenty years to complete. Pyir Rhone had said it had been begun the very day the last of Hodin's enemies had fallen to his sword and he'd proclaimed the beginning of the Order of the Makir.

From that day to now, no country had ever attempted to attack the island nation. A sardonic smile came unexpectedly to his lips. *Atlan withstands the world but crumbles from within.* Would a day come when Atlan was no more than memories, a myth handed down generation after generation until it finally became garbled and lost forever in the misty halls of legend?

And if so, what was man's purpose? Nothing lasts forever, except the Creator. He astonished that he could find comfort in this. Five years ago he would have never thought it possible.

But Atlan had not fallen yet, and if Pyir Rhone was successful, she would regain her vitality. The disease eating away at her had not yet become terminal. There was yet a cure.

The entrance to Hodin's Gallery was dotted with boats of every description. Many came this far simply to view the mighty statues; only a few would actually venture into Hodin's Passage. To most of the world, Atlan was a wonderful, distant land where mythical warriors still lived and ruled. He had held such fascination upon his first visit almost a year ago. Since then he'd made six more, and much of the magic had disappeared. Atlan was still beautiful, Atlan was certainly powerful, but her mysteries had faded with familiarity.

The boat glided past the sightseers into the passage and was engulfed in deep shadows. In another quartering the sun would stand overhead and turn these dusky waters a deep turquoise, but for now the stone canyon soared darkly upward toward a narrow slash of blue sky. Most of the canyon rock was an inky black, streaked in red, but some of it, like the stone at the entrance from which the figures of Hodin and Atla had been hewed, glowed milky white.

They passed under the first of six delicate, arching bridges connecting both sides of the canyon, spaced three thousand spans apart. The first time he had seen them, he was amazed that man could construct such airy structures of heavy stone. Later he learned they had been carved in place as the canyon had been shaped from the rock.

Once they entered Hodin's Gallery, the character of the walls changed. The roughness ended abruptly, and finely dressed stone took its place. Carved into the sides of the man-made canyon were hundreds of boat docks. Atlan was a seafaring nation. She boasted some of the most advanced boatbuilding facilities in the world. Atlanders used boats like Nodinites used three-points and carts.

Da-gore studied the canyon walls with the eye of a tactician. The dark stone held more than docking facilities. Less conspicuous were the battlements concealed high upon those polished walls. Up there a small army lived just out of sight in caves hidden behind the ornate colonnades. The caves secreted great catapults that could hurl fiery balls of destruction down upon invading ships. And few knew that Zorin had recently installed a battery of proj-lances, vastly larger than the small shoulder devices men carried. The carved columns disguised all that and gave the passage a look of elegance, a stunning entryway into Atlan, the jewel of the Great Sea.

Captain Akin made his way among the piles of cargo and stopped at Da-gore's side again. "We'll be pulling in for inspection shortly." The deeper shadow of an overhead walkway momentarily darkened the captain's ruddy features and inquisitive eyes.

"I'm prepared."

The captain nodded and went down a hatch. A mate had the helm, with only half the sweeps in motion. Although traffic in the passage was heavy, there was still room enough for ten boats abreast.

Ahead, two stone jetties split the passage into three channels: the left for incoming boats, the right for outgoing, and the center channel to remain open for official and military traffic. The oars snapped up, rotated inboard, and they slowed and stopped in the queue of waiting boats.

Da-gore removed the documents from the inside pocket of the cloak he held over his arm. The heat within the chasm pressed down on him, and the towering rock walls gave off a musty smell. Every voice, every thump of oar against gunwale echoed off the walls and flat water.

"Won't be long." Akin watched a crewman on the jetty with a hawser over his shoulder slowly haul his boat forward.

"Zorin doesn't take chances, does he?" Da-gore nodded toward the officials ahead inspecting each boat.

Akin frowned, looked around, and lowered his voice. "Tyrants have no choice but to keep the mast-line taut, Master Jael-ik." His eyes narrowed worriedly as if he suddenly regretted his words.

Da-gore smiled. "Don't worry. I won't mention it to the passage inspectors."

He flashed a quick but uncertain grin. "One of these days my tongue will be my undoing."

When their turn arrived, he took a deep breath and fixed an indifferent look to his face. Three inspectors came aboard with the standard questions: name, business, length of stay. Da-gore showed them his papers: Master Jael-ik; a merchant dealing in cloth, to meet with a business associate; probably no more than a few days, a week at the most.

Thankfully, the interviews were brief. The inspectors examined the cargo, impounded the lookouts' proj-lances, and said they'd be returned when they left. The formalities completed, Captain Akin received a three-day permit for the Merchant's Harbor. The oars dipped into the water, and the boat moved back into the crowded channel.

Once they passed the inspection point, the towering cliffs of Hodin's Gallery dropped rapidly behind them, and they entered a stretch of water know as Hodin's Canal. Atlan's mountainous terrain gave way first to thick, timber forests, then to rolling hills with broad, sweeping valleys filled with grain and fruit, root crops, and vast sweeps of bright red tomatoes or neat rows of keelit trees. In the distance, the hot clear sky appeared to be propped up on the craggy peaks of the Rim-wall that bound in the Atlanders' world. To the west, the land climbed gently away from the canal, gradually gaining height until it met the horizon.

Da-gore focused his attention ahead upon a handsome wall of dusky red stone that rose thrice the height of a man on either side of the canal and was several hundred spans wide. The wall—actually two walls—marched toward its twin, down to the canal's edge, ending in a pair of octagonal guard towers that dipped their stony toes in the water. An arching bridge, high above the canal, connected the two towers. He knew that this wall completely encircled Atlan's harbors. Pyir Rhone had carefully charted the entire land for him before his first visit. Da-gore counted eight guards in the towers and upon the bridge.

The boat glided past the wall—last barrier to the harbor—and the countryside beyond became a patchwork of small villages and country farms set on neat rectangles of land surrounded by low stone walls.

The waterway grew more congested as Akin's boat drew near the harbor. Soon battlements sprang up on each side of the canal, with towers evenly spaced every two hundred spans. Here and there, smaller canals shot off the main one, leading back to large stone buildings where Zorin had garrisoned troops and military vessels. Da-gore had noted these on previous trips.

"Those are the preparations of a country planning for war," Pyir Rhone had commented when first hearing of Zorin's defenses.

That had been a year ago, and since then, Da-gore had observed a buildup of men and boats along Hodin's Canal.

Merchant's Harbor—the most seaward one—was the largest of the three. It encircled the next, smaller harbor, called the Kinsmen's Anchorage, which in turn embraced the third, innermost ring of water—Haven Port. Haven Port surrounded the man-made island known as Hodin's Sanctum, where Atlan's official buildings stood. Few but Atlan's ruling class were permitted passage into these protected waters.

Merchant's Harbor, where most of Atlan's commerce was conducted, was by far the busiest. Akin nudged his boat into a slip at one of the exchange docks and paid the harbor recorder a shaved gleck for three days' anchorage. Da-gore disembarked, glancing at the busy merchants' stalls beneath betasseled shiverthorn canopies, then at stone warehouses along the wharves gleaming in the midday sun. Batok wasn't in sight, but then Da-gore hadn't expected him to be waiting. There was no way Batok would have known where he'd come ashore. Hooking his cloak over his shoulder, he made his way toward the wide bridge across the Kinsmen's Anchorage over to the island that bore the same name.

※

As Da-gore strolled eastward along walkways lined with shops, the massive red stone buildings beyond Haven Port held his eye. He had walked perhaps a half a league—maybe a quarter of the narrow island's circumference—when he spied a trellis arching over a narrow path into a shaded park. Bending his steps beneath it, he came upon another walkway—this one of black and gray stones, crafted into an undulating pattern as though a gigantic snake were crawling through the neatly groomed grounds.

The sounds of the busy waterfront muted as he walked, and now he could hear birds twittering, monkeys chattering, and small pocket dragons purring from treetops.

"Master Jael-ik," a soft voice rasped out from an airy drapery of green and silver feather palms.

Da-gore peered into a leafy alcove whereupon sat the ample bulk of Batok the cloth merchant, holding a keelit hull and sipping from it through a straw. Da-gore moved aside a wispy veil of feather palms. "I'd hoped I'd find you here."

"I got your message. I've been waiting a long time."

"Mainland boats keep to their own schedules."

Batok nodded severely. "I know." Then he grinned and glanced at the keelit hull. "Had too many of these. Another half quartering, and you'd be carrying me home, Master Jael-ik."

"I'm not sure I'm up to the task."

Batok laughed and heaved himself to his feet with the aid of an overhanging branch. "Fair trip?"

"Uneventful."

"Good. I need to limber some. Let's walk." He slurped up the remainder of his drink and cast the empty hull into the upper branches of a tree. A waiting pocket dragon snatched it out of the air by its teeth, and Batok laughed again. He slapped Da-gore on the back. "Excellent to see you again, old friend."

"Have you anything for me?" The park was not crowded, but he kept his voice low just the same.

Batok's tiny eyes widened like gray pearls within fleshy pale pockets. "My friend, you need to learn the art of small talk." His breathing wheezed as they walked upon the serpent's back. The pace seemed painfully slow.

A woman walking a canic strolled past. Once out of earshot,

Da-gore said, "Small talk is for old men and peaceful evenings. What have you learned?"

Batok's florid cheeks wrinkled into a fist of frowning dimples. "Always business first with you, my friend." He shook his head. "You have a taskmaster's bearing, Master Jael-ik. What were you before all this began?"

"A prisoner of a lie."

The gray pearls slid toward him with a glint of amusement. "Very well. Your past is your own, as it should be. Yes, I do have something." He went silent a moment as a man and woman passed by. "Zorin has moved Lady Darha to an unknown location."

"Why would Zorin do that unless—" he glanced at Batok— "unless he knows."

Batok's lower lip pushed out. "He suspects."

They paused at a fountain where Batok sat upon the stonework, puffing. Da-gore propped a foot on the edge. A glimmer fish slid past the toe of his boot. "I'll want to know where he's moved her, Master Batok."

The cloth merchant patted his forehead with a handkerchief. "My canics are already on Lady Darha's trail. It's only a matter of time, my dear friend. But that's not all."

Da-gore turned from the fountain and sat beside him.

"The Rim-wall Highwatches are being repaired and the ancient signal pyres rebuilt."

"So, Zorin *has* caught a scent."

"It would seem so."

"This is not the best of news."

"Sorry to be the bearer."

"And what of the others?" Da-gore watched a pocket dragon across a wide green lawn, eating scraps of food someone had left behind.

"Your army grows; each man is loyal to the cause. The Makir are coming out of the woodwork as well, and they grow restless to be bound again."

He smiled and turned his eyes back to the sweating man sitting beside him. "That is like them." This was encouraging news to take back to Rhone. "I want to speak with our captains."

"Of course. I'll hang the gold cloth outside my shop. Will tomorrow evening be soon enough?"

Da-gore nodded. He had plans for the day. "Now, what else have you for me?"

Batok thought a moment, then his flushed cheeks rounded like a ripe tomato. "Dinner? It's nearly fifth of the second quartering."

Da-gore smiled. "Now that *is* pleasant news to the ears of a man whose only breakfast was keelit mush."

Batok laughed, levered himself to his feet, blowing a long breath. He touched his face with the handkerchief again. "I know a place with a menu as long as Hodin's sword, and you'll not find keelit mush anywhere on it!"

24

Suspicion

Sari'el peered over Lamech's shoulder, the human completely unaware of the Messenger's presence. Even though Sari'el was out of phase with the realm of man by mere degrees, it did not prevent him from seeing past the boundary into Lamech's world. Nevertheless, from Lamech's point of view—if he had been in a position to judge such things—the separation might well have been a hundred million leagues.

Laes'el, Lamech's Guardian, said, "He works diligently, even though he detests what he is being forced to do."

Sari'el spent a moment watching Lamech carefully create the mechanical drawings, using a ruler and compass to precisely lay out the gears that activated a mirror array within the heart of the Oracle's Temple. "He understands that what he does here, he does for Elohim."

"Ironic, isn't it, but true. All things work toward good to the man who loves Elohim." Laes'el glanced over his shoulders at the stalkers, ever lurking in the shadows, patiently waiting. "Lamech does well so long as I keep them from whispering their words of discouragement in his ear."

"Have they challenged your authority?" Sari'el watched the Fallen Ones stalking around the edges of the room.

"No. Lamech's faith enables me, while their jealousy makes them weak." Laes'el hefted his golden staff, grinning. "And timid."

Just then both Sari'el and Laes'el looked toward the closed door. And a moment later there came a knock.

Lamech straightened up from the detailed work and rolled a shoulder, grimacing as he worked his stiff muscles. "Come in."

The door creaked open and the rumpled old man, dressed in a faded red robe, wandered in. Sor-dak's nose was pressed to a sheet of parchment, and he was mumbling quietly, "Found another one. Ha-ha!"

From the shadows, the stalkers moved toward Sor-dak like rats toward a trail of spilled grain.

Gorn'el, the Guardian who accompanied Sor-dak, leveled his ivory staff and made a threatening growl, and the Fallen Ones skulked back to the edges of the room.

"Another what?" Lamech asked, setting his pen in the inkwell as he pushed back from the worktable.

"Connection! Look." Sor-dak spread the parchment over Lamech's drawings, anchoring it in place with the tip of his long, big-knuckled finger.

Lamech bent close to study the paper a moment.

Leaning farther over his shoulder, Sari'el saw that Sor-dak had brought a star chart. Sari'el glanced to his two companions and smiled, nodding knowingly.

Gorn'el said, "Once he made the discovery, he could hardly contain himself. Practically ran up the stairs in leaps and bounds." A slow smile moved across Gorn'el's face. "And Sor-dak's faith grows in the same manner."

Sari'el said, "Lamech has succeeded in that task as well." His voice took a reverent pause. "He has almost finished the job

Elohim has commissioned him."

"What connection, Master Sor-dak?" Lamech gently moved Sor-dak's finger to see the star it was covering. "This is the gathering of Taleh, the Lamb."

"Yes, a gathering of sixty-six stars. You told me the chief star in the forehead of the Lamb is named El-nath, meaning wounded, remember? And that it referred to the Strong Man to come, the Creator's Redeemer, who would be wounded."

"Yes. Wounded for man's transgressions. A wound that in some unknown way would heal the race of man. So, what have you 'connected'?"

"Ah. Look." Sor-dak was bubbling as he plopped his finger back where it had been. "This star here, just to the left. Remember the prophecy made to Adam and Eve? The one about bruising his heel, while he would crush the head of the Deceiver?"

Lamech nodded. Gorn'el beamed a smile at Laes'el and Sari'el. "Sor-dak is working out the mystery. He knows."

Sari'el cast Gorn'el a sideways glance. "Is that pride I hear in your voice?"

Gorn'el immediately sobered. "No, of course not. I'm just … pleased for Sor-dak. For his growing faith."

Sari'el winked at Laes'el, and the two Messengers laughed. Gorn'el laughed too.

Sor-dak said, "I have wondered if that prophecy wasn't hidden in the gathering of the Lamb, and guess what?" Before Lamech could answer, Sor-dak said, "El-shr'ta. Right here." His finger ground against the paper. "It means 'The Bruised One.' Ha! Everything comes together. Marvelous. Such precision!"

Lamech laughed. "You're acting like a boy of fifty again."

"My Coming-of-Age Rite was never as exciting—or as rewarding—as discovering the Creator's message to us. What do you think?"

"I knew you'd find it eventually."

"You knew about it?" Sor-dak looked crestfallen.

"I wanted you to find it on your own."

"And I was so excited." Sor-dak gave an exaggerated sigh and smiled. "I'll just have to keep looking. I've surprised you before."

"And I'm sure you will again, Master Sor-dak. I'm amazed with your progress at discovering the Creator's story."

Sor-dak took up his paper and rolled it into a tight tube, glancing at the drawing that lay beneath it. "The mirror array."

"Massive, isn't it? What do you suppose the Oracle has in mind?"

At the mention of the Oracle, the stalkers around the edge of the room grew agitated, emboldened. Sari'el tightened his grip on the ivory staff.

Sor-dak's white-haired head shook. "I don't have the answer. Only the Oracle knows, and I'm sure he's hiding the truth from us. But this I do know. The way those mirrors will concentrate the light of the cap crystal, the energy will be tremendous."

Lamech frowned. "Far more than is needed to consume a few sacrifices."

Sor-dak huffed. "By the size of the altar, I'd say a few hundred sacrifices."

"Maybe that's it."

Sari'el sensed Lamech was unconvinced.

Sor-dak took a long breath. "Well, we do what we have to, you and I, Master Lamech—for the Creator's sake. Maybe someday, some good will come from our efforts."

The stalkers hunkered back into the shadows.

"Maybe." Lamech pulled his chair around and took up the pen again, shaking it once into the inkwell.

"I'll let you return to your work."

Sari'el said to Gorn'el, "Keep them from him."

Gorn'el glanced at the stalkers. "You know how it works. I'm strong so long as Sor-dak remains strong. But when he drifts away, as all men do from time to time, then the stalkers grow stronger."

Sari'el nodded at the grim truth. "If only we could tell them."

"If only that would make a difference." Gorn'el followed Sor-dak out of the room.

Sari'el said to Laes'el, "I, too, must leave. Rhone has let his faith slip, and his stalkers are tormenting him."

Laes'el nodded. "I understand. I'll manage them. Lamech's faith is a rock."

"You are fortunate."

"Fair journey, Sari'el"

Sari'el stepped briefly into eternity and emerged a moment later in the room where Rhone's Guardian was holding back the hoard of loathsome stalkers.

※

Rhone stood at the window in the upper room of his quarters, staring at pinkish bands of high clouds changing slowly to bright orange. "Could I have so misread the man?" In the low, slanting sunlight, the treetops suddenly flared with a greenish fire.

"When we first discovered him following us, I suspected he was a spy," Klesc said at Rhone's back. "I have never completely trusted him."

"But I did." The sunset beyond his window glowed like molten gold in the heart of a crucible.

Leenah momentarily stopped her pacing. "He wouldn't betray us. I've never seen anyone more committed to a cause than Master Da-gore. And I know his faith is genuine. He couldn't hide something like that very long without the truth showing through."

"Faith has nothing to do with this," Klesc snapped. "Da-gore is a leader—a leader without followers. What might he betray to be given warriors to command again? Zorin could provide what he wants."

Rhone turned from the window. "So can I." He felt weary.

Klesc stood with arms folded across his broad chest, eyes narrowed, his mouth a thin, unsmiling slash. Leenah resumed pacing with a vengeance, as if determined to wear a track across the hard sten-gordon floor mat. The only one there who hadn't yet spoken was leaning nonchalantly against a stone column. Rhone shifted his gaze to the gray-haired man who'd once been his father's closest adviser.

"What first aroused your suspicion?"

Larik pushed off the column and stepped forward. "Da-gore has had the opportunity. Even now he is in Zorin's realm."

"Doing our business," Rhone reminded him.

Larik shrugged. "Perhaps that's what he wants us to believe."

His words stirred the doubt he had been working so hard to suppress. "Opportunity is not evidence of guilt. Here, this close to Marin-ee, opportunity is all around us."

Larik frowned, and his voice took an ominous tone. "There is something else."

Leenah ceased pacing.

The muscles across Rhone's shoulders contracted. "What?"

Larik frowned and shook his head. "I'd hoped to confirm what I say next, Pyir Rhone, but since you ask, I must speak. Word has reached me that *ex*-Captain Da-gore is raising an army of his own within Atlan."

"No," Leenah blurted.

The growing tightness moved from Rhone's shoulders to his chest. He drew in a long breath and let it out slowly. "Who?"

Larik hesitated. "Ka-Larik heard whispered words, and he rightly came to me about it. I don't know who first started the rumor."

"Idle gossip?" Rhone said, wanting to believe that.

Larik's thin smile turned cold. "Call it what you wish. But I ask you this. If it is true, could such a thing happen under Zorin's very nose without his consent?" Larik's tone darkened. "We must keep our eyes open wide, Pyir Rhone." Scorn snarled from his lips. "We have far too much to lose to rely on an ... *off-lander*."

Leenah glared at him. "Off-lander?"

Even Klesc looked a bit dismayed.

"Do we have so many warriors that we can afford to be selective, First Statre Larik?" Anger pinched her brow and flamed in her narrowed eyes. "I'm half Atlander. Does that make me half off-lander?"

"Of course not, Mistress Leenah," he said soothingly, but his eyes remained hard as sparkrock.

Rhone said, "Let our tempers not get in the way of clear thinking." As he spoke, he reminded himself there was a hand in this more powerful than man's. The Creator's purpose was larger than merely regaining a kingdom. He was securing a future refuge for Noah. He couldn't allow circumstances to cloud that commission. "Our immediate concern is to determine if there is any truth to this rumor." He looked at each of them. "Our suspicions must not leave this room."

Larik nodded. "Of course. What would you have me do, Pyir Rhone?" He seemed to have easily shrugged off the disagreement, but Leenah had not.

Rhone moved to her side, hearing her sharp breathing. Wishing to defuse the soaring tension, he said to Larik, "Find Kev-nn. Tell him I wish to speak with him in the morning. Then see if you can track down the source of this rumor."

Larik bowed stiffly and departed.

Rhone glanced back at Leenah. "What is it?"

"I dislike that man," she said quietly.

He put a hand on her shoulder and gave it a gentle squeeze. Her muscles were tighter than a walking strand in a javian's web.

Klesc's face, no longer frowning, had assumed an expressionless mien—his way of keeping his thoughts to himself.

"Klesc, return to the prisoner. See what more you can learn from him."

"There may be nothing left to learn. I'm convinced he's only a castaway piece in Zorin's game."

"Perhaps, but try anyway."

Klesc nodded. "I'll wring what's left from the rag."

"Just talk to him."

Klesc left.

Rhone took Leenah by the arm and guided her to a long sofa. She sat stiffly upon the soft cushions. Standing behind her, he began kneading her shoulders and neck. "This matter has affected you more so than I'd have thought."

She rolled her head back as his thumbs dug into taut muscles. "I refuse to believe he's a traitor."

"I know how you feel. Da-gore had earned my trust as well."

"You speak as if you already believe him guilty."

"I am trying not to."

"I never have cared for Larik." Her muscles bunched beneath his fingers. "But the longer we are in this together, the more his haughty demeanor grates on me."

"It's just his way. My father trusted his advice."

She rolled her head forward then back again. "And you?"

"Trust has never been a question. He was loyal to my father—and mother—since before I was born. He is loyal to me."

"I'm not questioning Larik's loyalty, Rhone. I just don't like the man. My spirit is troubled whenever we are together."

"Our problem is not Larik. We must find the spy among us, and if it turns out to be Da-gore, I will deal with him." His thumbs worked her shoulders.

"Mmmm." She closed her eyes.

He felt the knots melt beneath his fingers.

"When is Master Da-gore to return?"

"Four days, maybe five."

She looked up. "What is he doing there this time?"

"Touring the countryside."

Leenah stared at him a moment, then shut her eyes again. "You and your secrets, Rhone."

It was just as well she didn't see the frown that pulled at his lips. Touring the countryside … and what else?

The morning Katrahs and Kimahs were in progress when Kev-nn's three-wheeled cart came sputtering up the road. It turned into the compound, its iron-rimmed wheels crunching to a stop in the old garrison. Kev-nn sat a few moments on the device's leather saddle, while its sputtering cycler filled the air with the fumes of unburned vera-logia. He seemed to be listening to the way the cycler popped and stuttered, his dark head cocking first left then right. Finally he shook his head, shut down the machine, and swung off the saddle.

Rhone and Larik descended a flight of steps and met Kev-nn coming up to them. As Atlanders went, Kev-nn was only about medium height, which put him about half a head shorter than Rhone and half a head taller than almost any other man not of Hodin's lineage. Size aside, he was a brilliant mechanic who'd made a generous living constructing cycler-powered carts and boats for the well-to-do merchants of Marin-ee. Kev-nn's face and neck were streaked with green grease. His large hands were callused and stained, as if he'd recently had them buried deep in the guts of some mechanical device.

"Pyir Rhone … First Statre Larik." He nodded to each of them. "I came as soon as I could get away. I've been at the gormerin's cycler most of the night."

"I need to know when the gormerin will be ready." They started down the steps, Rhone at Kev-nn's side, Larik a few paces behind.

Kev-nn shook his head. "Not long. How soon are you wanting it?" He pulled a greasy rag from his pocket and began absently cleaning his blackened nails.

"Zorin may already be aware of what we are building. The sooner the better."

Kev-nn glanced at him, his brown eyes widening. "Has that fellow you caught yesterday talked?"

"No. But I had Klesc work on him last night."

He grinned. "I wouldn't want to be that fellow."

"We'll eventually get the information we seek," Larik said.

Rhone wondered. Klesc had yet to report back on what he'd learned, but maybe he was right. Maybe Lorun had no information to give. They left the steps and started toward Kev-nn's machine. "What still needs completing?"

"Very little. The tail fin functions, but the watertight seals have yet to be installed. The air bladder pipe work is nearly complete. The bellows are already in place. The hull is sound but untested. The cyclers are nearly assembled. That's what I was doing just before I came here. I've built the piston. It's in my shop. I'll be going back to Marin-ee later to retrieve it."

"When can it be moved from the boathouse to the sea cave?"

"Two months."

"If Zorin suspects what we are up to, he will send others. I want to move them in two weeks."

"Two weeks!" Kev-nn shook his head and shoved the dirty rag back into a pocket. "I'll need more time."

"Pyir Rhone!" a voice shouted.

They turned as Ka-Larik came sprinting up the passage that led
to the underground rooms.

Larik seemed surprised at seeing his son and cast a worried
glance at Rhone. Ka-Larik halted, gave his father a brief look, and
then turned to Rhone. "I just came from the prisoner, Pyir Rhone."

"Yes?"

Ka-Larik took in a breath and let it out. "The prisoner's dead."

Kev-nn whistled. "I better get back to work. You have matters
to address here." He went to the cart, sparked a flame, and in a
moment the cycler began popping, settling down to a regular
cadence. Kev-nn grinned with delight at the sound of his little
mechanical triumph. He put the cart into motion and rumbled
away.

※

The subterranean tunnels rang with their hurried footsteps. "I
was bringing a tray of food," Ka-Larik said. "When I arrived, the
door was locked, and two guards were in the anteroom. They'd said
the prisoner hadn't made a sound since Klesc left him."

Overhead, high windows set in narrow shafts of stone spilled
a weak light across the stone floors, showing the narrowness of the
place. Shadowed doors led off to either side of the long, musty
burrow.

"How was he killed?" Rhone eyed a bend up ahead in the corridor. Lorun had been imprisoned in a room that, in ages past, had
been one of many troop quarters. Now the abandoned underground barracks were home to rats and jikloos—and one dead spy.

"His neck was broken." Ka-Larik gave a wan smile. "He looks
pretty roughed up."

Two guards, Togar and Borin, were waiting outside the room
when they rounded the corner. "He's in there, Pyir Rhone." Togar
pointed at the door, which stood open.

Lorun lay upon the hard floor, half in shadow, half in a hazy shaft of light streaming down from a grated opening high overhead. On a table sat the tray of food Ka-Larik had been delivering.

Rhone knelt beside the body. Some of the bruises had already begun to turn purple. Lorun's split lip was crusted over, and dried blood clung to his forehead and cheek. His head lay at a distinctly unnatural angle, his neck indeed broken. Rhone felt the dislocated bone, then examined the skin. There were no marks to reveal how the neck had come to be twisted almost three-quarters around his shoulders. Not even any scars. Only a single bead of dried blood.

"We won't be learning any more of Zorin's treachery from this one." He stood. "Who was the last one with him?"

"Klesc," Borin said.

Ka-Larik said, "It's hard to believe Klesc could do such a thing."

Footsteps echoed in the hallway outside the door, and a moment later, Leenah and Klesc appeared. They stopped, looked at Rhone, at Lorun, then stepped quietly inside.

"We heard," Leenah said softly, staring.

"From whom?" Rhone demanded.

Klesc scowled at the body. "The news of this is already making the rounds."

Rhone looked to Ka-Larik. The young Makir managed an apologetic smile. "I guess I must have mentioned it on my way to find you, Pyir Rhone."

As if to draw the heat off his son, Larik said, "Klesc, what happened here?"

Klesc slid a slow look toward Larik. "I don't know."

"You were the last one to see him alive."

"Was I?"

"He was," said Togar, who'd been guarding the door that night. "After you left him last night, no one else went inside the room."

Rhone looked back at Ka-Larik. "This is exactly as you found him?"

Ka-Larik nodded. "Borin and I found him like this. I was the first at his side, though. I hurried to check if he was still alive, while Borin turned to call for Togar."

Rhone said to Borin, "Is that the way it happened?"

"Yes, Pyir Rhone. Ka-Larik went to the body, and I summoned Togar."

Togar nodded. "We three found him just like you see him."

Rhone looked at Klesc. The warrior folded his huge arms and said evenly, "He was alive when I left him."

Larik scowled. "I find that difficult to believe."

Leenah glared at the First Statre. "If Klesc said he was alive, then he was."

Rhone studied his friend. Klesc would have no compunction over using force, but he also was no liar. Still, the evidence against him was serious.

"You're not going to believe Larik over Klesc," Leenah said.

Larik stiffened slightly and held her in a long, impatient gaze. "My own son bears witness."

She sent him a burning stare. "There has to be another explanation."

"I will investigate the matter." Rhone looked back at Lorun. He had a wife and son back in Atlan, and Zorin had held their safety over Lorun's head to ensure his loyalty. The muscles in his neck grew taut. "Take him out of here."

"What will you have us do with him, Pyir Rhone?" Togar asked.

What indeed? Lorun had only been a castaway piece in Zorin's game, and Rhone might never know what circumstances had set in motion the cascade of events that ended here. He drew in a long, thoughtful breath. This should not have happened under his watch.

"Send him to sea. It is a fitting end for an Atlander."

"By Dirgen's sword, he was a spy!" Larik protested.

Rhone glared at Larik. "He was a grandson of Hodin."

※

The gentle lap of waves against the stone wharf seemed to soothe Leenah's impatience. The sea comforted her anxious soul in a way she didn't understand. She stepped closer to Rhone's side and slid her hand under his arm. He put a hand over her fingers. At the end of the jetty, two Makir Warriors lowered Lorun's body, tightly bound in seavine and weighted with rocks, into a boat. A Makir would have been weighted with his weapons.

The air was cooler here at the water's edge. She filled her lungs with the sea breeze, which carried the vital scent of teaming life. She had inherited her mother's blood, for the sea spoke to her as she knew it did to Rhone—and to all Atlanders—unlike the dry, stony fortress that had become her home. She narrowed her eyes up toward the harsh, umber cliffs, rising two hundred spans. The crumbling gray walls of Imo-suk stood far above them, hoary with age, forever staring out to sea.

Imo-suk had become her prison. Few of the women who lived there cared for the place. Rhone's warriors, on the other hand, seemed invigorated by the rugged simplicity of the ancient fortress and the rigorous training each of them endured. This was the life they had been born to live. She'd seen these traits in her uncles. She understood the patience of the Makirs … intellectually. Emotionally, the waiting grated.

Gur and three dragons soared out over the cliffs and flapped powerfully toward the east, toward Atlan. In a moment of whimsy, Leenah wanted to leap upon the back of the scarlet dragon and soar away with him, if only for a little while—if only to steal a glimpse of the homeland she left behind as a child.

The body in place, two men lowered themselves behind oars and rowed out to sea.

She put such daydreaming aside, reminding herself why they were all gathered here. "Klesc didn't do it," she whispered softly. Rhone gave no indication that he heard. She sighed as the boat shrank in the distance. What was he thinking? Sometimes he guarded his thoughts as though they were gold.

"Perhaps," he replied finally.

So he had heard. The boat shrank to a speck and stopped. She couldn't see what was happening, didn't need to. Sea burials were a strong Atlanian tradition. Her mother had talked of them. Her uncles, too. There would be an ode to Dirgen, and then the body would simply be dropped over the side.

"That's over," Larik said, turning brusquely. He glanced at her, then Rhone. "I must see to the warriors' training."

Rhone nodded. "We will speak later."

Larik and Ka-Larik strode toward the long switchback steps hewed from the cliff.

Four other Makir stood about, awaiting orders.

"Stay here until the boat returns," Rhone instructed them.

He took Leenah's hand and led her along the paved walkway to the steps. A flock of yellow and green divers, strutting along the white sand, squawked their indignation and reluctantly gave way to them.

"What will you do next?" She spoke openly once out of earshot of the others.

"Talk to Klesc."

"I don't like what's happening. First Master Da-gore, now Master Klesc."

Rhone gave her a probing look. "You think the two are connected?"

"Two accusations in as many days? Both trusted men? Is that not quite a coincidence?"

They started up the steps. "Coincidence, yes. Perhaps no more than that."

His reply didn't sit easy with her. "It makes me suspicious."

"Of whom?"

That was the big question. "I don't know."

"Then I have no choice but to question Klesc."

"You don't really believe he lied to you?"

"Only Togar and Borin had access to Lorun. Why would they have killed him?"

She crossed her arms angrily. "I don't know why, Rhone. But I do know this: I don't like coincidences."

❦

"I have no explanation, Pyir Rhone." Klesc's thumbs were hooked in the wide sword belt, which, at the moment, held no weapon. His broad chest expanded the loose-fitting training shirt, and he exhaled sharply. "I never touched Lorun. He was very much alive when I left him."

"Yet he turned up very much dead."

Although Klesc's eyes remained unflinching, the muscles of his neck and his naked arms rose like cords of twisted rope, his anger restrained in the presence of his Pyir.

Rhone glanced at Leenah, sitting in a chair. She refused to believe Klesc guilty, and he wanted to also. Yet what other answer could there be?

"Sit down, Klesc." He motioned to a chair. His questions would be answered more easily if everyone wasn't so defensive.

The warrior hesitated, then reluctantly lowered himself into the hard seat. Rhone sat across from him. "Tell me everything from the time you arrived until you left. Perhaps there is a clue we've missed."

"Lorun was determined but frightened. The Makir are all but

extinct in Atlan, but their reputation still lives on in the minds and the hearts of the people." Klesc gave a brief smile. "Lorun did not wish to tangle with one again." The smile vanished. "But an even stronger fear kept his tongue from wagging."

Leenah said, "Yet you did not touch him?"

His gaze shifted. "I knew my Pyir would not want me to use the techniques my training had given me." Klesc's eyes returned sullenly to Rhone. "Lorun's fear was for his family and how they would suffer if he did not return with the information Zorin wanted."

Rhone's fingers curled into a fist. "How had Lorun become Zorin's castaway piece?"

"He said he owed a debt, and he was repaying it."

"What else did he say?"

Klesc seemed to relax. "Lorun spoke only of his family and how he wanted to protect them. I reminded him that there was little he could do to help them while being held here at Imo-suk. He seemed to grow despondent at that."

Leenah's eyes widened suddenly. "Could he have killed himself?"

Rhone looked at her. "How does a man break his own neck?"

Her hopefulness faded, and she shrank back in the chair. "I'm clutching at the wind now."

"Lorun was fearful for his family; he wasn't suicidal. And I didn't kill him."

In spite of how it appeared, Rhone believed him. "Then who did?"

"The spy among us."

She straightened again, her eyebrows giving a speculative hitch. "And just how many spies do you propose there *are* among us, Master Klesc? Master Da-gore is in Atlan."

He apparently hadn't thought of that. His broad forehead wrinkled in frustration. "Maybe ... an accomplice?" It was a lame try, one that obviously didn't even convince him.

Leenah looked pleased with his answer. "Now *you're* clutching at the wind."

She stirred Rhone's admiration. Her intelligence and her convictions made her a worthy granddaughter of Hodin—a worthy leader of Hodin's people. More and more he was beginning to see her in that light. In times past, when such thoughts sprang to his head, he would immediately push them aside. Now, however, he did not.

He stifled a smile. "You got no more out of the man?"

Klesc thought a moment. "He did mention something about Zorin's new fear."

"What does that mean?"

Klesc's shoulders rolled. "I don't know."

Rhone stood and stared at a shaft of sunlight spilling through a window and glaring upon the ancient stone floor. "It's a puzzle. One we will work on. Strengthen the guards at the boathouse. I've told Kev-nn I want the gormerin able to move in two weeks. Zorin suspects its presence; it's no longer secure where it's berthed."

"If he suspects the gormerin, what of the rest of our fleet?"

"Indeed. Send word to our boat captains that there may be attempts on them. Double the Makir aboard each boat."

"I'll do it immediately."

Once Klesc had gone, Leenah rose from the chair. "I should look for Gur. I spied him and some others winging eastward over the Great Sea."

She was distracted, and Gur was only the excuse to leave. "Scarlet dragons fly to Atlan all the time. It's the wild bdell-m growing on the lee of the Rim-wall that attracts them. You know that. What's wrong, Leenah?"

She went stiff in the hazy light of the arched portal and

looked at him. When she drew herself up and squared her shoulders like that, she looked as determined as any Makir. She was indeed an Atlander, even if only on her mother's side. The longer he knew her, the more he saw Hodin's courage. The few traits imparted to her by her father she'd somehow managed to submerge. Perhaps it was from her father that Leenah inherited her impetuousness?

"What good will moving the gormerin do? Or doubling the guard on the fleet? The longer we wait, the more vulnerable they become."

So, it was that again. *Courage and spontaneity*, he mused. Two opposing strengths—like the Katrahs and Kimahs. But did they complement each other?

"You would have me rush off to war with Zorin? Although we grow stronger with each day, Zorin's army is far stronger yet."

"He has no Makir," she countered. "One Makir is worth fifty of Zorin's soldiers."

He went to her and took her by the shoulders, peering into her blue eyes. "But in the end, we would all be dead, and Zorin would still hold the island."

Those azure pools flashed a careless indifference. "We may lose men, Rhone, but you underestimate the unrest of the people. It would take but a spark, and they would be on fire for our cause."

"Don't you think Zorin knows that?"

"Certainly. Why else do his dungeons overflow, and why else is your mother still captive? You know where she is held, yet you've made no attempt to free her—to even contact her."

"Contact is impossible right now. You know that."

She shook her head. "I don't understand. I could go in and take her out of there myself."

He smiled. "I believe you would try. And you would lose your pretty head to the executioner's sword for your effort."

She scowled and turned out of his grasp. "I need to find Gur." She paused before stepping out into the lengthening shadows and gave him a faint smile. "Evening peace, Rhone." Then she was gone.

Impetuousness. He smiled briefly—then a sobering thought tugged at him. In all that had happened here with Lorun's assassination, he'd put off thinking about Da-gore. He stood by the east window, peering out at the darkening sea. Atlan lay just below the horizon—just out of his sight.

"Da-gore, my friend, are you true? Or have you become a Turnling?"

25

Batok's Secret Meeting Room

Once the sun dropped behind the Rim-wall, evening descended swiftly upon Atlan. The sky was a deep purple, striated by high pink clouds when Da-gore's hired boat chugged into the Kinsmen's Anchorage. Harbor traffic was light this time of day, and the boat-man kept the cycler thumping at full throttle until his home dock came into view. He stopped the cycler, swung the boat hard to the right, and expertly eased it into a narrow slip between two red stone jetties.

Da-gore slung his cloak over his shoulder and disembarked with the other passengers, making for the Hodin's Sanctum Bridge, hoping to have some time to survey the High Councilor's residence before he completely lost the light. He paused a moment at the turned-stone railing upon the bridge and buttoned the cloak's inner pocket where he kept a slim book. Then he continued over to the center island, presenting what he hoped would be a casual attitude. No sense raising suspicious eyebrows. Especially since it would be difficult to explain the notes he'd penned in a code no one but himself could read.

Atlan's royal residence and official buildings were built mostly of the red stone removed from Hodin's Passage during its digging. They towered above him, a few ending in sky-piercing spires with blue roofs. Some of the higher projections still caught a glint of sunlight. Atop each spire fluttered Zorin's pennant—dove gray with red borders and bearing the likeness of a minck with its black wings stretched up, tips touching above its back. The minck, a night hunter, was a fitting symbol for a man who stole a kingdom and used his imprisoned mother as a shield to maintain his power.

Zorin, like Rhone, was a sensitive. Da-gore had heard that the gift runs in families. Pyir Rhone's gift was to javian spiders, Zorin's to the minck.

He strolled slowly along the broad, paved lane called Atla's Fair View, which encircled the soaring walls. Twelve gatehouses pierced this outer curtain, each with four guards. He noted, as he made his way to the far side of Hodin's Sanctum, that the guards, dressed in gray jerkins with the red trimming, seemed to fade against the stonework as night fell. He must record that in his book later.

Atla's Fair View, the royal promenade around the Keep, had been skillfully paved with tightly fitted black stone, the seams so precise that not even a slip of paper could be inserted between them. Once in a while the road spanned a narrow canal that flowed from beneath the red walls through bronze grated stone arches. Sometimes the effluent bore partly gnawed jikloos or the gutted and plucked corpses of other birds; sometimes it bore dark, foul-smelling things. It all spilled into Haven Port, presumably to sink out of sight and eventually be carried out to sea by tidal action.

A wring serpent slithered through the bars, its head held high out of the water as its long, slender body propelled it under the bridge. Da-gore moved to the other side as it reemerged, its scales a lustrous, iridescent green in the failing light.

"Nasty creatures, those wrings are," a voice nearby him said.

Da-gore turned. The man wore a long gray cloak, trimmed in

red. Da-gore smiled easily. "Some people say they are Turnlings." Had he alerted the Keep Guards by his snooping?

The Guard watched the greenish glow fade against the blacker water of the canal. "We've begun to kill them."

Da-gore turned and pointed. "It came from there."

The man glanced at the grate in the shadowy arch above the dark water. "They live in the lower levels. Come in through the rocks, into the Black Pool beneath the Keep."

Da-gore grinned. "It doesn't sound like a pleasant place."

The Guard eyed him. "You have business here?"

His heart thumped against his ribs. "Here? No. I have business there." He pointed to the Triumph Bridge crossing over to the Kinsmen's Anchorage. But it was the general direction of Atla Fair, on the far side of Merchant's Harbor, that he meant. "I just returned from the interior and was taking the short way across." He gave the Keep Guard another grin. "If I'd have thought ahead, I'd have boarded a boat housed on the north side of the Anchorage. I'm not familiar with the routes, you see."

The Guard considered him a moment. "You'd best be on your way."

He tried not to show his relief at the dismissal. It could have been worse. "Yes, it will be well after dark before I get back to my lodgings. Evening peace."

"Evening peace." The Guard said it without enthusiasm and watched after him as he made for the Triumph Bridge, glowing beneath arches of milky white moonglass.

He breathed a little easier once he'd crossed back over to the Kinsmen's Anchorage and hurried along a softly glowing path, still bustling with commerce. Unlike the mainland, business here didn't cease with the coming of night. He crossed the first bridge over Merchant's Harbor, into the city of Atla Fair.

Atla Fair, whose streets radiated outward from Merchant's

Harbor like the pleats of a fan, was home to some twelve thousand Atlanders. At one time the neat, wide avenues of crushed stone were well groomed and kept clean as a new spoon by a small army of sanitation workers. Now, Atla Fair did not appear so pristine. Zorin had conscripted most of the workers into his army.

The curbs were of the finest white stone, and beyond them were the baked-brick alcoves where shop doorways beckoned.

Batok's cloth shop resided in one such alcove, illuminated by 'gia lamps opposite each shop door. Inside, three customers lingered among the ranks of colorful cloth hanging from the ceiling. Master Batok, helping a man at one end of his shop, noted his arrival with a brief nod that folded his chins into one fleshy mass.

Da-gore stepped unobserved into a back room crowded with stacks of cloth, some still wrapped in reed-paper shipping skins. Looking around to make certain he was alone, he pulled open a small, heavy door, ducked under the timber lintel, and descended stone steps to a dark floor where a dampness enveloped him like a clammy fist. The stench that lingered in the air made him think of those carcasses he'd seen flowing from the red-stone walls.

An octagon of moonglass set into the stone wall cast barely enough light to discern the shadowy shapes of barrels and crates lining the narrow passageway. He wondered briefly what was wrong with the glass that it should put out such a feeble light, but the thought evaporated as he spied the brighter glow of 'gia lamps spilling from an open doorway.

Around a wooden table, Maelc, Baer-on, and Soo-tuk stared at him as he stepped in. Two chairs were empty. Da-gore wheeled suddenly. At his back was Sirt, pressed against the wall with his sword drawn. Sirt grinned and sheathed the weapon.

Da-gore nodded. "It pays to be cautious these days."

At the table, Baer-on set down a flagon. "We thought it might be you, Da-gore." Baer-on's long gray hair was pulled back and tied in a series of knots; his braided gray beard was vaguely reminiscent of Quort Whip En'tuboc's in all but coloring.

"As I said, Master Baer-on, it pays to be cautious. Here you call me Jael-ik."

Sirt looked out the doorway, glanced up and down the dark passageway, and then returned to his seat at the table. He strode with the distinctive bearing Da-gore had come to recognize living among the Makir at Imo-suk.

Maelc's face bore the welted scars of oil scalding, a reminder of the years he'd spent in Zorin's Deep Chambers. He shoved back a chair with his booted foot. "Good to see you again, Master *Jael-ik*."

Soo-tuk, skin dusky as the night and hair black as jikloo fur, drew out a short dagger. "Batok hung the gold cloth, and we came." He began cleaning his fingernails.

Da-gore took the seat, laying his cloak upon the table. He eyed each man there: Soo-tuk, the boat captain; Maelc, the cooper; Sirt, once a Makir, now a First Shield in Zorin's Royal Residence Guards; and Baer-on, a gate warder in Hodin's Passage. "Today I was at Far Gate. The Golden Hills are crawling with Zorin's Gray Bears. Can someone here enlighten me?"

"The Golden Hills overlook the Eastern Passage," Sirt said. "The land lies low and there is no Rim-wall."

Da-gore nodded. "The original harbor inlet." From a tactical point of view, it was a poor position to defend. "Why has Zorin taken an interest in it now?"

Baer-on tipped up his flagon, then dragged a sleeve across his mouth. "I have been told the passage is to be chained."

"Chained? The Eastern Passage is still in use."

"It won't be for long." Soo-tuk drove his dagger into the tabletop. "Zorin intends to force all sea traffic through Hodin's Passage. Whatever manages to go out or come in by way of the Golden Hills will be scrutinized like a counting clerk's ledger."

"As it is in Hodin's Passage," Baer-on added.

Sirt said, "Zorin is rebuilding the bastions along the Golden Hills inlet and moving catapults and proj-lances into position. He must expect trouble from that quarter."

"Reasonable expectation." Da-gore didn't mention that Pyir Rhone was considering putting just such an incursion of forces through the Golden Hills by way of the Eastern Passage. "How soon before the passage is chained and the fortifications in place?"

Sirt said, "Zorin hopes to have the chain forged in three months."

"Three months to forge a chain?"

"It's not just any chain." Baer-on made a rueful face. "He's weaving a net of bronze links to stretch across the passage and drape to the bottom. It's twenty spans deep at the place Zorin plans to anchor it."

"What's he attempting to keep out of the harbor? Leviathan?"

The men around the table smiled.

"The Creator only knows." Soo-tuk yanked his dagger free and slid it into a hidden scabbard under his left arm. "At the very least, it will keep whales from snarling harbor traffic." The boat captain sounded none too happy about the new restriction he'd have to deal with.

Da-gore removed the little book from his cloak pocket and noted the information in code. "Our plan was to garrison arms at Sea Watch Rock and bring them in at the last moment. How will this affect those plans, Captain Soo-tuk?"

The chair creaked as the big seaman leaned back. "The Eastern Passage has always been closed to off-lander traffic, but we Atlanders have had free use of it since Hodin dug his passage. Now?" He shrugged. "My hold will be searched. The swords and proj-lances will certainly be confiscated. And I'll find myself in Zorin's Deep Chambers along with the other insurrectionists."

"Then we'll have to find another way." Da-gore glanced around the table. "Any ideas?"

Baer-on said, "Zorin has forbidden all but the smallest knives.

Even Soo-tuk's dagger is no longer allowed on the island, although I can't imagine our independent sea captain relinquishing it voluntarily." He gave a short laugh, then slid a taunting glance at Sirt. "The Makir are furious over the matter. But the last thing Zorin wants is an armed force of disgruntled Makir pounding at his gate."

Sirt's mouth curled in disgust. "Atlan is a country under siege by its own government." His hand went to the sword under his cloak. "I am not restricted because I am trusted in Zorin's residence. But the Makir in my kal-ee-hon avow that the only way Zorin will get their swords is to pry them from their bloody fingers."

"Not to mention proj-lances," Baer-on said.

Sirt's snarl deepened. "A proj-lance is a coward's weapon."

Da-gore seemed to remember hearing Klesc express a similar sentiment on more than one occasion. He made another entry, then put down the book and looked at his small cadre of trusted captains. Although they were as different as bumps on a three-point's back, they were alike in one important fact. They all believed in the Creator. He had picked them with that in mind.

"The Eastern Passage is a problem we will have to work on. Now, I want to know about the Rim-wall Highwatch Towers. Batok says they are being rebuilt."

"Both the towers and the signal pyres," Maelc said. "I should know. I've been working day and night to build the barrels Zorin needs to store food to feed the workers." He laughed suddenly. "And I make certain every barrel that leaves my shop for Zorin's warehouses has a handful of weevils thrown in. No extra charge."

The men laughed.

Da-gore grinned. "We fight on all fronts and in anyway we can." He sobered. "Everything I've heard points to Zorin knowing our forces mount against him. How did this happen?"

Sirt said, "It's no secret he's put out spies to secure his power. Plainly, one of them has dug his way into Imo-suk. Zorin knows his brother is there, and it doesn't take much imagination to figure out why."

"Then why hasn't he moved to crush our efforts?" Da-gore's fist bunched in sudden frustration. He didn't like not being able to read the enemy clearly. If it had been he who sat on the high seat of the Council of Ten and it was made known that an upstart rebellion was forming on the mainland less than twelve leagues from his shore, he'd have immediately sent in forces to grind out the threat.

Sirt shrugged. "Perhaps there's a certain smugness that comes from holding power for so many years. A misplaced confidence in the forces at his command."

Da-gore shot a glance. "You would know the sentiment of the warriors under Zorin's command, Sirt. Tell me of it."

The ex-Makir's expression remained unreadable, but his voice revealed the depth of his feelings. "There is much unrest. Yet if called upon to defend the realm, Zorin's warriors would fight—to the death if need be. It is only those like me, who once were Makir, being bound, who yearn with the fire of youth for the old ways—for a council that rules in justice. My small kal-ee-hon is restless. I fear the Makir may tip their hand before Pyir Rhone makes his move." Sirt stared at the stone cellar wall as if seeing a far-off vista—a view that once existed but now lived on only in memories. "It is we who look for our Pyir's return. And it is us whom Zorin fears."

"Yet Zorin trusts you."

Sirt's eyes returned to Da-gore. "Many, such as myself, keep our feelings tightly held within our hearts, even though they burn like live coals. We did not abandon Atlan as our brothers did. Their consciences are perhaps purer than ours, but we truly thought we could do more good staying behind after the betrayal and assassination of High Councilor Khore and the swift takeover of the council by Zorin. Had Pyir Rhone been here, perhaps we might have resisted Zorin."

Da-gore knew a little of what had transpired a hundred years earlier. "I'd heard he was away when it happened."

Maelc said, "He was deceived. The evil twin knew he could never seize the council if Pyir Rhone was in Hodin's Keep."

"Deceived how?"

Maelc said, "Zorin staged Lady Darha's kidnapping, holding his mother in the Deep Chambers somewhere in the Black Pool Caves. Then he forged documents that convinced his brother to leave Hodin's Keep on a foray to rescue their mother from the old Rimwall Highwatch Tower at Dirgen's Naval. Once his brother was away, Zorin assassinated his father, shattered the Council of Ten, and secured his mother in the royal residence—an assurance that Pyir Rhone would not try his hand."

Sirt said, "Zorin would have murdered Pyir Rhone too, had he not survived the Pit of Ramor. As was the custom at the time, a survivor had to be set free. Zorin's hold over the people was still too tenuous to break that ancient tradition."

He had never heard Rhone speak of this, and out of respect for their leader, neither had the Makir bound under him. "Why was Pyir Rhone put in the Pit?"

Sirt said, "Zorin claimed the assassins who murdered their father were under Pyir Rhone's orders. Few in Atlan actually believed him, but by then he had the council behind him."

Da-gore was surprised he'd never heard this before. But it was old history, and he brought the conversation back to the present. "And what of Lady Darha? Batok says Zorin has moved her."

The already somber mood in the room darkened. Sirt peered at him through eyes smoldering in anger. "It's true. I spoke with Lady Darha only last week—that was the final time. Three days ago, she was secreted away in the middle of the night. Not even the Council of Ten knows where he's keeping her—only Zorin's inner circle."

Pyir Rhone's whole strategy revolved around a swift raid on the Royal Residence by a tight group of handpicked Makir. Once Lady Darha was safely in their hands, the invasion would begin. This new wrinkle would delay that, and the longer Pyir Rhone waited, the stronger Zorin's defenses became. "What is being done to find her?"

Soo-tuk said, "Our numbers are small, but our fingers stretch to the farthest corners of Atlan. I've already contacted my men, who are even now reaching out to their contacts. If she was taken away by boat, I will hear of it."

"Likewise here," Maelc said. "Some men conveniently forget their loyalties when I deliver twenty barrels but write eighteen. Such matters are not closely scrutinized by the counting clerks." He winked. "A gleck or two pressed into the right palm is amply rewarded."

"The word is moving through my circles as well, Master Jael-ik," Baer-on said.

Sirt nodded. "I, too. I have contacted my kal-ee-hon, but my position forces me to move slowly."

"I understand." Da-gore stood. "I'm afraid my report will not be well received, but Pyir Rhone will know what to do with the information." He took up his cloak, buttoned the book back into the pocket, and put it over his shoulder.

"There is one other thing," Sirt said.

Da-gore stiffened at the tone in the ex-Makir's voice. "What?"

"The Lodath of the Oracle has made overtures toward Atlan. Zorin is to entertain one of his representatives in a few days."

"The Lodath?" Visions of the tyrant, and the Evil One he served, swam clear in Da-gore's memory as if it had been only yesterday that he'd cast aside the crystal Pledge Pendant and broken the Deceiver's hold on him. "What business could he have with Zorin?"

"An alliance."

He was momentarily stunned. "An alliance between Atlan and the Land of Nod would strengthen Zorin's hand immeasurably."

Sirt nodded gravely.

Da-gore said, "Why would the Lodath seek an alliance with Atlan? The two countries have never had dealings."

"It's a mystery for which I have no answer," Sirt said.

"One thing is certain: The Lodath must see in this a way to advance the cause of that Evil One he serves. This is not good news." Da-gore had to get back to Rhone at once with this.

Sirt nodded. "It seems the sun moves against us. If Pyir Rhone delays much longer, all will be lost."

"Bad news heaped upon bad news." He shook his head. "I must return to Imo-suk immediately."

Sirt said, "Advise Pyir Rhone that saving Lady Darha might not be an option."

Da-gore stood there a moment as the reality of that sank in like a lead weight. "Time is certainly an enemy in this."

Their eyes leaped suddenly to the doorway at the sound of heavy footsteps in the passage. A moment later, Master Batok stepped into the room and gave out a long, wheezing breath. "I finally shooed the last of them out and barred the door." He looked at Da-gore. "Your meeting satisfactory?"

The news he'd received was hardly that. "I accomplished what I intended."

"Good, good." His small eyes gleamed in the lamp light.

"I must hurry."

"You'll want to be going out the back way, Master Jael-ik." Batok glanced around and lowered his voice. "Never know who might be watching."

"Your caution is wisdom in these dark days." Da-gore turned to his captains. "You are doing well. Let us ask the Creator for guidance in this matter."

They nodded and Da-gore led them in a prayer, then turned to leave.

Sirt spoke before he reached the doorway. "Master Jael-ik." The ex-Makir Warrior stood from the table and came to him. "My niece. How is she?"

"Mistress Leenah is safe at Imo-suk. You needn't worry about her."

A cloud of concern gathered in Sirt's eyes. "See that she does not come here ... at least, until this is all over."

"I'm sure Pyir Rhone would not permit it." Da-gore clasped him on the shoulder, then hurried after Batok.

26

Mansnatchers Attack

Out beyond the heavy walls of Imo-suk, Leenah turned an eye to the darkening sky. Where was Gur? Still feasting on wild Atlanian fruits? She shut her eyes and willed her thoughts to reach out. Nothing. She was angry. Not at Gur, for the scarlet dragon was but a young, wild beast off frolicking with others of his kind. And not at Rhone either—not exactly. Although not the wild beast Gur was, he too *was* with his own kind and content to play the waiting game.

But she was not!

In the long, late shadows, a herd of red deer bounded up the cliff side from the sea and scampered across the hard-packed road, making for the distant, dark forest.

She started down the road. It eventually would have taken her to Marin-ee, but she had no intention of walking that far. She needed to be free of Imo-suk's suffocating embrace. She needed to walk off her frustrations, to breathe the clean sea air … and think.

Rhone had confided much in her. It was plain his whole plan revolved around one thing, and once that was accomplished, there would be little stopping an invasion of Atlan. In spite of his concerns over Zorin's warriors, she had no doubt three ranks of determined Makir could rout ten times their number of Atlanian regulars.

She kicked at a stone and watched it skitter down the road. She remembered how Uncle Sirt had refused to leave Atlan, but Uncle Debne had fled to the mainland with her mother and father. He'd protected them on their journey to her father's homeland in Morg'Seth and then stayed on the mainland, refusing to align himself with *that conniving rebel,* as he most often called Zorin. She remembered Uncle Debne shaking with rage at the atrocities Zorin had committed—shaking more at his own impotence to right the wrongs.

And her mother.... In those days, all Leenah remembered was her mother's deep sadness. She hadn't wanted to leave Atlan, but after Zorin's takeover, there had been the purging. Leenah's father had been targeted, so they had to flee. Tears came to her eyes. She'd been a child at the time, and the fear had been so real that she felt it even now.

It was nearly dark, and she stopped and looked back at the vague hunkering shadow of Imo-suk. She hadn't intended to walk so far.

Where could Gur be? She scanned the sky. Stars were already twinkling, and a large moon was rising above the horizon right where she imagined Atlan lay—but no Gur. Her gaze swept around, then lurched back. A shadow had begun to emerge from the smooth, pale glow of the lesser light. As she stared at it, the shadow grew larger and became three distinct shadows. At first she hoped it was Gur returning. But no, the shadows weren't quite the right shape. They weren't scarlet dragons at all. Her stomach knotted as their shapes became clear.

Mansnatchers!

She cast about for cover, but the ground was a bare rock overhanging the sea. Wheeling around, she set her eye on the distant fort, now almost completely swallowed up by the night, and started to run. She heard their hunting screeches as they swelled in size as if emerging directly from the pale, milky smooth surface of the moon. They swooped up over the edge of the cliff, their long, spear-topped heads turning left and right, their huge black eyes glinting faintly in the moonlight.

Leenah put on a burst of speed. The three hunters banked toward her, their hunting screech grating in her ears. Panic exploded in her chest as she glanced over her shoulder, seeing the giant hunters dive out of the sky, their talons stretching out. In the blackness of the night, it was impossible to see exactly how near they were, but the mighty flapping of their long, pointed wings drummed as if inside her head. Her heart felt as if it would burst through her chest.

At the last moment, she lunged headlong and hit hard, the breath exploding from her lungs, her arms and chin grinding to a halt upon the rocky ground. The hunters whooshed over her. She saw one mansnatcher winging skyward as the other two hunters banked tightly for a second try.

And then she spied something else. A single, yellowish eye had suddenly appeared down the road. It glared at her from the darkness as it raced toward her at a ferocious speed, growling, but the drumming of blood in her ears nearly drowned the sound out. She scrambled to her feet, ignoring the stinging pain of her dive for safety. The mansnatchers were swooping back. Racing for the distant fort, she craned her neck at that hideous eye behind her.

Although her legs felt as if they were flying, she was losing ground. Overhead, the three hunters swooped in for the final kill.

Imo-suk might well have been a thousand leagues away—or not there at all—for all the hope she had of reaching it. She was trapped between the mansnatchers and whatever creature was growling on her heels. Even the blood and strength of Hodin flowing through her veins couldn't save her now. The hunting screech seemed to vibrate to her bones, but it wasn't going to be the mansnatchers who got her....

In her next breath, the creature was upon her, but instead of crushing her to the ground and ripping her apart, it snarled up alongside her, reached out, swept her off her feet, and deposited her upon a hard, bouncing spine.

"Hold tight!"

"Kev-nn?"

Kev-nn gave her a grin as he pushed a lever forward and the cart leaped ahead. A mansnatcher screeched. Kev-nn swerved hard. Leenah lurched and gave a sharp cry of pain as raking claws ripped away the shoulder of her dress and cut deep into her back.

The cart wobbled onto two wheels, then straightened out, its front lamp jittering wildly across the dark road ahead. She wrapped her arms about his waist, fingers dug deep into Kev-nn's heavy leather jerkin as she stared past his shoulder at Imo-suk growing nearer. The hunters wheeled in front of the moon and dove.

"Here they come again!" she shouted above the roar of the straining cycler. Imo-suk was still too far. Her grasp tightened.

Kev-nn glanced once at the creatures, then turned his face back to the road. The chilling cry of the diving hunters raked through her body. Kev-nn suddenly shoved one lever forward while hauling back on another. The cart spun to the right and careened toward the edge of the cliffs as deadly talons swept past, missing them again; but as the creatures banked away, a huge wing came around and batted her from the saddle. She slammed into the rocky ground and tumbled to a stop. Stunned, she watched Kev-nn's cart careen toward the edge of the cliff and finally grind to a halt on the brink.

Leenah shook the fog from her eyes and glanced for Kev-nn. The big man lay a few spans away near the wreckage. Overhead, the mansnatchers strove skyward on their powerful wings and pinwheeled for the final kill. She leaped to her feet, ignoring the raw pain that burned up her leg and hip, and rushed to his side. Bits and pieces of machinery were scattered about him. He was not moving when she reached him, but groaning softly, his wide eyes dazed.

"Kev-nn!"

His eyes went to her face. "Sorry," he said through clenched teeth, gritting back pain. Then his eyes widened, and he looked past her. She spun around. A mansnatcher was almost on her. Without thinking, she grabbed up a heavy metal cylinder that had spilled from Kev-nn's cart, long as her arm and thick around as a small tree trunk.

One of the hunters swept in, and Leenah shoved the metal into its shiny, black claws, sharper than harvesting blades. The mansnatcher tore the cylinder from her fists and with a violent wind, flapped skyward, carrying it out over the sea. Its horny beak stabbed ferociously at the object, and Leenah could almost feel its frustration at realizing it had not snagged flesh, but something hard and cold and unpalatable. With a nerve-fraying cry of rage, the hunter released the decoy, and it plummeted into the sea.

She tried to pull Kev-nn to his feet, but he gave out a cry and grabbed at his back. "Can't move. My back."

"We can't stay here!" She couldn't carry him, and she wouldn't leave him. She cast about and grabbed up a long bronze rod from among the scattered parts.

"Go!" Kev-nn ordered.

The rod was solid and heavy, though a poor weapon to use against mansnatchers. She stood to face their outstretched claws. Since the day the Mother and Father disobeyed the Creator's command and ate the forbidden fruit, death was the inevitable end to all men. She had always hoped that when the day came, and she stared her own mortality in the face, she would do it with bravery and dignity.

"Come get me!" she shouted, her voice ringing above the hunting screech that set every nerve in her body blazing. She steadied herself, drew back on the pipe, and took aim at the broad chest growing larger before her eyes.

And then with a booming rush of wind and a blur, something reddish, the size of a house, swept past and grabbed one of the mansnatchers in its immense claws, scattering the other two. The wind of its passing knocked her to the ground, and when she looked up, scarlet scales flashed like blood in the moonlight. Gur's long neck stretched for the sky, and his snaky tail flopped wildly as enormous wings strove heavenward.

The two remaining mansnatchers ceased tumbling through the air and righted themselves. Ignoring the plight of their fellow hunter, they turned dark, evil eyes back on her and Kev-nn, then started their dive.

Gur, not nearly as swift, wheeled heavily above them. With a single snap of his powerful jaws, he bit off the head of the mansnatcher in his grasp and dropped it. Circling back, Gur dove, red eyes seeming to burn with determination. As he got closer, his head drew back on his long neck and then shot forward. With a roar and a blinding glare that lit the night with crimson light, Gur spat a tongue of fire. Instantly one of the mansnatchers folded its wings and nose-dived toward the ground, trailing a spiral of smoke.

Leenah stood over Kev-nn and, with a lunge, thrust the rod into the belly of the last mansnatcher. The impact knocked her to the ground as the beast tore the weapon from her hands. She lay stunned and momentarily helpless. The third mansnatcher broke off the attack and dipped sharply toward the sea. Gur swooped after it, reached out a clawed foot, and snagged the hunter out of the air. Clutching the snapping beast, Gur soared out to sea, climbing higher and higher until he was only a smudge against the night sky. He turned a slow arc and dove back toward the cliffs. Gaining speed, he swept low.

Leenah feared Gur's red belly would scrape the ground, but at the last moment the scarlet dragon released the mansnatcher, slamming it with deadly results into the cliffs, and pulled up out of the dive, nearly impaling himself on the jagged rocks. He climbed skyward again and circled, searching with a hunter's eyes for more danger. Satisfied, he glided down and landed heavily nearby, folding his wings.

"Kev-nn!" She staggered to her feet, her back and shoulder burning where they had been raked by the mansnatcher's talon. She dropped to his side as Gur lumbered over to the charred remains of the mansnatcher and sniffed it.

Leenah heard men rushing down the road from Imo-suk, alerted to their peril by the air battle.

"Don't move. Help is coming."

"My cart!"

"It's wrecked."

"Oh no," he groaned.

"And so are you, so lay still."

The poultice stung at first, but as the healer promised, the bite of the acerbic roots and leaves soon faded as warmth spread down Leenah's shoulder and up her neck.

"The mansnatcher's talons contain a poison," the healer said as she tended to her other wounds. "Fortunately, it's easily remedied with lance willow and sweet temmon." She smiled. "As the poison works its way out of your blood, you may experience some confusion … or delusions. So, for the next several days, if you should get any strange or outlandish notions, like turning somersaults across the parade ground, don't."

Leenah was only half-listening to the woman. She'd hardly have any notions along those lines, she was sure. Her gaze kept returning to the tall, arched portal into the next room where the light from several moonglasses cast a shifting of shadows, as people moved about the adjoining room just out of her sight. "What about Kev-nn?"

The healer glanced up from her work, her brown eyes gentle. "I don't know yet. Mistress Delah and Seri will do all they can for him."

She'd been taken to this room, while Kev-nn, strapped to a wide wooden slat, had been whisked off to the other. She strained to hear their words, muffled by heavy tapestries just beyond the portal.

When the healer finished dressing her scrapes and scratches, Leenah slipped back into her tattered dress and went into the next room. Rhone was standing near Kev-nn, who was strapped to a table. The healers were working on his back. She moved toward Rhone. Sensing she was there, he turned.

"How is he?" she whispered.

Kev-nn rolled his head to one side and looked at her; a dreamy glaze dulled his otherwise alert eyes. He grinned. "I'm doing juuu-uuust fine."

"What did they give you?"

"I don't know, but it was good."

She glanced up at Rhone.

"Maribin," he said.

"Oh." She knew about that. She said to Kev-nn, "At least the pain is gone."

"For the moment." He gave her another silly grin as his eyelids drooped languidly.

She said quietly, "Is it broken?"

Rhone nodded, took her by the elbow, and walked her around the corner, out of earshot. "The healers are optimistic. Kev-nn still has feeling in his toes, so the chord was not severed. But he will be a long time recovering." He looked at her. "Are you all right?"

"Yes. The healers treated me for the poison, and the rest are mostly scrapes and cuts." She shrugged. "They'll heal."

"The healers got to you soon enough. If this had happened in the Wild Lands and you didn't have the remedy, it might have killed you. If not, the effects could've lasted for months."

"I thank the Creator that Kev-nn showed up when he did."

"And Gur," Rhone noted. "Kev-nn was coming from his shop in Derbin-ee. He had with him parts for the gormerin." He frowned. "This means there will be a delay in finishing it. It'll be months before Kev-nn is back on his feet and able to work on it."

Leenah's heart sank. Another delay. Sometimes she wondered if she would ever see Atlan!

※

The sun was high and hot, and the day seemed to stretch on forever as she sat on the stone ledge in the patch of wavering shade beneath Gur's wide wings. She stared out across the blue distance of the Great Sea, listless and distracted. It must be the poison. It even seemed to shape her thoughts. The healer had said it might be days before the poison worked its way out of her body.

"What's it like to fly?" She lifted a keelit from a basket in her lap and tossed it skyward. Gur's head snapped out and snatched it out of the air. "Can't you tell me?"

But the scarlet dragon seemed unaware she was speaking to him. She closed her eyes in the shade of his outstretched wings. If she could fly, she'd leap off of Imo-suk's highest battlement and wing free as a bird all the way to Atlan. She felt her lips rise in a long, slow smile. Maybe she could, and just hadn't tried before. Maybe it's like being a sensitive—a gift hidden until you reach out and take hold of it for yourself.

She opened her eyes and lifted them toward the tawny stone watchtower perched on the promontory of the cliff. Might she not leap from that precipice and soar to Atlan? A frown replaced the smile. At the rate Rhone was going, he would never get there.

The scrape of heavy footsteps coming up the stairs pulled her view around. "Klesc." She tossed him a keelit. "How high can you throw it?"

He grinned, heaved back, and flung the keelit far into the sky. With a whoosh of wings, Gur leaped after it, caught it, then stretched out and glided over the flat blue sea, banking slowly back around, flapping with a lazy, effortless rhythm.

Leenah shaded her eyes against the sunlight and laughed.

"You are looking well, Mistress Leenah."

"My brain is swimming." She looked at him and grinned. "You ever wonder what it would be like to fly? Klesc, I think that if I tried, really tried, I might be able to actually do it."

"Now that's the poison talking."

She returned her view to Gur. "I suppose so." She sighed. No one would ever believe her. She would just have to show them ... later. Right now, she was suddenly too tired to worry about it.

Klesc watched the dragon circle around the end of Imo-suk and then climb back toward the high wall. "I heard Gur lived up to his name last night."

"He was wonderful. I told you someday he'd strike fear in the hearts of his enemies."

"I just came from Kev-nn. He's wondering how you are doing."

"The healer's stopped giving him Maribin?"

Klesc nodded. "And he is not in such a happy state."

"I must go see him. He saved my life last night."

"So I heard."

"I'm sorry he got hurt."

"I don't think he is. I think he's proud to have been able to save you, Mistress Leenah."

She smiled. They all treated her so well here. Why couldn't she just be content to wait? But the more time that passed, the more anxious she became. She glanced back at the tower. One leap. One leap is all it would take. One leap and she'd be free. She'd soar off to Atlan with Gur at her side, rescue Lady Darha from Zorin's clutches, and open the way for Rhone to take back Atlan!

"Who's this coming up the road?" Klesc shaded his eyes to the south.

With a sigh, Leenah let go of the fantasy. She looked away from the tower and squinted down at the road, but the traveler was still too distant for her to make out. She could fly down and greet him. "I'll find out." She stood on the edge of the stone wall.

Klesc took her by the arm and pulled her down from the ledge. "Not that way."

With a rush of wind, Gur settled upon a crumbling merlon and sat there with his wings held out to catch the warming sun.

After a moment Klesc said, "It looks like Da-gore."

She followed him down twisting flights of stairs and out into the open parade ground. Rhone had already gotten the word and was waiting there as Da-gore strode beneath the tall, arched portal.

"You're back soon," Rhone said.

Da-gore eyed each of them but didn't smile. "I have pressing news, Pyir Rhone."

He stiffened slightly. "Let's go to my quarters."

Leenah sensed the tension in both men. She knew what colored Rhone's voice was his suspicions about Da-gore's loyalty. But what news could Da-gore be bringing to lend such a grave countenance to his face?

※

"Two things," Da-gore began, carrying a glass of water to the window and staring out over the sea. He paused to slake his thirst from the long walk up from Derbin-ee, then turned and said, "First, they have moved your mother."

"No!" Leenah reeled as if hit with a fist. This could only mean yet another delay in the planned invasion.

"I'm afraid it is true, Mistress Leenah."

Rhone folded his arms, his expression unreadable. "Moved her where?"

He left the window and set his glass on a table. "Don't know yet. Batok has his canics sniffing the woods. So far they've come up empty-handed, but it's only a matter of time. We'll know soon enough."

Rhone drew in a breath and exhaled sharply. "And the other thing?"

Da-gore shook his head. "This may be much worse. The Lodath of the Oracle has approached Zorin with the intention of forming an alliance."

"An alliance?" Leenah blurted, staring at Rhone. He seemed unmoved. Was he made of stone? Her head began to spin, and she grabbed for the arm of a chair. How could he take it so calmly? "We can't fight Zorin's troops and Nod City!" As the initial flare of emotion passed, she saw that he too was struggling with this. She took a step toward him, suddenly wanting to reach out and comfort him. She stopped herself and gripped her waist. These mood swings frightened her. Leaping emotions were unfamiliar to her.

Rhone looked back at Da-gore. "He knows, then."

"Zorin?" Da-gore raised a questioning eyebrow.

"The Oracle. He's learned why I must take back Atlan and the Creator's plan to nurture the child there. The Oracle—the Deceiver—must suspect the future Redeemer of man will come through Noah. Now he moves to cut him off. I see the pattern developing. The more the Deceiver learns, the more he narrows his attack. Have you mentioned this to anyone else?"

Da-gore shook his head. "Of course not. I put to sea on the first boat bound for the mainland and came directly here."

"Our options grow small. It's almost as if the Creator is forcing our feet onto a different path." Rhone told him about Leenah's narrow escape the night before. "The gormerin will not move until Kev-nn is well enough to finish work on it."

Da-gore dismissed the problem with a wave of his hand. "It's probably just as well. It diverts our energies." He paced to the window and stared again at the horizon. "I fear Zorin already knows of the gormerin." His gaze remained upon the far horizon, where Atlan lay just beyond his view.

In some deep, gut-wrenching way, Leenah was jealous of him. He'd been to Atlan over and over again, while she, an Atlander by birth, languished here in this ancient pile of rock. Her thoughts drifted, and she raised her arms, almost feeling the wind beneath them lift her.

Rhone said, "Zorin does *know* we are building the gormerin."

Da-gore turned with a questioning look in his eyes.

"We captured a spy while you were away."

"What did he tell you?"

"Nothing. Someone got to him before we could learn anything. He's dead."

"Someone? In Imo-suk?"

Rhone nodded.

"Unfortunate." Da-gore frowned. "It seems we have a traitor among us, then."

"The idea has been discussed."

Da-gore went thoughtfully silent a moment, then drew in a breath. "By whatever means Zorin found out, he is making preparations. The Golden Hills are swarming with his Gray Bears, and he's reinforcing the redoubts at the mouth of the Eastern Passage. He intends to chain it. When he does, all traffic will have to come and go by way of Hodin's Passage. And finally, Zorin is rebuilding the Rim-wall Highwatches. He's expecting us, Pyir Rhone."

"Until my mother can be located, we are rooted here."

Da-gore considered him and seemed to be pondering carefully his next words. "It might be that we are forced to make a move regardless. Your mandate from the Creator was to take back Atlan. There was nothing in it concerning the safety of your mother, Pyir Rhone. As much as it pains me to say this, she is expendable."

"No. We're going to have to work around this new tangle. There has to be another way."

Another way? Another five years is what he means! Leenah was almost too tired to care. She turned, staggered, caught herself, and left.

27

A Little Poison

*T*he world plummeted away past the toes of her shoes. More than two hundred spans below her, the blue sea painted the rocky shore with white breakers. From so high up, the wharf where Lorun's body had been borne away in the boat was a little jut of rock stretching out into the deep blue water.

A breeze tugged at her dress, urging her to try ... to leap ... to fly away. It buffeted her shoulders and whispered encouragement in her ear. *Just one step ... then freedom....* She raised her arms, and the wind beneath them seemed to bear her up. Giddy with the sensation, she saw the rocky coast spiral in her mind.

One more step, Leenah, and you can fly away with the dragons. Fly ... fly ... fly ... to Atlan, where you belong.

"Atlan. It's where I belong." She swung her arms in a slow circle. How they wanted to lift her away! Was this the confidence a bird knew when it came time to fledge the nest? She stretched her foot out over nothingness and spread her wings wide....

"What are you doing?" Rhone's harsh words crashed in on her reverie, while his powerful hand caught her by the arm, picked her up, and hauled her off the tower's ledge. "Leenah! Look at me!" Rhone stared worriedly into her eyes.

"Rhone?" She frowned. Why had he stopped her? Didn't he know she was going to fly off with the dragons?

"What are you thinking, Leenah?"

"Thinking? I was going to fly away with the dragons." She swept an arm toward the precipice. Why was he angry? She was going to rescue his mother.

"Oh, Leenah." He hugged her to him, crushing her in his huge arms. She could feel them tremble, his heart racing. "It's the poison. Come with me; we need to get you somewhere safe until it's out of you."

"But I don't want to go down there." She dug in her heals. "I want to fly."

He overpowered her, dragging her along. "You can walk on your own, or I'll carry you."

"I don't want to walk. I want to fly."

He stopped and looked at her. "I once told you what sometimes happens when people are poisoned by mansnatchers. Delusions are common. Leenah, you almost stepped off that ledge!"

"I did? You did?" Her head was fuzzy.

"In the forest, on our way to Derbin-ee. Remember?"

"That was so long ago ... wasn't it? I can fly. I know I can."

Rhone gripped her by the shoulders, taking a controlled breath. "The air is not right for flying. You'll show me tomorrow how you can fly." He guided her down to her quarters and sat her upon a bench by the only window in her small room. "Now, you must stay here. Zorin can't know you can fly."

"Oh, you're right," she whispered, quickly looking around the small gray room. One of its stark stone walls was concealed behind a tapestry, purchased in Derbin-ee, depicting Atlan's wondrous harbor. The other three walls were bare stone. Her bed stood in one corner; four chairs and a table occupied the middle of the small room; and a long bench with cushions, upon which she presently sat, stood before a small window. The stone floor was covered with small woolen rugs, colorful but threadbare. There was no sign of Zorin's spies.

Rhone gave her a small smile and sat beside her, taking her hand. His hands were warm against hers, which lately always seemed chilled. "Promise me you won't try to fly without me."

"I promise." She didn't like it, but she knew Rhone was correct. The air wasn't right for flying, and Zorin mustn't find out.

He smiled. "I'll come back later, and we'll go to supper."

When he left, she remained awhile upon the bench, staring out her window at the forest and the flocks of bright birds that soared and sparkled in the sunlight. Her thoughts drifted. She couldn't see the water from here, but the smell of it filled her with longing. After a while, she stretched out across her bed and counted the ceiling beams as the room contracted about her.

She dozed throughout the warm hours of the second quartering, and as she did, a dream took hold of her and became so real that it pulled her from her nap and set her pacing the floor. Rhone would wait forever before making his move, but what if she could clear the way for him? What if she found where Zorin had hidden Lady Darha and set her free? If she could do that, Rhone would have no excuse to delay further.

She paced furiously, turning this over in her brain. In a moment her mind was set, and with the decision came a curious euphoria that spread through her like the warmth of a bright day. She touched her fingers, no longer chilled. Quickly she changed into a fresh dress and packed a shiverthorn backpack with the few things she would need.

The Makir were assembling on the parade ground outside her door for their second quartering exercises. Rhone would be among them, and so would most of the warriors encamped at Imo-suk.

Only the outpost guards would not be participating. Now was the perfect time. Taking a cloak over her arm and gathering the small pack beneath the cloak, she slipped out her door. She could simply take wing and soar to Atlan ... but she'd promised Rhone she wouldn't fly today.

Something nagged at the back of her brain, but try as she might, she couldn't remember what it was. A brief recollection of Rhone leaving her room was all, although she was sure there was more. She struggled a moment with the lost memory, then shrugged. Whatever it was she'd forgotten, it would come back to her—eventually.

Below her room, the men were beginning their exercises. Rank upon rank filled the parade ground, while on her level of the wall, First Statre Larik's booming voice called the moves and set the rhythm.

She made her way down a passage to a barred door. Lifting the bar, she stepped out onto a broad ledge. A short flight of steps took her down to the rocky ground outside the old fort's walls. Once free of Imo-suk, she strolled casually past an outpost, waved to the guards there, plucked a golden flower that sprang profusely along the cracks in the cliff, and descended the long switchback staircase down to the sea.

If she couldn't fly to Atlan, she'd take the boat, row to Atlan, scale the Rim-wall, find Lady Darha, free her, and then return. Leenah grinned at the simple elegance of her plan as she placed her cloak and pack in the bottom of the small craft. She cast off the line and shoved to sea, leaping aboard. Taking an oar in each hand, she gave the boat its first, tentative nudge away from shore. Soon her rowing fell into a steady rhythm. She shut her eyes and drew in a deep, exhilarating breath. It was the perfect plan. Why hadn't Rhone thought of it?

The boat lurched ahead, water rippling along its sides, the sweet smell of the sea all around her. She felt the wind rushing under her wings and imagined herself soaring among a flop of scarlet dragons. A vague concern as to the direction the bow of her boat was pointing momentarily brushed across her brain, then vanished as she swooped and stretched her scarlet wings to catch the sunlight.

❦

About the first of the third quartering, Rhone went to Leenah's chamber to escort her to dinner. He didn't think of the extra attention as watchfulness over her safety, more as a chance to spend a pleasant evening with the woman who had captured his heart. Captured it, she had, but he tried not to let his feelings interfere with the problems that seemed to gather about him like stalking mansnatchers. For tonight at least, he was determined not to think of them. Leenah's brush with death had strangely intensified his feelings toward her. To lose her was unthinkable.

When he didn't find her in her room, his concern was greater than the brief stab of annoyance. He should have left a guard outside her door. She wasn't well. His long strides drove him up the stone flight, three steps at a time. She wasn't on the wall where she often spent time.

A thought occurred suddenly, and dread tore at him as he raced to the tower. Grabbing the edge of a merlon, he leaned over, his breath catching at the dizzying height. With a surge of relief, he stepped back. At least her body didn't lie broken at the base of the cliff. Turning away, he went searching for her.

"We saw Mistress Leenah," one of the guards finally told him, after he had checked on three watch stations with no luck.

Isen said, "We didn't think anything of it, Pyir Rhone. The Mistress often strolls out to gather flowers."

"It's true," Glein said nervously. "We didn't know Mistress Leenah wasn't supposed to go down to the sea dock."

Rhone glanced to the cliffs. "She went to the dock?"

Isen nodded. "We'd have stopped her if we'd known, Pyir Rhone."

Why hadn't he alerted the guards? "If you should see Mistress Leenah, escort her to her chamber, then come find me. Understood?"

Isen and Glein nodded, glancing worriedly at each other. It wasn't their fault. Rhone sprinted down the zigzagging stairs, leaping them two and three at a time. At the cliff base, Leenah's footprints angled off in the sand toward the wharf.

"Leenah!" he shouted. He was nearly to the wharf when his heart bounded into his throat. The boat was gone!

Standing upon the stone quay and staring at the empty slip where the boat had been moored, he continued to deny what the evidence was telling him. *She wouldn't have!* He looked out to sea, glanced hopefully up and down the rocky beach, and called for her again and again. Then he spied the golden flower lying upon the stones. He scooped it up and glared out to sea. *She had done it!*

Anger and worry surged together as he crushed the flower in his fist and hurried back to Imo-suk.

�֎

"She's trying to reach Atlan."

"On her own? Can this be true?" Larik cast an incredulous glance at Rhone as the two of them strode through the now-empty exercise ground.

"She dropped this on the quay." He showed Larik the crumpled flower he still had pressed into his fist.

They stepped under an arched portal and up a flight of steps. Rhone had sent a runner ahead to gather his captains in his quarters, but he had personally gone to find Larik.

Larik scowled at the flower. "What can that woman be thinking?"

"It's the poison thinking for her." How long, he wondered, before she came to her senses? And once she did, would she be able to find her way back? Would she be terrified to discover herself alone at sea? Somehow, Rhone doubted she would—at least not right away. Leenah was made of sterner stuff. But the fear would come, eventually, and then the terror … if some Turnling didn't get to her before that.

He shoved that thought out of his brain.

Inside Rhone's quarters, Klesc and the others were already assembled. Rhone wasted no time explaining the emergency and giving each of them orders to ride swiftly to the captains of all their boats, which had been secreted in small harbors up and down the coast.

"I'm certain she's heading to Atlan. She may or may not have the strength to reach it, but regardless, we must find her before Zorin's lookouts spy her. Concentrate your search on the stretch of water between here and Atlan. She's alone in a small boat, and she will be difficult to find. If by some stroke of fortune she does reach Atlan and is spotted from the Rim-wall, Zorin's lookouts may dismiss her as of no threat. I pray that will be the case."

He looked at each of them. "Be alert, and remember our ships must not be seen. A single rowboat might not raise Zorin's suspicion, but our fleet abroad at sea will certainly force his hand. And one last thing. We must keep this quiet. Tell no one, except those few who must know. And warn them to silence as well."

His captains left, just Klesc and Larik remaining behind. Rhone said to Larik, "She's forcing our hand."

"Leenah has been impatient since the start," Klesc said. "She doesn't understand what is involved here."

"Maybe she understands better than you think." Larik leveled his view at Rhone.

Rhone chose to dismiss the insinuation for the moment. "Da-gore says Zorin has moved my mother, and that her new location has not yet been discovered. Leenah must think she can find her."

"Da-gore? Are you going to believe him?" Larik's gray eyebrows bunched together with the faint scowl.

"He has given me no reason to doubt him. I saw his concern when he returned with this news. I can't believe he's the spy among us." Neither Larik nor Klesc would be easily swayed, but Leenah believed in Da-gore, and right now, that was good enough for him.

Larik stiffened slightly. "Just the same, I would advise you to keep this news from him."

Rhone felt his anger rising, but Larik's advice was usually prudent. "He'll know something is wrong. How can we keep it from him? Leenah is gone."

"Then send him away on some urgent business."

"On some trumped-up business, you mean?"

Larik eyed him with a cool indifference. "Call it what you will, Pyir Rhone."

There it was again, that undertone of resentment. "Something is bothering you, First Statre Larik?"

Larik's jaw worked a moment, his eye hardening. "Might I speak freely?"

"Speak."

"You've changed, Pyir Rhone. You're not the same man Zorin exiled from Atlan. This new faith of yours has made you weak. You let your friendship with the off-lander Da-gore, who shares this faith, cloud your thinking. You showed leniency toward the spy Lorun, and you've yet to punish the man who killed him." Larik's gaze settled momentarily upon Klesc, then shot back and narrowed. "Your father would not have handled it this way."

"My father is dead."

"And that is truly unfortunate." Larik's hard gaze spoke what he really meant.

For months Rhone had sensed Larik's growing impatience. Like Leenah, Larik wanted action, not this endless planning. Were they right and he wrong? At times he didn't understand his own indecision and questioned his strength to rule. He'd be the first to admit it had changed him, but had it weakened him?

And did the other men share Larik's feelings? He returned Larik's stare. He was still Pyir. He was the leader of the Makir, and the invasion would proceed under his timetable, not Larik's ... or Leenah's.

"Your concerns are noted, First Statre Larik. Now, ready the Makir to move out at a moment's notice."

Larik nodded. "As you order, Pyir Rhone." He turned stiffly and strode out the doorway.

Rhone shifted his view. Klesc's mouth had settled into a faint frown, yet his eyes revealed nothing of his thoughts.

"You agree with him?"

"No, Pyir Rhone." But there was a momentary hitch of uncertainty in his reply.

"You don't think I delay too long?"

His eyes narrowed slightly. "I did not say that." Klesc seemed uncomfortable with the question. "I understand Mistress Leenah's impatience, and First Statre Larik's. I feel it too, and so do many others, but you are our Pyir, and we follow you."

Klesc was holding back something. Klesc had been with him from the beginning, and although their relationship had not begun on the most cordial grounds, over the years a close friendship had grown. Klesc, like Leenah and Da-gore, was one of his strongest allies.

"And what else, Klesc?"

Klesc let go a breath. "I was with you when the Messenger,

Sari'el, brought us out of the prison and guided us to safety. I know how the Creator touched your lifeless body with but a word, breathing life back into it. He is the One who sent you on this quest to secure Atlan as a refuge for the child, Noah. I do not claim to understand all that this portends, but there is a plan unfolding here. Do you not think he can empower you to victory, Pyir Rhone?"

"Of course I believe that, Klesc."

"Then why do you question our ability to take back Atlan now?"

"Atlan is a fortified country. Our numbers are yet few, Klesc."

Klesc considered a moment. "I wonder, Pyir Rhone, if you are relying too much on your own ability and not enough upon the Creator's strength?"

The question stunned him. Weak? Was that it? Was his faith weak?

After Klesc left, he stood at the window, watching the sea turn black with the coming night. Klesc's words weighed heavy on him. For years now he'd been forging ahead as if he were in control. How could he have so easily forgotten the One who had commissioned him to this task? It had been a long time since he had prayed to the Creator for guidance in this matter, and now, with Leenah missing ...

The sea was a treacherous place, and she was out there somewhere, alone. He'd done all that he could—yet there was one more thing that he hadn't done. Standing there watching the moon rising over the water, casting its silvery light across the black surface, Rhone bowed his head and prayed.

Leenah toiled at the oars as the third quartering lengthened out and the sky grew dark. Her arms and shoulders burned, and even her legs, where they braced against the gunwale, had begun to ache. She craned her head and stared into the darkness over her shoulder. How far could Atlan be? When the moon broke the horizon with a shimmering pool of silvery light, she was surprised to discover it rising not off her bow where she had expected, but directly to her left.

Exhausted, she shipped the oars, let out a soft groan, and leaned forward, kneading the muscles in her arms. Now that the clack of the oarlocks had ceased, she shuddered at how silent the night had become. Her eyes were drawn to the luminescent reds and greens and blues of sea creatures, some seemingly deep beneath the surface, others barely skimming it. The sea swarmed with the phosphorescence of life. She hadn't realized how beautiful it could be at night. Some animals, like the striped glimmer fish, she recognized. But most she didn't.

Rhone would have known them. Thinking of him made the loneliness tangible; she could almost taste it. And now she became aware of her thirst, and the gnawing in her stomach. She dipped up a handful of water. The sea was sweet, and it helped revitalize her. Fortunately, she'd had the common sense to bring a few pieces of fruit. Peeling a banana, she wondered in a distracted way, why the moon had risen in the wrong place.

She wanted to sleep, but Atlan was just over the horizon. It must be, for she'd been at the oars for hours. Reluctantly, she took them up again, her fingers closing achingly about them, the blisters upon her hands burning. Something important tugged at the back of her brain. She wondered again about the moon, but she was just too tired to think about it.

The agony of rowing clawed at her shoulders and tore at her back until the pain itself became the sedative that numbed her body and mind. The repetitious motion seemed to become strangely detached from reality. Finally the pain faded into a fog of unreality as she drifted in and out of consciousness.

Sometime before dawn she hauled in the oars, letting them

thump hard into the bottom of the boat, and slipped off the seat and stretched out on the bottom of the boat, hardly aware of the wooden ribs digging into her side. At once, she was asleep.

❦

The gentle rocking, the heat of the sun, and its glare against her eyelids pulled her awake. With consciousness, her body screamed in a score of places. She tried turning her face from the sun, but it beat down upon her from every direction. For an instant, she was disoriented. Then a sudden terror at what she'd done rose up.

Maybe it was all a horrible dream. But dreams seldom left her aching and wrung out, hanging to dry like an old rag. She moved an arm and groaned. It definitely had not been a dream. This was real. What had she done?

She was about to rise when the hunting screech of a mansnatcher paralyzed her. She lay frozen as the scream grew louder. A shadow momentarily passed over her, and as the shriek faded in the distance, the pounding of her heart filled her ears.

She did not move. Hardly breathing, she tried to take stock of her situation. Bits and pieces of the previous day came together, yet no matter how she turned them over, they made no sense. It must have been the poison. Trembling, she could think of no other excuse for such a stupid stunt.

Cautiously, she lifted her head and watched four dark shapes shrink against the hot, blue sky. She let go of a breath. They hadn't seen her. Where was she? She'd set off for Atlan, that much she remembered. Looking around, she could see nothing but blue water from horizon to horizon.

"What have you done to yourself, Leenah?" Groaning, she resumed her place behind the oars, her muscles a bundle of knots.

"All right. Think. Which way is home?" The sun stood nearly overhead; it was difficult to tell east from west. She recalled the moon off her left side the night before. She'd been rowing north! How far had she gone? And how far had she drifted during the night ... and in what direction?

The mainland might be leagues away and Atlan just over the horizon. Or the reverse may be true. Which should she try?

"Dear Creator, show me the way."

Dipping her right oar, she pulled hard, swinging ninety degrees. If the moon had been left, then the turn should put her on an eastern tract. But there was no way of knowing which way she had been pointing. She surely had been spun about with the current. In frustration she pulled again, swinging another ninety degrees, then heaved the oars inboard and sat there, fighting back her tears and anger.

28

Stranded

Leenah untied the bindings that held her hair and combed it out with her fingers so that it fell across her neck and down alongside her face. It helped a little to keep the sun off her, but the water was a thousand flickering mirrors, and there was nothing she could do to keep the glare from stinging her eyes.

She ripped strips from the hem of her dress and wrapped them about her hands, but they did little to ease the pain of ruptured blisters and raw skin. What pained her most was not knowing where she was. Her slow rowing might be driving her farther out to sea, or sight of Atlan's shoreline might be but one more oar stroke away. It was that hope that kept her straining, ignoring the pain.

"Strength and direction ... strength and direction." After a while, it was all she could mumble. She'd eaten the last of the fruit, and although she wouldn't die of thirst, she might well dry up like a prune beneath the hot sun. At times her burning skin carried her thoughts back to the Temple Prison, and she imagined hauling water to the prisoners again, the merciless sun pummeling her bare neck and arms. She worried about Lamech, but he had been protected by the Creator's Messengers. He must be all right.

"Dear Creator ... strength and direction."

The second quartering stretched on, thankfully, with no more mansnatchers. Once in a while great flocks of birds would pass overhead, their vast shadow a momentary respite from the sun's burning rays, but then they'd pass, winging their way to who knew where.

"Strength and direction." Her brain reeled.

Eventually the weariness overpowered her and drove her to the bottom of the boat. "Strength ..." A bit of shade beneath the seat slat was her only refuge. Her breath came slow and heavy. "... and ... direction ... strength ... direction."

The weight of her exertion was pressing the life from her. She didn't care. She withered in the bottom of the boat, drifting in and out of consciousness. Sometime later—she had no notion how much later—the distant sound of wings stirred her momentarily from the paralysis of fatigue. *Mansnatchers?* She opened an eye and peered past the angle of the seat and gunwale. Overhead a flop of scarlet dragons passed by, their slow, steady wings drumming powerfully in the still air.

Dragons fly to Atlan all the time. It's the groves of wild bdell-m growing on the lee of the Rim-wall that attract them.

"On the lee of the Rim-wall," she muttered as Rhone's voice faded from the memory. Opening her other eye, Leenah stared at the curved ribs beneath her face. "Scarlet dragons fly to Atlan. Strength and direction. Direction?"

Ignoring the daggers in her back, she clawed her way onto the seat and stared at the receding shapes. "They fly to Atlan. Direction?" A surge of strength seemed to energize her tortured muscles. "Yes, that's it. Thank you, Creator!"

Taking up the oars in her battered fists, she gritted her teeth to the pain and willed her arms into motion.

❊

Night spread its comforting coolness over the sea, extinguishing the sun's brutal burning rays. Three times that day she'd spied scarlet dragons, and each time she adjusted her course accordingly. Though she seemed to have no strength left, somehow the oars kept moving, and the pain throbbing through her body remained bearable.

Sometime after dark, she heard the breakers, distant at first, growing louder until they roared in her ears. The boat surged ahead with each crashing wave, and then unexpectedly it thumped against a rocky jut of land, reeled hard to the left, and ground to a halt. For a moment she did not grasp the meaning of it. Then she lifted her head from her chest and stared up sheer rock cliffs soaring darkly into the night sky, towering over her like shadowy sentinels, crowned with a frosting of stars.

"Land?" The word grated like a rusty hinge in her throat. The boat lurched around with the next wave. Grappling at the gunwale, she dragged herself over the edge and floundered a moment in the surf until her feet found the gravel bottom. A wave threw her headlong onto the beach. Her raw fingers sunk like sea anchors into coarse sand as another wave washed over her.

With a last bit of strength, she dragged herself into a small alcove of sand, ten or twelve spans from the breaking waves. When she reached the foot of the cliff, she collapsed, and the crashing sea vanished from her consciousness.

⁂

He was pacing again, as Leenah had done in that very room only a few days earlier. Rhone winced at the memory. Worry, like bands of iron, tightened about his chest. His head snapped toward the doorway of his chamber at the sound of pounding footsteps hurrying up from the parade ground. He went outside to investigate.

"Pyir Rhone," Captain Melik said, coming to a halt. He had a young man with him, dressed in the garb of a seafarer. "This is Hoarg-el, captain of the *Sprink*."

"I found her boat, Pyir Rhone," Hoarg-el said.

"Her boat only?"

"Mistress Leenah wasn't with it."

He immediately feared the worst, but at least Hoarg-el hadn't discovered a body in the boat. "Where?"

"Adrift, not far off the coast of Atlan. We hauled it in."

"You searched the waters?"

Hoarg-el's back took a defensive arch. "Of course we did. Over and over again. But we couldn't stay without arousing suspicions from the Rim-wall. And there were mansnatchers about. We weren't well armed."

"Mansnatchers." Had they finished what they had started a few days earlier? "Take me to the boat."

Mounted upon gerups, they rode swiftly down to the harbor in Derbin-ee where the *Sprink* was berthed. The *Sprink* was a midsize, seavining boat, twenty-five spans long and six abeam. It was like many of the others that Rhone had enlisted for the planned invasion. A rowboat was drawn up alongside. He boarded the smaller boat, immediately spying Leenah's shiverthorn pack shoved under one of the seats. It contained a few personal things—things she'd not carelessly leave behind. Again, his thoughts fell upon the worst scenario. Had mansnatchers ripped her from the boat and carried her away? He forced himself to consider other possibilities. Lifting one of the oars from its oarlock, he examined the blood on its grip— Leenah's blood.

"Captain Hoarg-el, take me to where you found the boat."

"Yes, Pyir Rhone. But it will be dark in another half-quartering."

"Then we'll be in position to begin our search at dawn. Captain Melik, return to Imo-suk and tell Klesc where I am."

Melik nodded and hurried down the stone pier to their waiting gerups.

❧

Leenah awoke with a sudden gasp and a fire raging up her back and neck. The nearby rush of waves and the cries of circling sea gulls helped drive some of the fuzziness from her head. Her arms refused to move at first, and when they did, she had hardly the strength to set herself upright. Her hair caught in the branches of a small viahliva bush growing out of a fissure in the cliff

Looking around, she discovered she was tucked back in an alcove of rock. The towering cliffs held her in cool, comforting shadows. A row of gulls perched nearby peered down at her. *Am I on Atlan or the mainland?* She leaned back against the rock, staring bleary eyed out to sea. The sun was just rising; the water beneath it glowed a deep orange. *The mainland.* Slowly she lifted one shoulder and rotated it, then the other.

The bloodied rags still clung to her fists. She carefully unwrapped her hands, set the rags aside, and stared at the raw skin. Working her fingers helped loosen their stiffness some, but the effort drove needles through her palms and wrists.

She didn't attempt to stand at once, but determinedly worked the kinks from her bound-up muscles. Her stomach cramped for lack of food. The viahliva provided her with a few gray berries. She ate the bitter leaves and stem too.

As she sat there watching the sun, a frown began to pull at her lips. The sun wasn't rising but setting. Experience told her the sun rose over the sea and set over the forests, but she was all turned around. This wasn't the mainland after all.

"Atlan."

Standing was a challenge. Once upright, she limped around the edge of the alcove and stared down a narrow strand that hugged the cliffs as far as she could see. A rope of washed-up sea-vine on the beach provided her with a single jelly pod filled with a sweet, brown pulp. She devoured it, then stood there peering along the dark stone cliffs.

"Atlan. I finally stand upon my homeland." The thrill dulled as she looked upward. The foreboding Rim-wall was mostly of black stone, here and there streaked in red. It was higher than the cliffs beneath Imo-suk....

Imo-suk! She turned, searching for the little boat. "Gone." She gave a short laugh. "No longer adrift, I'm now stranded upon a sliver of sand, sea to one side and insurmountable cliffs to the other."

She walked along the strand, waves licking to within a few spans of her feet. The sky darkened quickly, and she continued on in the moonlight, the sand in the wake of her footsteps shimmering with the iridescence of minuscule creatures. The sea also seemed to cast its own light upon her—the radiance of living creatures. In spite of her peril, she marveled at the beauty that filled the Creator's world.

After a while the sandy beach narrowed where the Rim-wall thrust a dark foot out into the sea, barring her way. She tried to find a pass over or around it. Stymied, she sunk to the sand and sighed, "In the morning."

She curled against the stone wall and peered up at the shadowy cliffs. "You think you've stopped me, don't you?"

The cliffs frowned down at her, silently chuckling.

"Well, you haven't. I'll find another way." She hugged herself, nestling her bottom into the sand, and went to sleep.

Invigorated by another night of sleep and a few sweet seavine pods, the *other way* turned out to be a small rill of cold water tumbling through a fissure in the wall. She'd walked right past it in the darkness the night before. She grabbed the sharp rocks in her raw hands and hauled herself up into the narrow rent. She paused to tear a bit more cloth from the hem of her dress and rewrap her hands, then began the long, exhausting climb to the top.

※

Driven by big-shouldered oarsmen and a brisk breeze, the *Sprink* sliced sprightly through the deep blue water. Rhone, stripped to the waist beneath the hot morning sun, stood upon its prow, one hand grasping a mast-line. His skin glistened in the humid sea air, the muscles of his arms standing out like thick ropes as he braced against the forward surge, shading his eyes toward the passing coastline.

During the night, Captain Hoarg-el had navigated his way back to the spot where he'd fished Leenah's abandoned boat from the water. Then studying the charts of Atlan's coastline, they planned their strategy—guesses at best. Rhone wished he had more to go on. Calculating the maximum drift of her boat, they decided where upon Atlan's rugged seacoast Leenah might have made shore—if indeed she had.

She had! He refused to let any other thoughts dampen his hopes.

They'd begun searching with the first hint of dawn. Now, with the morning full upon them, Rhone studied a point of rock as they came around it. Beyond stretched a long, narrow strand of beach, awash with the rising tide. He stared at a dark cleft in the Rim-wall, mostly hidden in deep shadows. How far back it went, he couldn't tell with the sun sitting just above it, glaring off the sea.

"Bring me closer in."

He scanned the heights for any sign of a Highwatch Tower. He spied one far to the south. Hopefully, if spotted, the guards would think they were only out gathering seavine. The boat heeled toward shore, and as it drew closer to the treacherous rock, Captain Hoarg-el came forward to study the water with the practiced eye of an expert seaman. Rhone also searched for the darker blue color that portended hidden rocks that could easily rip the bottom out of a boat. Finally Captain Hoarg-el ordered his men to take up their oars and heave the anchor overboard. The chain rattled through only three or four spans before coming to a halt.

"This is as close as I dare go, Pyir Rhone."

"Have your men put out the poles. We wouldn't want curious eyes up there thinking you're up to anything but gathering."

Captain Hoarg-el nodded. "All right, men, look busy and be prepared to smile and wave to any passing boats."

Rhone sprang off the deck and sliced into the sea, pulling himself toward shore with easy, powerful strokes. Soon the sea took over, and each wave surged him forward; it took all his strength to keep from being dashed against the jagged coast. Finally his feet touched the rocky bottom, and bracing himself against the relentless push and pull of the sea, he hauled himself up onto a narrow strip of sand.

The rift he'd spied from the boat was not deep: only a few spans before ending up against the Rim-wall. Another blind alley, like a fistful of blind alleys before. But he had to try each. She could have been lying unconscious in any one of them. He was about to turn away when he stopped and stared at the two pieces of cloth lying upon a rock. His heart leaped when he recognized the pattern from Leenah's dress. They appeared to be splotched with dried blood.

"Leenah!"

His call went unanswered. He spied her footprints leading away down the beach and jogged the long length of it until the sand narrowed and disappeared into the sea. He returned to the place where he had come ashore and swam back to the boat.

Captain Hoarg-el helped him aboard. "You found something!"

He showed him the cloth. "She used these to bind her hands

while rowing. She couldn't have scaled the Rim-wall without ropes and spikes, so someone must have picked her up."

Captain Hoarg-el peered at the long strand of sand. "She might have waved down a passing gatherer."

He nodded. "She's in Atlan."

Captain Hoarg-el looked at him. "And we're not, Pyir Rhone. What do you want me to do?"

There was only one thing he could do right now. "Take me back to Imo-suk."

🦑

Leenah faced her third night in Atlan, but this night she'd sleep not at its damp feet, but upon its strong shoulder! The climb had taken all day, and now she filled her lungs with the high, crisp air and thrilled at the sight that spread out below her. From the summit of the Rim-wall, the Great Sea was a flat, azure sheet of the finest glass, the low sun seemingly setting it afire. She waited, almost expecting to hear it sizzle. Reaching the summit made her almost giddy.

A pang tempered her delight. Was Rhone watching this sunset as well? How he must be worried for her! She slapped a bound hand against her forehead. "How could I have done such a stupid thing?" She desperately wanted to tell him that she was safe. He must be searching for her ... might she have put everything he'd planned for in jeopardy?

She turned her back to the sea and unwrapped her tender hands. On the leeward slope below her, a vast forest spread its leafy top to the fading light. At this elevation there were likely some qwall and apple trees among the others; both flourished in cooler temperatures, and both bore delicious fruit—the qwall produced the bdell-m that dragons craved.

The daylight was receding fast. She knew she must make it

down into the cover of those trees before darkness overtook her. Just then something caught her eye: a flicker of light in the distance, as if a 'gia lamp had been placed upon the very precipice of the Rim-wall.

"People!" With the gloom of night settling about her, thoughts of companionship, warm food, and perhaps a soft bed propelled her toward the light. It was farther off than she'd first guessed. She stumbled in the darkness over the uneven rock, more feeling than seeing the ground, careful to keep well away from the edge of the wall. As the light grew closer, she saw it was not one lamp, but several. Suddenly she stopped, staring at a tall, blocky stone silhouette—a Highwatch Tower!

A guard stepped from a bright doorway and strode toward her. She dropped to the ground, and her breath caught. The guard stopped and tilted back his head at the stars. He stood that way for a moment, then strode to a rail at the Rim-wall's edge and stood there looking out over the dark sea.

She watched him a moment, then shifted her view. Not far from the tower was a pile of wood stacked taller than two men. Near it flickered a flame in an iron brazier. In the old days, the pyre would be set ablaze in the event of a sea invasion. But those days were long gone ... except Da-gore had said that Zorin was rebuilding the Rim-wall Highwatches and signal pyres.

The guard arched his back and stretched so large that she imagined she could hear the crackling of his spine and his long yawn. Yet he just stood there, staring into the distance. Was he was ever going to leave? He stretched again and finally ambled back into the tower.

She scooted backward and, once beyond the reach of the lamplight, sprang to her feet and stumbled quickly down the uneven slope until the trees rose up around her.

❧

Rhone. "I want you to return to Atlan to learn what you can. Perhaps a seavining boat picked her up off the shore. Ask around, but be careful."

"As you wish, Pyir Rhone." Da-gore seemed reluctant to leave.

Larik wore an angry scowl. He would deal with him later. "Go now. There is no time to waste."

Da-gore seemed as if he wanted to say something more, then snatched up his cloak and left without a word.

He looked at Larik. "There was no way to keep this from him." At least he hadn't sent Da-gore off on a trumped-up mission. The need to return to Atlan was genuine. "Now that he is gone, you may speak freely."

Larik grunted. "I have nothing to say." But his smoldering gaze said plainly he disapproved of including Da-gore.

Rhone's gaze traveled slowly across the eight men gathered there. "Then this is how we will proceed. Larik will continue preparing the Makir to move out. He will begin provisioning the boats with food. You each ready your kal-ee-hon. Be ready to move at a moment's notice."

"Why delay any further?" Captain Maull asked. "The Makir are ready now."

Klesc said, "It is clear that Zorin already expects us. Arousing his suspicion seems the least of our problems, Pyir Rhone."

Rhone nodded. "Holding off now will profit us little." A tourniquet of helplessness tightened. His mother was just another of Zorin's castaway pieces, and so, maybe, was Leenah. His next move could very well be the sacrificial knife that slew them both. "Still, we will delay a little longer."

"For what reason, Pyir Rhone?" Larik asked. "The men grow restless."

Rhone shot him a narrow glance. "We will move when I say the time is right."

Larik folded his arms across his broad chest. "We all have our lives—our futures—invested in this venture. You are letting sentimentality get in the way of sound judgment."

Rhone's spine stiffened. "You have your orders, First Statre. See to them."

Larik held him a moment in a steady gaze, then abruptly turned on his heels and strode out of the room. Rhone dismissed them all, and once he was alone, he pondered Klesc's earlier words. He *had* been relying on his own strength when he should have been relying on another's. Now, with the stirrings of a rebellion within his own ranks, would he finally turn this over to the Creator?

29

The Kleimen

Noah, Mishah, and Amolikah sat at a table behind the cabin, shelling the peas they'd harvested from the little garden that Amolikah tended with an almost religious zeal.

Mishah loved this quiet time in the cool of the evenings when the sky began to darken and the Dancing Lights came alive. They had a huge basket of peas before them to complete, but as usual, Noah was spending more time entertaining the animals that seemed attracted to him like iron flakes to a lodestone.

Noah snapped open a hull and skimmed the small green beads into his hand, putting some in the big bowl in the center of the table, then passing one or two to an attentive little pocket dragon perched upon the corner.

"Busy hands make for happy hearts." The Gardener's gentle voice seemed to come like a wind blowing in from every direction. Mishah looked around and spied him strolling toward them from around the corner of the house. He glanced at the bowl of peas. "They are particularly sweet this season."

"Thank you for providing all this," Amolikah said, stretching an arm toward her garden. The colors were magnificent, and kept changing from month to month as new vegetables ripened.

"Everything tastes better than I can remember," Mishah said.

The Gardener looked pleased. "I watch over it carefully." He winked. "The plants that grow here are special to me."

She knew he was referring to all of the Creator's Garden, not just Amolikah's little patch.

"Noah." The Gardener sat on the bench next to the boy. "How many of those have you given him?"

The pocket dragon ruffled his green iridescent wings and extended a long orange neck, expertly licking a pea from Noah's fingers with a quick flick of its forked red tongue.

"I don't know, Sir. Ten? Twenty?"

The Gardener steepled his fingers under his chin in thought. Mishah noted his fingernails held good black earth.

"You ought to begin to keep a count."

"Why? There is plenty to eat."

The Gardener nodded. "There is no lack here, it's true, but someday, when you leave, you might need to know how much each of the Creator's animals eats. Take our friend perched on the corner of the table. He'll eat at least fifty peas before he's content."

"I'll count next time."

The Gardener nodded. "Here's a question for you, Noah."

Mishah smiled. She knew the Gardener's ploys by now. Never a chance missed to teach Noah a lesson.

"If a pocket dragon eats fifty peas a day, how many peas would it take to feed him for a whole year?"

"That's easy. Fifty increased by three hundred and sixty." He thought for an instant. "That's eighteen thousand peas."

The Gardener beamed and gave Noah a big hug.

Mishah's smile wavered a bit. How Lamech's arms must ache to hold his son like that. Even as her arms ached to hold her husband again.

The Gardener glanced up, His eyes seemingly penetrating to her soul. "Not long, dear Mishah."

He smiled at the older woman beside her. Amolikah always radiated joy whenever the Gardener visited. "Your patience is your crown." He stood and studied the darkening sky. "It will be a beautiful show tonight. Already my Dancing Lights make an appearance."

Indeed, the northern sky had begun to shimmer red and green. Mishah drew the sweet evening air into her lungs, and her spirits soared at the way the Gardener laid a loving hand upon her son's shoulder.

"Noah, you know what I want you to do for me?"

"No." Noah suddenly expanded his chest. "But whatever it is, I can do it."

"I know you can. I want you to help me discover how much each one of the animals in my Garden eats every day."

Noah looked bewildered by the task. "I will try."

"Good. And when you have solved each problem, write the answer in this book for me." There was suddenly a little brown book in the Gardener's hand.

Noah nodded, taking it.

"Then, when your father returns, we can show him how you helped me."

"When is my father coming for us?" Noah glanced at his mother and great-grandmother, then back at the Gardener.

"Soon."

※

With the morning mist burning off and the sun's warmth upon her face, Leenah descended the steep, forested slope and came upon a path wide enough for a cart and three-point. Earlier, she'd passed a grove of qwall trees. More than once she'd sensed dragons nearby, but whenever she reached out to them, they fled before her. If she could only coax one to return to the mainland ... yet even if she did, no one in Imo-suk could understand her summons for help. If only there was some way to get word to Rhone. *How he must be worrying!*

Now that she was deep in the forest, trees arched overhead hiding all but an occasional glimpse of the sun. Many were heavy with fruit, and she didn't suffer from hunger. In the muted light, the gnarled roots of gopher trees, green with ancient moss, thrust their bony joints from the rich earth like so many ankles and knees and thighs and shins. Occasionally a creature would rustle in the deep shadows, always just out of sight. More than once she walked into a spider's web spun across the trail—all but invisible until she actually stopped to study it. She wondered what sort of spider had spun it. Rhone would have known.

When she reached level ground below the Rim-wall, the path widened out into a road that wound on and on through the forest. She didn't know which direction she was heading, but she did know that if she ever hoped to secure passage out of Atlan, she had to reach Atla Fair and the harbor upon which that pleasant city abutted. She'd heard stories all her life of how Hodin had lavished his wealth upon the city. He and his wife had built it for his children and for all friendly off-landers who wished to enjoy the benefits of Atlan. For five hundred years the Makir had assured Atlan's peace and prosperity.

She sighed at a sudden sadness. That time of peace ended when Zorin seized power. It wasn't long after that that he began to "cleanse the island." Her mother and father had been among those forced to flee to her father's homeland, even though her mother had been a granddaughter of Hodin.

She had been but a little child when they finally settled in the green and fertile land of Morg'Seth, and for most of a hundred years she had become a Sethite in all but height ... and blood. When her father died, her mother moved to a wheat farm on the Little Hiddekel River, in the willow-bank village of Jubl-ee, south of Nod City ...

Leenah gave a sudden shiver and ordered her thoughts to cease, refusing to permit the terrifying memories she knew would follow.

"Morning peace, Mistress," a woman's voice said from seemingly out of nowhere.

She came to a sharp stop and looked around, but she only saw tangled tree limbs and a deep, misty gloom beyond them.

The voice laughed. "No, no, bend your eyes to Dirgen's Bosom."

Leenah looked down at the edge of the road at the tiny woman who stood near the crook of a twisted gopher tree root. The crown of her head barely reached to Leenah's hip. The woman smiled up at her out of a face furrowed with great age, yet her fair skin glowed as if she'd been a mere babe. Her wide, friendly eyes were greenish gold. Her black hair hung in three long braids from a wreath of pink and blue flowers encircling her tiny head. The braids nearly touched the ground. She wore a faded red dress, checked in fine green and gold embroidery, some of the threads beginning to unravel. Beneath the hem of the dress peaked out the scuffed toes of little green shoes. Across one thin, pale arm was a basket woven of yellow pipe reed. It held a large brown mushroom and smaller orange ones and some silvery mothwing moss. Her other hand held an airy, conical mushroom that she'd apparently just plucked.

Her Uncle Debne had told her of the little people who lived below the Rim-wall, but she put the stories aside as children's fables. She smiled and bent forward, placing tender hands upon her knees. "Morning peace to you, too, Mistress."

"My name is Ela. We don't often get big people way back here in Deepvale."

"I'm Leenah, and ..." she was embarrassed to admit it; "I'm lost."

"Lost?" Ela considered her a moment and frowned. "You've been through hard times."

"Indeed I have." Somehow, this little woman put her instantly at ease.

"And your hands!" Ela dropped the mushroom into her basket and set it down. "Let me see, Mum. They hurt bad?"

"Not too much." The needles had ceased their prickling pain, but the rawness still burned with every movement.

"Come with me, dear. I have just the thing to fix you up."

"Are you a healer?"

Ela twittered as she gathered up her basket. "No, no, but with twenty-three sons working the mines," she winked, "I've come to know a little of what it takes to mend bone and flesh." Ela's small hand folded about Leenah's wrist and led her down the road.

They turned off the main road onto a path that she would have missed altogether if she hadn't been looking for it. Shortly the path began to descend into a valley where the acrid bite of smoke grew strong.

"What is Deepvale, Ela?"

"It's our home."

Leenah searched her memory for the stories Uncle Debne had told her. "You're a Kleiman."

Ela looked at her with surprise. "Yes. Of course. What else?"

She gave her an apologetic smile. "I'm a stranger to this land."

Ela stopped and peered at her. "A daughter of Hodin is a stranger to Atlan?"

She shrugged. "I've been away for a long time."

The path wound down into the smoky vale, and the trees gave way to a little village of tents and pavilions. Some were whimsically shaped like dragons and eagles, some simply round or conical, and some wore tall spires, with tiny limp flags at their peaks.

The tents encircled a green lawn; in its midst was a pool fed by a trickling stream, surrounded with bright flowers. A delicately arched bridge, wrapped in shimmering ribbons, straddled both banks. Farther on in the vale, the vertical, black Rim-wall soared upward. Its face was scarred somehow, but Leenah couldn't see it clearly.

Between her and the wall were what appeared to be several forge pits, carved from the solid black-rock shelf. Each pit sat under a roof of stripped saplings, and each had a bellows. A smoky plume from each pit drifted skyward through a hole in the roof where it converged into a gray, hazy ceiling above the vale.

Leenah stared at the army of tiny people at the forges and bellows. A procession of red- and green- and gold-clad villagers marched like gaily bedecked ants from the Rim-wall to the forge pits, carrying reed baskets upon their shoulders.

The lawn was home to ten or twelve women sitting before their looms. Around its perimeter ran horizontal poles dangling an assortment of curiously shaped stones. And at one end of the lawn stood five long wooden tables with benches.

Ela led her through the community, causing work to cease momentarily and heads to turn. Leenah sensed a bit of uneasiness at her arrival. Two women hurried over to join them. Mia and Lil were their names, and after Ela made the introductions, she explained how she'd met Leenah on the road. Mia looked concerned, but it seemed Ela held some sway over the women, and Mia merely said a pleasant but reserved hello.

Leenah smiled, feeling conspicuous with all the attention she was getting. Here and there she noticed small, steaming pools of water dotting the rocky shelf that sloped up to the soaring black wall. At least one that she had passed smelled faintly of sulfur.

At a green and gold tent, Ela beckoned her inside. She ducked low under the door. When she stood, her head brushed the top. The material was of some shiny, tightly woven cloth, a little like spider silk. Her heart thumped faster as she thought of Rhone. She had to contact him.

Ela's tent was a neat place, with six sleeping mats arranged around the edge and a few fragile-looking chairs of splendid workmanship set about a small table.

"Sit down, Leenah."

She dared not attempt a chair. It couldn't support her weight even if she could fit in it. She settled to the floor, which was covered in a fur she didn't recognize. Ela pulled a little upholstered chest from under a small table and began rummaging through it. The other women asked if they could get her anything.

"I am a little thirsty."

Ela nodded to her two friends, and Mia and Lil set off to get her a drink.

Leenah noticed that the detailed embroidery, which decorated the walls of the tent, was similar to the needlework on Ela's dress. Although neat and clean, the tent was patched in many places and the material was threadbare. She didn't see any cooking utensils. That job must take place outside. Maybe behind the tent.

"What a lovely house."

"Thank you. I know it's not as fancy as what's down in Atla Fair, but it's comfortable." Her aged cheeks puckered with a smile as she set a green jar, decorated with a leaf motif, upon the table and dipped out a thick, yellow salve that smelled like ropesweets. Ela gently rubbed it into Leenah's raw hands. Almost at once, a soothing warmth radiated deep into her palms and fingers and moved up into her aching wrists.

"There. In two days you'll have forgotten they hurt at all. How did you ever come by such harm?"

She gave her an abbreviated account of the adventure, leaving out all remarks of Rhone, the Makir, Imo-suk, and why she'd even attempted the journey in the first place.

"You do look exhausted, dear." Ela came around and massaged her shoulders much as Rhone had. Another pang pricked her heart. "You are tighter than a kribbag. What you need is a long soak."

"A soak?"

Ela smiled. "You'll love it."

Leenah warily followed Ela outside. Out on the lawn, a fist of women had begun throwing cloths over the five long tables. There was now a bustle of activity beneath the canopies edging the lawn. Mia and Lil emerged from one of them; Mia held a pitcher in both hands, and Lil carried a glass.

"It's the largest I could find," Lil said handing it to her. Mia filled it from her pitcher. Leenah tasted it. "Lemon squeeze."

"We call it Lemon Lania-ya." Mia beamed.

"It's delicious."

Ela's, Mia's, and Lil's cheeks bloomed like ripe rose pods about to burst open. Leenah drank it down and handed the glass back to Mia. "Thank you."

Ela led her behind the tents and up a path toward the black stone cliffs. Leenah noted that the markings she'd seen earlier upon the cliffs were really fissures and cracks in the Rim-wall. Just then two men tromped out of one of them, each carrying a basket upon his shoulder. Before she could ask about it, Ela stopped before an enclosure of four bright sheets stretched between poles. Within it was a clear, shallow pool, trailing fine curling tendrils of steam into the air. The enclosure held the heat, and the sun shone warm upon the black stone around the basin, tempered by the haze that hung in the sky.

"Take off your clothes, dear."

Leenah stooped to touch the water—warm, but not uncomfortably so. "Where does it come from?"

"It wells up from deep beneath Atlan, dear. From Dirgen's belly. Some of our pools arise from shallower springs and smell horrible, but this one is different. Its salts will draw the weariness from your body."

Leenah looked around. The pool was entirely enclosed except for the top. "Are you sure?"

Ela smiled. "You'll love it. Now take off those rags and let me see what I can do to mend them."

Leenah slipped out of her clothes and lowered herself into the water. "Mmmm."

"Now you just soak. I'll be back to check on you in a whompa's whisker." Ela scurried off.

Leenah sank deeper into the liquid heat, inhaling the salty steam. She closed her eyelids against the muted light, and in a few moments her thoughts began to drift, suddenly unlatched from all the worries that had burdened her. Only one concern remained, and that was how to let Rhone know she was all right. But even that could wait now. Her head leaned back; she found a smooth concave in the stone, and as the aches seeped away in to the water, her weariness overcame her and she fell asleep.

30

The Prisoner in Highwatch Thirty-four

With a scream, Leenah bolted upright in the warm pool, and her lungs sucked in the steamy air. She stared wildly at the hazy sky, realizing it had only been a dream.

"What is it, dear?" Ela's high-pitched voice pulled her head around.

Leenah drew in another breath, and the dream faded from her brain. "Mansnatchers." She licked her lips and sank back in to the water. They had come back for her, spying her cringing at the bottom of the boat all alone and defenseless. They'd plunged from the hot sky, their horrid screams renting the air, their talons like the blackest stone and sharper than harvesting blades, coming right at her.

Ela smiled. "Sometimes dreams can seem more real than life itself."

She nodded. "Lately life has been pretty terrifying, Mistress Ela."

"Was it a mansnatcher that gave you that bad scratch?"

Leenah touched the hard scab on her shoulder and nodded. "That's why I rowed out to sea all alone." She stared back into the sky.

"Ah, the poison. I've heard it twists people's thoughts. Well, put mansnatchers out of your head. They don't come here."

"How do you keep them away?"

"It's the dragons." Ela stared at the enclosure's wall as if peering through the colorful fabric. "Our forests are filled with dragons, and mansnatchers fear them; oh, yes, they fear them." Her view lingered a moment, then shifted back to Leenah. "The soak was good, wasn't it?"

She nodded.

"Time to get out." Ela rose from the smooth black rock and gave Leenah a towel upon which she'd been sitting. Leenah dried herself, then stared at the new dress Ela held out to her. "But how did you ever—"

"I had help. We took the measurements from your old dress." A comb was suddenly in Ela's hand, and she had Leenah sit while she worked on the tangles. "There, that's better."

Leenah quickly braided it and turned it into a loose knot so that it would stay in place. "How can I thank you for your help? You … everyone … has been so kind."

"We only try to do Dirgen's will, and that's to treat strangers as though they are family."

Leenah smiled, but it pricked her heart that these sweet people were committed to Dirgen, the sea god, one of the Deceiver's many different guises.

Leenah followed her back into the village where everyone seemed to be gathering on the lawn near the five tables, which were now strewn with bowls of food and set with plates and goblets.

Ela guided her to a section of log set at one end of the table. It was polished smooth, and the red grain glowed in the late second quartering light. Ela sat in a small chair beside her. Was the log "chair" held in reserve for times when big people came visiting?

Once all the villagers were seated, Ela stood and introduced

Leenah. Although they were cordial, she sensed their suspicion of her, especially the men who had come in from their work. Starting at Ela's left, they began introducing themselves. One by one the names and greetings flowed like a rippling stream, wending up and down the tables until everyone at all five had been properly and formally introduced.

Leenah thanked them. She was famished and the food smelled wonderful, but there seemed yet another matter to be tended to first. A man at one of the tables stood, and the chatter died down to silence. He spoke kind words about their guest, then, raising his voice, declared, "Bring forth the keelit!"

Five women appeared from one of the canopied areas, carrying two large baskets a piece, and they each started a basket down the sides of the tables. The little people plucked up a slice of keelit and passed the basket. Leenah took one as well. Once all had taken a piece, the man held a slice in the air and said, "To long life. May Dirgen's will be done." And with that, everyone ate the fruit. Leenah followed along, perplexed by the short ceremony. Now folks began passing bowls and baskets and pots, heaping their plates. She dismissed the ritual as the food began to come around to her.

Everything was tasty, especially the spicy seavine pods, and she ate while answering the questions cast her way. The men, she noted, were fine boned with thin, regular features, all quite pleasant to look at. Upon closer study, each had either a prominent nose that first bumped up and then hooked down to a point, or they had large ears. The women also had these peculiarities, although far less prominent and easily overlooked.

The community meal seemed to be a time of camaraderie for these people. Afterward, they lingered long over dirty plates, chattering away, sipping a strong ale from flagons cleverly crafted of gold, with elaborate golden vines encircling them.

Time slipped away. Leenah hadn't realized it had turned dark until she looked up and suddenly discovered the lawn was encircled with daggers of moonglass dangling from thin golden wires. Indeed, the whole village was ablaze with moonglass basking the vale in a splendid radiance. The tents glowed like multicolored mushrooms, and even the cliff side was ablaze with magnetic light.

"Ela, where did you get all these wonderful glasses?"

"We make them here in Deepvale." Ela's wrinkled skin smoothed a bit with the smile.

Leenah glanced at the cliff sides. "So, that's what the men were doing."

"Some are miners and some are forgers." She looked to the man sitting across the table from her. "My Turi, he's a forger."

Turi grinned. "Right I am, Mistress Leenah." He had a gravely voice that sounded at first as if he were angry, but Turi's smiling face quickly belied that impression. "I'll wager you've never seen moonglass as it comes from the forge." Ela's husband was of the hook-nose strain of Kleimen.

"No, I haven't."

"Would you like to?"

"Yes."

Turi put his flagon of ale down; and he, Ela, and Leenah strolled across the lawn, which now was filled with knots of friendly, chattering Kleimen.

The forge pits twinkled, as if spattered with a million minute specks of moonglass. The fires were out, but the heat from them still radiated from the ground. Off to one side sat two large baskets. Turi dipped a hand into one and drew out seven or eight pebbles. "This here is Selum, Mistress." He dipped up a handful from the second basket. "And this, Dirgenium. You put 'em together in the forge and out comes moonglass." Turi lifted the lid of a wooden box filled with smooth nodules, each giving off a different hue of soft, magnetic light.

"We sometimes mix 'em or we sort 'em, Mistress, depending on what color we want to make."

She picked up one the size of a walnut, smooth as the moon and nearly the same color. "This is how it comes from the forge?"

"Indeed, Mistress. Later we'll fashion them into the pure sheets like what you're familiar with. My job is to forge the Selum and Dirgenium together in that crucible over there. Then I pour it into a barrel of pickling water from the pools you've noticed about. The moonglass settles to the bottom in neat little balls like you've got there in your hand.

"Later we'll remelt the balls of moonglass and pour the liquid into these molds." From the stripped saplings overhead hung iron forms—some round and oval, some jagged, others spiraling or dagger shaped.

"Fascinating."

"And where you find Dirgenium, you find gold. So we forge that, too, and make things that are useful here in the village."

She returned the stone to the wooden box. Turi dug through the pile and pulled out a nodule as large as her fist, glowing a bright yellow. "Now, you don't see many like this one." It shimmered like liquid gold in the palm of his hand. He grinned. "She's splendid, don't you think?"

"Very beautiful."

He smiled as if she had complimented him on a favored son and placed it into her hand. "A gift for you, Mistress."

The gesture brought a catch to her voice. "Thank you." These people had been so kind to her that she was at a loss as to what she could possibly give back to them. She cradled the glowing stone and imagined she was holding the sun in her hands.

"There was a time when a stone like that would have lit up your face like a lantern." His smile faltered as he stared worriedly at the mines in the cliff side, then back at her. "Been working those cliffs for most of six hundred years, and I'd swear by Dirgen's beard, the stones don't shine like they once did."

"Oh, Turi, it's just your old eyes." Ela threaded her arm through his.

He shook his head. "The veins must have run into poor ground ... or something."

Ela and Turi walked her back to the lawn where a bustling contingent of men and women was clearing the tables of the dirty dinner dishes. The scattered knots of conversations and the soft, throaty music from flutes and airy ripple of harps wafted in the warm air—fresh smelling now that the forges had been put to sleep. But the fires seemed to be the only thing that would sleep tonight.

"Are you celebrating something?"

Ela blinked and smiled. "No. Why do you ask?"

"It's just that it seems so festive. And there was the ceremony with the keelits."

"Oh, we're like this every evening after a hard day of working. And the Keelit Remembering too."

Leenah thought such gathering would wear thin after not too many days, but the Kleimen seemed to thrive on it. "What is the Keelit Remembering, Ela?"

"You don't do it? Hum. Well, I suppose you wouldn't unless you'd been given the Parting Word."

"Ah!" A glimmer of understanding flamed to life. The Parting Word came from years ago, when the firstborn left the Mother and Father to settle their own lands. At the time of parting, Father Adam would place a hand on the son or daughter and whisper a secret word. Not that it was a secret never to be shared; for, in truth, they were often spoken of. But the Parting Word was something each family took with it and built traditions around.

When two families were joined through marriage, the man and woman whispered their secrets to each other. Eventually, all the

Parting Words became known, although a few were still missing. It was a puzzle Father Adam had constructed—one that would take many generations to fit together.

What had Father Adam told Ela's ancestor about keelits? It was improper to ask for another person's secret, yet if the other wished to share it, nothing bound by tradition prevented it.

A dance was whirling under streaming ribbon and a hundred suspended moonglasses. Leenah caught snatches of conversations here and there as they returned to the table. Turi recovered his flagon, drained it, and went trotting off to a communal keg to rectify the problem.

Ela smiled after him; then her view shifted toward the empty keelit basket on the table. "Always eat your keelits, dear."

"Why is that, Mistress Ela?" Maybe she would volunteer the secret?

Ela's cheeks widened out. "I'll tell you." Her musical voice lowered a tone or two. "The keelit tree is first cousin to the Tree of Life."

"Really?" The tree was renowned in the legend of all people.

"Really. Its fruit renews the body and sharpens the mind. A special food given by Dirgen to lengthen our years, to harden our bones, and to keep us strong and healthy. Although it can't give eternal youth as its stronger cousin can, it keeps us vigorous for a very long time." Ela thumped her chest with a tiny fist. "I'm nearly seven hundred years old, and look at me."

Leenah's short 135 years made her feel like a child compared to Ela. But she wasn't, she reminded herself. She'd passed her fiftieth birthday and had her Coming-of-Age Rite long ago. She still had another six or seven hundred years ahead of her, maybe more. After all, Rhone had told her the Mother was over eleven hundred years old when she fell asleep against Adam's Bosom.

"You mean the common keelit that grows everywhere and is

eaten by everyone, this is what gives us our years?"

"Oh, not the keelit alone, my dear. But it's one of the important parts. This world was designed for man: Its temperature, its distance from the sun and moon, even the magnetic veil that protects us is just perfect." Ela looked up at the starry sky where strands of iridescent red and green light fluxed through the heavens like colored dyes trickling into the eddies of a stream. "It's all weighed on a scalepan, and man," she looked back at Leenah, "you and I, we're the fulcrum." Her cheeks dimpled again. "You eat your keelits, and you'll have a long, strong life."

"This was your ancestor's Parting Word?"

Ela nodded. "Klei the hump nose, the fifteenth son, was not as sturdy as his other brothers. He never grew any taller than this." She held a hand just above her head. "Father Adam chose this secret for him because he feared for Klei's strength." Ela laughed. "But Klei lived over eight hundred years and worked the mines until the very day Dirgen gave him his rest."

"Ela, you speak of the Mother and Father, yet you honor Dirgen. I don't understand."

"Who else is there to honor?"

It occurred to her these people truly didn't know. Somehow, the truth of the Creator had become blended with the lies of the Deceiver. Suddenly she knew what gift she *might* give these people for their hospitality. "Have you heard the Parting Word given to Seth, the ninth son?"

"No. We don't get many visitors here." Ela looked almost apologetic. "We keep to ourselves, except when we sell our moonglass in Atla Fair." She gave Leenah a puzzled look. "You're of Hodin. How do you know of Seth's Parting Word?"

"I'm only half Hodinite. My father was Sethite. Would you like me to tell it to you?"

A spark of curiosity lit her face. "Yes, if you wish."

"Father Adam told Seth that someday the Creator would send a Strong Man to redeem man from the Fall. He told him the whole plan of redemption is written out in the stars, and it was up to Seth and his kin to learn the story and then spread it to the rest of the world." A twinge shot through her as she remembered how Lamech used to explain the meaning of the names of the stars to her. His excitement for the prophesies had been so real that it was almost impossible not to catch some of it for yourself.

"A plan among the stars? What does it mean, Mistress Leenah?"

"It means redemption comes only through the work of the Creator, not Dirgen. And it means someday we will again eat the fruit of the keelit's stronger cousin."

"The Tree of Life?" Ela's eyes and mouth rounded.

Leenah smiled at her wonderment. "The fruit of eternal well-being."

"When will this all happen?" Her voice held sudden suspicion.

If only she knew. "No one knows, Mistress Ela." Leenah sighed. "It is a long time off, I fear."

Sadness tainted Ela's eyes and voice. "Then you and Turi and I and our whole village will be gone."

How easy it was to despair. She often did so herself, until she remembered the end of the matter. "Perhaps we will be gone from this world, Ela, but the good news is, if you trust in the Creator, then you will live again—and so will your loved ones."

Ela brightened. "My sons and daughters, too, and Turi … forever?"

"If you and your children and Turi turn from honoring things that can neither hear nor save and learn of the One True Creator who not only hears, but also has the power to save, then you will live forever in the world to come."

Just then the word *Darha* drifted over from one of many conversations. Leenah lurched, her attention riveted.

Which of the Kleimen had said it?

"What's the matter, Mistress Leenah?"

She looked at her. "Someone spoke the Lady Darha's name."

Ela shook her head. "Isn't it deplorable, the way that evil son of hers has locked her away like some criminal? Don't know why her people have allowed it this long, except they fear for her safety." She pointed out a group of four men. "Lael there, he knows most about it."

"Ela, might I speak with them?" She did not yet have a complete grasp on what was proper or not among these folk.

"Yes, certainly."

Leenah went to them. The talk stopped, and four pairs of curious eyes peered up at her.

"Excuse me, but did I hear you mention Lady Darha's name?"

The men cast worried looks at each other.

"Mistress Ela told me one of you has news of her." She glanced at the little woman standing at her side.

They looked at Ela—then one of the men cleared his throat. "Well, err, no, not really." He flashed a quick smile, fidgeting on his tiny green-shoed feet. "I mean, no more than hearsay, Mistress Leenah."

"Are you Master Lael?"

He gulped a quick drink from his flagon. "I am." Lael was a hump-nose Kleiman, as were two of his companions. The third was of the big-ear variety.

"Please, if you know of her whereabouts, tell me."

"Why is the Mistress interested in hearsay?" His chuckle wasn't convincing, his grin more grim than gleeful.

Leenah went to her haunches and put herself at eye level with him. "I must find her."

Lael's eyes shown with an odd hue of gold in the glow of moonglass. "Why?"

"Because—" She caught herself. She'd almost blurted that the Makir assembled at Imo-suk wouldn't invade Atlan until she was found. "Because I've heard Lady Darha has been moved from the Royal Residence, and that Zorin has secreted her away somewhere."

Lael's nervousness showed in his voice. "This is true, but why do you inquire of her?"

How much should she tell this man? She hardly knew these people or where their loyalties lay. What if she revealed her true mission and word of it got back to Zorin? But hadn't Ela said Zorin's treatment of his mother was deplorable? If Ela thought this way, perhaps the others did too. *Creator, what should I do?* She had to take the chance. A warmth infused her, giving her a peace with that decision.

"Lael, I'll tell you a secret." She caught each of them in a glance. "But you must promise not to repeat it."

Their wide, staring faces nodded. "Speak," one of the men said quietly as they moved closer.

She swallowed. Words once spoken can never be recalled, but the warmth was still there, gently reassuring her. "I've come to Atlan to free Lady Darha." There! The shuttle had been thrown, the weft laid down, and there was no tearing out threads now. Whatever pattern it would eventually weave, so be it!

Their stunned silence was punctuated by the flute and harp and the happy, twittering voices that filled the lawn. The four men exchanged astonished looks. Lael whispered, "Can this be true?"

She nodded. "But I don't know where Lady Darha is being held."

"How can you do it alone?"

"I don't know that either ... yet. I suppose it depends on where Zorin has taken her." She saw Lael's lingering uncertainty.

Lael cleared his throat. "I need more ale." He strode to the communal keg and seemed to take longer than necessary topping off his flagon. He was considering. Weighing the outcome of revealing too much. Leenah understood that better than most. Had she revealed more than was prudent?

Lael came back, took a long drink, and sleeved a foamy mustache from his lips. His eyes shifted warily. The light struck them differently this time, turning them the color of polished walnut shells. "My Uncle Faeg who lives in Watervale was down in the tunnels of the Black Pool, beneath the Royal Keep last week, quietly chipping Dirgenium from the tunnel walls—it's the only place in Atlan where the brown variety of the stone can be found."

The other three nodded. "Very rare," one of them said.

"Aren't the tunnels guarded? It would be most careless of Zorin not to post men at the entrances."

"Guarded? Oh no, Mistress. No one bothers. It's a royal rat's warren down there. If you don't know your way around those tunnels, you might be lost in 'em forever. They riddle most of Atlan."

"You can crawl and pinch your way from one end of Atlan to the other if you know the twists and turns," another said.

Lael nodded. "What Gali says is true, Mistress Leenah. But Zorin doesn't worry about them 'cause only us little people can squeeze through them—at least far as he knows—and we're not a threat to him."

"What do you mean 'as far as he knows'?"

Lael gave her a knowing look. "There are a few passages where big folk like you might make it through, Mistress, but only we know how to find them."

The idea of a maze of underground tunnels intrigued her, but she had no desire to explore the tight passages herself. "What did your uncle hear?"

Lael cleared his throat. "He was working near the Black Pool, where Zorin holds prisoners, keeping ears wide open 'cause of the serpents that live in the water, you see."

Uncle Debne had told of the wring serpents. They had become Turnlings even back in the days before he'd fled Atlan.

"He overheard a couple prisoners talking. It seems Zorin had imprisoned Lady Darha's drivers, so they couldn't tell where they'd taken her. The drivers were angry, as well can be imagined." He hissed. "I'd be complaining too. Poor treatment for service well done, if you ask me."

Lael's three friends hissed and stabbed their fingers at the ground.

"What did he hear?" she pressed.

"An earful, Mistress Leenah. Zorin's taken her to the Rim-wall."

"Where on the Rim-wall?" The Rim-wall extended for hundreds of leagues, nearly surrounding all of Atlan.

Lael pulled the light brown beard at his chin. "It's one of the Highwatches Zorin is patching together."

"Which one? What's it called?"

"They go by numbers, Miss. Uncle Faeg said they'd taken her to Highwatch thirty-four."

"Can you tell me where that is?"

Lael puckered his lips and nodded. "I can, Mistress, but there's one more thing I might warn you about before you go running off to rescue the old High Counciloress. The word has gone out that if the Rim-wall pyres are lit, Lady Darha is to be killed at once."

Ela gasped. "He wouldn't."

Lael's expression sobered. "He would. You remember what he did with the little folk of Bright Canyon Vale?"

Ela paled.

"What did he do?" Leenah asked.

Lael looked away. "It was the Bloody Pikes for every man, woman, and child," he grated angrily.

The Bloody Pikes. She shivered. Just the sound of it sent a chill through her. "He murdered the whole village?"

Lael nodded severely.

The crime stunned her. She was more certain than ever that if Lady Darha was to be saved, there was no time to lose. Once the invasion began, those signal fires would almost certainly be set ablaze and Rhone's mother would be dead.

31

Leenah's Daring Mission

Rhone had gone down to the infirmary where the healers had Kev-nn bound upon a board with a poultice of herbs and minerals packed against his injured spine. The healers were pleased; the vertebrae appeared to be responding to the medicines that slowly penetrated his skin, bathing the fractured bone with their restorative fluids. The mechanic, happily sedated, seemed in good spirits in spite of being immobilized.

Afterward, he stood upon the wide ancient wall of Imo-suk, stared up into the night sky, and said a prayer for Leenah. He cared for her more than he'd ever let on. Why hadn't he opened his heart to her? Now it might be too late. That thought brought a sting to his eyes, and he started back to his room. He had preparations to see to.

He rounded a corner, instantly alerted to the strong presence of eyes watching him. Passing a shadowed alcove in the ancient walls, he lurched suddenly to his left. His fingers found the cloak of a man hiding there, and he heaved the Watcher out of the shadows.

"Da-gore?"

Da-gore appeared as startled as he. Rhone's suspicions rushed back. Had Da-gore been spying on him? Had Klesc and Larik been right all along? "What are you doing here?"

Da-gore looked down at the fists that held him. "Waiting for you, Pyir Rhone."

"I told you to return to Atlan." Rhone released him.

Da-gore straightened his cloak. "I know Imo-suk has been penetrated and her secrets whispered in Zorin's ears. It doesn't take much imagination to know I'm a suspect. I saw it in Larik's eyes, and the others'. They don't trust me. I'm neither Atlanian nor Makir. It's why you sent me on my way while the others remained."

His perception and boldness were admirable. It wasn't surprising he had risen to the rank of Captain of the Lodath's Guard. "What you say is true. And now you want to plead your case before me?"

He smiled. "If I thought I had to, I'd have simply disappeared. I will let my actions of the past seven years be witness to my loyalty, Pyir Rhone. Do you require more?"

"Times are perilous, Da-gore. Sometimes I feel I'm fighting too many fronts at once."

"So far you haven't been beaten back."

That wasn't exactly true. He tried not to think of Leenah, but she was always there at the edge of his mind. "What's so important that you had to follow me out into the night?"

"I dared not speak in front of the others. To do so would be to risk the information."

"What information?"

"The people of Atlan grow more dissatisfied with Zorin's heavy-handed rule. And now he's begun conscripting them into his army. He swells the ranks of his guards with men who will cut and run at the first sign of the enemy. Further, his fist tightens about the neck of the people, and dissidents are being rounded up in greater numbers. Execution Ridge displays their bodies as a deterrent to others who would tread their path.

"My spies tell me there is a growing resistance that can be tapped to our advantage. I've already ordered my captains to begin assembling the dissidents. And Sirt has been forming a kal-ee-hon of unbound Makir. Just say the word, Pyir Rhone, and I can raise an army of a thousand men right under Zorin's very nose—some well placed within the Royal Residence."

"We've known for years the people have been ripe for revolution."

"True, yet up to now it's been only grumbling. But Zorin continues to press more men into service and raise taxes to rebuild ancient fortifications. Many Atlanders are ready to fight to overthrow his heavy hand." His gaze intensified. "You see why I dare not mention this in front of the others? If there is a spy among us and word of it should get back to Zorin, he'll expunge the land of all who don't swear loyalty to him. The Pikes will gorge themselves on the blood of Atlan's people, and the Rim-wall will flow red down to the Great Sea."

"You did well to bring me this news privately, Da-gore."

"What word would you have me pass to my captains?"

He thought a moment. "Gather your army of rebels. It may be that the time has come to make our move."

Bathed in the soft, magnetic glow, Leenah, Lael, Gali, Orve, Tek, Turi, and Ela crowded around a table in Gali's small tent. Spread out before them was an old map of Atlan, drawn up in happier times, when the Makir kept peace and Hodin sat upon the high seat of the Council of Ten.

Lael put a slender finger on the map. "This is Highwatch thirty-four. It's about two days from here if you know the way

along the Rim-wall. Six if you first go to Aulm's Lake and catch
the road from Atla Fair." His finger described the alternate
route—then he looked up at Leenah. "You're certain this is what
you want to do, Mistress Leenah?"

A tightness spread across her chest. Common sense spoke
against what she was planning, but the determination in her
heart overruled it. "Can you guide me?"

The Kleimen glanced at each other with concern in their
faces. Lael tried unsuccessfully to clear his throat.

"It's not that we wouldn't want to help, but if Zorin should
hear of this ..." He shuddered. "When the folk of Bright Canyon
Vale opposed his new taxes and refused to send the tribute to
him, he sent his soldiers to seize the village. When a few of them
escaped in the tunnels, his soldiers sent in a pack of canics to
pursue them. Of more than a hundred villagers, only five
escaped. The rest were either mauled in the tunnels or impaled
on Execution Ridge." Dread darkened Lael's face. "Zorin made
the entire village an example to those who would refuse his
rule."

The others nodded and looked grim.

The crime appalled her. "And no one spoke up in their
defense?"

"No one who wished to stay alive," Gali said, shifting from
foot to foot.

She understood their fears. "I have no wish to endanger you
or your village. If you could just draw a map for me, I'll leave at
first light." She'd begun this quest alone, and she'd finish it
alone.

Gali quickly brought over a sheet of parchment and drew a
careful map, methodically noting each turn and each intersection
in the Rim-wall trail—labeling each way point so that she'd have
no trouble finding the place.

"It's mostly uninhabited countryside, this end of Atlan." His golden brown eyes peered up at her. "But you'll pass near several villages. They're tall folk, like you. They harvest bdell-m and are wary of strangers. Try not to be seen. They've aligned themselves with Zorin and might report a stranger in their land."

"I'll be careful."

"If you stay on the path I've indicated, you'll not likely meet anyone, save perhaps another traveler. Have you a weapon?"

"No." It had been foolish of her to embark on this quest without one, but then this whole affair had been conjured up in a mind twisted by mansnatcher poison.

Gali rummaged around in a dark corner of his tent and found a sword, which in Leenah's hand was the length of a long dagger. The grip was of carved ironwood, designed to be used two-handed, and rested in her palm quite comfortably. "Keep it out of sight," Gali warned. "Zorin has decreed such weapons illegal in Atlan."

"How shall I hide it?"

"Before you leave, I'll give you a cape," Ela said.

"Thank you." Where would she find a cape large enough for her?

Gali said, "The Highwatches usually are manned by four guards who are rotated once a month. But if I'm not very much mistaken, Zorin will have strengthened number thirty-four." Worry lines deepened in his face. "Mistress Leenah, I don't know how you will free Lady Darha without help, but we will implore Dirgen to strengthen your hand."

"No need to trouble Dirgen, Master Gali. I have a stronger ally in the Creator." But even as she spoke, she wondered if this fool's quest was in his will. Or was it something out of her own impatience? A thought occurred to her. "Do you have access to the sea?" She recalled the seavine pods she had eaten earlier.

Tek, a smiling, red-haired, hook-nose Kleiman, said, "The tunnels. A few of them pierce the Rim-wall clear to the sea."

"Have you a way to reach Marin-ee?"

They glanced at each other with bewilderment. Tek scratched his head. "Why would we want to go to Marin-ee, Mistress Leenah?"

"No one here has ever been to Marin-ee," Turi said in his gruff, low voice.

"That's right," Ela chimed in. "Farthest anyone here's been from Deepvale is Atla Fair, and we only go there when we have to sell our stitchery and moonglass."

"We don't even have a boat." Tek's scratching moved from his head to his red-bearded chin. "No one would know how to work one if we did."

Up until now Orve had remained silent. His voice was nearly as high as Ela's. "Why do you ask, Mistress?"

She sighed. The hope that had blossomed within her faded. "There is someone who must be very worried about me ... and Lady Darha." She reminded herself not to give too much away, even though she trusted these little people.

"A man?" Ela's eyes sparkled and shifted toward Turi.

"Yes, a man."

"We'd help if we could," Lael said sadly.

She believed him.

※

Leenah lay on a pallet of soft pillows beneath a shimmering canopy of orange, smooth as the finest spider silk yet strong as shiverthorn and hemp.

Sleep evaded her as her brain busily turned over the task ahead of her. The light from a hundred moonglasses strung about the village didn't help. She needed a plan! How could she hope to free Lady Darha from Zorin's armed guards without one? Eventually weariness won out, and the next moment, it was the dawn of a new day.

She ate a hearty breakfast with the village—and then Ela, Turi, Gali, and Lael took her aside. Dark shadows showed beneath Ela's eyes as she presented her with a pale red cape the same shade as Ela's dress. It appeared woven of that similar tough cloth that their tents were made of, except the cloth wasn't glossy.

It was hemmed in what at first appeared to be a simple border. The pattern, upon closer examination, was not simple at all. Tight, detailed knots wove in and out of each other. The thread was of pure spun gold. She fastened it about her shoulders and turned about. It fit her perfectly, falling mid-calf. She turned, and the cloak swirled and settled lightly about her. "How did you come by this?"

Ela smiled. "Some of us stayed up all night making it for you."

The gesture brought a tear to her eyes and she hugged Ela. "Your speed is amazing, Ela. And your skill is excellent."

Turi beamed as if the compliment had been directed at him instead of his wife.

She looked down at the cape, stared at it a moment in shock, then at Ela. "Wasn't it red?" The color had shifted subtly and now was closer to the green of her own dress.

"It was," Ela said.

"But ...?"

"It's a woodsman's cape," Turi said.

"A woodsman's cape will give you an advantage," Lael added. "You'll need every advantage you can come by to be successful."

"I've never heard of such a thing." She noted that a part of the cape had darkened to a shade of brown that nearly matched the nearby table.

"Very special and very rare. We don't make these to sell. Hardly anyone knows of them."

"How does it work?"

Ela said, "It's woven from the silk of the veiled blackglen spider. It lives in our forests, and its web is all but invisible at a glance."

"It drinks in colors," Turi explained. "Wearing that cape and standing perfectly still, you will blend with whatever is nearby. Most eyes will pass right over you."

Leenah studied the fine material. "This is marvelous. Will it really hide me?"

"Indeed, it will," Lael said. "I only regret not having more to help you on your way. But what we have, we give."

"Why have you honored me with such a gift?" She put a hand against the cloak and watched it slowly fade against a spreading swath that matched her skin color.

Ela said, "Because we all love Lady Darha, and we despise the evil twin who has treated her like a criminal all these years."

Turi handed her a rucksack, decorated in matching needlework. "Here's a few keelits, not that you'll lack for nourishment in the Rim-wall forests."

"Always remember to eat your keelits," Ela said.

"I will. And you remember to always thank the Creator for them."

Ela smiled. "I will ponder what you said."

Leenah fastened the dagger about her waist and hung the sack from her shoulder. "You've all been so kind." She bent and hugged each of them. "How can I ever repay you?"

"Freeing Lady Darha will be payment enough," Turi said, but Leenah heard doubt in the man's voice.

The Kleimen had proved themselves fine friends, and she regretted having to leave them so soon. The task ahead of her was daunting, but with her mind made up and her feet set upon the course, she was determined to see it through.

⚜

The misty forest was filled with pleasant sounds: rushing waterfalls, singing birds, and a menagerie of scampering creatures. The walk was both pleasant and interesting. The diversions helped lift some of the weightiness of the daunting task that lay ahead. The pathway was remarkably free of humans, and it was late morning when Leenah first heard voices around a bend, coming her way. Quickly, she darted a fistful of spans into the forest before stopping beside a dusky gray yew, grasping the cloak closed about her. A few moments later, a man with his small son strode into view. They each bore a yoke upon their shoulders— the child's being smaller than the adult's. Each yoke held two pails, the sweet tang of bdell-m sap wafting from them.

When a bend in the trail snatched them from view, she reemerged, loosening the woodsman's cape as she continued on her way. The cloak seemed to work as Turi claimed, but on the other hand, it may have been pure luck that prevented them from glancing her way.

At every intersection or fork, she paused to study the map. Gali's directions were excellent, and she was reassured that her feet were pointed in the right direction by his extensive inclusion of landmarks. After a while, she'd firmly committed the map to memory and only removed it from the cloak's pocket to check herself.

Night eventually darkened the path and spilled out across the forest. According to the map, she was near the villages Gali had warned her to avoid. She sought a hidden ravine or gully in which to wait out the dawn—someplace secluded enough so she might open one of the cased moonglasses the Kleimen had provided for her.

Something startled her to a stop. Listening, she heard only the sounds of the forest. Nothing out of place.... Slowly a thought encroached upon her brain, muddled at first. Her breath caught as she sensed terror. Terror and confusion. Somehow, she'd touched the frantic thoughts of a scarlet dragon.

32

Lady Darha

*C*oncentrating, Leenah attempted to reach out as she so often did with Gur. Now, distantly, she caught a glimpse of a flame that flickered briefly among the trees. Opening the lid of a cased moonglass for light to see by, she left the path. The terror grew stronger. She'd pinpointed the flare in her mind and pushed through tangled undergrowth toward it. Suddenly the trees gave way, and Leenah found herself standing on a groomed verge overlooking a dark grove of qwall trees; the bright moonlight faintly illuminated the pale paths between straight rows of trees. All at once an orange flare of dragon fire shot out, sending dancing shadows scampering through the ruler-straight rows.

The dragon seemed to be trapped, struggling against something Leenah couldn't make out. Leenah sensed the dragon's squeezing panic inside her own chest. As she stepped off the verge, the huge head swung around, moonlight glinting red off its eyes. Panic surged, achingly, and Leenah stopped. *Peace.*

The creature's fear flooded her brain. Now she saw the faint outlines of a heavy net, a part of it burned away, but the major part of it twisted about the dragon's wings. The more the dragon struggled, the more entwined it became. Leenah filled her head with soothing thoughts and advanced cautiously until just out of range of its fiery breath.

You've been caught in a harvester's net. They were often set to catch dragons invading croplands, and what could be more tempting to a scarlet dragon than all these qwall trees flowing with sweet bdell-m. *I won't hurt you. Do you understand me?*

The dragon's thrashing ceased, blood-red eyes holding her in a piercing stare. *You do understand.* The beast was a tight spring ready to explode apart at the least provocation. *Friend. Peace.* She took another step.

The dragon's thoughts were muddled with fear.

I am of the old blood. I understand. Leenah drew the dagger from her belt. *Permit me to free you.* She halted at the sudden rise of fear. *The trap was set by another, not I.*

The dragon's head arched back as far as the thick netting would permit. Leenah heard the muffled gurgling of juices within its throat sacks. It was preparing to mix them. Separately, the juices were harmless, but once combined it took only the briefest exposure to the air for them to burst into deadly flame.

She tried to remember the thoughts that soothed Gur when he was upset. The ability to cross the barriers between the created kinds was swiftly dying out. How much simpler it had been in the beginning when Father Adam and Mother Eve communed freely with all of the Creator's creatures. Her short stay in the Creator's Garden—the Cradleland of man—had been a tantalizing glimpse of what it must have been like before the Fall.

She returned the dagger to its sheath and slowly stretched out a hand, palm down, making a soft purring sound, imitating as best she could the purr of a contented dragon—the sound Gur made when he'd shielded her beneath his wings and rested his head lightly upon her lap.

The gurgling of fulminating chemicals ceased. Leenah released a breath and approached close enough for the dragon to sniff her hand. Gently, she tugged at the thick hemp ropes. With even greater care, she withdrew the dagger. The dragon's red eyes rounded warily. Leenah sawed at one of the strands.

"I'm called Leenah." She both thought and spoke it.

The dragon watched the blade as the strand parted.

"Do you know Gur?"

Its thoughts remained a blank. She wasn't surprised. Gur was a name she'd given him. Dragons knew each other by other means. She tried another tack. "Do you know the place called Imo-suk?"

The great head cocked to one side, eyes like swirling blood giving no indication it had understood the question.

Here was a way to get word to Rhone, but how to reach her? Leenah sensed the femaleness of this dragon.

"Gur roosts at Imo-suk." She wasn't getting through to the she-dragon. Her jaw clenched in frustration. Had Rhone struggled like this with spiders?

She turned the problem over in her head. Perhaps they knew each other by location or by deeds? "Gur nests across the wide water."

The dragon seemed interested but still didn't appear to grasp her intentions.

"Gur nests near Imo-suk."

Still no spark of real understanding. She pondered as her blade worked through the knotted ropes, freeing one wing, which instantly rose and flapped. Ducking around it, she went to work on the second wing.

"Gur kills mansnatchers."

Nothing. But then, all dragons killed mansnatchers. How might a dragon express it? "*Wings-of-Fire* consumes the black screechers?"

The great head swung around with interest in her eyes.

"So, that got your attention." She drew a vivid mental picture of Gur in her brain. "Gur—*Wings-of-Fire*—killed three black screechers near Imo-suk."

I know you.

The dragon's sudden, clear thought set Leenah back a step. "You know me?"

Wings-of-Fire-Nests-on-Stone-Pile?

Stone pile. She grinned. That was an appropriate name for the crumbling fortress. "Yes. Do you know where *Wings-of-Fire-Nests-on-Stone-Pile* is? Can you find him? Will you find him for me?" She'd let her thoughts run unbridled in her excitement, not sure how much the dragon had understood.

With the last strand severed, the dragon leaped free of the net and flexed her wings, rattling the branches on either side of the row. All at once she leaped skyward.

"Wait!"

The dragon circled and landed a few spans from her. *I know Wings-of-Fire-Nests-on-Stone-Pile.*

"Will you take something to him?"

The dragon shook her wings and folded them along the glinting ruby scales of her body. *Yes.*

Upon what could she write a message? She rummaged through her sack. In their thoroughness to outfit her, the Kleimen had overlooked including pen and parchment. And why should they have? To whom had they expected her to be writing? The inside of the bag glowed with various pieces of moonglass. She grabbed out the large round pearl of moonglass Turi had given her; the golden glow spilled through her fingers, reflecting like burnished bronze against the dragon's scales.

She sat upon the ground, in the midst of the qwall trees and the sweet scent of flowing sap, and with the point of her dagger inscribed upon the golden surface:

Darha held Highwatch 34
Will be killed if signal pyres lit
Leenah

In the stone's glow, the letters stood out clearly. She took Gali's map from her cloak, wrapped the moonglass in it, then unwound a ribbon from her hair and bound the package tight, forming a loop.

The dragon eyed the thing curiously, and with a tentative clawed foot plucked it from her outstretched hand.

She understood! "Fly swiftly. Give to *Wings-of-Fire-Nests-on-Stone-Pile*. Do you understand?"

She got the strong impression the she-dragon had understood. "When you give it to *Wings-of-Fire-Nests-on-Stone-Pile*, tell him to take it to Rhone. *Rhone*—do you understand? *Wings-of-Fire-Nests-on-Stone-Pile* will know who Rhone is."

The dragon stretched her wings and bound into the sky, flapping slowly but powerfully toward the starry sky until she was but a glint of blood in the moonlight. And then she was gone.

"Creator, keep her on course," she prayed, knowing the whimsical nature of dragons, their curiosity and distractibility. But she'd done all she could. Taking up her sack, she returned to the forest.

❧

The following day, traffic on the path all but ceased as it narrowed and began switchbacking. A carpet of thick moss was squishy and slippery beneath her feet.

Suddenly, as if a garden tender had set an edging and said, No more, the trees halted and gave way to an army of stark, black-rock spires, standing as if to bar her way. But the narrow trail continued steeply upward, winding through the rocks, crooked as a dead snake in the road. A brisk wind blew in off the sea, still hidden from her eyes by jagged spires of rock. She pressed onward until the broad top of the Rim-wall leveled out and the Great Sea, a flat gray slate in the late light, stretched before her, touching the horizon in every direction.

She inhaled the freshening air, exhausted. She couldn't stop to rest. Highwatch thirty-four lay still farther east, a goodly distance off.

The path forked, and she set her feet upon the left branch of it, remembering the way from the map. The trail was no more than a faint, smooth discoloration upon the ancient rock. *How many feet must have gone before me to have worn it down so?* she wondered as hers added their own imperceptible bit of polishing.

It was long after dark when the tiny flicker of light appeared in the distance. She pushed onward until the old Highwatch Tower loomed suddenly from the darkness, its unlit signal pyre rearing up before her like a shadowy giant. The pyre's brazier burned lowly, casting an uncertain light upon the solid block walls of the tower. She halted in its shadows and studied the layout. Lady Darha was somewhere inside it, or in one of the three smaller outbuildings.

Being but an observation post, and not a defensive structure, the Highwatch Tower was attached to a small building designed to billet four or five men in relative comfort. From its three leeward windows, lamplight stretched out across a rocky patch of ground, partly illuminating a road down off the Rim-wall.

She studied the two other buildings not attached to the tower. From one of them, a faint glow showed through one of the windows.

Moonglass. Nothing else produced that soft magnetic light. And now as her eyes more precisely picked out the details, what she'd first suspected was another lamp turned out to be a small fire a little distance away. A man sat before it on a folding bivouac chair, peering into the struggling flames. Around him, stretched upon their sleeping mats, lay the shadowy forms of four men. *Extra guards.*

Leenah crept to the small stone building and sidled up to a barred window. The opening was covered with a reed-paper curtain. Cautiously, she moved the curtain aside and peeked inside.

She'd never seen Lady Darha before, but the woman asleep upon the low bed could be none other. Her long black hair, shot with gray, fell over a shoulder and hung in a braid off the edge of the bed. Her face, peaceful in sleep, bore the straight nose and thin, well-formed lips Leenah knew so well from another face. Rhone's mother. On a table sat a half-shuttered moonglass, and upon the floor at the woman's side lay an open scroll, as if she'd fallen asleep reading.

Lady Darha's quarters appeared well attended with the necessities of comfort. This might have been the Tower Captain's quarters before it became Lady Darha's prison. From her limited vantage, Leenah noted the floors covered in luxurious skins, the stark stone of the walls softened with colorful tapestries. A dinner tray holding dirty dishes sat on one end of the table. Three water urns stood in one corner. To the left, a door to a second room.

Leenah was just about to *pssst* Lady Darha awake when the guard by the fire stood. She drew the cape about her and pressed against the outbuilding's stone wall.

The guard stretched. Leenah spied the key dangling from a thong around his neck. He walked slowly toward the edge of the Rim-wall and peered at the sea for a while, then strode around the camp. She held her breath as he started in her direction. But his gaze passed over her—and he only came as far as the door to the building, stared at it a moment, and then wandered back toward the fire. He paused at a barrel, ladled out a drink of water, then returned to his chair and chucked a small log onto the struggling fire.

She couldn't risk making a sound now. An idea came to her. She'd trained with a healer once, before being enslaved in the Temple Prison. She frowned, trying to remember something she'd been taught.

As soon as the guard appeared mesmerized by the flames, she slipped silently away from Lady Darha's window, backtracked far along the black, savage Rim-wall, and then found a nook in which to wait out the night.

Come the sky's first graying, Leenah scouted a path down into the forest and began searching for the plants she required.

It took most of the morning to find what she needed, and then most of the second quartering to pound them to pulp and extract their sap. She collected about a tenth of a kab of the milky white fluid in a keber nut shell and carried it back to the Rim-wall, careful not to spill a drop.

Once the night was well advanced, she crept back to the corner of Lady Darha's prison and hunkered down to wait.

The stars wheeled slowly overhead, and eventually everyone was asleep except for a single guard—a different man this night—sitting by the fire and reading by the light of a small moonglass. She waited, something she was not gifted to do. Impatience began to gnaw at her. She fought her natural impetuousness. It seemed as if she'd have to wait the whole night. Then the guard stood and roused one of the sleepers. He handed his replacement the key. The man slipped it over his head and took the retiring guard's place by the fire. More time passed. Leenah chewed her lips, keeping an eye on the eastern sky. Finally the guard stood and strode to Lady Darha's building, checked the door, and then made a circuit around the camp, momentarily disappearing behind the tower.

Her heart pounding, Leenah dashed to the water keg, spilled

in the concoction, and then, just as swiftly and silently, dashed back into cover. No sooner had the shadows concealed her than the guard returned, sat back by the fire, and stretched out his legs.

Leenah frowned up at the sky, imagining dawn just below the horizon. For a while the guard sat so still she imagined he'd fallen asleep, except when the cocking of a knee or the recrossing of his arms warned her otherwise. Finally, he threw back his arm, gave a yawn, and stood, this time walking stiffly to the water keg.

She held her breath as he ladled up a drink of water, then stopped and stared at it. She urged him on with her thoughts as though he were a scarlet dragon. Suddenly casting the contents aside, he scooped out a second drink, peered at the water, and then quenched his thirst.

A short time later, the guard was sound asleep.

Leenah crept in among the sleeping men, removed a heavy key from around the drugged watchman's neck, and backed quietly away.

❧

"Who are you?" Lady Darha bolted up from her bed, startled from a sound sleep at the soft scuff of the shutting door.

Leenah put a finger to her lips. "You'll alert the guards."

Darha fumbled for the moonglass, snapping open its shutters. "Who are you?" This time she spoke not much above a whisper as her view leaped from Leenah to the door and back again.

"My name is Leenah. I'm a friend of Rhone."

"Rhone!" Her eyes rounded, and she sprang from her sleeping pallet. "My son Rhone?"

"Yes."

"Where is he? Is he here in Atlan?"

"He is near, Lady Darha."

Dread instantly filled the woman's face. "No, he mustn't come for me. Zorin will have him killed."

"He knows that, Lady Darha. Now, quickly, get dressed. We must be away from here before dawn, and already the night is nearly spent."

Darha threw on her clothes and grabbed a few items that she packed into a red velvet and gold tote, drawing it closed and tying the strings. She snatched a yellow cloak from off a peg. Leenah stopped her. "Have you something not so bright?"

She thought a moment, then dashed into the adjoining room, and came back with a heavy, deep-red cloak. "It's all I have."

"Then it will do." Leenah cracked open the door. The sky had begun to gray, yet the guard in the chair slept. He would be unconscious for the next quartering, if she had blended her plants correctly. "Now."

The two women slipped outside. Rounding the little building, Leenah led the way past the hulking shadow of the Highwatch, emerging from the night's dark embrace.

They made it just past the signal pyre when from atop the tower a shout raised the alarm. Leenah grabbed Darha's hand and put on a burst of speed. "Stop!" came the order again, followed by the urgent peal of a warning bell.

They raced across the rocky ground toward the forest, looming darkly below them, but as yet Leenah could find no way off the Rim-wall, and it was still too dark to attempt a blind rush down among its unseen crags. A backward glance showed two men drawing up behind them. Others would be joining them in moments. Her heart pounded, and dread rose in her breast. The older woman did not move as quickly as she, and Leenah feared any instant a misplaced step would throw one of them to the rocks or twist and break an ankle.

She scanned the downward slope. The men were gaining; they

were young, powerful, and used to the uneven footing. Alone, she might have outdistanced them.

Then she spied a narrow trail into forest below and dove down it, Lady Darha struggling to keep up. Rhone's mother couldn't maintain this pace much longer.

"Go on without me," the older woman puffed. "They won't hurt me. Save yourself."

"No." How could she face Rhone knowing she'd abandoned his mother on the cusp of freedom? There had to be another way.

They rushed past the first of the giant Rim-wall trees, the game trail twisting down the steeply sloping terrain. "Quick, give me your cloak!"

"My cloak?" Darha wheezed.

The trail made a sharp turn, momentarily hiding their pursuers. "Give it to me now."

Lady Darha fumbled with the ties and swept it off. Leenah flung off her woodsman's cape and gave it to the panting woman. "Put it on."

The trail turned again, and Leenah pulled her off it, into heavy brush. "They can't see you if you don't move. I'll lead them away. Flee to the little folk in Deepvale. They'll help you." Leenah yanked the hood down over Lady Darha's head, then sprang back onto the trail, fastening the red cloak about her as she flew down the slope, deeper into the forest, praying Darha would not be seen.

The Rim-wall guards rounded the bend a moment later. No longer held back by the older woman, Leenah opened the distance. A glance over her shoulder sent a surge of energy straight to her legs. They were only twenty or thirty spans behind her, and she now spied three more men not far behind them.

Would Lady Darha's red cloak alone be sufficient to fool them? It was a slim hope suspended on a hair-thin thread, but she clung to it as she stretched out, her lungs beginning to burn, the muscles in her legs tightening. Unburdened by either sword or spear, she flew down the trail. She suddenly realized she was missing the small rucksack the Kleimen had given her. Where had she dropped it?

Another glance confirmed she was pulling ahead. Now it was only a matter of endurance …

Her toe struck something in the trail. She lunged off balance, her shoulder slammed into a tree, and her head smacked a low branch. Trees, sky, brown earth, and green shrubs whirled—her eyes jumbling them all up. She tried to sit but fell back as her dazed ears filled with a thumping of approaching feet and muddled voices. Then rough hands grabbed her and hauled her to her feet. She cried out as needles of pain shot up her neck and down her arm.

The hood was yanked off her head, and garbled words tumbled into her brain. She was shaken. Her shoulder screamed. Slowly, the words all came together in a meaningful way. "Where is she?"

Leenah moaned and reached for her shoulder. Her arms were wrenched back and gathered behind her. The pain nearly drove her to her knees.

"Where is she hiding?"

In spite of the torment, Leenah forced her brain to clear. She had to think quickly. "Lady Darha went through the woods, down."

"Who are you?"

She set her jaw, refusing to answer.

"Who sent you on this task?"

Her burning glare of defiance enraged the guard. He struck out, backhanding her. "High Councilor Zorin has ways to loosen your tongue. Garit, Wos-nn, take her back to the Highwatch and put her in irons. The rest of you spread out. I don't have to tell you that if Lady Darha escapes, it'll be the Pit or the Pikes for all of us."

Leenah gritted her teeth against the fire in her shoulder and her jaw as they pulled her along the trail. Her legs were still getting mixed signals from her brain, stumbling, trying to keep up. When they passed the bend in the trail where she had left Darha, she stole a glance. Rhone's mother was gone, and there beneath a shrub was the nearly invisible rucksack of woodsman's cloth. She whispered a prayer for Darha's protection and hoped she had taken her advice and was making quickly for Deepvale.

33

A Plan Unfolds

*R*hone stood at the bow of the boat, studying the dark walls rising in the pale moonlight. His impatience, great as it was, couldn't increase the speed of the rowers by even one stroke. They all knew the urgency and were pulling with all they had.

"If I'd only deciphered it sooner!" His fist balled into a knot, and his teeth clenched. He took a breath to ease his tension. It didn't help.

Klesc, steadying himself beside Rhone on the plunging deck, said, "The Fates have moved the pieces, Pyir Rhone. It's now in Dirgen's hands."

Rhone shot him a glance. Klesc's lips hitched upward. "I meant the Creator's hands."

He should have scrutinized the stone as soon as Gur had winged overhead and dropped it at his and Larik's feet as the two of them had been crossing the exercise ground. Arriving as it had, wrapped in the map and bound with Leenah's hair ribbon, he'd set the stone aside to ponder the map. It sat on his table all that day until night, when in the moonglass's golden light, Leenah's hastily-scratched words suddenly stood out.

He'd lost a day, a night, and now another day in transit. Yet the timing worked out. He needed the cover of darkness for what he and his twelve handpicked Makir had to do. He glanced back at the warriors sitting quietly on the benches. Clad in their black sutas, the fighting clothes of a battle-ready Makir, they might have appeared as shadows to the casual observer. Among them was Ka-Larik. Rhone felt a frown. He only chose him because his father had requested it. Rhone wondered if it wasn't a father's attempt to bolster his son's standing among the other warriors, or was it an old man's way of vicariously living one more battle? Whatever Larik's reason, out of respect for his First Statre's years of service to his family, he had brought Ka-Larik along.

The boat lurched as a surging wave grounded the keel upon the gravely shore. He looked back at the Rim-wall. They had arrived beneath the soaring cliffs. A distant prick of light marked the location of the Highwatch. The twelve leaped ashore while the rowers remained with the boat, making it fast against the pounding surf. He wanted it ready for a speedy departure. No words were spoken. Each Makir knew exactly what was required of him as they unloaded coils of rope and bags of iron stakes.

Dressed in their sutas, they all but disappeared against Atlan's rugged shoulder. Swiftly they buckled on swords. Rhone peered at the cliff that soared darkly upward. The moon cast just enough light for him to determine where to begin. Hefting a coil of rope over his shoulder, he found his first finger- and toehold and started upward, quietly driving the iron pegs into minute crevices with a hammer muffled by thick leather padding. Securing the rope, he ascended a few more spans and repeated the process.

As the night advanced, the Makir silently worked their way toward their goal. Rhone, in the lead, managed to find fingerholds where none appeared to be. When one rope played out, a fresh coil was handed up from below. In this way, they crept up the sheer cliff, cresting the top of the Rim-wall as a weary moon dipped toward the far horizon.

Three men sat around a fire. Rhone motioned to two of his Makir to take them. The rest slipped into the tower and silently secured it; the guards within startled awake to discover the black warriors and their deadly swords. Rhone ascended the Highwatch Tower and easily took the lone watchman up there. It was the work of a few moments, and the lookout station was in his possession.

"Where's Lady Darha?" he demanded of the officer in charge once all the prisoners assembled together in the main tower house.

"Gone. Escaped into the forest," the officer said, his view shifting warily about at the twelve masked warriors. "Makir?" He sounded incredulous. No doubt he was, since the Makir had fallen into legend and memories.

"How and where did she flee?"

Rhone put his sword to the officer's throat when he hesitated. "A woman poisoned the guard on duty and stole the key."

A *woman? Leenah!* The surge of hope was tempered with dread. "Where is this woman?"

"She was apprehended and is even now being transported to Hodin's Keep."

Hodin's Keep meant that Leenah would soon be in Zorin's hands. His dread took on weight and texture. "When?"

"Yesterday, about the beginning of the second quartering. After we'd searched the forest for Lady Darha and could find no trace of her, the Captain of the Guard and a few others took the woman to Zorin. The rest of us remained behind to continue the search. But Lady Darha's trail ran cold." His eyes rounded. "As if Dirgen himself took her away."

Yesterday. If he'd deciphered Leenah's message sooner, he'd have arrived in time! By now she must nearly be in Zorin's custody, and his mother was somewhere in the forest. He glanced out the arched stone window. The dawn had come, and he had not a moment to lose.

"Take me to the place where Lady Darha disappeared."

"What should we do with these?" Egbin asked, his sword covering two trembling men.

"Lock them in one of the outbuildings. You and Gorlid keep watch."

Once the prisoners were secured, Rhone and the rest of the Makir followed the officer along the Rim-wall and down a steep trail into the forest.

"The woman was captured here. Lady Darha escaped somewhere in this area."

Rhone began backtracking, his eyes taking in every detail. The ground was too hard for footprints, but here and there crushed vegetation showed that a chase had transpired. He knelt from time to time to examine a snapped stem or the outline of a foot upon a patch of softer soil. Then he spied the small bag off the trail, tucked under a bramble—he'd almost missed it. The bag was expertly made and curiously embroidered. He knew of only one village that used such a distinctive pattern. He looked down the trail where apparently no one had recently trod. A single, freshly snapped vine and a timnerin leaf crushed upon a wedge of black stone was as clear as a road map. He glanced at the bag, certain now where she was heading.

He momentarily weighed both sides of his heart. His mother was alone in the forest, seeking refuge. Leenah was soon to be a prisoner in Hodin's Keep. Zorin would surely interrogate her and make life unpleasant in the process. But interrogations could sometimes take a long time—and his mother held the truth about

Zorin's ruthlessness; truth the people would need to hear if he was to retake Atlan....

Surveying the men with him, he chose the one he could best do without and took Ka-Larik aside. "I and the others are going after Lady Darha. I want you to return to Larik and tell him to move forward with the invasion. We have no time to lose."

A momentary spark of indignation narrowed the young man's eyes, but it passed almost at once. "As you order, Pyir Rhone."

"Take this prisoner with you. Tell Egbin and Gorlid to accompany you and the prisoners back to Imo-suk."

Ka-Larik nodded, retrieved the prisoner, and marched him up the trail.

Rhone watched after him a moment, feeling a scowl come suddenly to his face. What was it that had made him uneasy? Then he turned his mind back to his mother, setting out now with nine Makir at his side. The sooner he found his mother, the sooner he could turn his quest back to Leenah, and then to the task of wresting Atlan from his brother's bloody fist!

❦

It was nearly evening. Da-gore and Batok stood upon the promenade in front of the cloth merchant's shop, Batok listing all the reasons why he'd not yet learned of Leenah's whereabouts. As he expounded on the efforts being made, sudden shouting down the street intruded upon their talk. A crowd had begun to assemble.

"What is this?" Da-gore moved to the curb and studied the racket, drawing nearer to them.

"Your guess is as good as mine, Master Jael-ik." Batok grunted and strained to raise up on his toes, to see over the gathering throng. "It appears to be a prison cart."

A moment later a heavy wagon pulled by a lumbering three-point rumbled into sight along the main road through Atla Fair. As it drew nearer, Da-gore stiffened. "You needn't search any further for the woman."

The cloth merchant looked at him wonderingly, his fleshy eyes widening. "Is that she?"

Da-gore nodded, watching Leenah, who was sitting in the rear of the prison wagon between two of Zorin's guards. As the prison cart groaned past, he could see the iron shackles about her slender wrists, the bruises upon her face, and the careful manner in which she cradled her arm.

He glanced to Batok. "Send word to Pyir Rhone. Tell him Leenah is a prisoner of Zorin. Then inform my captains that they are to pass word to their men to be ready to move out at a moment's notice."

"I'll release a bird to Imo-suk immediately. What will you do?"

"I'm going to stick close to that wagon." Da-gore stepped off the promenade and joined the press of onlookers. They crossed over Merchant's Harbor and then the Kinsmen's Anchorage. Da-gore trailed with the crowd over the Triumph Bridge into the heart of Atlan—Hodin's Sanctum.

A line of Zorin's guards stood at the ready as the procession marched along Atla's Fair View. The wide, red-stone thoroughfare encircled the red wall—Hodin's Keep—that protected the official buildings and Royal Residence. The tall bronze gates were swung open, and guards moved in among the crowd, putting themselves between the curious onlookers and the wagon. Once Leenah was within the Keep, the gates swung closed, and the people began to disperse. Da-gore lingered with a few others, peering through the thick bronze bars as the wagon drew to a halt before the Sanctuary of Justice. In the old days, the Sanctuary had meant justice for the innocent of Atlan. Now the sort of justice Zorin meted out there brought more scorn than praise.

He watched as the guards unchained Leenah. Six of them escorted her through tall, double doors. Once the doors shut, Dagore stood a moment longer, peering at their boldly carved panels. They bore the once-proud images of the original ten council members, with Hodin standing above them, symbols from a happier day.

It was getting dark. He strolled back along Atla's Fair View, trying to devise some plan. Any way he looked at it, getting to her seemed impossible.

Leenah would stand before Zorin, but what after that? Torture? Imprisonment? The Black Pool Caves deep beneath Hodin's Keep? Few prisoners who entered the Black Pool caverns ever returned. The wring serpents and Zorin's executioner finished off most of them, and the rest succumbed to poor nourishment or went mad in the perpetual gloom. The cooper, Maelc, was one of the lucky few who had survived.

He strolled through the growing darkness. The light of recently lit torches flickered across the wide avenue—while an edging of moonglass bathed Atla's Fair View in a soft glow that turned the red paving stones the color of rose petals. He paused from time to time to stare up the high red walls. At one of the many gutters flowing from beneath them, he paused to study the bronze grating, hidden in deep shadows now. Did the bars go clear to the bottom or end somewhere above? And might a man hold his breath long enough to squeeze beneath it? The notion of crawling through that filthy gutter repelled him, but if he truly thought it possible, he knew he'd at least attempt it.

There was nothing he could do now. Rather than risk drawing the guard's attention, he returned to Atla Fair and Batok's little shop.

"And you know of no way past that wall?" Da-gore drummed his fingers upon the table in Batok's cellar. "There's got to be a way."

The ponderous cloth merchant sat across the table from him, still puffing from the climb down the stairs. He'd locked up his shop early, in spite of any suspicion it might have drawn toward him. "None, Master Jael-ik. The gates are all heavily guarded, as you well know, and unless you could float over the walls in a sky-barge and lower yourself down on a rope or burrow under them, I know of no other entrance than the main gates."

Da-gore recalled something a guard had mentioned to him. "Under them? I heard there are tunnels beneath Hodin's Keep. Is it true?"

"True enough, but you can forget about using them."

"They are guarded?"

"Not that. You could never fit into them. They are narrow, winding passages fit only for jikloos, rats, wring serpents, and, of course, the Kleimen."

Kleimen? He tried to recall where he'd heard that name before. Then he had it. Rhone had mentioned them in his briefing ... but that had been a long time ago, and the details escaped him now. "Who are the Kleimen?"

Batok shrugged his meaty shoulders, patting his glistening forehead with a handkerchief. "The little folk who live along the Rim-wall. They keep to themselves. Hardly ever come to Atla Fair except to sell their moonglass and needlework. Ah, the needle-work. Splendid!" His jowls folded upon themselves as he frowned. "But you'd not fit in the tunnels, even if we could locate an entrance. And I?" He grasped his belly and laughed. "Might as well stuff me through the eye of a needle."

"What about the sewers?"

Batok's mouth wrinkled, the flesh at his cheeks and eyes

puckering. "I wouldn't know and wouldn't care to learn, either."

"Who would know?"

Batok rolled his shoulders and turned his palms to the dark, webby ceiling.

Da-gore fell into a thoughtful silence, pondering the Deep Chambers ... and suddenly the answer came to him. "Maelc!"

34

The Deep Chambers

At least there were no broken bones. Leenah was thankful for that. But a night and a day riding upon the hard seat of the prison wagon had driven the pain deep, like a red-hot prod pressed against her neck. The heavy iron shackles had rubbed her wrists raw.

When they had left the tower, Lady Darha had still not been found. Leenah prayed that Rhone's mother was still free. The guards assigned to deliver her to Zorin had been in a sober mood the entire trip, mumbling about Zorin's wrath or the Bloody Pikes. A runner had been sent ahead, and Zorin's anger would have had enough time to flame into a dangerous state.

Now, upon arriving at Hodin's Keep, the wagon was immediately surrounded by guards. Six armed men escorted her up the wide red stairs to a massive pair of doors that swung open as they approached and silently closed behind her as they passed through.

Their footsteps echoed in a cavernous welcoming room as the entourage turned left and followed a wide hallway hung with pictures of Hodin and others. In spite of the grinding apprehension sinking its fangs and sucking the life from her, she couldn't help but notice the similarity in face shape and the strong jawlines of Hodin and his kin.

The company came to a stop. A squeezing fist seemed to wrap itself about her throat as the Captain of the Guard stated their business to a door attendant who immediately slipped inside the room. A moment later, the door whispered open, and she was whisked inside.

Her guards formed up in front of and behind her. The room was bright in spite of the failing light beyond a wall that opened in tall arches to what appeared to be a polished stone veranda outside. She was vaguely aware of a man retreating slowly toward that long porch, his back to her, as her guards came to a halt.

"The woman, High Councilor Zorin."

Past their broad shoulders, she caught a glimpse of a man with a dark gray minck perched upon a leather patch on his shoulder.

"Let me see her."

The guards stepped aside. Leenah gasped, staring at a face that, if she'd seen it any other place, she'd have sworn it was Rhone. Her blood ran cold. The eyes, nose, mouth, the strong jaw, and the prominent cheeks were all Rhone's. Even the hair was identical.

Zorin's eyes narrowed as if something loathsome had been shown to him. There were differences. Although the eyes were the same color and shape, they held a harder edge. This was not Rhone's warm, caring gaze settling upon her. His face was paler than the man she had come to know so well, the folds of skin beneath his eyes fleshier, their surrounding skin shadowed as if sleep were sometimes hard to come by. Scowl lines radiated deeply from them and etched his furrowed brow.

"Your name?"

The pain of her ordeal still hadn't softened her resolve. She clenched her jaw.

A smile stretched tightly across his face, and he bent nearer. "Why have you interfered with my business?"

She flinched at his hot breath, but said nothing.

"Stubborn? Well, you'll talk soon enough. I have ways. You will beg to tell me all, and then you will die." Zorin glanced at the captain who had escorted her. "Has my mother been found?"

"She's not been located yet, High Councilor."

His view shot back at Leenah. "How did you find her? Who is your informant?" When she didn't reply, his hand shot out. The slap wrenched her head and started the fire in her shoulder burning again.

"Who aided you in this?" Cords of rigid muscles stood out along his neck.

She stared back at him. "I'll tell you nothing."

Zorin drew in a long, slow breath, as if forcibly calming himself. Then all at once he smiled and glanced at the minck perched upon his shoulder. "What do you think, Pia?" he whispered, gently stroking the minck's furry back.

The minck squealed and dipped its head twice, as if it had understood the question.

"Yes, I think we will both enjoy seeing her beg the executioner for death." Zorin looked back at Leenah. "I have most exquisite ways to make women talk."

A cold dread tightened the muscles of her chest.

The captain said, "We found this on her."

Zorin took the Kleiman sword from the captain. "I know this workmanship." He looked at her, then her dress as if seeing it for the first time. He fingered the fine embroidery about her neck. "And this too. It's a Deepvale pattern. So you've been with the Kleimen."

"No." But she'd spoke it too quickly, and her eyes must have showed a sudden rise of fear.

"Was it those pesky wall rats who told you?" His frown lengthened. "It was them. You'd have thought they would have learned by now."

Leenah remembered being told of the attack on the other Kleimen villages, and Turi's and Lael's reluctance to become involved in her quest. They'd helped the only way they could, and had left enough evidence for Zorin to implicate them in her crime.

"They did nothing."

"The Kleimen need a fresh lesson on what happens to people who practice treason. Captain Link, order a full fist of warriors to Deepvale. Take the canics with you. Burn their village, and drive them from their filthy mines. Then bring the survivors here to be hung on Execution Ridge as a reminder to all who come near of what happens to rebels."

Link bowed curtly and strode out of the room.

"You mustn't," Leenah cried. "They're innocent. All they did was feed me."

"And you will hang on the Pikes beside them. But first I will learn who you are and who sent you."

"I think I can be of some help." The man Leenah had seen strolling toward the terrace was now standing near her. She turned, and her mouth went slack.

Captain El-ik smiled. "So, you recognize me."

She swallowed hard, recovering from the shock.

"You know this woman?" Zorin demanded.

The Captain of the Lodath's Guard glanced at Zorin. "She was a prisoner of the Lodath seven years ago. She attempted to murder the Lodath and escaped with another prisoner ... one of your own."

"One of my own?" Zorin raised quizzical eyebrows.

"A Hodinite. A Makir showman named Klesc. And another. We eventually learned his name. It's one that might interest you, High Councilor Zorin."

Zorin's anger rumbled. "Cease with the drama, Captain El-ik. What name?"

"Rhone."

Zorin's eyes widened as he stared back at her. "So, you're one of those rebels my brother gathers across the water." His dark eyes suddenly narrowed. "Don't look so surprised. My spies keep me well informed. It seems the list of charges against you grows. Tell me, what is my brother planning? Does he believe he can unseat me from the High Council?"

His hypocrisy snapped something in her brain, and her words burst forth without thought of consequences. "The High Council? You had the High Council murdered when you seized power! Those who sit in rule over Atlan are mere puppets, and you hold all the strings." Saying it somehow swept aside concerns for her own welfare, freeing her. She was doomed to die anyway—how much better to do so on the attack than in retreat. Perhaps a bit of her uncle's Makir blood coursed through her after all! "You have no more right to sit as High Councilor than I. It's your brother's rightful place. It belongs to Rhone."

Zorin's mouth tightened, his neck crimsoned. The minck on his shoulder hunkered forward and glared at her, its wings rustling like dry leaves underfoot. "If my brother thinks he can take Atlan, let him try. The people know how he arranged the murder of our father, the assassinations of the High Council, and how *I alone* managed to protect our *dear* mother from his treachery."

"That's a lie!"

Zorin grinned. "Is it?"

Her anger flared, and suddenly Zorin's guards were restraining her, pinning her arms and surrounding her.

"First Shield Oert, take this *escaped prisoner*—" he gave Captain El-ik a thin, acquiescing smile, "—down to the Black Pool. Inform Prison Master Sayor that I will be there shortly, and we can begin loosening her tongue immediately."

The door opened and a servant entered, glancing timidly at the men gathered there as he approached Zorin.

"What is it?" Zorin demanded, impatient at the interruption.

The servant whispered something in his ear. The High Councilor's eyes widened with interest. "Send him in at once."

The servant retreated, and a moment later, Leenah glimpsed the tall man who strode in. He wore the black suta of a Makir, and although she hadn't yet seen his face, she instantly recognized his swaggering gate.

He stopped before Zorin, and saw her. His shock was clear ... and so was hers. "Ka-Larik," she whispered.

He studied her a moment, his eyes hardening, then looked at Zorin. "I have urgent news." Ka-Larik glanced cautiously at the men standing there.

"You can speak freely. I'm surprised to see you here. The reason better be worth the risk."

Ka-Larik gave a confident grin. "I think you will find it so, High Councilor. I've just arrived from Highwatch thirty-four."

Leenah gave a small gasp.

Ka-Larik glanced her way, then back at Zorin. "Pyir Rhone is in Atlan."

Her heart leaped with sudden hope. Rhone was here.

Zorin's expression turned worried. "The invasion has started?"

"No. Just a small incursion. To find her."

Rhone was coming for her!

"Where is he now?"

Ka-Larik shook his head. "I don't know for sure. He sent me

on a mission back to Imo-suk. Needless to say, I disobeyed." He grinned. "I left two dead Makir at the tower and freed your men who were being imprisoned. Pyir Rhone has gone after his mother, but once he finds her, he will be coming here."

Zorin ordered First Shield Oert to assemble the troops immediately.

Ka-Larik said, "There are only ten of them, including Pyir Rhone. They shouldn't be too much of a problem for your forces, High Councilor."

Zorin said to Oert, "Send men to every corner of the hinterland. Find my brother and bring him here—alive, if you can." His fiery stare shot back to Leenah. "We'll have a double execution."

Ka-Larik said, "Do you know who you have here?"

Zorin looked at him.

"This woman holds a special place in Pyir Rhone's heart. She might be useful."

She fought down the urge to spring for the traitor's throat. How could he betray Rhone and the others? They were Makir— closer than brothers.

"Really?" Zorin slid a cunning look at her. "It seems I've learned all I needed to ... without your help." He turned to one of his officers. "Captain Jik, take this rebel to the Deep Chambers and lock her away from the other prisoners. We wouldn't want her spreading lies to them, would we? Then inform my executioners that soon I will have another job for them. The Pikes will run red with her blood ... and my brother's. The people of Atlan will again see what happens to traitors and rebels."

❧

The blackness would have been nearly complete if not for the distant braziers on either side of a hewed-stone staircase. Their wavering flames were too weak to worry the deep shadows filling the small cell in which Leenah had been cast—a dim reminder that there was but one way out of the Black Pool. She rotated her shoulder and winced. They'd practically thrown her down those hard, sharp-edged stairs, hewed from the rock beneath Hodin's Keep. Then the guards had pulled her roughly along a ledge of black rock, torchlight reflecting off the black water that snaked the length of the cavern from one unseen end to the other.

She shifted upon the hard stone and rubbed her hip. They'd tossed her in here, bragging how the next time she saw daylight, it would be from the point of a pike. The slamming of the door and that awful resounding clack of the lock being snapped had stolen any zeal for her quest she'd managed to cling to up until then.

The air was cold and damp and smelled of things dead and dying, and of human excrement. She shivered and hugged herself. After her captors' receding footsteps had been swallowed up by the vastness of the underground rooms, the silence had rushed back with a deafening nothingness. But like those far-off specks of light shaking a defiant fist at the blackness, even the silence wasn't absolute.

Slowly, she had become aware of the echo of dripping water from maybe eight or ten different locations. Now and again a nearby splash and ripple set her spine rigid. Straining, she thought she could almost hear the murmur of men's voices from the direction of the braziers, faintly distant, like a light breeze in the treetops.

Zorin had ordered her to be kept separated from the other prisoners. "This is about as separated as I can be," she mumbled, then loudly, "Do you hear me?" The cavern must have been vast to absorb her shout. She deflated and huddled in a corner.

"Rhone, I'm so sorry. I didn't know what I was doing." She shivered and tried not to permit her imagination to paint in the details the blackness hid from her. Tears began to sting her eyes. She wiped them with her sleeve and crouched in the corner of her cell, her uninjured arm beneath her head for a pillow.

Ela and Turi and Lael. Doomed because of her. *And what of Lady Darha?* Had she found her way, or was she lost in the depths of Atlan's forests? It occurred to her that if Darha had reached the Kleimen, Zorin's troops would find her. She scrubbed the tears from her cheek with the palm of her hand. *How have I helped Rhone's mother? How have I helped Rhone?* She'd only made matters worse and had doomed her friends in Deepvale to certain death. Surely Rhone was looking for her right now. She had forced his hand before the time was right and likely jeopardized everything he'd worked toward all these years.

Zorin had known Rhone's plans all along. Ka-Larik had been the spy. Ka-Larik must have devised a way to kill Lorun, too, for Lorun was the only man who could betray him to Rhone. *How had he managed it?* She filled her brain with this puzzle to keep it from conjuring monsters out of the soft sounds that she could not identify.

After a while she dozed, but the chill of the deep cavern soon woke her, and she sat up, her arm buzzing where it had pressed into the bars. How much time had passed? It was impossible to know. She leaned back against the cold iron bars and imagined fingers stretching through them from the blackness to strangle her. She scurried to the center of her cage, glaring into the darkness. The distant braziers still cast their feeble light against the stone steps. If only she had a moonglass or a candle—a candle would provide a smidgen of warmth.

Reluctantly, she sat upon the cold stone floor and heard a faint, distant sound. She stilled her breathing and listened. Was that a pattern, or was it her imagination? No, there was a definite pattern. Three or four soft taps and then a pause. Three. Five. Three again ...?

Then something cold and wet slithered across her leg. She screamed and leaped to her feet, grabbing an iron bar and clambering up it half a span. *Wring serpents!* Her pounding heart drove the breath from her lungs. The Black Pool was infested with them—Uncle Debne had told her; Lael had told her. She forced a breath. How would she survive with wring serpents slipping through the bars?

Her shoulder burned. Hesitantly, she lowered herself to the rock, clinging to the bar and shaking, not caring anymore if hairy fingers were reaching through the cage to strangle her. Her heart slowed; the rush of blood left her ears. The tapping had ceased. Had her scream silenced it?

She hunkered in the corner of her cell, knees drawn tight to her chest. In a few moments the tapping resumed. She was certain it wasn't a natural sound. Too steady, too much of a rhythm. It seemed to be coming from her left where not a glimmer of light plumbed the depth of the darkness.

She remembered something Lael had told her. She glanced toward the brazier. The guards who usually lingered by the stairs were away from their post. She stared back into the darkness and called, "Faeg!"

As the depth absorbed her shout, the tapping suddenly ceased.

"Faeg! Can you hear me?" She listened. Only the echo of dripping water. "If you can hear me, please answer!"

The silence remained, and despair pressed in. She glanced back at the guard station, then drew in another deep breath. "Faeg, I'm a friend of your cousin, Lael. I must speak to you!"

Nothing. She slammed a frustrated palm into the bars and fell against them, wishing for the strength of a dozen Rhones so that she might bend them apart.

Time stretched on. The tapping remained silent. She dozed,

then awoke with a start, casting about, the hairs on her neck tingling. The chill of watching eyes surged through her. She sat up, suddenly aware of soft breathing nearby. Scrambling away from the bars, she stood in the center of her cage, hugging herself. "Who?" she whispered, her heart racing, her clammy skin beginning to sweat.

The quiet crept back.

She shivered again. This heavy blackness was eating away at her. She would have taken the hot glare out on the baking Temple construction site over this oppressive nothingness any day. Burnishing heat into her arms, she sat back down. Her stomach told her dinner was long overdue. "Maybe they intend to starve me first," she whispered to herself.

"Prisoners are fed but once a day."

Leenah leaped to her feet and spun toward the voice. "Who's there?!"

"How do you know Lael?" the high-pitched voice whispered from right beyond the bars.

She gulped, peering into the blackness. "Faeg?"

The voice did not answer her.

"Lael told me you mined Dirgenium in the tunnels beneath Hodin's Keep."

"Who are you?"

"My name is Leenah."

"Why have you been imprisoned, Mistress Leenah?"

"I helped Lady Darha escape. Lael told me where she was being held. He said you had heard it from some prisoners."

"Lady Darha is free?"

She nodded. Perhaps he could see her. "We fled into the forest. I told her to make for Deepvale."

"Deepvale?" he said softly, thoughtfully.

"Yes. The people there must be warned. Zorin knows they

helped me. He intends to make examples of them. Even now he sends his soldiers to murder them and burn their village. I must get word to them."

A light glared suddenly, and she flung a hand before her eyes. In a moment they adjusted to the soft, pale glow of a gray moonglass. The light moved away from her, and a disembodied hand floated in the darkness. Then something like a veil fell away, and the little man appeared standing right beyond the bars. Faeg's lithe frame was clad in brown britches and a red and gold shirt. Across his arm he draped a woodsman's cloak.

He glanced worriedly about. "I'm not supposed to be down here."

"Can you free me?"

He shook his head, his pale blond hair brushing softly across his shoulders. "The bars are set deep in the stone." His view went briefly to a red tote bag at his tiny, booted feet. "It would take me a week to chisel you out."

"Then you must warn them. The Kleimen of Deepvale must flee or be killed. And Lady Darha, too."

"What will become of you, Mistress Leenah?"

She hesitated. "The Pikes."

Faeg's eyes widened. "Then I mustn't leave you."

"But you have to. You have to warn your people. There's nothing you can do for me." She saw his reluctance, but also his understanding of the situation.

He grabbed up his tote, dug around in it a moment, and came out with a small, cased moonglass and a bag. "This will comfort you some, though it doesn't glow brightly down here for some reason. And here is something to eat."

Leenah took the bag and thanked him. His faint light bobbed along an unseen path alongside the Black Pool and was gone.

She opened the wooden-cased moonglass and a soft, rosy light pushed back the gloom. As she suspected, her cell was littered with dried dung and unidentifiable moldy lumps she tried not to speculate on. She could make out the still water of the Black Pools, not five spans from the bars of her cage, and the stone bridge over which her captors had led her.

She peeked into the sack and smiled at its content. *Don't forget to eat your keelits.* Leenah took up a slice and whispered, "I won't, Ela." Then lifting her eyes to the void overhead, she pleaded softly, "Creator, give wings to Faeg's feet. Protect the little ones in Deepvale and Lady Darha. And give me courage."

⚶

The next day Batok, through his network of moles, passed a coded message to First Shield Sirt. Then they waited. Finally, after night had come again, Sirt's reply was delivered. Immediately Da-gore set off across Atla Fair to Maelc's shop.

Maelc, the cooper, was busy forging iron hoops for a row of newly crafted barrels when Da-gore arrived.

"I can do it, I suppose," Maelc said, thoughtfully stroking the old scars that marred his face. His eyes clouded. "But what you're attempting is mighty dangerous, Master Jael-ik. You get caught, I'll get caught."

"These are risks we take in this quest. You risk getting caught every day. We've all known this time was coming. You got my message, did you not?"

Maelc's face widened, his dark eyes brightening some. He glanced quickly around his busy shop; none of his helpers was nearby. "The invasion?" he whispered.

Da-gore nodded. "I've sent word to Pyir Rhone. It can't be delayed much longer. Leenah is his future consort, if I read the two of them correctly. She's forced his hand coming here. If I know Pyir Rhone, he'll come for her, and when he does, he'll have to bring Makir."

"Makir," Maelc whispered reverently. "You know how long the people of Atlan have waited for this to happen? Some thought it would never come about." He drew himself up and flung his forging hammer onto a nearby bench. "We haven't any time to lose, Master Jael-ik. I have a load of barrels ready to be delivered to Hodin's Keep. Was supposed to deliver them day after tomorrow." He glanced around his shop. "But look at this place. I've no room left."

Da-gore grinned. "No, indeed. You must make more room."

Maelc untied his apron and tossed it after the hammer. "Kelin!"

A young apprentice who'd been sharpening a drawknife at a honing wheel hurried over. "Yes, Master Maelc?"

"I've decided to make the delivery tonight. Have the barrels loaded aboard the wagon, then hurry to the Keep, and inform First Shield Sirt I'll be there within the hour."

"Tonight?"

"Something wrong with your ears?"

"No, sir." Confused by this sudden change in schedule, the lad nodded obediently and ran off to do Maelc's bidding.

Maelc eyed Da-gore's clothes and cloak. "You'll need a different outfit."

"What have you in mind?"

He led him to a back room, shoved a heavy crate out of the way, and then swept aside a pile of wood shavings. The outlines of a trapdoor appeared. He bent and pulled it open. Beneath it lay a collection of uniforms. "Been acquiring them for years. I figured someday they'd come in handy."

"They will all be too large for me."

Maelc gave a short laugh. "Too bad you don't have even a drop of Hodin's blood in you, Master Jael-ik, but poor breeding can't be helped. We'll roll up the cuffs. So, what's your fancy? A lieutenant? A Shield? A First Shield?"

Da-gore slid him a sly smile. "I've always fancied myself a captain."

"A captain you shall be!" He rummaged around until he found a captain's uniform and held it up. "Stand on your tiptoes, and you should pass all right."

35

Herc

Enclosed in darkness, Da-gore smelled the pungent resin from newly sawn wood. The smell, coupled with the rocking motion of the wagon, made his stomach queasy; the barrel staves pressing against his shoulder and pushing his knees into his chest made him vaguely claustrophobic. Suddenly the rocking ceased as the big wheels ground to a halt. He heard the approach of footsteps; then faint, vertical lines of light appeared through the staves.

"Master Maelc? What are you doing here this late?"

"Another load of barrels for the supply room."

The light brightened through the gaps in the barrel staves as the sentry shone it into the wagon bed. "You're not due to deliver tonight." His voice was puzzled, not suspicious.

Maelc yawned, and Da-gore pictured him putting on an unconcerned expression. "Had to get them out of my shop to make more room. I've already sent word to First Shield Sirt about this. Check with him."

The guard ordered another to fetch the First Shield. Da-gore's backside and shins had begun to cramp and go numb, making him impatient.

When Sirt arrived and authorized the delivery, the sentry said, "We weren't expecting Master Maelc tonight. I have no one to escort him to the depot."

"I'll escort the wagon," Sirt said.

Da-gore exhaled an impatient breath, relieved to be moving, and anxious to be freed from his wooden cocoon.

In the storeroom, more voices penetrated the barrel. Then came the squeak of the wagon sides being lowered and the thumping of barrels being off-loaded. Da-gore felt himself lowered to the ground; Maelc lent a hand lest someone should be suspicious by the extra weight. The job completed, Maelc chatted with the workers while they waited for an official to sign for the delivery. Finally Da-gore heard the wagon leave, and the storeroom grew quiet.

He waited. His tailbone began to tingle. He tried shifting his weight ... and waited some more. The bitter aromatic sting in his nose was working on his stomach, and when he about thought he could stand it no longer, approaching footsteps alerted him. They stopped nearby, and there was a soft rap upon the barrel.

"It's safe now. We must move quickly."

Da-gore lifted the lid and looked cautiously about the big, dark room, then at Sirt. "Have you learned where she is being held?" he asked as he extracted himself from the barrel.

"The Black Pool. But I can't go there without raising suspicions, and neither can you." Sirt looked at Da-gore's uniform. "Where did you get that?"

He stretched and rolled his shoulders. "It seems Maelc has made a business of collecting them."

Sirt frowned. "It's too big on you." He tugged the cloak around, straightening it, and glared down at the baggy trousers. "Try not to be seen."

Da-gore rolled up the cuffs a couple turns. "I'll do my best."

"Even if you make it past the guards, only Sayor, the Prison Master, holds the keys, and he hands them out only to men he knows and trusts." Sirt's frown grew into a scowl. "I was opposed to this dangerous scheme when I got Batok's message. This puts us all at grave risk."

"Sirt, she's your niece."

The large man's expression softened a little. "Yes, but there will be other opportunities. Zorin has temporarily put aside his plans for Leenah. He knows that Pyir Rhone is in the land."

"How could he?"

They started for a dark, arched passageway. "One of his spies arrived with the news."

"Do you know his name?"

"No, I wasn't privy to that information." They entered the passageway and moved quickly along a dim corridor.

❧

His mother's trail was clear, and it was plain she was making for Deepvale. Rhone knew the way and pressed on all night. What would he say to her? He'd not seen her for so long that he had trouble picturing her face in his thoughts. Now that he was so close, his heart ached for the years lost. Why hadn't he come back sooner? He'd chosen to abdicate his rightful place at the head of Atlan's Council of Ten in return for her safety. But what kind of life had it been all these years? He should have moved sooner!

He'd been a fool to have tried to bury his past, collecting Web and pretending the man he once was no longer existed. He'd successfully hid it from friends, but in the end, the Makir inside him had won out. Looking back, he saw how the pattern had been woven. It had begun that day on the Meeting Floor in Nod

City, that day his life had been wrenched from his control and his feet placed on this road. And now, again, matters had been wrenched from his control, and he was being moved further along that road, and where it would end, only the Creator knew.

Rhone shook his head. He'd known this time would eventually come, yet it had taken the hand of the Creator to break his resistance.

He glanced around at his men, no more than shadows marching swiftly through the darkness of the Atlanian night. Strong, fearsome fighters, each one. They'd waited patiently all these years, unbound. He had let them down as well. Rhone put these thoughts out of his head. Tomorrow they'd reach Deepvale, and with any luck, his mother would be there too. By now Ka-Larik would have returned to Imo-suk, and Larik would have the Makir ready to move.

Once his mother was safe, he'd take his small company on to Atla Fair. He could only pray that he reached Leenah in time. But what then? His nine Makir could hardly take on the troops garrisoned at Atla Fair and the forts along Hodin's Passage. He had to come up with a plan. He paused on that thought. *Again, I'm trying to do this with my own strength.* Rhone found that relying on the Creator for something like this was still difficult.

But enough of this ruminating. This also was not his nature. His path was that of action, that of a warrior. Whatever would come tomorrow, and the day after, its outcome was in the hands of the Creator.

"Then she's told Zorin nothing so far?" Da-gore's eyes were in constant motion, his ears alert, as he and Sirt hurried along the underground passage from the supply depot to the Sanctuary of Justice.

"I wasn't present to hear, but I do know that Zorin discovered Leenah was aided by the Kleimen of Deepvale. He's dispatched six fists of soldiers to raze the village."

"Only thirty?"

"The Kleimen are like children."

"Zorin's confidence borders on arrogance."

"Arrogance is too mild a word for the tyrant!" Sirt expelled a sharp breath and looked at him, a sad resignation in his eyes. "The Kleimen will not put up a fight. Their only defense is to flee into their tunnels where Zorin's canics make short work of them." Sirt frowned. "Zorin enjoys making examples of rebels."

"So I've heard. The Bloody Pikes on Execution Ridge speak to that."

His frown lengthened. "That would never have been permitted under the old council."

Da-gore grinned. "We are going to tear the Pikes down, aren't we, Sirt?"

The ex-Makir nodded. "So we hope."

The tunnel angled upward, and then they were above ground and striding along a well-lit hallway in the Sanctuary of Justice. He had never been here and was impressed with the beauty of the place: the gleaming stone columns, the tapestries, the marble and onyx floors that rang beneath their rapid steps.

When they passed servants and officials, Da-gore would draw himself up as tall as his spine would permit. Still, he was nearly a head shorter than Sirt and every other man in Atlan who had come from Hodin's line.

Sirt maintained the look of a man on a mission. A First Shield and a captain would cause little suspicion, and so far no one had stopped to question them.

They came to a great hall, and Da-gore paused to look into it. Sirt said, "This is where Zorin holds court." He nodded to the golden chair raised from the floor upon an exquisite island of gleaming red marble. "More men than you can count have heard their death sentences read to them from that chair." On both sides of the hall stood towering statues of the original ten council members and their consorts. At the far end of the chamber, Hodin's statue soared taller than the others, glowing in the lights of four golden braziers. It appeared to be carved of the purest white stone, and he stood upon a dais of gleaming gold, his sword point down in the customary Makir watch position. The pose was strikingly similar to the image carved into the white-stone cliffs at the mouth of Hodin's Passage. The whole place was lit by a ceiling of the purest white moonglass.

Sirt said, "Hodin built this three hundred years ago, shortly before he fell asleep and was taken to Dirgen's Bosom. At one time, the chair was called the *Heart of Justice*." He scowled. "But no more."

Leading off the great hall were arched portals to smaller rooms. Da-gore was about to move on when a voice he recognized reached out from one of those portals. He glanced at Sirt. "Has the Lodath's emissary arrived from Nod City?"

"Yes, just a few days ago."

Da-gore started for one of the nearby portals.

"Where are you going?" Sirt caught him by the shoulder, turning him. "He's meeting with Zorin. You can't just walk in there."

"I'm sure I know that voice, but I need to make certain. Pyir Rhone will want to know."

Sidling up to the portal, he peeked around the corner. Captain El-ik of the Lodath's Guard was standing with Zorin. Da-gore was struck with the resemblance between Zorin and Pyir Rhone. Another man stood with them, dressed in a black suta, which he'd seen often in Imo-suk. Although his back was toward

Da-gore, he had the bearing of a Makir. But what had riveted Da-gore's eyes was not the men, but the giant!

Herc! He felt his heart thump hard against his ribs as the memories tumbled back. Herc was an Earth-Born, a monstrosity formed from the unholy union between human women and the god-like Messengers of the Oracle. He had commanded a detachment of Earth-Borns when he'd chased Mishah and Rhone halfway across the civilized world into the Ruins of Eden where they had finally escaped into the Cradleland.

The sight of Herc brought those memories back with ferocious clarity. The Earth-Borns were unpredictable, powerful creatures, taller than Hodinites and broader than a horse. They had six fingers on each hand and six toes on each foot. And when they opened their mouths, their two rows of teeth were a frightening reminder that what had been born of gods and humans had gone wrong in some mysterious and terrible way.

Zorin was speaking. "... curious why, Captain El-ik. What does the Lodath have to gain by this alliance?"

Da-gore signaled to Sirt, waiting for him in the hallway, nervously watching the long corridor, that he'd only be a moment longer.

"It's simple, really," Captain El-ik said. "Nod City is poised to rule the world. Atlan is already the queen of the sea. It's the ideal fit."

"And what of King Irad? All you've spoken of so far is the Lodath."

El-ik lowered his voice. "The King has become a mere figurehead. The Lodath has successfully consolidated his hold over the land." He paused. "I wouldn't be surprised to soon learn that King Irad is no more."

Zorin gave a short laugh. "So, the Lodath is not above assassination?"

"Not the Lodath. His followers."

Zorin glanced at Herc. "Like this one?"

"Herc and others. There are many like him now, and their numbers are growing. The gods have taken to wife all whom they desire. The nursery in the Mountains of the Singing Skies has perhaps a hundred children. Now that the Oracle's Temple has been completed, they will be brought to Nod City. The Oracle himself will take up residence among the children of men soon to oversee the transfer."

Da-gore raised his eyebrows. *So, that much of the Lodath's plan had already been completed.* The dwelling place of the Oracle was finally finished, and the next phase of the Temple complex was about to begin.

"The breeding of gods will go forward?" Zorin's skepticism was clear.

"Yes, of course."

Zorin glanced at Herc. "When will they get it right?"

Herc growled lowly.

El-ik said, "This is but the first stage in the advancement of the human race. In two or three generations, the problems will be eliminated. Man will have leaped ahead a million years, and Atlan can be part of this, High Councilor. That is, if Atlan survives under your rulership."

Zorin's face flushed with anger. "What are you implying?"

El-ik remained poised and cast a glance at the man in black who so far had not spoken. "He has brought the very words you've feared, High Councilor. But it comes as no surprise to either of us. The Lodath knows of the rebellious nature of some of your people and what is in the mind of your scheming brother, High Councilor, as our friend here has now confirmed."

El-ik peered a moment longer at the tall man, then glanced back to Zorin. "An alliance with Nod City could prevent all that, but time is short. Perhaps it is too late. An army of warriors like Herc, however, can defeat even the legendary Makir now on your doorstep."

On your doorstep? What had El-ik meant? Did he know the invasion was imminent? One thing was clear: Zorin was well informed of Pyir Rhone's plans! He had to get word back to Rhone. Da-gore was about to leave, when all at once Herc's massive head turned toward the portal, his black eyes staring. Zorin and El-ik peered at Herc, then at the portal.

Da-gore backed away, feeling the giant's probing eyes, as if he were watching him through the thick wall. He'd forgotten how closely these Earth-Borns were tied to the realm of the Oracle— that other world just beyond men's awareness. Somehow the beings of that world must have alerted Herc to his presence. Zorin gave a shout of alarm. Da-gore turned to run. A swarm of guards rushed from an adjoining room into the great hall, and in an instant he and Sirt were surrounded.

Sirt's sword leaped from its sheath, and the ex-Makir turned a slow, wary circle, prepared to fight a hopeless battle. Pikes and swords pressed in on them. A contingent of guards bearing proj-lances came pounding out of a small alcove.

Da-gore turned to his companion and put a hand on the sword.

With a snort, Sirt slowly lowered the tip of his sword to floor.

"Disarm them," an officer ordered.

Their weapons seized, the troops parted, and Zorin and El-ik came forward. Herc remained behind, towering over the heads of the guards, his lips slowly peeling back, misshapen, as if smiling were not a natural thing to him.

Zorin looked from Sirt to Da-gore and then back again. "Explain yourself, First Shield!" he demanded. A tingle rippled up Da-gore's spine. Zorin's eyes might have been Pyir Rhone's eyes in shape and color.

Sirt remained silent. A brooding anger clouded his eyes, directed at Da-gore.

He could hardly blame Sirt.

"And who are you?" Zorin glanced at the marking upon the shoulder of his cloak. "You are no captain I know."

El-ik laughed. Zorin gave him a stormy look. "Don't tell me you know this one as well."

"Unfortunately, I do, High Councilor. And the irony of it is, he *is* a captain—or he was at one time. It seems you have been infested with renegades from Nod City. If this is how easily spies enter your land, an alliance with the Lodath could prove profitable."

Zorin's anger boiled. "What do you know of him, El-ik?"

Da-gore's luck couldn't have been any worse if it had been the Lodath himself standing before him. Captain El-ik and he had never liked each other, and now El-ik was gloating over his predicament.

"His name is Da-gore. He was once Captain of the Lodath's Guard ... until he failed the Lodath. The Lodath was kind to him, however, and merely demoted him to First Shield. He could have had him executed. And how did Da-gore repay his kindness? By abandoning his post and leaving his pledge pendant behind—a blatant slap in the face to his master. That was over seven years ago, and now it seems the turncoat has somehow found his way into the rebels' camp."

Zorin looked back at Da-gore. "And he will soon find his way into the Deep Chambers. My executioners will make a long and painful work of him—both him and the traitor in my household." Zorin glared at Sirt.

"High Councilor, if I might be so bold as to request the prisoner Da-gore be given to me to be taken back to Nod City. If you grant this, I'm certain the Lodath will look with fondness upon your graciousness. It could be the beginning of a strong alliance between our two lands."

"You may have him. But the other," Zorin's seething glare had not left Sirt, "I will personally oversee his execution."

"Thank you, High Councilor."

At that moment the Makir in the black suta walked up beside Zorin.

36

Makir in the Land Once Again

Faeg hurried through the night, doggedly following the dimly lit forest path to Deepvale. He didn't like being in the forest alone, in the dark where night creatures roamed the shadows. Some of them were Turnlings, and some of them ate little Kleimen with a rapacious lust. But fly he must, if Leenah's warning was to reach Deepvale before Zorin's troops.

On this night no creature threatened him, and with the coming of dawn, he stood upon the path to his cousin's village and prayed to Dirgen that he was not too late. Finally he crested the ridge overlooking the peaceful tents and the smoking embers of last night's fires.

"Thank you!" He rushed down to the green lawn, heavy with the morning mist.

"Flee! Flee! Wake from your sleep and flee!" He ran from tent to tent, shouting, and in a moment, tent flaps were cast back, and a startled group of Klei-folk, abruptly roused from their sleep, emerged to learn what the emergency might be.

Breathless, he told of the impending carnage at the hands of Zorin's soldiers. He'd almost finished when one of the tent flaps opened, and a tall woman, obviously not a Kleiman, stepped out. Faeg stared at her, and his knees went weak, and his words caught in his throat. "Lady Darha!"

"Tell us more," Lael insisted. "How did you learn of this? What proof have you?"

Faeg swallowed and looked at his cousin. "A prisoner told me while I was working the Black Pool tunnels. She said they were coming here and pleaded that I should warn you."

Lady Darha came to him. "What woman? Did she give you her name."

"Yes, dear Lady Darha. Her name is Leenah."

Darha's face went slack, her eyes filling with sadness. "They caught her. She gave herself so that I might gain freedom."

"We won't have freedom much longer," Faeg said. "Zorin's soldiers might be here any moment."

"To the tunnels!" someone cried.

"No," another trembled. "The tunnels are death traps! We'll be torn apart by Zorin's canics. Just like our brothers and sisters of Bright Canyon Vale."

"The sea tunnel then," another suggested.

"Yes, yes! The sea tunnel," several of them echoed.

"But Lady Darha can't make it through the sea tunnel," Lael reminded them.

"You mustn't worry about me. Save yourselves."

"You'll be captured and taken prisoner," Turi protested. "There must be another way."

"Escape into the forest. That's the only way!" Ela's hands fisted as her bright, dread-filled eyes shifted among the gathering crowd. Faeg sensed Ela's panic in the tightness across his shoulders and the tingle at the back of his neck that kept his head pitching back over his shoulder, expecting to see Zorin's soldiers at any moment. They all felt it, each of them ready to flee in twenty different directions—and maybe that would be best. Zorin's men couldn't follow them all.

Faeg was about to suggest just that when nearby the low growl of a canic chilled his blood. He spun about. A rank of armed soldiers stood at the forest's edge, canics straining at their leashes. More soldiers stepped out to block the road leading into the village, while yet a third contingent marched down the Rim-wall trail, barring the way to the tunnels.

A wail of fear arose from the people as they huddled near Lady Darha. Faeg cast about, but all avenues of escape were blocked. His chest squeezed, driving the breath from it as the soldiers advanced in a pincer of certain death.

❀

Rhone recalled the few times he had escorted his mother's entourage to Deepvale. He'd been a young Makir at the time, not yet ascended to the status of Pyir. His mother had been inclined to visit the far-flung villages of Atlan, saying that she could not help folk she hadn't met. Most of Atlan shunned the little people of the Rim-wall for their quaint ways and diminutive size, but his mother held all of Atlan's people close to her heart.

He remembered the way as if he had traveled it only yesterday. Not much in this part of the world had changed in the hundred-plus years since those peaceful days when his father sat upon the high seat of the Council of Ten.

Now, as they neared the village, his pulse quickened at the thought of seeing his mother once again … and from a peculiar dread that he simply put off as the uncertainty one feels when renewing an old and lost acquaintance.

❀

The officer of the guard ordered the frightened Kleimen herded together. Faeg quavered beneath the points of drawn swords and leveled pikes. There were about eighty souls in Deepvale, and Faeg never imagined he'd be numbered among them. But here he was! Jostled among the tightly packed people, bumping shoulders with his cousin.

"Burn the village!"

Lady Darha pleaded with the officer, but he ignored her. Trembling Kleimen huddled together as soldiers lit torches and went from tent to tent. Kleiman cloth did not burn well; here and there a flame struggled up a brightly colored side. The job was moving too slowly for the commanding officer, and he ordered more torches. Slowly a sickly odor like burning hair filled the little valley and drifted out into the thick forest that surrounded it.

"Tear them down," the officer shouted, growing impatient. He glared at the captives. "As enemies of Zorin, you are to be made examples of." He glanced to his second in command. "Remove the High Councilor's mother from them—then kill the vermin. Make sure to leave a few alive to decorate the Pikes!"

"You cannot do this awful deed," Lady Darha pleaded.

"You have no say in this matter. The orders are from High Councilor Zorin." He signaled his men to seize Lady Darha from among the little people. "Remove twenty for Zorin's delight—then kill the rest."

The soldiers grabbed men and women at random, marching them aside under the cold iron of their blades. Faeg, shaking in his miner's boots, found himself among them. As they were jostled aside, he tripped and fell. One of the soldiers drew back and plunged his pike at him. Instinctively, Faeg curled himself into a ball. The long point skittered along his back and buried in the grassy turf. Blind terror taking hold, he leaped to his feet, ducked under the man's spread legs, and dashed for the forest.

"Stop that one!" the commander barked.

Faeg dodged as a spear whizzed past his ear and thunked into the ground ahead of him. A second ricocheted off a tree trunk, and then the forest closed in around him. He flew as fast as his short legs would carry him—three soldiers on his heels and closing in fast. Raw fear glazed his vision, and it was all he could do to avoid bashing into a low branch or running into a tree.

Something grabbed him by the shoulders and swung him to one side. His reeling brain instantly told him he'd been snatched in the jaws of some fierce beast. When the pain of piercing fangs and crunching of bone failed to materialize, he forced his eyes open.

"It's all right, little one," a man whispered, passing him back to another. Faeg looked wildly about at the black figures crouched silently in shadows. Friend or foe?

Just then Zorin's soldiers came crashing through the trees, coming to a startled halt as the way before them was suddenly blocked by a single man. They stared at the lone swordsman, surprise turning to recognition, and recognition to fear as the color began to drain from their faces.

Faeg became aware of a long-dormant memory beginning to rise to the top of his consciousness.

The three soldiers began a slow retreat, but the way was barred by another black-clad figure. Glancing at each other, they tossed down their swords without a fight and raised their hands to the sky.

The memory, that had been slowly percolating up into Faeg's brain like a soap bubble, burst suddenly upon his consciousness. *Makir*! His breath caught. The Makir had been gone from Atlan so long that most had forgotten.

"Bind them," the man ordered, and the three were trussed up against a tree.

There was something about the leader.... He resembled ... Suddenly Faeg remembered the others. "The village! Zorin's soldiers are going to kill the villagers!"

"How many?" the leader asked.

"Very many. Thirty? Forty?"

With a silent nod from the man, the Makir melted into the shadows.

❧

Rhone hadn't counted on engaging Zorin's troops with only nine Makir. Halting at the forest's edge, he saw the little people gathered for the slaughter and heard their wailing for mercy. He motioned two of his Makir to the eight lancers blocking the road. As they moved off silently toward them, he gave the rest of his men the ready sign.

Zorin's captain was about to give the order to begin the slaughter when the two Makir fell upon the lancers. The warriors' swords flashed like mechanical harvesting blades, and before even one of the lancers could raise his proj-lance, they had been cut to the ground.

The stunned officer ordered his forces to attack. Rhone gave the signal, and his warriors burst from the cover of the trees.

What had once been training became instinct. He moved in among the clashing swords, his brain noting and marking each of his enemy as he turned and slashed, parried and dodged. His strength swelled rather than diminished as the battle progressed. He felt the energy from each of the battling Makir flowing through him, and he knew they felt it too.

Time seemed to stop, and it was only as fewer and fewer men swarmed in over the bodies of the previous wave that he was able to see the passing of the moments.

And then there were no more swords coming at him. He whirled to take in the scene, noting with relief that all of the Makir were still standing.

Klesc slowly drew himself up in the center of a ring of carnage. Eight bodies lay about him. Rhone and each of his Makir had taken their share. A few terrified soldiers had managed to flee into the forest. Rhone sent Makir to track them down lest word of the encounter reach

Zorin. He had to buy all the time he could. Certainly by now Ka-Larik had returned to Imo-suk and delivered his message to Larik.

The Kleimen had scattered to the forest, and now that the fighting was over, slowly began to return. Among them was his mother. She halted at the edge of the village as she saw Rhone.

His heart leaped and he started toward her, sheathing his sword. She hesitated, as if not believing her eyes. "Rhone?"

The smile came unbidden to his face.

She rushed to embrace him. He engulfed her in his arms and held her tight, feeling her sobs of joy racking her chest.

"Is it truly you?" She looked up at him, eyes glistening.

"I should have returned sooner."

"No." Her joy turned to dread. "Your brother would have killed you."

"No doubt he'd have tried. It was fear for your safety that held my hand all these years."

"I know the threat he held over your head, Rhone. But Zorin is strong. His army grows day by day."

"Yes. He fears the return of the Makir."

"The Makir?" She stared at the warriors making their way among the dead, checking for any survivors, then back at him. "Are they in the land?"

"These nine are, but soon there will be many."

"But the Makir are unbound?"

He shook his head. "The cord has been retied."

"Retied," she breathed. "And their Pyir?"

He nodded.

Sadness suddenly filled her eyes and pulled at her face. "Then there will be war!"

"It was inevitable from the beginning. I should have seen it sooner." He hesitated. "But it took other things to open my eyes and Leenah to force my hand."

"Leenah? Zorin holds her in the Deep Chambers."

"How do you know this?"

"Master Faeg brought word of it moments before the soldiers arrived." She clutched his arm. "She freed me. She knew she would be captured, yet she did it ... for me."

"We've taken Highwatch thirty-four. The watchmen told us everything. I sent word to Larik."

"Larik is still alive?"

"I left him in command of Imo-suk. And as we speak, he and two hundred Makir are making their way to Atlan. I must go to Leenah."

"You can't penetrate the Keep, Rhone. It's too heavily guarded. If Atlan is invaded, Zorin will surely have Leenah killed or use her as a castaway piece to bargain for his realm."

"That is why I need to go to her now, even if I must go alone. A single warrior might make his way past Zorin's fortifications."

"I can take you to her," a high voice declared.

Rhone looked down at the little Kleiman he'd saved from Zorin's guards. "What's your name?"

"Faeg, Master ... err ..." He hesitated, staring with big eyes at Rhone.

"You can get me past Zorin's troops?"

"I do it all the time. I mine Dirgenium in the Deep Chamber tunnels. That was where I spoke to Mistress Leenah."

"But can you get me in?"

"Not only you, but all the Makir ... Pyir Rhone," he added with a breath of awe. "I can take you through the tunnels."

"No Makir can fit through those narrow cracks." Klesc planted his hands upon his hips, his slashed shirt showing a streak of blood across his massive chest.

"You're mistaken, Master Makir! There are two ways large enough for big people, but if you don't know them, you'll wander helplessly until you go mad all alone in the dark."

"Take me there."

"I'd be honored, Pyir Rhone."

Rhone turned to his mother. "You stay here until this is over."

"No, Rhone. If there is to be war, I need to be back with our people."

"The Kleimen are our people as well." He looked at the little people gathered about, some marching in circles around the bodies of their enemies and piling curses upon their dead heads.

Faeg smiled. "Zorin doesn't consider us so. We've been outcasts since your father, the mighty Khore, was murdered."

His mother's face softened toward the little people. "You're right, my son. These are our people." She gazed back at him. "Nevertheless, I am going with you."

❦

In the light of the moonglass, Leenah watch a rat fall into the Black Pool from somewhere above. It splashed about, swimming for the rocky edge, and almost made shore when suddenly the water erupted in a swarm of wring serpents.

She huddled against the bars, her moonglass open and shedding its weak but comforting light across the dark stone. She had only closed it once, when the prison guards had brought her a bowl of gruel. That had been many hours ago, and she was hungry.

She watched the rippling wake of a wring serpent. Footsteps upon the stone stairs alerted her, and she snapped the cover on the moonglass, throwing her little nook into darkness.

A company of guards marched along the narrow ledge, the flames of their torches flickering against the walls close to their right side, yet shedding no light into the distant depths and soaring ceiling. They crossed the stone bridge to her cage, unlocked the door, and shoved in two prisoners.

Da-gore! She looked into the face of the second prisoner and sucked in a startled breath, but waited for the guards to leave before saying anything.

"Uncle Sirt!" She hugged him, burying her cheek into his powerful chest.

"Leenah." He engulfed her in his arms, and she felt tenseness in them.

She quickly drew out the moonglass and opened the cover.

"What's happened? Why are you here?"

Da-gore went to the bars and gripped one, giving it a shake. She'd done that too. Maybe it was what all prisoners did upon finding themselves caged. "We were trying to rescue you."

The bigger man gave a low growl. She looked back at her uncle and in the dimness saw him glaring at Da-gore. "Uncle Sirt?"

"The plan went awry," Uncle Sirt said. His strong arms fell away from her.

"The effort proved valuable," Da-gore replied.

"How so?" she asked.

He turned from the bars. "Do you know who is suing for an alliance with Zorin?"

"Nod City and the Lodath," she answered at once. "Captain El-ik is here in Atlan. I saw him."

Da-gore's short laugh came from the darkness. "Well, that news is old news, but here is something I'll wager you didn't know. The spy is here in Atlan as well."

"Ka-Larik," she said, shaking her head.

"You know?" Da-gore sounded surprised.

"I saw him too. It begins to make sense. It was Ka-Larik who found the spy Lorun dead in his cell at Imo-suk. And it was he who was quick to point the finger at Klesc and plant the seeds of suspicion toward you in Larik's ear. Even Klesc believed you might be the spy among us."

"Did he? The pieces come together."

Uncle Sirt rattled the bars, then paced the length of the cage and back again.

"Watch where you step. This place is infested with wring serpents," she said absently, her thoughts on Ka-Larik and how he had betrayed Rhone.

"It's hard to watch for them in this light," he answered.

"Oh." She opened her moonglass. "It's not very bright. Something is affecting it."

Uncle Sirt drew to a halt, staring. "How did you come by that? They're not permitted."

"Faeg gave it to me." She suddenly realized that was something important, something they ought to know. "He's a Kleiman, and Zorin has sent his soldiers to wipe out the Kleimen village."

Da-gore turned on his heels and clutched the bars with a sudden desperation. "I have to get a message to Pyir Rhone."

She said, "I tried to send one, but I doubt it got through."

"For Lady Darha's sake, I hope it did." Uncle Sirt suddenly lunged and slammed his heel down on the head of a serpent. The writhing body thrashed and coiled about his leg as he ground it into the stone. "But for us, I'm afraid it's too late. They would not have locked us all together if they intended to keep us alive very long."

37

To the Bloody Pikes

*T*he entrance was a dark, narrow crack in the stony foot of Mount Kebaal, not far from the outskirts of Atla Fair. Faeg, handing out moonglasses to each of them, said, "They grows dim the deeper we go, but there will be enough light to see by." He shook his head. "Must be something in the surrounding rock."

"It's the magnetic veil," Rhone said. He recalled the long, flooded passage beneath the walls of Chevel-ee and how their moonglass had dimmed then. Cerah, the young ward of Mother Eve, claimed it was the breaking of the veil.

"What of the veil?" his mother asked.

"It's failing, growing weaker every year."

Klesc glanced at the smooth amber stone in his hand, encased in a wooden frame and a hinged lid—unremarkable in the light of day. "How long before they don't shine at all?"

Rhone shrugged. "No telling. A hundred years … a thousand? One thing is certain: Unless the Creator restores the veil to what it was in the beginning, all moonglasses will surely fail."

His mother gave him a curious look.

"Is everyone ready?" Faeg peered into the dark slash in the rock.

"It will be a tight squeeze at first, but soon the way will open up."

"Lead on." They had marched straight from Deepvale to here, and his mother was weary, but Rhone couldn't afford to waste any time. Leenah's life might well rest upon a balance weighed in moments.

The first fifty spans were nearly impossible. By removing their weapons and emptying their lungs, they squeezed between rocks that any rational man would have backed away from. But Faeg assured them they could make it, and when suddenly the way opened up, the little man just grinned and forged ahead.

The Makir, bent low to keep from knocking their heads, followed, stone grinding against their shoulders and pinching their hips. The tunnel wound ever deeper. Where larger, more inviting passages led off in a different direction, Faeg kept to the narrow one, sometimes saying, "That way will run you in circles," or "This one will squeeze you in so tight you'll never get out."

Hours passed. Their moonglasses grew dimmer but never faded completely. The air became heavy, stale, and more damp and chilled the deeper they descended. At first Rhone tried to build a map of the way in his head, but there were so many turns and side tunnels that he finally abandoned that idea, putting his trust in Faeg to take them where they wanted to go … and then to lead them back again.

❧

Leenah shivered in the light dress Ela and the other skilled Kleimen seamstresses had sewn for her—one that had been designed for Atlan's warm climate. The persistent damp was slowly getting to her. She cupped the moonglass as though it could cast some heat, but the dim magnetic light was as cold as the hard stone she sat upon.

Da-gore rose and draped his cloak over her shoulder. "Are you all right?"

"Yes. Thank you." She gathered it tight.

Uncle Sirt shot a glance over his shoulder at her, then turned back to the bars he had been examining. He gripped one of them and, bracing a leg, strained against the unyielding iron. It barely budged under even his powerful muscles.

"It's no use." Da-gore returned to his place across the way.

Uncle Sirt expelled a breath and folded his arms. "Unless one of us can get free, Pyir Rhone won't know that Zorin has been alerted to the invasion."

Their heads turned at the sound of approaching footsteps. Leenah quickly shut the moonglass. Far down the black cavern, flickering torches brightened the stone steps as a contingent of Zorin's guards descended them and approached along the narrow ledge beside the Black Pool.

The guards stopped outside the cell and leveled their proj-lances at them as the door was unlocked. "You and you." The officer in charge indicated her and Uncle Sirt.

Leenah removed the cloak, hiding the moonglass in its folds, and gave it back to Da-gore. Heavy shackles were clamped about their wrists, and as she and her uncle were led away, Leenah looked back at Da-gore until he faded from view as the darkness, held briefly in abeyance by their torches, flooded back.

The climb up the stairs seemed longer than the descent. The air slowly warmed as they mounted level upon level, each as dark and dreary as the previous one, with shadowy hallways leading off in different directions. Heavy ominous doors pierced the walls at irregular intervals, but not a glimmer of light leaked from their barred windows.

The ascent ended in a wide corridor within the Sanctuary of Justice. They marched along high, arching passageways, lined with small golden statues, then turned a corner. Before her stretched a great hall filled with what appeared to be officials and dignitaries of

Atlan. The gallery shone of polished marble columns and towering statues. At its far end stood Hodin, sculpted in gleaming white stone and standing upon a platform of gold, his sword in the traditional watch position. He loomed above all the others, surrounded by four golden braziers burning brightly, and appeared to stare straight at her—some trickery of the sculpture's art.

At the back of the gallery huge tapestries had been raised like curtains, opening the hall to the outside where sunlight streamed in past the statue. Gold and ivory and brilliant red stone glowed where the bright light touched it. Beyond the raised tapestries lay the courtyard outside, filled with people.

The body of guards remained to the rear of the gallery, out of sight from the crowds, while the officer in charge and two armed escorts led her and Uncle Sirt into the center of the hall. They halted before a golden chair, upholstered in green and red cloth. The chair rested on a raised circle of polished red stone, and upon it sat Zorin, resplendent in his purple and gold robes. His minck perched on a rod of ivory, its tiny eyes staring unblinkingly at her, its scaly tail flicking back and forth.

Zorin peered down at them with indifference, his eyes as cold as the Deep Chambers she'd just left. Slowly his mouth hitched up on one side in a cruel smile, and he raised a short black staff and tapped a bronze gong. The booming reverberated throughout the great hall, and the undercurrent of murmuring voices hushed. She noticed that sound mirrors had been placed strategically around the hall so that all might hear what Zorin said.

As the silence settled about the dignitaries in the hall and the crowd outside, Zorin ordered the court scribe to read off the charges. Did he know that she and Uncle Sirt were related? She doubted it, for if he had, other charges surely would have been added to the litany of crimes—a family conspiracy, perhaps.

Zorin listened with an icy stoicism as the charges were read, as did her uncle. But Leenah's heart was pounding, and she couldn't help it. Her quick breaths were beginning to make her dizzy. The court scribe finished, rolled up the scroll, bowed low, and handed it to Zorin.

Zorin rose from the gaudy chair, and when he spoke, his words bounced off the sound mirrors and boomed out into the crowd. "Open rebellion and disregard of Atlan's authority. That is what these two represent!" He looked directly at Uncle Sirt and slowly shook his head. "One, an officer within my own house. We live in a day when no one can be trusted. It saddens me."

Zorin shifted his gaze to Leenah. "But what saddens me more is that this rebel, a daughter of Atlan and ancestor to Hodin, should try to harm the Lady Darha whom we all love. In spite of my effort to protect her all these years from an exiled son who means only harm for her, this rebel managed to penetrate her stronghold, her place of peace and safety, and nearly succeeded in murder."

Leenah gasped. Did the people actually believe these lies?

"Fortunately, my loyal guards thwarted her evil plan," he continued glibly.

A murmur rustled through the crowd. Zorin raised his voice. "Lady Darha is safe and in hiding, and we have the two rebels in custody. Now what shall I do with them?"

"The Pit!" some shouted. "The Pikes," others insisted. Apparently Zorin had been careful about whom he permitted into the courtyard. This was all for show; her fate had been determined the moment she'd been captured.

Zorin held up a hand for silence. "My heart counsels leniency, but such crimes as you yourselves have heard require the severest punishment."

Neither she nor her uncle was going to be allowed to speak in her or his own defense. Zorin couldn't risk the people hearing what she might say. Any earlier thread of hope she may have falsely clung to left her at that moment. She glanced at her uncle. No hint of emotion. That was the Makir way. She grimaced. And if she had the strength, it was going to be her way too.

She closed her eyes. Fear buzzing inside her head washed away Zorin's words. She turned her thoughts and her heart to the Creator and prayed for the strength to face death. Would the Creator's Messengers be waiting on the other side to carry her to Adam's Bosom, to await the coming of the Strong Man Lamech had told her about—the Creator's Redeemer spoken of in the star pictures, who would break the bands of death and open the way for men to walk again with the Creator?

A roar from the crowd snapped her from her prayer. She hadn't heard Zorin's proclamation, but there could be no doubt about their fate as the guards moved in, surrounded her and Uncle Sirt, and led them through the long gallery, out to the crowded courtyard.

The people chanted, "The Pikes ... the Pikes ... hang them on the Bloody Pikes."

They wanted a spectacle, and Zorin was going to give them one. *Where were those who opposed Zorin?* According to Da-gore, Atlan was ripe for rebellion. She would never have guessed it by the hundreds of jeering supporters gathered in the courtyard.

Guards escorted them down the steps as a corridor opened for them in the midst of the crowd—a solid line of armed soldiers restrained the people on either side. Her impulse to break and run would prove fruitless among this mob clamoring for blood. Uncle Sirt glanced at her, and as if he'd read her thoughts, said softly, "Don't give them the satisfaction of seeing your fear. Remember who you are."

"I'm not a Makir." Her voice sounded weak.

"You are a daughter of Hodin. Draw on that strength now."

Hodin was long dead, and the dead knew nothing. There was only one strength she could draw on now: the living Creator who held the whole world in the palm of his hand.

Behind them, Zorin, protected within a double circle of guards, descended the long flight of steps. She saw a waiting prison wagon, its ironwood bars shining like burnished walnut shells in the midday sun. They were shoved into the cage. As the door closed and the lock turned, she saw Zorin mounting an ornate coach, which was immediately surrounded by the guards.

He must live in constant fear for his life.

With a lurch, the prison wagon started forward. Leenah's heart felt as if it were a leaden lump in her chest.

Ahead of them marched a company of soldiers and behind another forty or fifty. After them came Zorin's coach, and yet farther back swarmed the throngs of spectators, eager for blood. The procession passed through the bronze gates and made for the Hodin Keep Bridge.

Leenah fought to calm her breath, but she could do nothing about her racing heart. Her uncle's face revealed nothing of his fear, and she desperately wanted his courage, but that kind of fortitude was something gained only through hard training. Hodin's blood or not, she didn't have the strength to accept the inevitable.

She willed her breathing to slow as she forced herself to remain outwardly stoic, like Uncle Sirt. Even so, her white-knuckled fingers clutching the ironwood bar revealed her true fear. All the while, her brain cried out for help, leaping between fervent prayers and wild, crazy thoughts of bursting the bars.

38

Race to Execution Ridge

*S*uddenly the tunnels ended, and Rhone straightened up in what felt like a massive, underground room. The Deep Chambers. The smell of the place brought back memories. He listened to the sound of his own breathing, interrupted only by the distant plop ... plop of dripping water and the scuffing of their feet. The feeble glow of their moonglasses showed the narrow ledge upon which they stood and the pool of black water not four spans distance. A ripple caught his eye. As a wring serpent swam past, its head held up out of the water, its long, flexing body swiftly driving it beyond the reach of his moonglass.

"Which way?" His memory of the Deep Chambers was vague. It had never been one of his favorite places.

Faeg pointed. "To your right, Pyir Rhone."

He took the lead, staying near the cavern wall, his long sword occasionally scraping the black rock. Faeg came next, and behind him were Rhone's mother and then Klesc. The others brought up the rear.

Faeg said softly, "I was working around here when I first heard her calling to me. She's just up ahead maybe two, three hundred spans."

Rhone refrained from hurrying, although his heart urged him on with uncustomary impatience. One slip could send him or one of the others into the Black Pool, and if the wring serpents swarmed…. He spotted a faint glow ahead, and beyond it the distant flicker of flames where the stone stairs landed upon this, the lowermost part of the Deep Chambers. Finally he spied the regular shape of a cell and the indistinct form of someone sitting within it. He shut his moonglass and motioned for the others to stop—then, alone, he silently crept forward. When the shape inside it stirred, he knew immediately that this prisoner wasn't Leenah. With heavy disappointment, he opened his moonglass and shone it through the bars.

The man inside the cage lurched around.

"Da-gore!"

Da-gore leaped to his feet and clutched the bars. "Pyir Rhone! How did you get here?"

"Where's Leenah?"

"They took her. I don't know how long ago. An hour. Maybe two. It's hard to keep track of time down here. They took Sirt, too."

"Sirt? Explain!"

He drew in a breath. "Leenah managed to set your mother free, but she was captured."

"I know. What about Sirt and you?"

"My carelessness put us here. You must go quickly. I suspect Leenah and Sirt are headed for the Pikes."

"No!" his mother exclaimed, stepping from the shadows.

Da-gore looked at her, then questioningly at Rhone.

"This is my mother."

His eyes widened. "Lady Darha! I'm pleased to see you are well."

"My son mustn't do this!"

"I pray not," Da-gore said, "but he's ruthless."

She bit her lip, a heavy sadness coming to her eyes and pulling at her face. "Yes, I know," she breathed quietly.

Rhone motioned to the Makir. "Test the bars."

Klesc and Orn took one side, Tabic and Birn the adjoining bar. Bracing their feet against the others' bar, the four pulled, their massive arms bulging beneath their black sutas while their legs strained against the iron. With their eyes closed, they focused their thoughts and strength. Rhone felt the gathering energy, as the four seemed to become one. Through the training of the Katrahs and Kimahs, they drew strength from one another.

Da-gore stepped back, watching with wide wonderment. Metal creaked and then groaned as the two bars spread slowly apart. When the Makir finally stepped back, Da-gore turned sideways, expelled his breath, and squeezed through.

"Amazing." He stared at the bent bars.

"These were never built to hold Makir," Rhone said.

"But Sirt was helpless against them. He and I both tried."

"Sirt was alone," Klesc said. "The Makir draw their strength from one another. It's part of the binding."

He shook his head in amazement. "I'd known being bound was important, but I didn't realize ... no wonder a small band of Makir could outfight far greater forces."

Rhone's thoughts shot back to Leenah. He'd been so close, and again she'd been plucked from him at the last moment. Could this be the Creator's will? Was he about to lose her now? Or was this the work of the Deceiver?

The more he thought about losing her, the more he realized how much he'd come to love her. Why hadn't he told her? The party hurried along the ledge alongside the Black Pool toward the stairs ahead. He glanced behind himself at the others. He should have insisted his mother remain behind. She was in danger here, as was Faeg.

Da-gore said, "It was Ka-Larik, Rhone. He's the spy among us."

"Ka-Larik!" He frowned. "I sent Ka-Larik back for help."

"You can bet that message was never delivered."

"And that Larik won't be arriving with the Makir."

"Zorin will know you are on the island," Da-gore added.

Rhone halted at the stairs that soared into gloomy shadows. With no hope of help arriving now, he would have to rely on just his handful of Makir. "Faeg, you need go no farther. Take Lady Darha back to the tunnels and await word from me that it is safe."

"No, Rhone. My place is here." His mother stared at him with a determination he recalled from his youth. Whenever she got that look on her face, there was no budging her.

He glanced back up the stairs. "All right. But stay behind the Makir. Faeg, you may return to your people."

"Pyir Rhone, I think it best I remain with Lady Darha, to protect her."

Darha smiled at the little man. Rhone grunted and shook his head. "You're both stubborn. All right, but stay to the rear, and at the first sign of trouble, scatter to the winds and hide."

The sound of voices echoed down the stairs from above. He motioned them up against the cavern wall. The Makir instantly melted in with the shadows. When he looked to his mother, both she and Faeg had managed to disappear.

The voices grew louder, and footsteps rang upon the stone. Eight soldiers emerged from the shadows above. Replacement guards, Rhone guessed. He cast a glance farther down the cavern where prisoners were kept, then ducked out of the reach of the light from the braziers.

The final soldier to come off the steps must have spotted one of them. He drew to a halt, stared into the gloom, and shouted a warning. Swords leaped from scabbards faster than a heartbeat, and just as swiftly Makir sprang from the shadows, making short work of all but one of the guards. Rhone spared the last man, holding him beneath the point of his sword.

"The prisoners Leenah and Sirt. Where are they?" he demanded.

The guard stammered, his eyes huge and staring at the long blade reflecting the dancing light of the burning braziers. "They're on their way to the Rim-wall."

"The Pikes?" Rhone growled.

The frightened man nodded. "High Councilor Zorin sentenced them not more than an hour ago."

"We still have time," Klesc said. "It takes at least two hours to reach Execution Ridge."

"Even longer," the man blurted. "There is a great crowd following them, and High Councilor Zorin will want to wait until all have arrived."

Klesc sneered. "Zorin wouldn't want to disappoint the people, would he?"

"Finish this one, Pyir Rhone, and let's be on our way," Tabic said.

In the old days he would have. Maybe Larik was right. Maybe he'd grown weak, but there was something inside him now that called for mercy. He swung the hilt of his sword alongside the man's head, knocking him cold.

"Live enemies sometimes come back to kill you," Klesc mumbled.

"And sometimes not." Rhone passed one of the fallen men's sword to Da-gore. "You might need this."

"I'd rather it was a proj-lance," Da-gore said.

"A coward's weapon," Klesc snarled.

"A pragmatist's weapon, Master Klesc," Da-gore replied. "Swords will soon be a thing of the past. Mark my words."

They hauled the unconscious man out of sight and then dragged the bodies into the Black Pool. Greedy wring serpents swarmed and the water boiled.

His mother and Faeg emerged from the shadows. His mother stared at the pool, frowning. "Did you have to?"

"Where did you disappear to?"

"We were here all the time." She momentarily pulled her cape about her and faded against the stone wall in spite of the firelight flickering upon it. "A woodsman's cape. Leenah gave it to me."

Leenah! Rhone hustled his men up the stairs. The Makir moved silently through the building, falling back into alcoves or darkened rooms as guards and servants approached and passed by. The great hall was mostly empty except for a few lingering court officials. Servants were busy lowering the tapestry wall that shut the hall to the outside. The *Heart of Justice*—the golden throne at the hall's center—was empty. Rhone felt his ire seethe. The name used to mean something in his father's day. Now, the sort of justice Zorin meted from it made a mockery of the once-proud title. How Leenah must have despaired standing before him.

He would rush the stables, overpower the guards, and appropriate gerups upon which they would easily overtake the procession up to the Rim-wall where Zorin intended to carry out the executions. Just the same, any rescue he might attempt was a long shot. With only nine Makir and himself, success seemed unlikely.

They'd nearly made it to the Sanctuary and the long corridor leading to the stables when a servant descending a flight of stairs spied them. He wheeled, prepared to silence her—but instead of shouting an alarm, the woman's eyes sprang wide, and at that instant he recognized her too.

"Wana Rhone?" she gasped.

"Amah Selika!" A lump lodged in his throat at the sight of the old woman who had once been his amah, his nurse.

Her eyes glazed, and she threw her arms about him. "Is it really you? You've returned." She looked at his mother. "And Mistress Darha!" Sudden concern filled her face. "I'd heard you'd been freed, but High Councilor Zorin said he'd found you again."

"My son lies, as usual." Darha's voice held a mother's disappointment. "I was freed by the woman he has condemned."

"I heard the sentencing," Selika said. "She wasn't even permitted
to speak in her own defense. It was never like that in the old days."

"I intend to change that," Rhone said.

Selika looked at him, touching the black sleeve of his tunic. The
affection in her eyes was almost that of his mother's. "The Makir have
been out of the land too long, Wan—I mean Pyir Rhone. What can I
do to help?"

❧

Half an hour later, five men dressed in the gray and scarlet of
Zorin's personal guards strode from the Sanctuary of Justice, escort-
ing a prisoner in irons.

The red stone stable, fifty paces behind the Sanctuary, was
fronted with twenty stone arches of the whitest marble, tooled and
polished by Atlan's finest craftsmen. They were confronted by the
commander of the guard, a Second Shield with a stern mouth and
sharp cheeks beneath sea blue eyes. Hair the color of late flax fell
shoulder length from under his leather casque.

"I need a coach and swift horses to draw it," Klesc demanded as
the small company of men halted behind him.

The Second Shield glanced to the emblems upon the shoulder of
Klesc's cloak. Rhone averted his face, hoping the officer would not
notice his striking similarity to Zorin.

"I don't know you, First Major."

"I don't know you either, *Second Shield*."

The man stiffened at Klesc's subtle rebuke.

"High Councilor Zorin wants this man at the Pikes." Klesc slid a
glance at Da-gore, bound in chains. "If he misses his appointment
with the executioners, I'll be certain to let High Councilor Zorin
know how we were delayed."

❧

In short order they were all piled into a fleet two-wheeled mer-non pulled swiftly along by a pair of excellent horses, nearly as tall at the withers as Rhone. The mernon rattled out upon Atla's Fair View, hoofbeats thundering along the wide avenue toward the Hodin Keep Bridge. Once across the bridge and upon the ring of land known as the Kinsmen's Anchorage, Rhone hauled back on the reins and brought the mernon to a halt.

Da-gore leaped from the coach, rubbing his wrists where the shackles had abraded the skin. "That was almost too easy."

"Do what you have to do, and may the Creator's hand be with you."

"You, too, Pyir Rhone." He turned at once and broke into a jog, heading toward the far end of the plaza and the bridge over Merchant's Harbor into Atla Fair.

Rhone urged the horses into motion again. He and Da-gore had begun as enemies, but the Creator, in his wisdom, had drawn them together. He had been wrong to doubt Da-gore's loyalty. Da-gore was a man he could trust as much as a Makir ... and more than some. A heaviness settled in his chest as he thought of Ka-Larik. He resigned himself to the certainty that he'd get no help from the Makir at Imo-suk. It was just he and his Makir against Zorin's army. Success seemed impossible, yet failure would certainly spell the end of the Creator's commission to him. Could the Creator fail? He cut short that line of thinking and glanced heavenward. *The outcome is in your hands.*

The mernon raced over the Kinsmen's Anchorage, then Merchant's Harbor, and turned with its wheels thundering onto the Rim-wall Road.

❧

Darha stood at the window long after her son's carriage had sped through the bronze gates and disappeared down Atla's Fair View.

Faeg had to grip the windowsill and stand on tiptoes to see out. The courtyard was slowly emptying as guards circulated among the lingering knots of people, hustling them toward the gates.

"I heard the lies High Councilor Zorin spoke, My Lady," Selika said at her side. "He said Wana Rhone was intent on harming you," her voice cracked under the emotion of that, "and the people believed him."

"Not all the people," Faeg said. "There are still many who remember the way it was."

Darha looked down on the town of Atla Fair, visible in the distance beyond the wall that encircled Hodin's Keep. "Those loyal to Zorin are mostly the younger ones, those who have never known the truth." Her heart ached. How could a mother favor one son over the other? How could two sons be so similar yet so different? Birthed within moments of each other, it seemed incredible one could rise through strength and honor to be the Pyir of the Makir, while the other could gain power only through lies and murder. She shivered.

"You are chilled. I'll fetch you a wrap."

"I am chilled, Selika, but no covering of wool will help. Only justice can warm my blood now."

Selika's eyes held a blank look. "I don't understand."

Darha gave her a quick, thin smile and touched the servant on the shoulder. "The people need to hear the truth. But for them to believe it, they must hear it from me. Fetch a carriage."

"But My Lady, when I'm asked by whose authority I do this, what shall I say?"

Darha scowled. With Zorin's guards prowling the halls, she was yet a prisoner within her own home. "Is there no one still loyal to the old ways?"

Selika thought a moment. "There are a few here."

"Take me to them."

She looked at Darha. "You'll be seen leaving."

Darha snatched the woodsman's cloak off the back of a chair. "What about the underground tunnel to the supply houses?"

"It's used mostly by servants," Selika said.

"Behind the supply houses are my old gardens. There is a gate in the wall that was always barred. The gardens have long ago returned to weed and thorns, but I'm sure I can find it."

"If you're seen, you'll be captured again."

She fastened the cloak over her shoulders. "I'll take that chance. You go ahead of me by a good distance and speak in a loud voice if anyone approaches. I'll hide"

Selika nodded. "I can do that."

Faeg went to the door of the upper room where they had hidden themselves, opened it a crack, and peeked down the long, deserted hallway. "All clear."

They slipped out of the room and made for a flight of narrow wooden stairs, built out of sight so that the servants might be able to move more discretely about the residence.

39

The Makir

Sirt put an arm around Leenah's shoulder. For the stern ex-Makir, it was an unexpected display of tenderness. Was his coolness toward life something inborn in all Makir? Or was it the training? Leenah took comfort in his touch. Rhone also found it difficult to show her he cared, though she knew he did. Small things told her so. Sometimes it was simply taking her hand as they walked. Other times, when his guard was down, he'd say things that made her believe their relationship was deepening. But always he came to that place where the Makir inside him would take over the man he was ... that wall ... that place of secrets that he kept under lock and key.

Sirt said, "When the time comes, fill your mind with a thought and hold on to it until the light fades."

She looked into his stern eyes. "I can't focus like you can, Uncle Sirt. I've never used the Katrahs and Kimahs."

"You must stretch your mind. Do it now and try to reach out. Try to touch my thoughts. If we can do this, I will lend you my strength when the time comes."

"Touch your thoughts?" There had only ever been one whom

she could reach and touch ... except in the Creator's Garden, the Cradleland, where all creatures seemed able to touch one another.

"You can do it, Leenah. You must. It is a gift that runs strong among us who carry Hodin's blood."

If that was true, could it explain why she was a sensitive? Why she was able to touch dragons, and Rhone the spiders?

"Close your eyes and cast your thoughts to the wind."

Free her thoughts! On the road to Execution Ridge and the Bloody Pikes, she was to cast her thoughts to the wind? Impossible as the task appeared, she shut her eyes and tried to force the fear from her. Instead, she merely became more acutely aware of the jolting of the wagon, reviving the ache in her neck. She tried again. Slowly the smell of the forest filled up her senses—the trees, the rich earth, the sweet perfume of the lambent creepers snaking along the forest floor with giant, pale flowers spread wide filling the air ... but that was all. She concentrated harder, stretching her mind as she had many times with Gur, but struggle as she might, she could not sense the man at her side.

"It's not working."

"You're straining too hard, dear. Clear your mind, fill your lungs and let them drain slowly, then try again."

She set her jaw as she shut her eyes, broadcasting her thoughts as grains of wheat across freshly turned ground. But there was still no perception of Uncle Sirt at all. Nothing—

Just then something unexpected touched her brain. *Gur!*

Her eyes snapped open. Had she only imagined it? A shadow passed suddenly overhead, but it was only a skybarge. Likely carrying dignitaries for a bird's-eye view of Zorin's planned entertainment. Despair washed over her again. It must have been only her imagination.

She cast off any further attempt at the Makir way. She just

didn't have the ability. "I'm sorry; I can't do it."

Uncle Sirt watched the great sky vessel pass slowly overhead. When he looked back at her, there was a ghost of a smile upon his face. He squeezed her hand. "Then have faith, daughter of my sister." He turned back as the skybarge glided swiftly away.

Faith? That sounded odd coming from him, a believer in Dirgen. Yet it was true. Faith was all she had left, and up until now she'd not shown him any of it. She nodded and straightened up on the hard seat, focusing her thoughts upon the Creator. Death was simply passing from one world to the other. She'd had a glimpse of that other world when the Messenger Sari'el had led her and Rhone past the Lodath's soldiers and into the Cradleland. There was nothing to fear, she told herself, shivering nonetheless at knowing what must happen first. She was a true follower of the Creator, but what of Uncle Sirt?

"If today is to be our last day on earth, are you ready for what waits beyond?" she asked him.

Her uncle looked at her strangely for a moment, then a thin smile creased his face. "I go to Dirgen's Bosom."

That wasn't the answer she had hoped to hear. "While I go to Adam's Bosom, to await the Creator's call. Uncle Sirt, I want you to be there with me, but you won't if you don't put your trust in the Creator."

He stared a moment longer, then shook his head. "Why do we deceive ourselves, Leenah? There is nothing beyond the here and now. We may draw some comfort in fables, but in truth, the Pikes and death are the only reality." He gave her hand a tender squeeze. "Try not to let fear overcome you. The pain will pass soon enough."

The pain will be over soon, and then the Messengers of the Creator will carry you to Adam's Bosom where pain and tears are gone.

The procession wound higher along the road toward the Rim-wall where death awaited them like a stalking mansnatcher. From time to time, she heard Uncle Sirt give the chain that connected his wrist shackles a sharp snap and heard his muffled groan as he tested it as he had the iron bars in the Deep Chambers. The Warrior inside him wouldn't allow for a complete surrender.

She drew in a quick breath when the wagon came to a halt. She stared out the bars at the stark platform, her chest tightening. Uncle Sirt, grim-faced, gave her hand a gentle squeeze. "Fill your thoughts," he whispered.

Soldiers surrounded the wagon and unlocked the door. Her knees went weak, and she nearly tumbled out. A pair of guards grabbed her and led her away. Her head spinning, she was only vaguely aware of the huge skybarge hovering a hundred spans overhead, casting a great, oval shadow across the Rim-wall.

She stumbled up a tall flight of steps to the raised wooden platform, ringed with guards. Her vision cleared some. A little distance away stood an open-sided booth, roofed in gray fabric and trimmed in red. Gray pennants bearing the crimson image of a minck fluttered in a sea breeze coming from behind her.

She became aware of a steady puffing, like heavy breathing, and turned. An ugly iron brazier burned and crackled not five spans behind her, its belly glowing red, the bitter smoke of resinous wood stinging her nose. Fear hardened in her throat at the sight of a fist of iron rods poking from the blackened rim, their tips buried in a pile of charcoal that flared with each stroke of a bellows.

She forced her view past the brazier to the Pikes, their sharp bronze points piercing the sky. A hundred or more of them stretched away in both directions. Her eyes traveled down the row, her stomach convulsing. Here and there hung the remains of Zorin's victims, their skeletons picked clean by the birds. Beneath some of the Pikes lay piles of bones mixed in with shreds of clothing. In spite of the heat from the brazier, a cold, sticky sweat prickled her skin. She looked down at the black rock of the Rim-wall where rust-colored stains flowed off in every direction, much of it spilling profusely over the lip of the Rim-wall to the sea far below.

"Faith," Uncle Sirt whispered beside her, a small smile lifting a corner of his lips. His eyes flicked downward, and he raised his shackled wrists. She didn't understand until she spied one of the iron links had broken and now was stretched just enough to allow the chain to become unhooked.

"You won't suffer," he whispered. "I'll see to that."

Her heart raced. "You can't take on his army, alone!"

He gave her an amused look. "Are we alone?"

Her skin tingled. What did that mean? She gulped. *Faith*. She needed it now more than ever. She squeezed her eyes shut and prayed for strength. Whatever happened, she knew where her destiny lay. That assurance brought an unexpected comfort, and she drew herself up tall as Zorin entered the booth across the way, accompanied by several lower councilors, Captain El-ik of the Lodath's Guard, and a huge man she'd never seen before. His head was oddly misshapen, his eyes deeply hooded beneath thick brow ridges. Upon each of the giant's hands was an extra finger. She remembered Rhone telling her of the giants he'd battled while fleeing to the Cradleland. Was this one of them? The creature didn't seem quite human.

A contingent of guards moved in around Zorin's booth. Their alertness was more telling than anything else. With a surprising clarity, Leenah understood now that the High Councilor lived in constant fear for his life. Somehow, that emboldened her. As he settled upon the plush cushions in the booth, she caught his eyes and stared unflinchingly into them.

He seemed taken off guard by that. He scowled, then glanced

away from her and whispered something to one of the councilors.

"What are you doing?" Uncle Sirt whispered as guards mounted the platform and formed a line behind them.

"Telling him I don't care anymore. That he can kill my body, but he can't harm my spirit." She looked at him. "And if you trust in the Creator, you can have that same assurance."

Uncle Sirt grinned. "You have the mettle of a Makir after all." He casually brought his hands together so that the open link dangled near his fingers. "I'll put my trust in two spans of sword steel."

That wasn't the reply she'd hoped for. Her heart quickened, and she tried not to think about what he was planning. "Who is that one, the giant?"

"A new breed of warrior. I don't think he's fully human."

"I can believe that."

Zorin waited as the crowds that had followed them up from Hodin's Keep finally all gathered in the viewing area. She had already settled it in her mind that she'd not cry for mercy, and she felt a strange peace about this that seemed to go beyond human understanding.

Overhead, the skybarge lowered an anchor line to some men on the ground who hooked it onto an iron ring embedded in the stone. A dazzling brilliance stung her eye. She had to look away as the skybarge's crew adjusted the tracking mirrors that focused blazing sunlight upon the great silk balloon's vast black underbelly.

Finally, when all was ready, Zorin stood and raised his arms to the hoard of blood-seekers. The murmuring faded.

"A land at peace cannot tolerate rebels and anarchists. You are here to witness the final end to all such traitors to Atlan and her duly appointed council." He looked at Leenah and her uncle. "I commit these two into the hands of the great ruler of the deep.

May you not find Dirgen as merciful as I! Let the executions begin!"

The crowd raised their voices in roar of approval. Two soldiers went to the Pikes, lifted a pair of them from sockets bored into the rock, and leaned them against the platform.

Uncle Sirt stiffened, and his thoughts seemed to focus. He glanced over his shoulder at the Rim-wall, then up at the sky-barge. A scowl sprang suddenly to his face, and his eyes leaped back at the Rim-wall.

"What's wrong?" she whispered.

"No more talking!" A guard drove the barrel of a proj-lance into her back.

She glared at him.

Two burly men dressed in scarlet tunics, wearing black sashes about their waists, appeared at the foot of the platform.

The crowd cheered.

"Be ready to move," Uncle Sirt warned, his whisper barely audible above the crowd's roar as Zorin's executioners ascended the stairs.

Move where? They were surrounded by Zorin's guards. Her thoughts raced. If she could make it to the rear of the platform, she might leap to the ground and flee along the Rim-wall. But if she became trapped between Zorin's guards and the sheer drop.... She drew in a determined breath and exhaled sharply. The plunge to the rocky beach far below was preferable to the slow torture Zorin's executioners were famous for.

The executioners moved slowly, in no hurry to do their job. Her heart was trying to batter its way out of her chest. *Move where?* She wondered again, but then the question became irrelevant.

Uncle Sirt flung apart the chain and snatched a pair of swords from the guards at their back. The weapons slashed with a fury she had never seen in the mock practice battles upon the training grounds at Imo-suk, and three guards fell dead before they realized he'd broken his bonds. Turning the whirling blades upon the executioners, the men fell a heartbeat later, then two more guards. Stunned, the platform guards backed off, while below, Zorin's soldiers rushed up the stairs.

Leenah scrambled to the back of the platform, about to leap, when half a hundred ropes tumbled from the skybarge, and the next instant black-clad Makir with gleaming swords slung across their backs were dropping to the ground and onto the platform. Zorin didn't have Makir Warriors!

Uncle Sirt's face wore a grim smile as his sword flashed in the sunlight, holding off the upswell of guards at the top of the steps. Feeling an unexplainable surge of energy, she snatched up a fallen blade and sprang to his side. The clanging of steel rang in the air, and the shouts and groans of men fell like leaden hammer blows upon her ears as the platform slickened with blood.

"You knew!"

"My kal-ee-hon. I felt their presence."

Below, people were scattering even as Zorin was shouting orders to the soldiers in the rear to press forward. Like a black cloud of death, the Makir from the skybarge advanced upon the platform, mowing a wide swath through Zorin's guards.

From her high vantage point, she could see the vast number of troops that had followed them up from Hodin's Keep. Her stomach clenched, and a pang of despair shot through her. Hundreds of Zorin's gray-clad soldiers were fanning out across the rugged Rimwall. Her uncle's small band of warriors was mighty, but in the end, Zorin's numbers must work against them. Already many had fallen, and with each of them she'd felt a stab of pain, as though it had been she who had taken the deadly wound. Her senses came achingly alive; somehow she lived inside every one of them. Was this the *binding* Rhone had tried to explain to her so often?

She felt it! And now that she finally understood, it was too late to tell him.

❧

Rhone had almost reached the top of the ridge when the sky-barge hovering above the Rim-wall suddenly bristled with black-clothed warriors dropping swiftly to the ground on ropes. He gave Klesc a puzzled glance.

Klesc shrugged his massive shoulders. "Sirt's kal-ee-hon?"

"It must be." As the road became congested with fleeing civilians, he brought the panting horses to a halt and sprang off the mernon. Still dressed in the uniform of Zorin's guards, he and his men pushed unchallenged against the tide of people. The Makir fighting about the execution platform were far outnumbered, and more soldiers were rushing up from below.

When he spied Leenah atop the platform, his heart took a joyous leap. Seeing her there wielding a sword among a double fist of Makir filled him with admiration, and the love he felt just then was almost overpowering. He had to get to her side! Tearing off the gray cape and gray and red jerkin, Rhone flew through the crowd and plunged into the battle.

❧

Leenah, her wrists encumbered by half a span of chain, aware of her lack of training, swung her sword and took her hits where she could find them. She stayed among the Makir, feeling their energy—that connectedness that Rhone had told her about. Surrounded by a double fist of Makir swords, leaping and striking as if under the control of a single mind, she heard a shout making its way like a rushing wind through the warriors.

"Pyir Rhone! Pyir Rhone!"

A burst of energy swept through the Makir. She felt it too, rising steeply in the center of her chest and moving out into her arms. Strength gathered in her muscles. It was as though a frayed rope had suddenly been rewoven. It was the *binding*! She peered through sweat-blurred eyes but couldn't pick Rhone out from among the mass of Zorin's soldiers crashing up against the Makir wall of deadly, whirling blades. Even as this thought sprang into her head, the wall began to crumble. Facing overpowering numbers, the Makir at the front of the stairs began a slow retreat to the back of the platform.

Those warriors on the ground still held a tenuous line and had so far kept the rear of the platform clear of Zorin's guards. Now with their heels against the back edge of the platform, they began springing lightly to the ground.

She tottered, ready to jump, when someone swooped her up and lowered her to a pair of strong hands waiting below. The warrior swiftly set her upon the rocky Rim-wall and immediately turned back to the battle.

Standing a head taller than everyone else, the giant who had accompanied Zorin had suddenly appeared in the midst of the fighting men, swinging an immense sword. At once two Makir fell beneath its crushing blow.

Leenah looked for Rhone. She'd lost sight of Uncle Sirt, too as the battle pressed in closer around her. The Makir were now in retreat. By the growing shouts of men and the ringing of swords, Leenah knew that Zorin's reinforcements had arrived. She cast a glance over her shoulder at the precipitous drop of the Rim-wall looming ever closer.

The giant had cut a swath through their crumbling forces and was advancing on them even as Uncle Sirt's dwindling kal-ee-hon was being pressed closer and closer to the edge of the Rim-wall. Leenah suddenly became aware of a familiar presence. She cast quickly about at the sky, not seeing him, yet certain this time that

Gur was somewhere nearby. Marshaling all her concentration, she stretched her mind and tried to reach out to him.

✼

Rhone drew strength from the fighting men with him, even as his presence lent vigor to them. With Klesc at his side, he punched a hole through Zorin's forces and mounted the stairs to the platform.

Makir now at their back, Zorin's guards quickly fell apart, leaping off the steps. Rhone mounted the blood-slick platform, and he and Klesc drove the remaining Gray Bears from it. In a glance, he saw the ragtag remnant of Makir pushed dangerously close to the Rim-wall. Leenah was still among them, but impossible to reach now.

And then Rhone spied the giant.

Herc! He'd fought this one before, at the entrance to the Cradleland. Back then, their great strength had been hampered by poor training. A grimace nudged at his face. It appeared the Deceiver's Messengers had been busy teaching their misshapen offspring a thing or two.

He turned to Klesc. "That one needs to be stopped."

Klesc glanced over and seemed to go rigid for an instant. "What is it?"

"A devil from the Prince of Devils. If the Deceiver has his way, that's what will infest this world in another couple generations. Try to make it to Leenah." He sprang off the edge of the execution platform, landing in the midst of ten or twelve of Zorin's guards being repelled by three tired Makir. He helped dispatch the Gray Bears, cut his way through another four or five guards, and then he was facing Herc.

Herc turned from the body of a Makir and stared at Rhone. His face widened with surprise, then pinched in a sudden, questioning gaze. "You're not Zorin?"

Rhone tightened his grip upon his sword. "No, but you do remember me."

Herc's forehead furrowed. "You killed Hepha," he rumbled.

That had happened years ago; his first encounter with an Earth-Born.

Herc's snarl showed rows of twisted teeth, and with a sudden growl, his sword leaped and slammed against Rhone's blade. The blow might well have shattered the sword, had it not been a Makir blade, forged in Atlan one hundred and fifty years ago by the Makir artisans.

Rhone turned out from under Herc's sword and drove for the giant's heart. The Earth-Born bent aside and came around with another blade-ringing strike.

They lunged and parried across the Rim-wall, each holding his own—Herc by sheer strength, Rhone by skill. The battle around him faded into the background as his concentration focused on this one adversary.

The last time Rhone had fought one of these Earth-Born, he'd been alone. Now, the energy of the Makir all around him surged through his muscles. Herc swung ferociously, his power greater than any Makir, and Rhone called on every trick he knew.

Rhone struck, missed, and leaped out of the path of Herc's sudden thrust. His heart was pounding, and his lungs began to burn. Herc feigned a jab and nearly caught Rhone by surprise, but he'd seen the ploy at the last moment. Rhone dove low. Herc's mighty sword clanged and knocked Rhone's blade aside.

The duel moved them closer to the thin black line of Makir now among the Bloody Pikes, barely holding ground at the edge of the Rim-wall.

Their swords momentarily locked, and Herc hissed, "I already killed you once!"

Rhone gritted his teeth. "But Elohim had other plans."

At the mention of the Creator's name, Herc shuddered, and in that brief moment the monster's sword faltered. Rhone drove for his heart. The point of his sword cut through the leather cuirass and pushed into hard muscle, but Rhone felt it deflect off a rib.

Herc's fingers sprang open, and his sword clattered to the black rock. He stared at the sword impaled through him, fear filling his eyes. He opened his mouth and roared, "Noooo!"

There was a sudden flash of light, and all around the giant the air began to shimmer like a slowing rotating wheel, forming a vortex of black smoke. The wheel cracked across its center, and a rift tore a ragged hole in the air. Herc, still staring, was sucked off Rhone's blade and into the fracture, and in an instant, the Earth-Born was gone.

The stinking fumes of sulfur tinged with the sweeter scent of lilacs spilled out from the rupture. Rhone caught a glimpse of the Messenger-warriors of the Creator and the Deceiver fighting. Then the shimmering wheel of light rushed in on itself, sealing the tear between their two worlds.

For a moment the fighting on the Rim-wall ceased as all eyes stared. Zorin, standing atop the platform, swung his sword in the air and cried, "Drive them off the Rim-wall. Kill them all now!"

Rhone dashed for the Makir, slashing a path through Zorin's guards. He leaped in among the black line, grabbed a long pike from its socket, impaled three of Zorin's Gray Bears, and then rushed to Leenah's side.

"Rhone!"

Holding a heavy sword in both hands, she looked exhausted—and beautiful. "I've found you at last." His breathing came hard and painful. He drove his blade though another of Zorin's soldiers.

"I knew you'd come." In spite of the iron cuffs, she was making a valiant stand alongside the few remaining Makir surrounding her. "Now I can die."

His muscles tingled with a sudden surge of energy. He cast a quick glance at the edge of the Rim-wall, now but a few spans beyond their heels, and felt a tight smile push at his lips. "Die? Perhaps, but I think not today. Where's Klesc?"

"I haven't seen him."

Neither had he, since leaving Klesc on the platform.

40

Zorin's Fall

Following Da-gore's orders, Batok had contacted Maelc, and Maelc had sent out word to his under-commanders to assemble the men they had been recruiting in secret for.

By the time Da-gore reached Batok's shop after leaving Rhone and the coach, more than a hundred men awaited his orders. Armed with picks and axes, shovels, spades, and stout clubs, they marched under Da-gore's command for the Rim-wall. Among the small army were forty gerups. Taking his best-armed soldiers, he and his "cavalry" mounted the animals and raced ahead of the larger body of fighting men.

He had just reached the battleground when a sudden flash of light set the air whirling into a whirlpool of black smoke. Hauling back on the reins, he and his men stared at the sight. Many years earlier, when he had commanded a small band of Earth-Borns, their inhuman fathers—the Messengers of the Deceiver—would appear and disappear in the midst of shimmering light just like that.

Were the Messenger-warriors involved in this conflict now? As the shimmering vanished, he spied the meager line of Makir perched precariously at the edge of the Rim-wall, barely holding on against Zorin's overwhelming numbers.

Before him lay more than a hundred bodies of Zorin's guards and Makir Warriors. Sirt's kal-ee-hon had made a proud showing for themselves, even if they now appeared doomed to die upon the points of Zorin's swords or to be broken upon Atlan's rocky coast far below.

Zorin, standing atop the execution platform, whirled a sword high above his head, encouraging his own fighting men on. Bile rose in his throat. If this was how it was going to end, so be it. He'd not let the Makir and Pyir Rhone die alone. Da-gore tipped his eyes upward. *Your will be done.* Turning back to his men, he shouted, "Dismount. Arm yourselves with Zorin's swords." His army of civilians leaped from their gerups, dropping shovels and rakes and snatching up fallen weapons.

As his men rushed forward, shouting and brandishing their weapons, something had begun to take shape behind the stout-hearted Makir perched upon the very edge of the Rim-wall. A black line seemed to be emerging all along the wall's length, growing thicker.

Standing on the execution platform, urging his men on, Zorin suddenly went stiff as more than a hundred Makir Warriors swarmed up over the Rim-wall. Almost at once the tide of the battle turned. The Makir's backward retreat halted and surged forward. Zorin's guards were instantly in disarray as shouting and the ringing of swords swelled across the Rim-wall.

Zorin spun around and fled down the steps, accompanied by his bodyguards.

Da-gore took some men and moved to cut off his escape, while the rest of his army rushed toward Zorin's retreating rear flank.

As Da-gore rushed to intercept the High Councilor, he heard the sound of wagon wheels rumbling up the road behind him, and a high-pitched voice shouting, "Make way for Lady Darha. Make way, make way!"

※

Rhone had sensed the binding strengthen. How could he not, with half his Makir brothers from Imo-suk mere spans beneath the brink of the Rim-wall? Somehow, Larik had gotten the message in spite of Ka-Larik's unfaithfulness. All he had to do now was hold on a few moments longer.

As the wave of Makir flooded over the top of the Rim-wall and crashed down on Zorin's army, Zorin's fighting men broke off their advance and scattered. Rhone took Leenah's arm and followed in their wake, his muscles trembling from exertion, his heart and breath battering his insides almost as violently as Zorin's Gray Bears had worked him over on the outside.

Leenah stared into his eyes, her face and arms blood-streaked, her hair in wild disarray ... and the loveliest sight he'd ever seen. "You knew they were there," she gasped, struggling to catch her breath.

He nodded as they made their way among the bodies of Zorin's troops and the fallen Makir. "I felt them there."

"I felt them too, Rhone," she said.

He saw the wide look of discovery in her eyes.

"I understand now what you tried to explain to me. The binding. I felt it!"

He put an arm around her waist and drew her close to him. "I thank the Creator for this victory and for bringing you back into my life."

Leenah gave him a surprised look.

He smiled. "And I don't intend to let you leave again."

She lifted her shackled wrists over his head and kissed him.

"People of Atlan, hear me!" It was his mother's voice—a feeble attempt against the clamor of battle. He looked about, then saw her standing atop the execution platform, trying to get the attention of the people still fighting in scattered groups.

"Hear me, hear me," she called.

Faeg's high voice declared beside hers, "Listen to Lady Darha! Please, everybody listen!" But they both may as well have been shouting to an empty room.

Rhone took Leenah's hand and hurried toward the platform. As they made their way to her, one of Rhone's statres fell in step beside them. "Good to see you well, Pyir Rhone. And you, too, Mistress Leenah. You had us all worried."

"I'm so sorry for that."

"Don't be." Rhone tightened his grip on her arm. "Your boldness was the spark that set all this in motion. And it looks like we've made a good start."

"We have indeed, Pyir Rhone," the officer said. "We'll have the Rim-wall secured shortly."

"Good. Where is Larik?"

"He took the rest of our forces through Hodin's Passage early this morning, after landing us on the coast below last night. By now, First Statre Larik will have secured the passage and captured Zorin's first line of defense."

"How did Larik get past Zorin's fortifications?"

"The gormerin went in underwater and dropped off a triple fist of Makir." He grinned. "Like a guppy giving birth. Once they seized the caves, the passage was ours."

Rhone stared at the officer. "The gormerin is asea? Kev-nn finished the work?"

He gave a short laugh. "Kev-nn commanded that he be moved to the boathouse while still strapped to his bed. Flat on his stomach, he oversaw the completion."

"He'd said it would take weeks!"

"Maybe Kev-nn exaggerated." The officer grinned again. "Tell the Pyir weeks and deliver in days. From such feats commendations spring."

Rhone laughed. "Kev-nn will have his accolades!" This was good news, but he was still puzzled. "How did Larik know to put you off below Execution Ridge?"

The commander smiled wryly. "I call it luck, although that's not what he will tell you. First Statre Larik claims he was told to land us there. He's hearing voices now." The commander's eyes shone with amusement. "Perhaps it's time for the old warrior to take a council seat instead of a sword?"

Voices could only mean Sari'el, or others like him, were again moving in the lives of men. He recalled his momentary glimpse into that other realm as Herc was drawn into it. There had been a battle there too. What forces were in motion now, just beyond the knowledge of man?

The commander was saying, "Hodin's Sanctum and the Keep should be secured shortly."

"And what of the Golden Hills Passage?"

He shook his head. "Not yet."

They were almost at the platform. "Then that will be our next move. Once the Rim-wall is secure and our wounded tended to, begin running down the Gray Bears who fled ahead of us. We'll have to capture Zorin before he marshals in his troops from the inland or turns tail and slips the country."

The officer nodded. "I'll pass the word at once."

"Have you seen Klesc?"

"No, Pyir Rhone."

Rhone inhaled deeply to loosen the bands of worry beginning to squeeze his chest. Leenah gave his hand a gentle squeeze.

They mounted the platform and his mother hurried to him, the hem of her dress soaked red with the blood of men, relief in her eyes.

He went to the iron brazier that still glowed red from the coals and struck it with his sword, ringing it like a dull bell. Over and over it clanged while he called out to the warriors below. The fighting ceased as Zorin's failing defenders saw that the Makir had taken control of the battle.

Once he had their attention, his mother cried out, "You must stop this! We are all Atlanders, and we must not fight among ourselves."

Rhone suspected that most of these people had never seen Lady Darha before. They'd only heard of her through Zorin, who claimed he was only trying to keep her safe. His stomach knotted at that thought. *Safe by keeping her a prisoner in her own home!* Zorin had twisted the story over the years to make it appear as if he had been her real threat.

Lady Darha took his arm and turned back to the people drawing closer around the platform.

"My son Rhone! The rightful heir to the high seat of the Council of Ten has returned."

They seemed confused, and who could blame them after the lies Zorin had spread?

Weapons lowered, what remained of Zorin's Gray Bears moved toward the platform. The people who had come to see an execution began returning, and now there was a great number of people gathered around the platform, pressing in to hear his mother's words.

A sudden stir moved through the crowd. People stepped aside as a knot of men forced its way through them. As it drew nearer, Rhone saw Da-gore in the lead. The knot loosened at the foot of the steps, and Da-gore escorted Zorin up them at sword point.

Rhone felt his mother tremble, then draw in a calming breath. Resolution filled her eyes as she watched Zorin climb the steps. The reaction, he knew, had been a mother's sadness at seeing a child gone bad.

"Well done, Da-gore," he said.

"Pyir Rhone, Mistress Leenah." Da-gore grabbed Zorin's arm and moved him before Rhone. "A present for you. Gray Bears. We ran him down before he reached his coach."

"My guards will crush you!" Zorin growled.

Rhone studied his brother. It was uncanny seeing his own face staring back at him. Again he wondered how two men, seemingly so alike, could be completely different in the important matters. "Not today, my brother."

"Don't call me that!" Zorin glared at the people gathered around. "Why are you standing there? Rise up against these invaders. This is your homeland. Defend it!"

"No!" Lady Darha shouted. "Enough blood has stained the Rim-wall. Where there once was justice, there is now a land ruled by the heavy hand of fear." She lowered a long finger at Zorin. "Though it breaks my heart to proclaim it, I must. It was Zorin who murdered my husband ... his father ... the High Councilor Khore. And although he now holds the Council's high seat, it is a position he has stolen from Rhone, your rightful ruler.

"Zorin has kept me under heavy guard lest I speak this truth to you. He held me under the threat of death, to keep Rhone from returning. But today, that threat is lifted. Zorin is your real enemy, not Rhone!"

The crowd grew angry. Shouts for Zorin's blood rose from among the people, and they surged for the stairs. In a moment of distraction, Zorin drove an elbow into Da-gore's stomach and snatched the sword from his hand, grabbing Leenah and pressing the blade to her throat.

Leenah stiffened under the pressure of cold steel.

Rhone stopped short as the blade drew a thin crimson line from her throat. "I'll kill her if you come a step closer, Rhone."

"And you'll be dead a heartbeat later." He saw the desperation in Zorin's eyes. Backed into a corner, like a trapped hook-tooth cat, anything was possible. There was wild fear in Leenah's eyes. Rhone stared into them, drawing her fear into himself. He might reach Zorin's hand before he reacted, but he couldn't risk it. He'd lost Leenah once. He wouldn't lose her again, not now.

"Zorin, don't do this." Darha took a step toward him.

Rhone stopped her.

Zorin backed a step with Leenah held firmly in one arm, the blade biting into her skin. "Don't give me that doleful look, Mother. It doesn't work on me. It never has."

Darha's hand fell to her side. "I know. You never understood things like love … honor. Your father and I despaired over you, but we never expected you to become this. Let Leenah go. You will be treated fairly, I promise." She looked to Rhone for confirmation, and he nodded.

Zorin's minck flapped overhead and settled upon his shoulder. Zorin glanced at it and gave a thin smile. Then he looked back at Rhone. "I'll not stand before the council. I'll not spend my life in the Deep Chambers or end it on the bloodstained sand in the Pit of Ramor! I want safe passage out of Atlan." He glanced at the sky-barge that still hovered overhead. "In that. With a crew of my own men. I'll take the woman with me and leave her on the mainland."

Rhone knew that the moment Zorin lifted off with Leenah, her life would be over. "You can have what you ask for, but leave the woman here. I promise you no one will try to stop you."

"You promise? I'm to believe that?"

Rhone felt the anger burning suddenly within him. "A Makir promise!"

Zorin gave that momentary consideration. "No good. I take her with me. Make up your mind now."

Rhone suddenly tingled at a new sensation. It was Leenah reaching out to him, as if she were trying to tell him something, but the thoughts were garbled and indistinct. He had a vague recollection of the thought patterns he'd felt around javian spiders, only these were somehow different, more coherent, but not— human!

She lifted her wide eyes to the sky. He looked up and breath froze in his lungs. Zorin, being a sensitive—felt her thoughts too. A hint of confusion darkened his face. He glanced around, then heavenward, and his mouth gaped in terror as the shadow fell over them.

With a shriek, Zorin threw up his arms to protect his head as a rush of wind swept over the platform. Gur caught him in his mighty talons and snatched him up, sending the minck tumbling through the air.

Darha gasped and gripped Rhone's arm, her nails digging into his skin. Leenah stumbled to his side. Thrashing wildly about, Zorin grew smaller as the dragon carried him far out over the Rim-wall to the sea. Gur shrank in the distance, then released him and winged skyward as the speck tumbled toward the blue water, his arms flailing the air. Darha pressed her face into Rhone's shoulder. He put an arm around his mother.

Leenah stretched her arm around both of them. "It's over," she whispered.

But the struggle for Atlan was far from being over, even though they'd made a strong start.

Rhone and Leenah walked between the long rows of bodies. When they found her Uncle Sirt, she fell to her knees and wept over him.

Rhone put a hand upon her shoulder.

"It's not that he's gone," she said, sniffing back tears, "but that he died not trusting in the Creator. What will become of him now?"

He shook his head. "I don't have the answer to that. But he died a Makir. It's what he would have wanted."

She nodded, standing back from the fallen warrior. "If not for Uncle Sirt's kal-ee-hon, we'd all be dead now, and Zorin would still be in control."

He put an arm around her and drew her to himself. Holding her like that felt so right. She was indeed a woman worthy to lead his people, as his mother, at his father's side, had once done. As he stood there, he scanned the long row of dead. *Where was Klesc?*

He looked past the bodies of men he did not know. Some of the faces stirred memories of long ago. Sirt had recruited all the Makir who had remained in the land, and now most lay before him.

Rhone took Leenah's arm and guided her past the men gathering up Zorin's fallen guards and casting their weapons into a pile. Not far away, the healers were hurrying about, quickly and efficiently tending to the worst of the wounded. Rhone's eyes moved methodically down the rows. Here were faces he did recognize. His Imo-suk Makir had fared better than Sirt's unbound kal-ee-hon.

"Pyir Rhone," a voice rumbled weakly.

He came about. Two women were bent over Klesc, packing his wounds with poultices and wrapping them with linen bandages.

"Klesc!" He rushed to his side, gripping his hand and feeling a lingering strength there in spite of his condition.

The big warrior gave him a wan smile. "I tried to reach Leenah, but a triple fist of Gray Bears fell upon me." A grin crept up the side of his sallow cheeks. "I gave them a Makir welcome, but somewhere during the pleasantries, one of them drove a sword into me." He frowned. "I took his head off, and sent another fist of 'em on to Dirgen's Bosom."

Leenah took his other hand. "It's over now."

Klesc gave a small nod, then a laugh that brought a spasm of pain to his face. "I heard what Gur did. That beast is indeed living up to his name, Mistress Leenah."

Rhone looked at the healers. "How bad are his wounds?"

"He's lost a lot of blood," one of the women said.

"I think you ought to leave him now," the other said as she gently took Klesc's arm and began cleaning an ugly gash that had laid the skin open to the bone.

"Later, my friend."

Klesc gave a small nod and closed his eyes as his lips drew back in a grimace of pain.

Da-gore found the two of them a few minutes later.

"Pyir Rhone. I just received word that our forces engaged Zorin's guards as they fled back to Hodin's Keep."

"How did it go?"

Da-gore gave a short laugh. "Zorin's Gray Bears had no idea how many Makir were coming up over the Rim-wall. With nothing but memories and childhood legends to fuel their imaginations, they were ready to throw down their weapons. They surrendered completely to my ragtag band armed with their picks and hoes and shovels."

"This is good news."

"It gets better. Batok sends word that First Statre Larik's forces have secured Hodin's Sanctum." His expression flattened. "Larik, to his surprise, discovered Ka-Larik there."

A stab of regret pricked Rhone's heart. "He knows that Ka-Larik was a traitor?"

"It was quite clear. They found him hiding in Zorin's personal chambers. Statre Barav said that Larik personally ran Ka-Larik through with his own sword." He shook his head. "It must have been terrible. His own son betraying the cause he had pledged his life to."

Leenah shivered. "How horrible. Poor Larik. He must be devastated."

Rhone heard the heartfelt sadness in her voice toward a man she never much cared for. Her compassion would go a long way toward endearing the people to her. Rhone grasped Da-gore's shoulder. "It's unfortunate about Larik, but you and your men have done well. Now it's on to the Golden Hills Passage."

A shadow swept overhead, and Gur settled upon a rocky crag nearby. Leenah released Rhone's arm and went to him.

Rhone watched after her. "She's just perfect."

Da-gore smiled. "It's about time you noticed that."

41

Rise of the Nephilim

Lamech and Sor-dak stood upon the observation roof beside the large starglass tilted toward the sky. But it wasn't the stars they were studying this night. The Oracle's Temple, now complete, sat in a pool of light from a ring of specially crafted "energized" moonglasses, each nestled into a magnetic band that made it shine brighter than the failing magnetic veil could have allowed. Lamech thought it ironic that the very discovery he had made would one day be employed to glorify the Deceiver's Temple.

"I wish I understood the nature of the crystal capstone," Sor-dak said, staring at it, glowing with a life of its own. "Whatever elements were used in its forging have given it qualities far beyond anything we have here on earth. The power that thing might generate must be vast."

Lamech nodded, recalling bits and pieces of Mishah's dreams. Over the years he'd combined them with what his grandfather, Enoch, had taught him—coming up with a theory of his own. Rahab, the fifth stone of fire circling the sun, apparently had been very special to the Deceiver at one time. Could it have been his stronghold during the Rebellion, when he tried to usurp the

Creator's glory?

"One thing you can be sure of, it is not meant for man's good, in spite of what the Lodath preaches."

Sor-dak laughed. "Yet so many people think Sol-Ra-Luce wise."

"They are deceived."

"By the Deceiver who will one day be crushed beneath the Strong Man's heel." He nodded gravely.

Lamech glanced at the old stargazer. "You've learned your lessons well, Master Sor-dak." He stared back at the Temple as a frown pulled at his face. "I wonder about its true purpose. There is more to it than just a place of worship. It's far too complicated." He had such a close hand in building it that he practically carried the plans for it inside his head.

"Time will tell."

Time. A heaviness pressed down on him whenever he thought about the years. He'd used up more than half of his fifteen-year sentence building this abomination. *I mustn't dwell on that. The Creator had a purpose in it.* Perhaps Sor-dak had been that purpose? He had taken Sor-dak from a place of skepticism to belief, and finally, to faith. He'd taught the stargazer how to read the Creator's message in the stars, and that knowledge had filled Sor-dak with a light of understanding brighter than an energized moonglass. Sor-dak never tired of deciphering the Creator's story of redemption; he sometimes became giddy upon discovering some nuances that even Lamech had overlooked.

Sor-dak drew in a long breath and sighed. "One day soon the Oracle will arrive to dwell in his Temple."

"Yet the complex is far from finished." From here, Lamech could see the sprawling network of structures beginning to fill the Plains of Irad and what had once been the forests beyond. Someday it would be a huge city in itself, laid out in the shape of a great pentagram etched upon the earth. Another hundred years from now, nothing would be the same. More than ever, he felt the old world slipping away. The advances he'd seen in the time he'd been in prison had been staggering—much of it from knowledge imparted directly from the Oracle through his emissaries.

The two men left the rooftop.

Alone in his room, Lamech stared at the pile of scrolls he'd worked on over the years. He dropped into a chair before his desk and thought of Mishah and Noah. Reaching into his pocket, he took out a small leather case and stared at the tiny braid of hair that Rhone had given him so many years ago; his only tangible link to his wife and son. Although far away, they were always right at the edge of his thoughts. And so real in his dreams that he sometimes wondered if he hadn't somehow been transported to the Creator's Garden.

How he ached to see his son face-to-face and to hold Mishah again—to kiss her, to be with her forever. His eyes stung as he bowed his head to the desk.

"Creator, in all things I want to do your will. And I understand that your purposes are higher than man's, and unknowable to us on this side of Adam's Bosom, but if it be within your will, bring this trial to an end. I long for my family, and my soul is daily tormented here in Nod City, the bastion of the adversary. I know our time is short. You told my grandfather, Enoch, that when my father is taken to Adam's Bosom, judgment will fall upon this world. Will you keep me here in Nod City until that day comes? Methuselah is already three hundred and seventy-five years old." He took a rattling breath and felt moisture creeping down his cheeks. "Creator, you know my heart. If it be your will for me to remain here, so be it."

He had just finished his prayer when a flash of golden light filled his tiny room. He lifted his face from his desk as the air shimmered then split apart.

Sari'el, and a second Messenger Lamech didn't recognize, stepped into his world.

※

The tunnel had appeared suddenly, as such tunnels always did in the Creator's Garden, and its shimmering light faded a bit when she and Noah entered it. Oftentimes the colors would brighten, but not today.

"What's troubling you, Mother?" Noah noticed it too.

Mishah forced a smile to her face. "What makes you think it is I who made the light dim?"

He fixed her with a knowing stare. "Because I am not thinking any unhappy thoughts."

Her smile faded—as the tunnel had. "I was thinking about your father."

"Oh." The colors deepened further, and she was glad when they had reached the end. The mood tunnel opened up onto a pretty little patio that overlooked an immense river, so wide that its distant shore was lost to view in the billowing mist of a wonderful waterfall cascading over escarpments of golden yellow and ruby-red stone. The river, she understood, had its source among the Mountains of Eden. There a tremendous spring boiled up from the depths of the earth, where the Creator had reserved vast seas of water in deep storehouses. The river flowed through the Garden, and upon leaving, it branched into four mighty rivers.

She sighed, remembering the journey from Morg'Seth. They'd ascended the Little Hiddekel River to Nod City, and then joined the Hiddekel up to Far Port where mighty torrents finally made the river unnavigable. That had been almost eight years ago. It seemed incredible. Eight years of longing for Lamech; for his smile, for his arms to crush the breath from her and his lips to smother her with kisses.

The Creator's Garden supplied all their needs in abundance, and there was no fear of harm from any creature … but it was not home. It would never be home without Lamech.

She sat upon an ebony bench at the edge of the patio as Noah skipped to a black railing that lowered slightly to fit his height. He was growing so tall. He definitely had Lamech's eyes and his nose.

"It's so beautiful, isn't it, Mother?" He turned, pointing at the bow of light that arched from the waterfall to the roiling river.

"Yes, it is beautiful."

"It was meant to bring delight to the eyes of man," the Gardener said beside her.

Mishah turned with a start, a flutter of surprise in her chest.

He smiled as if amused that after all these years she still startled at his sudden appearances. "I've sent smaller bows into the world, but for now I'm keeping this one in my Garden."

Noah left the railing and came to them. He'd grown up with the Gardener's curious comings and goings. Mishah knew he thought it not the least peculiar.

"Is it special?"

"Yes, indeed, Noah. I call this my covenant bow."

"When will you let it leave the Garden?"

"When the time is right."

Noah turned back to the shimmering arch of color in the sky. "Will I ever see it again after I leave here, after my father comes to take us home?"

The Gardener's face became suddenly somber. "Someday you will see my special bow, and when you do, know that it is a promise from me to you and all your descendants. But that is still many years hence. You must first grow up with your father and mother."

"When will my father come for us?"

"Soon. Very soon."

Anguish wrenched at Mishah's heart. How often had he promised this? *Soon.* The word had lost its meaning. To the Gardener, *soon* might mean tomorrow, or a thousand years from now. Good thing she wasn't inside one of his wandering tunnels now. It's color would have surely turned muddy.

Though his attention had been directed upon Noah, the Gardener turned and looked at her. "You're troubled."

She could hide her feelings from men, but she could never hide them from him. "When? When will we be together again? All you say is that it will be soon." Her eyes began to sting as the longing she'd kept locked away in the vault of her heart burst free and surged upward. "What does *soon* mean?"

He took her hand. "What does it mean to you, Mishah?"

She sniffed, tears tumbling down her cheeks. "It means today. It means now." She didn't want to break down, and she was appalled to be speaking so frankly to the Gardener now, but something inside of her had burst, and it was impossible to put it back together again—at least not right away. She'd be all right in a little while, but now she needed to cry.

He drew her gently to her feet.

"What?" She patted her eyes, embarrassed at having crumbled so easily.

The Gardener gave her one of his soothing smiles and started her along. "The desire of your heart waits for you just around the bend."

She stared at him, not certain of what she had heard. In answer to her questioning look, His smile grew wider and he pointed. Mishah inhaled sharply and put a hand to her chest. *Did he mean that Lamech …?*

She looked to the bend in the path, caught up her dress, and ran. As she rounded a silver wimisa bush, she stopped and stared at the man coming toward her. He was still some distance away, but at once she recognized Lamech's tall, lean frame, his easy gait, that shock of unruly black hair.

"Lamech!"

He looked up, seemed to freeze for an instant, and then ran to her. She met him and threw open her arms, and they embraced.

"Mishah, is it really you?" He was sobbing too.

"Oh, Lamech! Yes, it's me. I've dreamt of this moment forever!" Tears choked off her words as he smothered her in kisses and held her with an urgency that defied anyone to take her from him ever again.

After a little while, she became aware of the presence of the Gardener, Sari'el, and Noah. She unlatched one arm and pulled the boy to them. "This is our son, Noah."

Lamech stooped, looked into Noah's round eyes, and then threw his arms around him as joyful tears spilled down her cheeks. They were finally together—all three of them. And she was going to keep it that way forever.

※

"You cannot go back to Morg'Seth, Lamech," the Gardener said somberly. "The Deceiver will be seeking for every chance to get to Noah."

He put a protective hand upon his son's shoulder. "I understand." He took Mishah's hand and looked out the portal, past the immense legs of the cherubim standing guard before it. "If this is what the Creator wants, then so be it." All he ever wanted to do was obey the voice of the sovereign One who'd spoken everything into existence.

"Where will we go?" Mishah asked. "All these years I've thought of only Lamech and home."

Although this news was a blow to her, Lamech knew Mishah could accept it, now that she had her family back together.

The Gardener said, "My servant Rhone has secured a place for you. He has swept it clean of his enemies, and there Noah will dwell until the fullness of time."

"Rhone! In Atlan?" she asked.

The Gardener nodded.

She looked up into Lamech's eyes. "Rhone was the man who helped us. He gave everything to see us safely into the Cradleland." She hesitated. "Even his life. But the Gardener raised him from the dead." A sudden surge of joy filled her heart. "Rhone has won back his land!"

Lamech smiled and gave her shoulder a tender squeeze. "I know all about Rhone."

She collected herself. "Yes, of course. You've already met."

"In prison." He withdrew the small leather pocket and showed her the braid of hair Rhone had given him from her.

She smiled and put her head against his chest. But the moment passed when, with a start, she looked back at the Gardener. "But why go to Atlan? Why can't we stay here if my son is in danger?"

"The Garden has served its purpose. Now, like all things once new, it too must fade and pass into stories, legends, and fables—the way of most truth."

Lamech saw Mishah didn't understand, but she nodded anyway. "What of Grandmother?" She glanced at Amolikah who had remained quiet so far.

"Amolikah can return to Morg'Seth, or she can accompany you. It's her decision."

Mishah looked hopefully at her grandmother. Amolikah still didn't speak, but her struggle with this decision was apparent in her aged face. "I want to go with you, Mishah, and to watch my grandson grow tall and wise, but I have many children back in Morg'Seth and many grandchildren, and I miss them all as much as you've missed Lamech. I want to return home." Her small smile filled with bitter-sweet joy.

"I ... I understand, Grandmother." Mishah's voice cracked under the strain of a breaking heart. Lamech put an arm over her shoulder.

Amolikah hugged her. "Oh, my dear, dear Mishah, don't cry. I love you more than you can know." Tears streamed down

Amolikah's face. Lamech's eyes filled, and he wrapped his arms around both women.

Amolikah sniffed and pressed her cheek against Mishah's. "If I am able, I will come to you someday."

Mishah let her tears flow unabated, nodding, her words all choked up in her throat.

Lamech fixed a smile on his face. "Of course you will." But Amolikah was an old woman, and it was not likely she'd ever make such a trip again.

The Gardener looked at Noah and the small boat the boy held under one arm. "Remember all that I taught you, Noah. Someday, it will be important."

"Here." Noah handed him a book. "I didn't finish it, but I've learned about many of the animals. It's all written down for you. I hope it helps."

The Gardener gave the book back to him. "You'll not be so easily shed of the task, Noah. You keep the book, and you continue studying all the animals and writing down what you learn." He smiled. "The exercise is for your growing and learning. As you did with the boat, someday you will understand."

The Gardener looked at all of them. "Sari'el will see you safely to Atlan. And Isot'el will take Amolikah to Morg'Seth."

A second Messenger was suddenly standing by them. Lamech hadn't seen where he had come from—he was just there.

Amolikah gave them all hugs, the strongest for Mishah and the longest for Noah, before rising and kissing Lamech on the cheek.

"Watch over my children, Lamech."

"You know I will."

Amolikah made a brave smile. "I know; otherwise, I would never leave Mishah and Noah." She broke down again, and when she had her emotions under control, she added, with unconvincing brightness, "even if it is only for a little while."

He knew she had to say that as he forced a smile too.

"Fair journey. I love you all." Amolikah reclaimed her brave face.

Mishah, still sobbing, clung to her hand until the last moment, and then the air parted in a golden light, and Amolikah was gone.

Lamech held his wife until she stopped crying and then looked at the Gardener and Sari'el, who had waited quietly nearby. The Gardener's smile reached down into his heart and soothed away the sadness. Mishah had felt it too, and patted her eyes dry.

"We're ready now," she said.

※

As they climbed out of the valley, on the road to the Ruins of Eden, they paused and looked back at the gleaming white walls that encompassed the Creator's Garden. From their higher vantage point, Lamech could see the pure stone stretching off in both directions, vanishing in the distance. The two cherubim were but a blur of gold before the tiny portal that led into the home of their first parents, Adam and Eve. Lamech felt a sudden, overwhelming sadness. The enormity of that loss, and the high cost he knew the Creator would one day have to pay to reclaim for mankind the Tree of Life that grew within the Garden, brought a renewed sting to his eyes.

"What are you thinking?" Mishah asked.

He looked at her. "According to his witness in the stars, someday the Strong Man, the Redeemer, will pay a dear price for you and me and all of mankind. Then his Garden will again be opened to welcome us." He smiled at Mishah and kissed her gently. "But that time is still far in the future." He glanced at Sari'el. "Isn't that right?"

Sari'el, who wasn't one to show emotion easily, leaned upon his ivory staff and gave a sly smile. "I don't know, Master Lamech. You see, like you, we too are watching this struggle. This is as much for our benefit as it is yours, for it was from among our kind, through pride, that the Rebellion first took root." His head turned suddenly back toward the Cradleland.

The air around the distant Garden had begun to waver, the stone walls going out of focus like a dream fading with the dawn ... and then they were gone.

Mishah looked up at Lamech, wonderingly.

Lamech stared a long moment. Had it even been real, or a mirage all along? He drew in a long-overdue breath. "The Gardener said it had served its purpose and must now pass into stories, then to legend, and finally ..." He shook his head.

There upon the Eden road, Mishah, Noah, Lamech, and Sari'el set off to discover what the Creator had planned next for their lives.

❦

Captain El-ik's muscles tensed as he stood before the tall doors, waiting for them to silently swing open. The Lodath's summons had been terse and immediate, and he had not even time to return to his quarters after his long trip from Atlan, first by ship, then overland to Far Port, and finally by a cranky riverboat to Nod City.

The doors finished their slow swing. He drew in a long breath and strode into the Lodath's grand gallery where court officials and representatives of King Irad had already assembled. He avoided their stares and hardly noticed the tapestries, the bronze sculptures, or the gleaming floor reflecting the light of the crystal ceiling. His eyes remained focused on the brooding figure sitting in the ornate chair.

The Lodath's blue-painted nails drummed impatiently on the chair's wide, sculpted armrest as he approached. The gallery pulsed with a nerve-fraying energy he had encountered before. *The Oracle.* His heart began to hammer in his chest as his view shot to the tall finger of smoky crystal upon its pedestal behind the Lodath. The crystal, twice the height of a man, was slowly pulsing with a reddish beat.

Nearby stood the Lodath's bodyguard, Bar'ack. Bar'ack never strayed far from Sol-Ra-Luce's side since the Lodath's brush with death years earlier—one that he'd never fully recovered from. Now Bar'ack's sullen eyes tracked El-ik as he approached, his hand resting upon his sword. El-ik glanced away. Bar'ack's eyes disturbed him in a way he didn't understand. The body, he knew, belonged to a man, but the life forces that inhabited it were from outside this world ... from the Oracle's world.

"Your Eminence." El-ik bowed stiffly at the waist. "I came as soon as your runner brought word that you wished to speak with me."

Sol-Ra-Luce leaned forward. His eyelids lowered, and his finger stretched out a long, blue fingernail at him. "I sent you to Atlan to secure an alliance." The voice from the damaged throat grated like gravel crushed underfoot. "Why did you fail?"

"Unforeseen events, Your Eminence. There was a revolution. A change in power. Zorin was—" How did one say it? Now two months after Zorin's fall from power, the vision seared into his brain was so incredible that he hardly believed it himself. "—overthrown, and the new ruler would not have consented to the alliance. I barely made it off the island." He stopped suddenly, his head lurching up as the air around him began to buzz.

The crystal's throbbing cadence matched precisely the rushing of his own blood. As the Lodath turned to stare, the limpid spire of rock gave off a burst of scarlet light, and the shape of a man formed within the beating heart of the stone.

Tall and slender, with broad, square shoulders, the Oracle stepped into the world of mortals. In contrast to Bar-ack's stark, lifeless eyes, the Oracle's eyes were a startling blue and seemed filled with the very essence of life. His skin had an almost pearlescent quality. He had a straight, handsome nose and well-formed lips, bent slightly—not quite a frown, but definitely not a smile. The face was perfectly symmetrical, and if it was not that the Oracle was obviously male, El-ik could almost think of him as beautiful.

The Lodath sprang to his feet and bowed, while El-ik and the men standing about the gallery instantly dropped to their knees. El-ik's hand went to his tunic and gripped the pledge pendant under his shirt; it had begun to warm against his skin.

"Sol-Ra-Luce," the Oracle intoned, his voice deep, resonating as if off reflectors, yet none had been erected in the gallery.

"My Lord."

The Oracle's slender finger lifted the Lodath's chin, and he peered down into the Lodath's eyes. "We have lost a valuable opportunity." His voice held an odd neutrality.

"Yes. We were just discussing it." The Lodath's strident tones sent an electric shiver down El-ik's spine. The Lodath glared over his shoulder at him. "El-ik has failed us. What manner of punishment do you wish me to mete out?"

The Oracle stared at El-ik, his eyes hardening ever so slightly, like blue ice across a high-mountain pool. In some remote place in his brain, El-ik thought that the Oracle was nearly as tall as a Hodinite. He exhaled, realizing the Oracle was waiting for his answer.

"I was in negotiations, My Lord. High Councilor Zorin would have joined us, had not his brother, Rhone, stirred the people to revolt." El-ik took another breath and tried to swallow.

"I once had Rhone in my hand." The Oracle closed a fist. "But he slipped though my fingers, much as Atlan has now." His view swung back around toward Sol-Ra-Luce. "That's twice I've been thwarted."

"As you know, I punished Captain Da-gore for the first failure, My Lord. Captain El-ik came to me highly recommended. I trusted him, which I now see was a mistake."

"Yes. A mistake, Sol-Ra-Luce." The Oracle's words hissed.

The Lodath took a trembling breath and drew himself up taller. "I have El-ik's replacement ready, My Lord."

El-ik hardly felt the hard marble beneath his knees. So, that had been the purpose of this meeting all along. He was to be pushed aside for another.

"Have you?" A sudden smile crept to the Oracle's face. "As you once told Captain El-ik, 'No one is indispensable.' I, too, have chosen a replacement."

"Of course, your man will command in his stead. Only name him."

"In a moment."

"Certainly, My Lord. What would you have me do with El-ik?"

At the Oracle's glance, a spark came to life in Bar'ack's eyes. El-ik went numb, and a sudden breath rammed into his lungs as Bar'ack slowly drew his sword.

The Lodath grinned.

El-ik's breath caught. With the gallery filled with the Lodath's guards and the Oracle himself present, he knew it would do little good to try to run. And it was useless to plead for mercy. All he could do was brace himself.

The Oracle nodded, and Bar'ack's sword drew back. El-ik shut his eyes.

The Lodath gave a startled cry. El-ik's eyes sprang open, and he looked up in time to see the Lodath slump to his knees, a wide, stunned look on his face. Bar'ack gave the sword a hard twist. Sol-Ra-Luce made a strangling gasping noise, then fell dead.

The Oracle nodded. Bar'ack withdrew the bloody blade and stepped back.

"No one is indispensable, Sol-Ra-Luce. Fair journey to your place of torment. Abaddon is expecting you." His view shifted, and El-ik gasped as pain completely filled him and seemed to radiate from every pore in his skin. The pain drove him to the floor. He writhed in anguish, hardly able to breath. As he squirmed, words filled his brain. *Your next failure will be your last.* Slowly the agonizing torment dissipated, leaving him exhausted, nauseated, and trembling upon the cold marble.

The Oracle turned to the crowded gallery, engulfed in stunned silence. "The Tyrant of Old is moving. Already he has intruded into my kingdom in order to subvert my plans. He thinks he can preserve the seed of man in its present, low state, but he will fail. From this day onward, there will be a new order, and you will have a new Lodath."

The air shimmered with a reddish glare, then tore open, and the giant stepped through.

Herc! Gasping for breath, El-ik half raised himself. He'd seen Herc run through the heart! He'd seen the Earth-Born die on Atlan's Rim-wall. But here he was, alive, yet somehow different. The grotesque features had been reshaped, almost as if this were a revised version. It was still Herc's face, but now it was almost handsome. El-ik's brain reeled.

"Behold, the next Lodath! The firstfruits of a new race of man." The Oracle's voice boomed. "From this day forward, you will see the rise of the Nephilim!"

Readers' Guide

*For Personal Reflection
or Group Discussion*

QUEST FOR ATLAN
Readers' Guide

*D*ouglas Hirt continues his compelling story about human origins in this sequel to *Flight to Eden*. Once again his account of mankind's beginnings differs sharply from paleontologists', but accords with events recorded in the Bible. We see an earth that, although fallen, retains a good deal of its glory. We see men and women made in God's image who were meant to be in fellowship with their Creator but instead find themselves separated from him. In just a few generations, almost everyone has forgotten the true account of creation. Most regard that story as merely myth or legend. Many also find themselves alienated—from God, others, and even themselves. Some are in open rebellion against their Creator. A few have remembered the old stories, or been reached by others who've retained the ancient knowledge, and found a way back to God.

Sound familiar? In many ways, the situation depicted in Hirt's trilogy closely resembles our own. We too are skeptical about creation, alienated, and often in rebellion. We too have lost our way. We too find it difficult to believe in a supernatural world that lies just beyond our senses. We too experience fear, distrust, enmity, hatred, family tragedy, and war. We too wonder why God—if there even is such a being—seems to have withdrawn from our world.

Just as the Christian story suggests answers to these age-old difficulties, so does *Quest for Atlan*. We're talking about faith, conviction, courage, commitment, and trust. Another great modern storyteller, C. S. Lewis, believed that every square inch of the universe, every millisecond of time, is a battleground over which the forces of light and the forces of darkness contend. Hirt's story shares that worldview. Every decision, every action, every commitment, every choice either promotes the Kingdom of God of the kingdom of the great deceiver.

Does all this seem unlikely, even highly improbable? Nevertheless, the details presented in this book closely follow the pattern of Scripture. We invite you the reader to search the Word of God to see if you can find answers to your uncertainties. We hope that the following questions will assist you in your quest for the truth about science, faith, human origins, and the natural and supernatural worlds. Even more, we hope they will stir you to take a close look at your own relationship to the Creator.

Chapter 1

1. Lamech, a real character in the Bible and the father of Noah, finds himself in prison just like another famous Bible character, Joseph. What are the similarities between Lamech's and Joseph's situations? The differences? Do you have any ideas why God might allow his people to be locked up in prison?

2. The scenes showing the building of the Temple of the Oracle depict engineering and mechanical feats of rather astounding proportions. Do these strike you as plausible? Why or why not? Why do you think ancient humankind is so often thought of as backward by modern people?

3. Lamech is called Preacher by his fellow prisoners. Do you think this is a term of respect or disrespect? Why? Does it strike you as a little bit odd that there would need to be preachers at a time when the earth is only a couple of generations removed from Adam and Eve? What is the substance of Lamech's preaching?

Chapter 2

4. What do you make of the scene where Lamech stands before the authorities of Nod? Does it seem realistic? Can you see any parallels between Nod's policies and those of modern states? How can Christians be effective witnesses in situations where speech is restricted? Do you think Lamech went too far in his exchanges with the authorities?

5. Lamech's brief encounter with Sor-dak resonates with the experiences of another famous prisoner in the Bible (besides Joseph). Who might that be? (Hint: He was a prisoner in Babylon, and also followed a simple diet.) Lamech is obviously a man of considerable learning, skilled in both astronomy and mathematics. What does this say about the value of "secular" learning?

Chapter 4

6. The angel Sari'el is a character of some importance in this book, as he was in *Flight to Eden*. What do you think of how he is portrayed? Is he too otherworldly? Too human? What about his discussion of eternity? Does it make any sense? Sari'el apparently eats and drinks when he takes on human appearance. How can that be?

7. Before Lamech attempts to free Leenah from those who would take her to be the Lodath's object of pleasure, he offers up a quick prayer to the Creator asking for guidance. Was his prayer answered? Did he make the right decision? Why or why not? Should we always make decisions based on likely results, or are there times we should just do the right thing no matter what the consequences?

Chapter 5

8. Given the outcome of the rescue attempt, did Lamech act too rashly? Was what happened part of the Creator's plan, or was

Lamech acting entirely on his own? Does it make any difference if we try to discern the will of God and cooperate with it?

9. Deep in the bowels of the prison, Klesc makes a confession. What is it? Is it possible for nonbelievers to have a sense of God's presence? Does God ever use those who are not a part of his Kingdom to effect his plans? What are some examples from the Bible?

Chapter 6

10. This chapter is titled "Children of the Gods?" Who are these children? What name do they go by in this book? What are they called in the Bible? What plan does the Oracle have to bring forth these "children of the gods"? What is the real reason the Lodath takes so many women as his consorts?

11. Are there any modern parallels with the breeding program described in this chapter? What are they? How are they similar? How are they different?

Chapter 7

12. When Rhone meets with Ker'ack, Bar'ack's father, we learn more details about what happened to Bar'ack. What does Rhone say happened to him? What were the two main reasons Rhone gives for Bar'ack's transformation? Is this a plausible explanation for demon possession?

13. Sari'el claims there were additional factors involved in the demise of Bar'ack. What were some of these? What parallels are there between the culture of Nod and that of modern Western nations, such as the United States and those of the European Union?

14. Sari'el makes some interesting observations about the nature of power. What is one to make of these? Do they line up with scriptural understandings of power? What does the Bible have to say about "principalities and powers"? (see Ephesians 6)

Chapter 8

15. Near the beginning of this chapter, there's an interesting scene involving Messengers like Sari'el and fallen Messengers. Does this scene seem realistic? Is this how you would imagine spiritual warfare? Sari'el makes an interesting remark about authority in our realm and in the realm of the supernatural. What does he say, and does it make sense? Why or why not?

16. When Sari'el first appears to Lamech and Klesc in their prison cell, Klesc mistakes him for a spirit of a dead person. Why does he react this way? If this is not a common reaction for a modern person from a secularized culture, might people from other cultures react in this fashion? If so, why? What does this say about modern Western cultures?

Chapter 9

17. After Sari'el frees them, Klesc and Rhone set out to rescue Leenah. Along the way they talk about their former lives, and Rhone accuses Klesc of breaking a solemn oath. Is this a fair accusation? Could Klesc have avoided breaking the oath? Must he still honor the oath if he is no long bound to a Pyir?

18. Rhone and Klesc disable guards to get information from them. After they get it, the two knock the guards out and bind them up instead of killing them. Wouldn't it have been smarter to kill them so that they wouldn't be discovered by other guards and thus endanger the mission? Did Rhone and Klesc do the right thing? Is it ever right to kill people in circumstances like these?

Chapter 10

19. How does Leenah find out that the necklace is affecting her ability to concentrate? How does the necklace work? Does this seem plausible? Why or why not? How does Leenah act after she puts the now-glazed necklace back on? Is her act convincing?

20. The Lodath catches on to Leenah's plan to stab him with a nail file. How did he find out? What does he say about it? Did he have supernatural help, or was he just observant? If the former, how would that work? How does this relate to Sari'el's observations about realms of power and authority?

21. Leenah and the Lodath struggle as he tries to overpower her. What resources does she use to resist and wound him? If the only thing she could do to prevent him from violating her would be to jump out the window and face certain death, would that be the right thing to do? Why or why not?

Chapter 11

22. In his prison cell, Lamech has a fascinating discussion with Da-gore. When Lamech says the world is being prepared for destruction, what does Da-gore say? Have you ever heard similar ideas from non-Christians? Are they convincing? What kind of answer can Christians give to such ideas?

23. Da-gore seems to think Lamech's confidence in the Creator's promises amounts to smugness. Is this fair? Is there a way to present the truth about the world without appearing smug? In our postmodern times, anyone who argues for absolute truth is often accused of smugness. Isn't this relativistic view itself a kind of smugness?

24. How does Rhone overcome Bar'ack's attack? Could anyone do this, or are there certain requirements for it to work? Is this a kind of magic or something else? Did Rhone do the right thing in allowing Bar'ack to live? Why or why not?

Chapter 12

25. The night before his scheduled execution in the morning, Lamech struggles with doubt concerning Sari'el's prediction that he will not die. Is this a lack of faith on Lamech's part, or a natural response to his circumstances? Can Lamech really rely on Sari'el's word? Could Sari'el be mistaken? If Lamech knows Sari'el is right, why does he doubt?

26. Lamech goes on to berate himself for his lack of faith. Is that what's really going on here, or is it something else? Does Lamech's response remind you of any scene from the New Testament? Can you recall a time when the disciples found themselves unable to pray, even when it was extremely important that they do so? What is the last thing Lamech prays before Dagore comes to get him next morning?

27. What do you think motivated Sor-dak to have Lamech's execution stayed and have him released into his service? Is it simply because he needed help with his star calculations? Or is there something else at work here? What could it be? Is there any evidence that Sor-dak is anything but a tool of the Deceiver and the Lodath? If so, what is it?

Chapter 13

28. Who is the Gardener? Is he the same person as the Creator? The Father? If it is Jesus, does he look like he will when he becomes Incarnate later on in human history? Are there any places in the

Old Testament where beings that appeared to people could have been Jesus?

Chapter 14

29. Lamech appears to be involved in a counterfeit project designed to subvert the deepest and most sacred purposes of the Creator. How does he justify his participation in this project? Does this make sense? Is there another course of action he could take, or does the Creator have a way of bringing good out of this work that is directed toward evil purposes? Are there any places in the Bible where similar principles are at work?

30. As Lamech gazes out on the stars, he ruminates on the idea of the extent of the curse—so great that it affects "even the far flung stars." Is that an accurate account of the extent of the curse? Did it really affect every corner of creation? What does that say about the Creator's plan for humankind and the importance of our place in the universe? Is this a common way to think about man's status in today's scientific/naturalist world?

Chapter 15

31. Rhone's decision to allow the group's "shadow" to continue following them rankles Klesc. What is his objection to Rhone's decision? Is it a fair assessment? Is Rhone acting out of wisdom or fear? Is Klesc being insubordinate?

Chapter 16

32. What does the Lodath's servant say the real purpose of the Temple is? How does this line up with what Satan's first temptation of Eve was? Are there any ways in which modern godless science participates in similar activities?

33. How does the religion of the Oracle mimic and pervert the true idea of sacrifice as practiced among the Creator's people? How does this relate to the Bible's idea of Satan as an angel of light?

Chapter 17

34. Da-gore reveals himself to be the one who was following Rhone, Klesc, and Leenah. Is this a surprise? Does Da-gore's faith seem real? Why is Klesc so suspicious of Da-gore? Does he have grounds for his suspicions?

Chapter 19

35. Sor-dak reveals that he was once a believer. What caused him to lose his faith? For Sor-dak, science takes precedence over faith. Are faith and science at odds? Science works on the basis of judgments formed in light of observations. What can happen if the observations are imperfect or partial? What are some cases in which partial or defective observations have produced wrong scientific conclusions?

36. Rhone asks Sor-dak if science is about finding truth or merely a thin disguise for philosophy. Is this a fair question? Does science ever operate as the handmaid of philosophical dogma? Are there any current examples of this?

Chapter 20

37. What ruse did Sor-dak use to test Lamech's knowledge and character? Did it work? What did Sor-dak learn about Lamech? What does Lamech's diligence in performing his tasks say about his character? Does the Creator honor Lamech's hard work? What lesson is there for us in how Lamech approaches his duties?

Chapter 22

38. Is it possible that Da-gore is the spy? Does Klesc have good reasons for suspecting him? What else could be at work in Klesc's suspicions? If the spy is not Da-gore, do you have any ideas who it might be?

Chapter 24

39. Not for the first time, Sari'el observes that the Messengers' ability to protect those to whom they are assigned is directly related to the strength of the faith of their human charges. Is this possible that our faith affects angels' ability to protect us? Is there any scriptural basis for this idea?

Chapter 25

40. For the first time Da-gore hears the truth about how Zorin killed his father, kidnapped his mother, and imprisoned his brother, Rhone. How was he able to succeed in all this treachery? Are there examples in history of such ruthless behavior? What about in other works of literature? Does this chapter finally prove Da-gore's innocence? What actions and responses of his can be given to support his innocence? If the traitor isn't Da-gore, who could it be?

Chapter 26

41. What is Rhone's reaction to the news that Da-gore brings from Atlan? What does his reluctance to take action come from? Prudence? Indecision? A proper waiting on the Creator's timing? Defend your answer from the text. What does Leenah think? Who's right?

Chapter 27

42. Given the known effects of the mansnatcher's poison, do you think Rhone has been keeping a close enough eye on Leenah? What could or should he have done differently? Does he do a good job of convincing Leenah not to fly? Is what he tells her a proper thing to say? Is it possible that the Creator is using Leenah's actions to force Rhone's hand?

43. What observation does Klesc make about Rhone's behavior? Could the mantle of leadership have caused Rhone to be too

self-reliant? Is this a common pattern among Christian leaders? Doesn't it seem paradoxical that those who are most gifted need to rely most on God? If he's given them gifts and abilities, why can't they just use them without depending on God's help?

Chapter 30

44. What is a Parting Word? How does it function in the various cultures? How does Leenah use this custom to help impart the truth to the Kleimen? What does this say about how we can use other cultures' traditions as an entrée for sharing the gospel?

Chapter 34

45. Was it a surprise to find out that Ka-Larik was the traitor? What kinds of things make people betray trust? What could Ka-Larik's motive have possibly been? Money? Power? Desire to be on the winning side? Jealousy?

Chapter 35

46. When Rhone is on the path to meet his mother in Deepvale, he begins to worry again that he lacks the strength to overthrow Zorin. Why is it so hard for Rhone to trust the Creator? Was it ever hard for people in the Bible to trust God? Can you think of some examples of famous people in the Old Testament who struggled with trusting God? Do you ever find it hard to trust God? When?

47. What does El-ik, the Lodath's emissary to Atlan, propose to Zorin? What would likely happen to Zorin if he allowed his country to become an ally of Nod? Are there any examples in history of two evil empires forming an alliance? How long did they last?

Chapter 36

48. Why do the people of Deepvale hold a special place in their hearts for the Lady Darha? What did she do to win their trust? What does this say about her as a leader of people?

49. When Rhone and Lady Darha meet in Deepvale, she is saddened by the return of the Makir. Why? She seems to believe war is inevitable. Is there any way that war could be prevented? Would it be possible for Rhone to try to negotiate a settlement with Zorin? Can war ever be justified? If not, why not? If so, under what circumstances?

Chapter 37

50. When Zorin reads off the charges against Leenah and Sirt, they are little more than a tapestry of lies. Is it possible that anyone believes him? If not, what is the point of holding this farcical mock trial? Can tyrannical regimes gain any credibility by conducting charades like these? It has been said that a lie repeated often enough takes on the appearance of truth. Could it be that Zorin has come to believe some of the lies he tells?

Chapter 40

51. All along, Lady Darha has insisted on accompanying her son
    Rhone on his mission to free Atlan from Zorin's grip. What key
    role does she end up playing? How do the people react to her
    disclosures? Would the stout fighting of Rhone and his allies have
    been enough, or was Lady Darha's speech the decisive element
    in defeating Zorin?

Chapter 41

52. After Rhone has defeated Zorin, Lamech returns to the
    Cradleland by a special means. What does he do just before the
    Creator opens the passageway? Why did the Creator make
    Lamech wait years and years before allowing him to be reunited
    with Mishah and Noah? A good portion of this book has to do
    with timing—man's and God's. What might be some reasons
    God's timing differs from ours? Have you ever had to wait on
    God's timing? What was it like?

Coming soon…

the exciting conclusion of
the Cradleland Chronicles…

THE FALL OF THE NEPHILIM

It's the dawn of humanity, and civilization is rapidly advancing—and something's not right ... not right at all.

CRADLELAND **1** CHRONICLES

DOUGLAS HIRT

FLIGHT TO EDEN

1-58919-053-X • Item # 104176
512 pages

A dark power is at work, intent on gaining complete control of the Cradleland—the birth place of the still-young world. All that stands in the Power's way is one troublesome line of humans: the descendants of Seth. They are of the only remaining clan clinging to an all-but-dead faith. And yet it's from that faith that a prophecy threatens all plans of world dominion—a promise, spoken from the heart of Eden, warning of a human son yet to come who would strike back with a crushing blow. The darkness is determined to stop that from happening. This redeemer must be born of a human, so an incredible scheme is launched to prevent the prophecy from coming to pass. First, pollute the human bloodline; and second . . . kill the only one who could be humanity's deliverance!

The first of the three-volume Cradleland Chronicles, *Flight to Eden* is fantastic page-turning fiction at its best!

The Word at Work Around the World

A vital part of Cook Communications Ministries is our international outreach, Cook Communications Ministries International (CCMI). Your purchase of this book, and of other books and Christian-growth products from Cook, enables CCMI to provide Bibles and Christian literature to people in more than 150 languages in 65 countries.

Cook Communications Ministries is a not-for-profit, self-supporting organization. Revenues from sales of our books, Bible curricula, and other church and home products not only fund our U.S. ministry, but also fund our CCMI ministry around the world. One hundred percent of donations to CCMI go to our international literature programs.

CCMI reaches out internationally in three ways:

· Our premier International Christian Publishing Institute (ICPI) trains leaders from nationally led publishing houses around the world.

· We provide literature for pastors, evangelists, and Christian workers in their national language.

· We reach people at risk—refugees, AIDS victims, street children, and famine victims—with God's Word.

Word Power, God's Power

Faith Kidz, RiverOak, Honor, Life Journey, Victor, NexGen — every time you purchase a book produced by Cook Communications Ministries, you not only meet a vital personal need in your life or in the life of someone you love, but you're also a part of ministering to José in Colombia, Humberto in Chile, Gousa in India, or Lidiane in Brazil. You help make it possible for a pastor in China, a child in Peru, or a mother in West Africa to enjoy a life-changing book. And because you helped, children and adults around the world are learning God's Word and walking in his ways.

Thank you for your partnership in helping to disciple the world. May God bless you with the power of his Word in your life.

For more information about our international ministries, visit www.ccmi.org.

Additional copies of *QUEST FOR ATLAN*
and other RiverOak titles are available
wherever good books are sold.

If you have enjoyed this book,
or if it has had an impact on your life,
we would like to hear from you.

Please contact us at:

RIVEROAK BOOKS
Cook Communications Ministries, Dept. 201
4050 Lee Vance View
Colorado Springs, CO 80918
Or visit our Web site: www.cookministries.com

RIVEROAK®
Good News in Fiction